BETH REVIS

razOr
bill

An Imprint of Penguin Group (USA) Inc.

Shades of Earth

RAZORBILL

Published by the Penguin Group
Penguin Young Readers Group
345 Hudson Street, New York, New York 10014, U.S.A.
Penguin Group (USA) Inc., 375 Hudson Street, New York, New York 10014, U.S.A.
Penguin Group (Canada), 90 Eglinton Avenue East, Suite 700, Toronto, Ontario,
Canada M4P 2Y3 (a division of Pearson Penguin Canada Inc.)
Penguin Books Ltd, 80 Strand, London WC2R 0RL, England
Penguin Ireland, 25 St Stephen's Green, Dublin 2, Ireland
(a division of Penguin Books Ltd)
Penguin Group (Australia), 250 Camberwell Road, Camberwell, Victoria 3124,
Australia (a division of Pearson Australia Group Pty Ltd)
Penguin Books India Pvt Ltd, 11 Community Centre, Panchsheel Park,
New Delhi – 110 017, India
Penguin Group (NZ), 67 Apollo Drive, Rosedale, Auckland 0632, New Zealand
(a division of Pearson New Zealand Ltd)
Penguin Books, Rosebank Office Park, 181 Jan Smuts Avenue,
Parktown North 2193, South Africa
Penguin China, B7 Jaiming Center, 27 East Third Ring Road North,
Chaoyang District, Beijing 100020, China

10 9 8 7 6 5 4 3 2 1

ISBN 978-1-59514-399-0

Library of Congress Cataloging-in-Publication Data is available

Printed in the United States of America

For my readers, who followed me across the universe.

Dei gratia.

I have loved the stars too fondly to be fearful of the night.
—Sarah Williams

1: AMY

"Wait," I say, my heart clenching.

Elder's finger hovers over the launch button. He glances up at me, and I can see the worry in his eyes, creasing the corners and making him look old and sad. The planet shines through the honeycombed glass in front of us—blue and green and white and sparkling and everything I have ever wanted. But the emotion twisting my stomach is fear.

Terror.

"Are we ready for this?" I ask, my voice barely a whisper.

Elder leans back, away from the launch button. "We've moved everything from *Godspeed* into the shuttle that we can take," he says. "Everything's been strapped down—"

"Even the people," I say. We used the big, heavy-gauge tethers like the one Elder used to go outside the ship in a spacesuit to wrap the people as best we could around the cryo chambers, against the walls, anywhere we could to make sure they wouldn't be tossed around like rubber balls when the shuttle lands on Centauri-Earth. It's makeshift at best. I'm worried that our jerry-rigged seat belts won't be enough, but it's all we could do. We are as prepared as we'll ever be.

But that's not what I meant when I asked if we were ready.

I meant: are we ready for what's down there?

Am *I* ready?

Probes were sent to the planet—many of them before *Godspeed* even arrived—and they all said Centauri-Earth was habitable. But there's a big difference between habitable and home.

And there are monsters.

I shake my head, trying to clear it from the disturbing thought. The last probes all reported some sort of unknown danger, something Orion called "monsters." Something so bad that the first Eldest decided it would be better to trap everyone on *Godspeed* rather than land.

What's worse? Monsters . . . or walls?

I spent three months trapped, the walls of the spaceship more cage than home. But at least I was alive. Who knows what the planet will hold, what new dangers we will face?

All I have now are questions, fear, and a big blue and green and white planet looking up at me.

We have to go. We have to face the world below. It will be better to die quickly with only the taste of freedom on our lips than to live long lives pretending not to see the walls that imprison us.

I tell myself, it *will* be worth it. No matter what price is paid, it *will* be enough to escape *Godspeed*. I tell myself these things, and I try to believe them.

Lights blink up at me from the control panel. Elder and I sit directly in front of it, a huge metal lever set into the floor between us. The main Bridge— the big room designed to control the entire ship—had six chairs and dozens of control panels, but this smaller bridge has only two of each. I hope it's enough. I hope we're enough.

I reach up—toward the window with the shining planet beyond or toward the control panel, I don't know which—and Elder grabs my shaking hand.

"We can do this," he says, no doubt in his voice.

"We have to," I say.

"Together?"

I nod.

Both of our fingers press the INITIATE LAUNCH button.

2: ELDER

A computerized female voice fills the bridge. "Initiation of shuttle launch."

Amy sucks in a shaky breath.

"Probe relay with directional input detected. Manual or automatic landing sequence?" the computer asks. Two new buttons light up on the control panel in front of me: one illuminated with a red **M**, the other with a green **A**.

I push **A** firmly.

"Automatic launch sequence initiated," the computer says cheerfully.

A grinding metal-on-metal, thunking, crashing noise reverberates throughout the shuttle. It sounds as if giant saw-like teeth are gnawing on the roof.

"What is that?" Amy squeaks. She holds onto her seat as if it will anchor her to safety. The metal arms of the chair are smudged with her fingerprints, her body pressed into the heavy foam padding.

My mind spins through the possibilities. The noise sounds like something breaking—ominous and terrifying. My stomach lurches as the entire shuttle shifts down and forward, as if on a giant arm swinging it from the rest of *Godspeed*. I'm pressed against my seat, breathless. Screams and shouts of fear from the other side of the shuttle door leak onto the bridge. Amy glances up at me, her face pale and worried.

"That was normal," I say, not sure if I'm trying to assure her or myself. "We're separated from the main ship now."

Something above us goes *ka-THUNK*, and the entire shuttle sinks a few feet before stabilizing.

"We're separated from the main ship *now*," I say. Amy laughs, but the sound is high-pitched and nervous, dying quickly on her lips.

"Detachment rockets initiate," the computer says matter-of-factly. A burst of three small rockets built into the top of the shuttle pushes us down, and our view shifts, the planet looming in the window, filling our vision.

"I'm glad we have the window," Amy says, staring through the honey-combed glass in front of us. The stars glitter, and the planet — our new home — shines brightly up at us. In some of the old texts from Sol-Earth, the planet is referred to as a blue-and-white marble. But that couldn't be further from the truth. Maybe in a picture, the planet looks like a marble. But here, with it hanging in front of me, it looks almost *alive*. The colors are vibrant, a stark contrast to the nothingness-black of the universe.

But even if it is beautiful, we're not there yet. The shuttle lurches forward again, and shouts and screams — short, muffled sounds of people who cannot contain their fear — erupt from beyond the bridge door.

"Let's get this over with," I say grimly.

"Orbital maneuvering system check," the computer chirps.

Amy gasps as a thunderous *boom!* fills the shuttle.

I want to grab her, wrap her in my arms, and whisper that everything will be fine. But I can't move. My heart is pounding in my ears, thudding so loudly I can't hear anything else. The shuttle knows what to do — probes were sent from *Godspeed* to Centauri-Earth that are now sending signals to the shuttle's systems, guiding it to the safest landing point with the best environment for us to land in. All we have to do is be strapped down for the ride.

A sick feeling rises in my stomach and radiates out, the same feeling I get — used to get — when I'd free-fall for that moment before the grav tube would kick in and suck me down to the next level of the ship. My head feels light. My brain screams at me: *I'm falling!* I panic, my arms and legs flailing, trying to hold onto something, anything, but there's nothing but air, and it doesn't matter anyway because I'm *not* falling. I'm floating.

"Shite!" I shout, staring down at my now-empty chair, just out of reach as I hover several feet above it.

A nervous giggle escapes Amy's lips, but her eyes are wide with fear. "Didn't you strap into your chair?" she asks. Her hair is floating around her face in a cloud of red, but the wide, foam-covered belts across her lap and chest keep her rooted in her seat.

"I . . . forgot," I say. My arms and legs swing wildly, but I'm not moving. *Of course*—the grav replicator was on the main ship. I twist my head toward the closed bridge door. I wonder how my people feel now, when I've taken everything from them, including gravity.

"Hold on!" Amy says, laughter still in her voice. She unbuckles her own seat belt, and, as she starts to rise, she slips her foot into the strap and reaches up for me with both her arms.

"Stupid hair," she mutters, blowing a stream of air out to make the gold-red-orange strands fly away from her face. Her hair floats around her head like a halo of soft tendrils, reaching up and out. It reminds me of when I first saw her, when her sunset hair swirled around her face like a cloud of ink.

"Probe communication detected," the computer chirps. "Probe indicates suitable landing area. Target shuttle to probe? Select yes or no." Two buttons light up: a red **N** and a green **Y**.

"Frex!" I say, reaching for the control panel. It's useless—my body is a weightless mass, and the control panel is hopelessly out of reach.

"Hold still!" Amy shouts at me. Her ankle is barely hooked around the twisted strap of her seat belt. It's not enough—she's straining to grab me, but I'm hovering just out of her grasp.

"Please select: yes or no," the computer reminds me.

"Oh, damn," Amy mutters. She wiggles her foot out of its grip, kicks up from the chair, and launches into the air.

She slams into me — I fly up against the roof of the bridge, and she bounces off me, toward the floor. I ricochet down, missing my seat by several feet, but my fingers slide over the metallic edge of the control panel, and I punch the blinking **Y** button.

Amy growls with frustration as she bounces from the floor to the ceiling again. She kicks off, aiming for her own chair.

I pull myself hand over hand along the edge of the control panel until I reach my chair, then slide in and tighten my seat belt around my lap and over my chest.

"Initiate orbital maneuvering system," the computer continues automatically, ignorant and uncaring, oblivious to the way my body is shaking so badly that I don't think I could stand now even if there was gravity.

The shuttle glides into motion. The stars dip out of view, and the planet fills the entire honeycombed-glass window. It feels as if my entire body is put on hold as I drink the image up with my eyes. It's different, somehow, seeing the planet without the blackness of space around it. As if the colors will wrap around us and swallow us whole.

"Oh," Amy breathes, barely audible as she grabs the armrest of her seat and pulls herself down. She wiggles back into the seat belt and straps herself in.

A monitor blinks on in front of her, showing three bright red dots over an outline of the shuttle. "These must be the rockets moving us," she says. She touches the screen, and her fingertips glow red from the lights.

One of the lights blinks out — Amy gasps, snatching her hand away — and our view shifts again, lurching up just in time for us to see the home we're leaving.

Godspeed.

It looks broken, crippled, with the shuttle missing from its underside.

Emotion clogs my throat. I — I didn't expect this. I didn't expect to look out the window of the shuttle as I left, and think of everything I was leaving behind, and wonder if it was worth it.

Godspeed. My whole life is . . . was on that ship. Everything. Every memory

I have, every feeling I felt, every important thing about me came from within those battered steel walls.

And I'm abandoning it.

And over eight hundred people who are still inside.

A crazy thought fills my mind: I want to reach out, cancel the rockets, point the shuttle back to *Godspeed*. I don't want to go. I don't want to leave home.

But then the red dots on the monitor light up again, and the rockets burst with power, and the shuttle dips back toward the planet, and it doesn't matter, it's too late.

I can never go back to *Godspeed*.

The red lights on the monitor blink on and off as a series of bursts from the rockets align the shuttle into position. Between it and the weightlessness of no gravity, I'm disoriented—the only steady image in front of me is Centauri-Earth.

"It's so weird," Amy says. "It's like we're upside down, facing the planet, but it doesn't *feel* like we're upside down." She swipes her hand over her hair, futilely trying to smooth it down, but it just floats up again.

"Orbit break initiating," the computer says.

All three of the big red lights blink on and stay on. The shuttle is pushed forward, straight toward the planet. I glance at Amy: her eyes are wide with fear, her fingers curled over the edge of the armrests of her chair. But I know— this is what she wants. Giving her Centauri-Earth is the only way I'll ever be able to make her truly happy, to make up for the fact that my careless actions trapped her in the cage of *Godspeed* with the likes of Luthor and people who will never be able to accept her.

"Deorbit burn," the computer announces.

"Ready?" Amy whispers.

"No," I confess. I want to give Amy the planet, but I wish it wasn't at the cost of the only home I've ever known.

The shuttle picks up speed, aiming at a downward angle toward the planet. All three red lights on the monitor in front of Amy glow brightly. A few smaller lights, scattered between the bigger one, blink on—more rockets are firing, increasing our thrust toward Centauri-Earth.

"Entry interface acquired," the computer says.

The planet fills the window. Blue-green-white. I can just see the nose of the shuttle, a dull grayish-green that starts to glow red. Something bright silver sparkles in the corner of my eye, but as I turn my head to see it, the shuttle dips again. Flashes of orange and yellow and red flicker around the window.

I glance over at Amy. Her little gold cross floats around her neck. She snatches it with one hand, clutching it so tightly that her knuckles whiten. Her mouth moves silently, forming words I cannot hear.

Lights blink chaotically across the control panel—rockets are bursting on and off, making our descent veer into an angled zigzag, designed, I suspect, to slow us down. I occasionally catch glimpses of the planet, but for the most part the windows are blurred with orange and red—flames? Or just heat from the deorbital burn? I don't know, I don't *know*, and by all the stars, how did I ever think we could land a frexing shuttle *by ourselves*?

Something smashes into the side of the shuttle—or at least, it feels that way as the entire shuttle wobbles and veers suddenly off course. A dozen lights flick on and off, and the computer chirps, "Landing signal disrupted. Manual mode on."

"What's going on?" Amy yells.

Red lights on the ceiling of the bridge flick on, casting a bloody glow around us. I look to Amy, and I can tell that she realizes the same thing I have: something's wrong. "Ground impact in T minus fifteen minutes," the computer says in a perfectly calm tone.

"Ground impact?" Amy parrots, her voice high and cracked. "We're crashing!"

My heart stops as I realize she's right. I grab the small steering wheel that juts out from under the control panel and do the only thing that makes sense— I jerk it back as hard as I can, hoping that somehow I can at least make it so we don't hit the planet head-on. The horizon wobbles on our screen, and more lights flash on and off on the control panel.

"Eighty kilometers above surface," the computer says. "Active deceleration initiated."

Several of the lights blink out, and the shuttle seems to drop—or maybe it's just that gravity kicks back in, slamming us into our chairs fully. Amy screams, a short burst of sound that is nothing but vocalized terror.

Something—a rocket failing? a computer malfunction?—knocks the shuttle off course again. I can see features of the planet's surface now: mountains and lakes and cliffs.

And we're going to crash into them.

3: AMY

I've heard that when you're in a life-or-death situation, like a car accident or a gunfight, all your senses shoot up to almost superhuman level, everything slows down, and you're hyper-aware of what's happening around you.

As the shuttle careens toward the earth, the exact opposite is true for me.

Everything silences, even the screams and shouts from the people on the other side of the metal door, the crashes that I pray aren't bodies, the hissing of rockets, Elder's cursing, my pounding heartbeat.

I feel nothing—not the seat belt biting into my flesh, not my clenching jaw, nothing. My whole body is numb.

Scent and taste disappear.

The only thing about my body that works is my eyes, and they are filled with the image before them. The ground seems to leap up at us as we hurtle toward it. Through the blurry image of the world below us, I see the outline of land—a continent. And at once, my heart lurches with the desire to know this world, to make it our home.

My eyes drink up the image of the planet—and my stomach sinks with the knowledge that this is a coastline I've never seen before. I could spin a globe of Earth around and still be able to recognize the way Spain and Portugal reach into the Atlantic, the curve of the Gulf of Mexico, the pointy end of India.

But this continent—it dips and curves in ways I don't recognize, swirls into an unknown sea, creating peninsulas in shapes I do not know, scattering out islands in a pattern I cannot connect.

And it's not until I see this that I realize: this world may one day become our home, but it will never be the home I left behind.

"Frex, frex, *frex!*" Elder shouts, pulling so hard against the steering wheel that the veins on his neck pop out.

I swallow dryly—this is no time to be sentimental. "What should we do?" I shout back over the sound of beepings and alarms from the control panel.

"I don't know; I don't frexing *know!*"

A yellowish-brown cliff looms high, seemingly parallel to the shuttle, and it isn't until we pass over it that I realize we aren't going to crash into it.

"Ground impact in T minus five minutes, shuttle off course from initial landing sequence," the computer says in a perfectly bland voice, and I wish it was a person so I could punch it.

"*Are* we going to crash?" I gasp, ripping my gaze from the image through the honeycombed glass window to face Elder.

Elder's pale and his face is tight. He shakes his head, and I know he doesn't mean, "No, we're not going to crash." He means, "I don't know, we might."

My eyes dart to a circular screen on the control panel—it shows a horizon line that dips and spins chaotically.

A lit button near me flashes, and I read the words engraved onto it: STA-BILIZER. That sounds good? I don't know—but Elder's straining to keep the ship steady, and it can't hurt, and I don't know if I should, but—I push it.

The horizon dips all the way down, then all the way up, jerking me around like some sort of sick combination of a roller coaster and the whirling teacup ride at Disney World. Indicator lights show us tiny rockets that are bursting at the bottom of the ship, making us even out until the entire shuttle steadies and slows.

"What the—" Elder starts, but he's cut off when the rockets sputter, and we drop straight out of the sky.

I scream as we plummet toward the earth.

Elder slams his fist against one set of controls, then another. We're drop-ping so quickly that the image outside the windows blurs and all I can see is murky colors smeared together.

The horizon dips again as Elder's button-pushing works—and then fails—and we're crashing down, down. Rockets flare, casting red-yellow streams of fire around us—

"Ground sensors feedback: suitable landing site," the computer says over the sound of the alarms. "Initiate landing rockets, yes or no?"

The green Y and the red N light up again.

"Push it!" I shout as Elder slams his fist against the Y.

I can see streams of white-blue fire shooting out the front, and the shuttle jerks, then slows, the sudden movements leaving me breathless. And just like that, all my other senses kick in. Everything becomes real again. I taste copper in my mouth—I've bitten my lip so hard I've drawn blood—and I can already tell that I'll bruise from the too-tight seat belt on my chest and around my hips. The noise from the other side of the door seems deafening, but I can pick out individual cries of pain and alarm from the 1,456 passengers in the cryo room.

And then we stop.

We haven't landed—we're hovering over the treetops—but we're not moving forward anymore. We're not crashing.

The shuttle isn't completely stable, and I can hear a *hiss-shh* sound from under our feet: the rockets are shooting down straight into the ground, keep-ing us over the surface.

"Land shuttle? Please select yes or no," the computer says evenly.

Elder and I exchange a glance. There is no meaning, no words behind the look—just one shared feeling. *Relief.*

Instead of reaching for the blinking green Y, he grabs my hand. His fin-gers slide between mine, and they're slick with sweat, but his grip is firm and strong. No matter what happens, what awaits us on the other side—we'll face it together. Elder pulls our joined hands toward the last button, and we push it.

The *hiss-shh* slowly fades as the shuttle sinks down and down toward the ground. I realize that somewhere in our mad descent, gravity's returned, and everything feels heavy again, especially the seat belt strapping me down. I throw it off and race to the honeycombed glass windows. I can see that our landing has decimated the area—the trees nearest us are nothing but smoldering ash, and the ground is black and shiny, almost as if it has melted. Trees—trees! Real trees, real ground, a real *world!* Right here!

With a sudden lurch that nearly knocks me to the floor, the rockets cut out and we drop the last few feet to the surface of the planet.

"Well," Elder says, staring out the window at the burning earth, "at least we didn't die."

"We didn't die," I repeat. I look up at his shining eyes. "We didn't die!" Elder grabs my wrist, pulling me into his lap. I melt against the warmth and security of his arm, and our lips collide in a kiss full of all the fear and passion and hope this new world brings. We kiss as if it were our first kiss and our last, all at once. Our lips meet in desperation; our bodies wrap around each other with a sort of fervent fury that exists only in the joy of surviving the certainty of death.

I pull away, gasping for air. I look into Elder's eyes . . . and for one brief moment, I see nothing but the boy who taught me about first kisses and second chances. But then the image shifts, and I don't see him. I see Orion. I scramble up out of Elder's lap, and even though I tell myself that Elder isn't Orion, I can't forget about the way Elder insisted Orion be on this shuttle with us, as if his crimes should be rewarded with a whole planet instead of only ice.

Elder reaches for me again as he tries to get up from his chair—but can't. "Stupid seat belt," he mutters, unfastening it.

I turn around.

The world is there, on the other side of the glass window.

The world.

Our world.

"We made it," I say.

"Yeah," Elder replies, unable to keep the surprise from his voice. "We did. . . ." His words are a breath of warmth at the back of my neck.

I turn around to meet his eyes, but my vision slides past him, to the door that leads to the hallway that leads to the cryo room.

"My parents," I whisper.

I can finally have my parents back.

4: ELDER

Without saying another word, Amy turns and runs through the seal-lock doors. Her footsteps clatter across the metal floor, the sound rising over the distant shouts from the 1,456 passengers in the cryo room. I take a deep, shaking breath. I still can't believe we've actually made it. Despite my incompetence, despite whatever it was that caused our near-disastrous crash landing . . .

I pause. What *was* it that made us nearly crash? It felt almost as if something *hit* us. . . .

"This concludes the landing of the shuttle," the computer says. "Please shift operational command of the mission to the highest-ranking officer in cryogenics once reanimation is complete. Do not leave the shuttle until you are commanded to do so. Thank you for contributing to the mission of the Financial Resource Exchange."

The computer's voice crackles and dies, leaving me in silence. In its place, the monitor on the control panel lights up, flashing a single phrase:

Military Authorization Code: - - - - - - - - - -

That word—*military*—makes my stomach jerk with the same intensity of the ship's sudden stop earlier. Orion would have been in my place if he hadn't feared the military of Sol-Earth so much that he tried to kill them, convinced they would turn us into soldiers or slaves.

It's hard for me to think of Orion as Amy does: a psychopath murderer. Because if I hadn't had Amy, I might have been Orion. What choice would I have had? I'd have become like him . . . or like Eldest.

And no matter what's happened, I can't help but believe that Orion and his tactics were preferable to Eldest and his lies.

The military authorization request blinks at me, waiting for a code I don't have. I cast one last, longing look at the world beyond the window, the never-ending sky, and then turn my back to it. I can already hear fear and pain rising up in the voices of my people, and the next step belongs to the frozens in the cryo room, not me.

When I reach the cryo room, Amy stands in front of her parents' cryo chambers, leaning over my people strapped to the row. As they pull aside the tether that anchored them to the cryo chambers for safety, Amy pushes past them, her eyes bouncing over the informational readout with such single-minded focus that she doesn't notice the way my people are fumbling, struggling to stand after being bound to the chambers.

I'm surrounded by chaos. Kit, our doctor, has a group of people dashing about, unlatching the tethers we used to strap people to stable objects. It is immediately apparent that the tethers were not a good idea. My stomach twists as Kit shoves a man's shoulder back in joint, and nearly everyone has the same sort of shocked, horrified expressions that I've only ever seen on disaster relief videos from tragedies on Sol-Earth.

A woman near me starts screaming, the sound ricocheting around the metal walls of the cryo chamber, piercing every ear with its horror.

Kit's group of helpers rush forward, disentangling her and the woman beside her from the tether, but it's obvious that it's too late—a deep red mark wraps around her neck. The tether that was supposed to save her life slipped and choked her instead.

I step toward the woman. Her screams have stopped, replaced with sobs.

Amy gasps, an almost inaudible sound, but I whip around to find out what's wrong.

She shoots me a satisfied smile of triumph, and it is only then that I notice the little doors in front of the cryo chambers have all snapped open.

"Frex, do you have to do this now?" I ask, striding toward her.

"*Yes,*" she says fiercely.

"*All* of them?" I ask. I could almost understand her need to awaken her parents, but we don't need to add nearly a hundred frozen people to the cacophony of voices around us.

There are dozens injured and at least one—no, two—no, more than that—dead. We don't have time to worry about the frexing frozens, not now, not after we just crash-landed.

I start to tell Amy this, but then she says, "They can *help.*" I think she believes this, but I don't think she thought of it until I questioned her.

Kit rushes over to me. There's a cut on her head leaking blood down the side of her face, but it doesn't look too bad. "Is everything okay?" she asks, worry making her brow crease.

I look around me. Everyone seems to have a glazed look in their eyes—shock, I realize. It's clear that while the tethers did keep people from bouncing around during the crash-landing, they also cut into people's skin or slipped around their necks or jerked them around so violently that they got whiplash.

"Yeah," I growl. "Everything's brilly."

"No, I mean the landing—is it—the planet—" Kit doesn't know how to say what she's really asking.

One half of my lips curve up, and for a moment, I don't see the metal walls wrapped around the despair of my people as they try to recover from the crash. I see only the sky. "Yeah," I tell her. "That part really is brilly."

She breathes a sigh of relief, and I know what she was really worried about was: is all of *this* worth all of that? And I wonder—has it been? My mind flashes to Shelby, the Shipper who taught me how to land. Without her, we really would have crashed. Whatever the cause of us being knocked off course, the only reason we weren't killed is because of the training she gave me.

And because of the choices I made, she's dead anyway.

The rows of cryo chambers hiss to life. With a clattering crash, the chambers shoot out, dropping support legs onto the floor. Thin robotic arms slide over the top of the cryo box, lifting away the glass lids and sucking them back into the chambers.

A mechanical hum fills the room, drowning out the sounds of pain and fear coming from the passengers. The metal arms shoot back over the cryo chambers, this time with sharp needles sticking out from one side. The arms slam straight down, driving the needles into the ice. I can see tiny streams of bubbles—jets of hot air?—bubbling through the frozen cryoliquid. Already, water drips down, pooling on the ground below. A slope so slight I've never noticed it before draws the water under the chambers.

Amy's eyes are glued to cryo chambers 41 and 40—her parents.

We don't need this. The frozens will cause nothing but trouble now. We need to help the injured.

And . . . and I need *her*. I need Amy. With me, not staring at some frozen boxes. Even now, I can feel the way every person *except* Amy is looking to me, waiting for me to be everything they need me to be. And I'm not sure if I can stand without her by my side.

"What can I do?" I ask anyway, turning away from Amy toward Kit.

Kit leads me to the far wall, where she has formed a sort of triage, setting up the nurses who can aid with the minor cuts and bruises, but there are still dozens of people with much more urgent needs. The tethers were too narrow; they cut into people's flesh, and even I, with my inexperienced eyes, can see that they'll need stitches. More than one person has a dislocated shoulder, like the man Kit helped earlier, and there are so many people sitting against the wall that I'm not sure if it's because they've hurt themselves and can't stand or if it's something else, something less serious, or more.

I meet Kit's eyes. She's desperate. Until a few days ago, she was only an apprentice—Doc is the one who should be here, the one who could efficiently solve everyone's problems. But Doc was a problem by himself.

In Kit's hands, I can see square, pale green patches. Phydus.

"No," I say, the word a command. Phydus was a part of *Godspeed*; it drugged us into submission for centuries. It has no place here; it has no place in any world without walls or lies.

Kit opens her mouth to protest, but she must see something of Eldest in the way I stand now, because she silently puts the Phydus patches back in her pocket.

"Amy," I bark over my shoulder.

"In a minute," she calls back, breathless, her eyes still on her frozen parents.

"*Amy,*" I order.

She looks up at me, hurt in her eyes.

"We need help."

"In a *minute*," she says again.

"Now."

I can tell from the venomous look she shoots me that she can see something of Eldest in me now too.

But she leaves the cryo chambers and approaches us. Her sullen attitude changes as she notices the injured around us, seemingly for the first time. "What can I do to help?" she asks, her voice sincere.

Behind her, the cryo chambers drip as the ice melts.

5 : AMY

Kit makes me watch as she gives a man stitches over a gash in his leg. "What's your name?" I ask, trying to distract both the man and myself from the amount of blood pumping past his knee.

"Heller," he grunts. He's in the middle-aged generation of people from *Godspeed*, but while most of the others who are forty are starting to show the frailty of age, Heller looks as if his bones are made of steel and his skin is leather. He looks down at his wound in disdain, as if mad that his body should betray him with any weakness.

"What happened, Heller?" I don't want to watch the way Kit pulls the surgical thread tight through his flesh, oddly pale with spots of red blood. My eyes dart to the melting cryo boxes, and I force myself to pay attention to the injured man before me. I've let myself be distracted too much already.

"Frex if I know," he growls. "I was sitting there, all trussed up, and a sheet of metal slid over my leg, sliced it right open."

"The door to one of the rabbit hatches broke," Kit says, tugging the surgical thread tight. "It got several of the others too."

"What happened to the rabbits?"

Kit jerks her head to the wall near the gen lab. A dozen bright red-and-white splotches dot the gray metal wall. I swallow back the bile rising in my throat.

"Did you see that?" Kit asks me, tying a knot around the stitch. "See how I did it?"

"Just like sewing cloth," I say. Not that I've sewed much in my life, but I had to learn how to hem my pants on the ship.

"Exactly like it." She hands me the needle and surgical thread. "Now go do the next person's."

"You want *me* to stitch someone?"

Kit nods.

"What about that foam stuff?" I ask, thinking of the last time I was here, the time Doc shot me, and how Kit squirted foam into my wound and sealed it up better than stitches or any bandage could.

"We don't have much. We should save it for emergencies."

"This is an emergency!"

Kit shakes her head, already kneeling beside the next person. "Not enough of one."

I stand awkwardly for a moment, unsure of what to do with myself. Elder is nearby but focused on helping others. My heart swells with pride at the way they turn to him, trust evident on their faces despite everything.

A woman near the wall moans. Her eyes are on the three dead bodies lined against the shuttle wall at her feet, the people who didn't survive the landing. I think for a moment her exclamation of pain was for that, but then I see the river of blood snaking down her arm.

I squat beside her, but she barely registers my presence. I peel back her shirt—a ragged cut mars her back shoulder, the red a stark contrast to her dark brown skin.

"I'm going to stitch you up, okay?" I ask, hoping that I sound confident.

She glances up at me, a look of fear in her eyes. I wonder if she doesn't want me to work on her because of who I am and how I look, but she turns away again, angling her shoulder more toward me, offering it up like a sacrifice.

"Do you know how to do this?" she asks, her voice hollow.

"Yeah," I lie, because honestly, what else am I supposed to tell her?

The first time I pull too tight, ripping the thread through her. She hisses in pain, and I try to apologize, but she's shaking her head, eyes closed, wishing, I know, for it to just be over.

"What's your name?" I ask, trying the same diversion tactics I used with Heller.

"Lorin," she says shortly. I start to make small talk with her, but then I notice the way her lips are pressed tightly together, her eyes squinched shut.

She doesn't want to talk.

I plunge the needle back in, and out, and in, and out, and then I can breathe again because it's finally done.

"Thanks," she mutters.

I spray the cut down with disinfectant and start on the next person.

I lose track of time and how long I have left until my parents awaken, my body slipping into a machine-like state as I try to separate my mind from my actions. I try not to think about how the needle pierces flesh, not cloth; I try not to notice the wet sound of the thread sliding through bloody skin. I am so focused on what I'm doing that when a harsh, shrieking scream echoes throughout the chamber I jump back, dropping the needle.

Like everyone else, I look up—but all I see is the metal ceiling.

"That was outside," Elder says, his voice deep and low as he crouches beside me.

My eyes round. "What was it?"

"Something—outside," he repeats.

The man whose leg I'd been stitching looks up at us, fear in his eyes. "Is that one of them monsters Orion warned us about?" he asks, and I'm ashamed to admit that was the same thing I—probably everyone—was thinking.

I look around me. All 1,456 sets of eyes are watching us. Are watching *him*. Elder. They are waiting for their leader to react. If he shows fear now, their new world will begin with fear.

Elder lowers his voice. "I've got to go," he tells me in nearly a whisper. "I'm going outside," he says, this time loud enough for everyone to hear.

I grab his wrist, leaving a bloody handprint there. "Why?"

Another screeching cry echoes above us. Whatever it is—it's close.

Elder pulls me up, dragging me away from the man I was working on. One of Kit's nurses kneels beside him and takes over, disinfecting the needle I dropped.

"Remember the way the shuttle was knocked off course?" Elder asks me softly. I nod. "What if that was no accident?"

"We were, what—attacked?" My voice sounds doubtful. "And you were mad at me for trying to wake up the frozens? If we were attacked, we need them even more!"

"Shh!" Elder says, his eyes darting over my shoulder. No one heard me, though. Still, even Elder seems to agree that the idea that we were attacked seems a little ludicrous. The shuttle *did* seem to be pushed out of trajectory—but the shuttle is also old. One of the rockets could have blown. Something could have malfunctioned.

"We have to know what we're up against," Elder says.

I bite my lip.

"I'm going," he repeats.

"Then I'm going too." I say this immediately, without thought, but as soon as the words are out, my eyes flick to the cryo chambers. It will be soon now.

Elder notices. He touches my arm. "You should stay," he says. I think he's only saying this so I don't feel guilty. "I *have* to go."

When I look into his eyes, I know that his sense of responsibility outweighs every fear I have.

"Well," I say, "at least go armed."

6: ELDER

"I don't know how to shoot," I remind Amy as she roots around in the armory.

"It's easy," she says. She thrusts a heavy metal gun into my hands. "I've already loaded it. Point this end at whatever's out there and pull the trigger. Bang. That's all there is to it."

She drops two small, green, egg-shaped objects in my hand. "Impact grenades," she says at my curious look. "If the gun doesn't work, just throw these. They'll explode once they hit something."

My eyes widen. The grenades don't seem fragile, but the idea of them exploding doesn't fill me with ease.

"And take this—" Amy adds, reaching for a large weapon with a tube the size of my arm.

"Enough!" I say. "I can barely carry these. I'm only going outside to *look*."

Another piercing cry cuts through the air.

"Wait," Amy says, her eyes pleading with me. Her fingers curl around my arm, gripping my wrist, holding me back with more strength than I knew she had. "Please. Just wait for my dad to wake up. The military can take care of whatever that is out there. That's their job."

"And what's my job?" I ask, gently breaking free of her grasp. "To protect *my* people. I have to do this." My people need to see me facing the world and whatever dangers it might hold. If I do, then they can too. But if I stay here, cowering, waiting for the frozens to save us, that will become their first instinct.

"Be safe." Amy says the words like a prayer. Her eyes don't meet mine, then she leans in, quick, and pecks me on the lips. Her cheeks flame up in a blush. All I want to do is grab her and crush her against me, to give her a kiss that's worthy of that blush.

"I'll be fine." It's not until I say this that I realize it's probably not true. My first reaction when I heard the screeching sound outside was to look, to calm the fear on my people's faces. But now my mouth is dry and my stomach twists as if the fear inside it was poisonous acid. I think it's the armory. Being surrounded by this many weapons reminds me that there's a reason why we have them.

My hand goes to the wi-com embedded behind my left ear, and I press the button down. Instead of the usual *beep, beep-beep*, there's nothing but a click as the button's depressed and released. I frown and push the button again, so forcefully that I wince in pain.

Shite. The wi-com network was on the ship. My fingers run over the edge of the button, a perfectly circular bump that has been a part of my body for as long as I can remember. Now useless. The frexing thing is useless. It's implanted into my flesh, its wires creep beside my veins, and it will never work again.

Amy grabs my hand, pulls it away from the button under my skin. "You don't need to tell them anything," she says. "They all know what you're about to do for them."

I've never felt so disconnected from . . . everything. It's one thing to know that the ship's unreachable, but now the connection I've had with my people who are here is gone too.

I wait until Amy's back in the cryo room before I turn toward the bridge. I don't think I could have kept my fear hidden from her as I opened the door, and I didn't want her to see me hesitate. I don't have a military authorization code, but Shelby showed me how to override the system for emergencies. I can't do much, but I could put the shuttle in lockdown, set an alarm sequence, or start the sprinklers in the event of a fire. And I can open the doors.

I stand, leaning against the control panel, staring through the thick glass of the honeycombed window. It's foggy now with condensation, but I can still make out the world that is ours. I touch the thick glass, surprised at the warmth it offers.

I know from pictures of Sol-Earth that the super-tall bushes are called trees and that the wood from them is the same kind of wood that made the table I used when working on assignments from Eldest. I know the dirt, although blackened from our descent, will not be the smooth, clay-like, evenly processed soil that filled the Feeder Level.

But I'm not looking at any of that.

I'm looking out, past the burnt ground and the broken trees, their limbs twisting and turning like tangled yarn, past the horizon and to the sky.

And no matter how much my eyes strain, there isn't a wall. Not a single frexing wall.

Something dark flashes in the blue sky, something unnatural, and my grip around the gun Amy gave me tightens.

I give my order to the computer: *open doors.*

It works. A cracking sound echoes throughout the bridge. I grab the control panel to steady myself—but my disorientation isn't from the shuttle moving. It's from the window breaking open. Just as I once saw the ceiling of the Keeper Level split in half, the honeycombed glass of the window lifts on one end, rising like a hinged lid.

The individual glass pieces were held together by metal solder, but now I realize that the metal is actually a part of an intricate mechanical feature. The hexagonal segments of glass move and shift, forming a ramp down the right side of the ship. The angle is steep, but the glass is long enough to stretch out past the burnt ground to the yellowish earth beyond.

I step past the control panel, brushing my hand along the exposed edge of the shuttle. The metal between the glass serves as a grip—I can easily walk down the sharp ramp formed by the window pieces and set foot on the new world.

A warm breeze blows past, filling my nose with the scent of ash and dirt, lifting the edge of my hair. The air is thick and humid, but the wind is as soft as Amy's shy kisses; and although it barely touches my skin, it spurs me just as deeply. I race down the ramp, skidding to a halt only when my feet touch the ground of the new world. The sandy soil shifts underfoot, making me feel as if I could plant myself into the earth as surely as one of the twisty trees.

My vision drifts up. How could I have ever thought the blue-and-white painted steel plates of the roof of the Feeder Level emulated the sky? They don't. They don't look anything like the gradient blues and grays above me, the wispy strands of clouds that move before my eyes. I'd never understood how Amy could miss Sol-Earth so much, how *Godspeed* was never enough for her. What's the difference between air from a spaceship and air from a planet?

Everything.

The two suns overhead beam down, so bright that staring at them makes me blink black dots. Two suns. Centauri-Earth is in a binary star system, unlike Sol-Earth, which had only one sun. The big sun is slightly higher in the sky than the littler one. The smaller sun has an orange-red color, a color that reminds me of Amy's hair, actually, and the bigger one is bright white, reminding me of her skin.

A high-pitched ringing pierces my ears, and I whip my head around to the forest. Something dark moves in the shadows, but as I try to squint through the tree branches, I hear another sound.

A horrific, bestial cry ringing across the sky.

I spin around, looking up at the direction of the sound.

And I see the monster Orion warned us of.

The bird-*thing* lands only a few meters in front of me, but it's so heavy that I can feel the *thump* of its body reverberating on the sandy ground. The creature towers over me, its long, pointed head tilted to the sky before peering down and opening its hard beak, exposing saw-like teeth. Green leathery skin that's so dark it's nearly black gives way to scaly claws and membrane-like wings. It's a horrible monster that seems cobbled together from creatures on Sol-Earth—a dinosaur head atop a lizard's body with raptor claws and bat-like wings.

My first instinct is to jab my finger into my wi-com and get help, but of course that doesn't work.

The thing stretches out its wings—each twice as long as I am tall and adorned with two-fingered hooked claws on top of the sharply angled joints. The claws spread apart and grasp at the air in my direction. The beast's feet grip the sandy soil as it leans forward, opens its mouth, and emits a piercing, ringing scream at me, a high-pitched shriek that feels as if it is vibrating my bones. Even though the creature is far enough away that I couldn't reach it, I can feel its hot breath on my skin, see its sliver of a black tongue raised as it screeches at me.

I fumble for the gun, the grenades, anything.

The creature launches up, pushing off from the ground and slamming into me with its hard, boney head. I crash to the ground, the monster on top of me, its body so heavy that I can't catch my breath.

It bends its long, snake-like neck toward me, its jaw opening, the black, saw-edged teeth foaming slightly as it nears my face.

A shot cracks out.

The beast whips up its head, startled. A bullet whizzes past, nicking it in the back. Its claws clench, and my skin rips along with the cloth of my shirt.

Another gunshot and the bird-like thing launches up, pushing against my rib cage as it leaps to the trees. I gasp for breath as it claws its way up one of the trees and takes off, flapping its voluminous wings as one final gunshot echoes after it.

"Get inside!" Amy shouts from the bridge of the shuttle. "Hurry!"

I scramble up. Blood drips from my chest, and my shirt is ruined, but the wounds are nothing compared to what could have happened. Amy grabs my arm as I reach the top of the ramp and jerks me into the shuttle.

7: AMY

As soon as the door slams shut, I spin Elder around, looking for wounds. All I can think is, *I almost lost him.* Every other thought — excitement about the planet, anticipation for my parents' return, fear of the monsters outside — all of that is gone as my eyes and my heart focus on the blood leaking down Elder's chest. He knocks my hands aside, taking off his shirt and using it to blot out the blood on the scrapes. They don't look deep, just jagged and rough. I grab some of the disinfectant Kit had me using to help with the stitches and spray Elder down.

"How did you know to come outside and help me?" Elder asks, still breathless.

"I heard that pterodactyl-looking thing scream — it sounded so much closer than before." I pause. "What was that thing?"

Elder shakes his head, looking at his ruined shirt. "One of Orion's frexing monsters, I guess. Did you see anything in the forest?"

I shake my head. "What was in the forest?"

"I . . . I don't know." Elder finally meets my eyes. "Think one of those things knocked into the side of the ship when we were landing? It was big enough to throw us off course."

"I don't know," I say, echoing Elder. I am only starting to realize how much I just don't know. Like, for starters, what the hell was that *thing*? It looked kind of like a pterodactyl, with a pointed head and massive wings and jagged claws, but there was also something distinctly *alien* about it.

Alien. That's what everything on this planet is to us. I suppress a shudder, my hands instinctively gripping the still-warm gun.

I should have been able to hit that creature; I should have killed it. But I was too scared, afraid that I might accidentally hit Elder.

And afraid of *it*.

Elder takes the gun from me. "I'll put this back in the armory," he says. "And I think I should take a closer look at what we have there."

I try to push the image of the beast from my mind as I head back to the cryo chamber, but I keep seeing the way it opened its mouth, lowering it toward Elder's face. . . .

Kit grabs me as soon as I re-enter the cryo room. A few people look up fearfully—they know Elder was outside, and they heard the monster's scream after he left the shuttle. They think whatever it was got him. "He's fine," I manage. "Everything's fine."

They are happy to believe the lie, at least for now.

"Nearly done," Kit says, pushing the hair out of her face and leaving a smear of blood on her forehead. "Two bones that need setting, and then the nurses and I will check the women, just as a precaution. . . . "

My stomach sinks. I'd nearly forgotten—the pregnant women.

"Anything else I can do?" I ask.

Kit gives me a watery smile. "You've already been a huge help."

I watch as she walks toward the last group of people waiting for medical aid. My hands are bloody, my arms are tired, and I want nothing more than to curl up in bed and forget about this day. Maybe this was all a huge mistake.

"Amy?" asks a voice I know, a voice I love, a voice I never thought I'd hear again, oh God, oh God, *oh God*.

I turn around, and standing there, looking exactly as I remembered him, is my father.

"Daddy!" I scream, and launch myself at him.

And his arms, his arms, they wrap around me, they pull me tight to him, and everything is fine, everything is *wonderful*, because I finally, finally have my dad back.

I'm sobbing and laughing and choking and sputtering and crying and speaking all at the same time.

"Amy," he says, a chuckle in his voice. "What's going on?"

I step back. My father's wearing a green surgical gown, not unlike the one that Doc tried to wrap me in when I first awoke. I can see that nearly every one of the cryo boxes is empty now that people are starting to get up, to pull the gowns off the little metal arms over the boxes to clothe themselves with. And Mom—

I run to her. I skid around the open cryo boxes and the other frozens starting to wake up. *Mom.* And though I've dreamed about seeing her with my eyes open a million times, my dreams were nothing, *nothing* compared to actually seeing her.

Mom's laughing—her voice cracks from disuse—but the music of her laughter is there, and it wraps around me just the way her arms do. "I told you that wouldn't be so bad," she whispers in my hair.

I choke out a sob. She doesn't know. She thinks I just woke up too. She thinks I've been sleeping beside her. She doesn't know about the three months I lived on the ship, the three months I thought I'd never see her again.

Mom's hands frame my face, and I notice that they're still as cold as ice. I glance past her shoulder, toward the hallway that leads to the armory, the bridge, and outside. I want Elder to be here; I want to introduce him to my parents. I want him to understand why I needed them, how everything is better now that they're with me. But he's not here.

"Oh, baby," Mom says, her eyes brimming with joy. "We made it! We finally made it!" She pulls me close to her again, squeezing me in a tight hug. "There's a whole new world for us to discover together," she says into my hair.

"I missed you so much," I whisper, the sound cracking as my voice catches.

Mom pulls back, tucking a piece of my hair behind my ear. "What do you mean?"

Suddenly, I notice the silence permeating the room. The people from the ship are watching the frozens awaken warily, and the frozens are eyeing the people from the ship with something like fear, something like caution.

My father steps closer, and this movement brings every eye to us. "Why are you dressed like that?" he asks, taking in my homespun tunic and pants.

I turn to face my mom, and I forget about everyone but the three of us. This is my world: my mother, my father, and me.

"I woke up early," I say, staring into Mom's green eyes that everyone says are exactly the same as mine.

A little frown shadows her face.

"How early?" my father asks.

The answer fades from my lips. At first I thought I was fifty years early and that my father and I would be having this conversation when I was an old woman. Then I thought I was a lifetime early and that I would die before having this chance.

"Three months early," I say, because until just this moment, I hadn't realized that the clock had stopped.

"Three months?" my mother gasps.

"Over a hundred days," I answer. I lost track at the end, when I realized the days on *Godspeed* didn't matter anymore because they were ending.

"What happened?" my mother asks, reaching for my wrist.

I open my mouth, but no words fall out. She's holding my wrist in exactly the same spot that Luthor held me down. *What happened?* I was promised a world, but I awoke to a cage.

There is so much I want to tell her. I need to tell her.

But as I look into her face, I know: it doesn't matter. Not now, not in this moment. What matters right now is this: we're each of us standing here, together, alive, *together*.

Dad steps closer to us, dropping one hand on my shoulder. He opens his mouth, and I'm not sure what I expect him to say, but it's not this: "What's going on?"

And the moment we shared melts like the ice dripping down the drain in the floor.

Dad looks out at the crowd of silent watchers from *Godspeed*—the wounded, the scared. "What is going on?" he repeats, authority ringing in his voice. He's looking for a leader, and Elder's not here.

The people from *Godspeed* don't know how to react. For a moment, I see my family, my people, the way they do. Strange. Weird. They just pulled themselves from their cryo chambers—cryo chambers that the people from the ship didn't even know existed until recently—and now there's this man with pale skin like mine, staring at them, demanding information from them. If they feared me, what must they think of my father? Of the ninety-six other people from Earth who are rising from their icy graves to take over?

After a moment, Kit steps forward. She doesn't speak, though. Her eyes go to me.

Slowly, my father turns, searching my face for an answer.

Mom strokes my hair one last time until the tension in the air makes her step back. She moves to stand beside my father, and I notice the way their hands brush against each other.

"Amy? Why were you over there, with those people? What happened?" he asks, each question dropping in volume until the last one is for my ears alone.

"Come with me," I say. This is one discussion I'd rather have in private.

Instead, my father looks around, scanning the chambers. "I'm not the one in charge," he says. "Robertson or Kennedy—"

"They're dead," I say.

His eyes snap down to me, and for a moment, I don't recognize him. He's never looked at me this way before. He's never looked at me like he was a colonel instead of my father.

"What's going on?" he orders.

"D-dad," I stutter over the name. "There was . . . I mean, the ship . . . It's not like what we thought it would be. These people were born on the ship," I say, waving my arm toward Kit and the others. I watch his face, carefully waiting for the moment when he finally notices that everyone from *Godspeed* looks the same. His eyes narrow in a calculating gaze. "You don't understand. A lot of stuff has happened. And we just got the shuttle to land. It—sort of crashed. And there are a lot of people injured, and we do have a leader, but—"

My father's eyes soften as I try to stutter through an explanation. He pulls me closer, wrapping his strength around me, and I feel safe for the first time in more than three centuries.

"I want to know more," he tells me in a low voice. "We'll talk later." Over the top of my head, he barks, "Bledsoe!"

A woman a few rows away stands at attention. I gasp—I know her. She's the woman Orion nearly killed, the one Elder and I saved while Theo Kennedy drowned in his cryo box. My mind goes back to the chart I made three months ago. Emma Bledsoe, thirty-four years old, a US Marine originally from South Africa.

"Sir," Bledsoe calls back to my father.

"Operation Genesis in effect," he says.

I don't know what Operation Genesis is, but Emma Bledsoe obviously does: she immediately begins calling out to individuals—the other military personnel who'd been frozen—and instructs them to line up in the space between those from *Godspeed* and those from Earth.

I glance over the heads of the military people and catch Kit's eyes. She's struggling to keep her nurses working on the remaining injured, but there's real fear in the way she holds her stiff body, the way she won't fully turn her back to us. Fear of my people—fear of my father.

"Dad," I say, "there are a lot of injured people. The crash was—"

"Sir!" Bledsoe calls back, interrupting me before I have a chance to mention Elder's theory that the pterodactyl-looking things caused the crash. Her voice is loud and clear, but she has an odd accent—British, maybe, or

Australian. "There are three casualties among the shipborn." She moves to stand over the bodies of the people who didn't survive the landing.

"What happened?" My father ignores me as he moves through the crowd to inspect the bodies. "This woman looks as if she was choked." In the crowd, I can see the dead woman's friend quietly sobbing as my father roughly tilts the woman's head to look at the marking around her throat.

I notice Lorin, the woman whose shoulder I stitched, standing to the side, staring down at one of the dead men. She shuffles nervously back as Bledsoe and my father draw closer to me, too afraid to try to move past them. Her panicked eyes meet mine, and I shoot her a sympathetic smile.

"What happened?" Dad barks again.

"We had to use tethers to secure the people during the landing," Kit says, trying to keep the quaking out of her voice. "It slipped around his neck, and—"

"Why didn't you use the magnetic harnesses?" Dad snaps.

"Magnetic . . . harnesses?" Kit asks.

Dad stomps over to the wall—Lorin squeaks in terror and darts out of the way—and he bends down at the floor. His fingers feel along the tiled metal, and he does something—a flick of his wrist, a push of a button—and the metal panel lifts up. Reaching inside, he withdraws a handful of canvas straps with big, black buckles. "There are three thousand harnesses in storage here just so that you can secure your people to the floors and walls in the event of an emergency shuttle landing. Why didn't you use them?" His voice is angry, accusing.

"We . . . we didn't know they were there," Kit says meekly, her eyes wide with shock.

I can't rip my gaze from the dead. What a stupid, stupid way to die. Killed just because we didn't know about the damn harnesses.

"The captain should have known about the proper procedures for emergency shuttle launch," Dad says. He exudes frustration and anger, and even though he's wearing a silly green medical gown that opens in the back, he still carries with him more authority than I've ever seen from him before, and everyone—people from *Godspeed* and those from Earth—is listening to his every word.

"It's not like that," I say. "You don't understand, Dad, things—"

He cuts me off with a glance, and I shut up. "This is a mess," he growls. "Bledsoe, where are the medical personnel?"

"Here, sir," Bledsoe says, drawing aside five people—three men and two women.

"Dr. Gupta," Dad says, addressing one of the men. "Have your team aid with the injured," Dad commands.

The medical professionals step forward, but I can already see this won't work. If the people from *Godspeed* worried about me with my pale skin and red hair, at least they've had three months to see I wasn't a threat. I can see these people through their eyes, and while I know it's silly, I understand why they flinch away from the Indian man, why they don't understand the woman with the Southern accent, why they rush to Kit instead of allowing the black man to wrap their wounds. I want to stay and help—but what good could I do?

"Let's suit up," my father tells Bledsoe. In shifts, the people from the cryo chambers go to the trunks on the far wall and begin dressing in the clothes they brought with them from Earth. My father and the rest of the military dress in fatigues.

Their clothes, so different from the homespun tunics and trousers made by the residents of *Godspeed*, do nothing but separate everyone even more. Synthetic fibers and bright colors pop up like blemishes among the browns and blacks worn by most of the crew from the ship.

The people from *Godspeed* are more than ten times the number of people from Earth, but they're cramped together all along one wall. The room is sticky and hot, and the air stinks of sweat and fear. And anger.

I open my mouth to call my father aside—if he can't prove that he's there to help, that he's not the threat Orion said he was, he's going to be labeled an enemy. But then he turns to Bledsoe and says, "Let's inspect the armory."

It's bad enough that suddenly ninety-seven people from Earth have woken up and are taking charge, but adding guns to this mix will *not* end well.

The door to the armory is shut and locked, and it doesn't open when Dad punches the code into the keypad.

"What's wrong, sir?" Bledsoe asks.

Dad shakes his head and punches the code in again. It still doesn't work. And why should it? Orion reprogrammed it long ago.

"Dad, I need to talk to you," I say, trying to emulate the authority in his voice.

"Not now, Amy."

I've waited three months that felt like a lifetime for him to say my name, but I did not think he would preface it with those words.

"Now," I insist.

"Amy," Dad says, turning away from the control panel to face me, "I don't think you understand. We're on a mission. This is work. We need to ascertain the situation, confer with the shipborns' leader, and take control of the outlying area."

"But Dad, I—"

"Amy, I would love to stop everything and talk to you. I would love to be your daddy right now. But this is a crucial situation, and what I really need to do is figure out why this code has been changed and talk to the leader of the shipborns."

"Well," Elder says as he pushes open the door of the armory, "then it's a good thing I'm here."

8: ELDER

The first thing I notice is the doubt etched on the man's face.

"Dad," Amy tells him, "I want you to meet the leader of *Godspeed*. Elder." She stares at me hard, and it takes me a moment to realize that she's analyzing my wounds. I tug on the clean tunic, careful not to wince when the skin made raw from the beast's claws rubs against the rough cloth. "Elder," Amy continues, "this is my father, Colonel Robert Martin. He's—after the deaths of the other two frozens, he's in charge of the military from Sol-Earth." Her voice catches over her introduction of her father. I can tell that she hadn't realized he would be next in line to command the frozens.

I step forward, my mind racing, trying to remember the proper way to formally greet someone from Sol-Earth military. I shouldn't bow, should I? That seems so archaic—but then again, so is he.

Before I can do anything, though, the man turns to Amy. "I don't have time for your games," he says. "Where's the real captain?"

Amy glares at him, her shoulders rolling back and her eyes flashing. "Elder is the leader," she says again, a steely edge to her voice.

Colonel Robert Martin casts me one disdainful look. "He's a kid."

"Sir," I say, my voice dripping with derision, "I *am* the leader of *Godspeed*, and if you want to get past any of the locked doors on this shuttle, including the one to the armory you're trying to get into right now, you're going to have to show me a little more respect."

One of the colonel's eyebrows shoots up, but he doesn't argue. "I need access to the shuttle computer," he demands.

Of frexing course he does.

I explain the situation: how the glass windows opened up to create the ramp, how there's no protection from the massive, reptilian bird that wanted to eat my face off, how the computer is outside on the now-exposed bridge.

"I understand," Colonel Martin says in a voice that makes it seem as if he's bored with my assessment of the monsters, "and we will be armed—but it is essential that I have access to the computer."

I step out of the way of the armory door, letting Colonel Martin and the woman with him select weapons. Amy shoots me a questioning look. "Let me handle this," I whisper, hoping my eyes communicate my need for her to let me meet her father on my own terms. If Colonel Martin wants to talk to a leader, I don't want him reminded that I'm younger than his daughter.

Amy doesn't look happy about this, but she nods and returns to the cryo room. When Colonel Martin and the woman finish arming themselves, I lead them down the hall to the bridge door.

Amy's father strides forward onto the bridge, one hand resting almost casually on the gun strapped around his waist. The woman with him, a tall, slender woman with darker skin than I knew was possible, follows him without even glancing at me. I close the door to the bridge, trying to ignore how vulnerable to the dangers that lurk in the skies we now are.

I can tell immediately that Colonel Martin and the woman with him are unimpressed by the world spread out before them. When the honeycombed glass dropped away from the bridge earlier, I was so overwhelmed by the boundless sense of freedom that I longed to rush into it, relishing every single thing I discovered. They are ambivalent at best. A warm breeze floats past us, and I want to close my eyes and savor the scent of plants and earth it carries, but neither of them even notices.

"It's not that different from Earth, is it?" the woman says in an undertone. Her voice has such a heavy accent that I never would have understood her if I hadn't already gotten used to Amy's.

Colonel Martin grunts. "Except for this *Lord of the Flies* shit going on."

The woman mutters something I can't hear, then moves down to the edge of the bridge. She sets up a rifle with a small tripod and angles it above us, pointed at the skies. There are two more guns and a series of grenades within her reach. At least they listened when I told them the bird-thing was dangerous.

"So you're the leader of the shipborns," Colonel Martin says to me.

"So you're Amy's father."

"I am Colonel Martin, and since General Robertson and Brigadier General Kennedy are out of commission, I'm the highest-ranking officer for this mission. This is Lieutenant Colonel Emma Bledsoe."

I take a moment to process this information. This means Orion didn't just target people in the military—he was going down the line, killing off the most important people first. I should have recognized Lieutenant Colonel Bledsoe from when I saw her under the ice, but I certainly hadn't expected Colonel Martin to be so unlike his daughter once awake. I do not see anything of Amy in his judging eyes, his stiff posture.

"I'm Elder," I say simply.

"Elder of what?" Colonel Martin snaps.

"It's my name. Elder. And also my title. It's what we call the leader of the ship."

Colonel Martin heaves a sigh, staring at me. From the corner of my eye, I notice Lieutenant Colonel Bledsoe's expression. She's much younger than Colonel Martin and not as good at hiding her emotions: I can see concern in her dark eyes, worry in the lines of her mouth.

"So you've been the one in charge of those people in there?" Colonel Martin asks.

"Yes." I don't tell him that I've been the leader for only months, that my reign ended with the shuttle launch, that my kingdom was so divided that a third of the people stayed on *Godspeed*. I don't want to be talking about this at all; I'd like for him to do whatever he needs to do on the computer so we can leave. My eyes keep flicking toward the sky; my ears are half-listening for a bone-chilling screech. I don't want him to see my fear, though, so I try to focus on what he's saying.

"I don't know what situation led to someone as young as you stepping up to a leadership role," he continues. "I don't know what's been going on that led to my daughter waking up early and becoming embroiled in this mess. But I can guess, judging from the sloppy landing I see here and the injured and dead of your kind in there, that things haven't been going well."

"Enough," I say, the word coming out as a growl.

A mask of compassion falls on Colonel Martin's face. "I just meant—it's clear that this has been difficult. For everyone, yes, but especially for you, as a leader called too soon."

I stare back at him, careful to keep my emotions from showing. There's truth to everything he's saying, but it's not the whole story. Yes, it's been hard. But I accepted the responsibility knowing it would be difficult, and that's different from the picture he's trying to paint of me.

It's not like I would have given up even if I'd had another choice.

"The situation at hand is simple," he continues. "We need to establish one leader for both the shipborns and the Earthborn people. I would like to suggest that you pass leadership over to me now so that we can begin this mission on the right foot."

My first thought: *This man looks nothing like Eldest, he sounds nothing like him, but he thinks in just the same way.*

Colonel Martin sits down in the seat in front of the control panel—the same seat Amy sat in as we landed the shuttle. He turns the chair so it faces the other seat and pats it. "Sit down, son," he says kindly.

And I do. I think I understand now why Amy wanted her father back so much. Colonel Martin speaks with such assurance in his voice that I almost believe he can make my problems go away merely by commanding them to do so.

Almost.

"Things are very different from how I expected them to be," he says, the words heavy. "I wasn't supposed to be in charge."

Neither was I.

"I'm not ready for this."

Neither was I.

"But everything has changed now."

I know.

Colonel Martin tips back in the chair, looking up at the sky. "Colonies have always had a difficult time surviving. When America was settled, the colonists were separated by an ocean and months of travel from any help from the home they left behind. We are separated by far more."

I follow his gaze skyward, but I'm not thinking about Sol-Earth and how far away it is. I'm thinking about *Godspeed*. It's much closer, but just as impossible to reach.

"Many people died in the first colonies. They called America 'the New World,' but *this* is the real deal, eh, son? Roanoke has nothing on us."

"Why are you telling me this?" I ask. I don't care if I sound rude.

"Son, I need you to think about the situation here. I realize that things have been happening while the Earthborns like me were frozen and that you had to take charge. It can't have been easy."

"No, no, no, no, no," Shelby said. Right before I let her die.

"And you might not believe me," Colonel Martin adds, "but I know how much pressure you must be under. Those people, the shipborns, it's obvious they're looking to you to solve all their problems. But you can't solve all their problems, can you?"

Three of my people are dead right now, just down the hall, and that's my fault. Bartie and over eight hundred other people are still in orbit around Centauri-Earth, and they're going to live and die in the remains of Godspeed, and that's my fault too.

"Son," Colonel Martin says, and I can't help it, I like the way he says that word. "I think you know what you need to do."

"They will make us slaves or soldiers," Orion said. "They plan to work us or kill us."

"I'm not just going to hand my people over to you," I say, turning away from him and toward the door that leads into the shuttle. A wind from the planet swirls through my hair, making me feel stronger.

"I'm not suggesting that, son."

"Quit calling me *son*." I am no man's son.

"Elder." Colonel Martin says my name as if it leaves a bitter taste in his mouth. "This is about more than you or me. We can't let egos get in the way."

"I'm not letting my ego control me," I say. "Don't let yours. I may be younger than you, but there are one thousand four hundred and fifty-six people inside that shuttle who stand behind me."

Colonel Martin stands up and lets the chair whip around. "I know that," he says, the kind edge gone from his voice. "I just thought I could reason with you—"

"You can," I say simply. "You're right—it hasn't been easy. And I'm very well aware that I am not in the best position." How could I not be aware of that, given the way Bartie rebelled? The way people would rather stay on the ship than follow me off it? The way three of my people have died already just because they trusted me?

"I'm not against you," I add. "But I don't think that it needs to be just me or you. I'm willing to let you guide us, but I'm not going to tell my people to blindly obey you."

"But you'll stand behind me? Support my orders?"

"If I find them reasonable, yes. I will stand beside you."

If he notices my subtle change of his wording, he doesn't comment on it. "The first order of business is simple: we need to establish communication with Earth."

"We haven't had com for gens," I say.

"What?" Colonel Martin barks.

"It's been centuries since we've heard from Earth."

Behind him, I see Lieutenant Colonel Bledsoe mouth the word *centuries*. But Colonel Martin lets no emotion show.

"There's this, though," I say, moving over the computer on the bridge. The metal is hot to the touch, warmed by the twin suns. The screen blinks, awaiting the military authorization code.

Colonel Martin strides over to the computer, then hesitates. He doesn't want to do this in front of me. I let one eyebrow twitch up as I stare him down. He turns back to the computer and quickly enters the code.

The screen comes alive as I step forward to get a better look. Amy's father reluctantly moves aside to make room for me. For several minutes, all the screen shows is a twirling globe and a blinking bar labeled PROCESSING . . . SIGNAL RECEIVED . . . PROCESSING. Then the screen flickers, and the globe opens up, revealing an image of a satellite. INCOMING COMMUNICATION flits across the screen.

Colonel Martin flashes a triumphant look in my direction, but I'm focused on the screen. Is it really that easy? A ten-digit code and suddenly we're talking with Sol-Earth as if there weren't light-years between us?

A voice fills the air, and typed words on the screen transcribe the message. My breath catches in my throat. We haven't had com from Sol-Earth for gens. And yet . . . here's a voice, traveling across the universe just to speak to us.

And all we ever needed to make this happen was a frexing military authorization code.

Congratulations, Godspeed! You have safely arrived at your final destination, the planet circling the binary Centauri system.

The deep voice speaks in a slow monotone, but I'm still grateful for the transcribed words scrolling across the screen.

We know your journey's been long, but we are excited to inform you that the probes sent prior to the ship's landing have indicated not only a habitable world, but profitable environmental resources as well! As such, we've been busy on Earth, trying to find a suitable way to aid in the growth and development of the colony you are starting.

They want to aid the colony? Why didn't they care about aiding the *ship*? When we lost com all those years ago, why didn't Sol-Earth work to re-establish communication? I know I should feel wonder at this new com link that's opened up, but truthfully, all I feel is rage. They could have helped us land. They could have helped us *before* we landed. Why did they abandon us, stranding us in the stars, waiting for us to land on our own?

In the time since the interstellar ark ship, Godspeed, departed Earth, we've continued with advancements in long-term space travel. A remote space station is already set in orbit around the planet you are currently occupying, which will aid in quicker satellite communication between the planets. Additionally, your first task is to locate one of the probes sent from the ship—the probes are equipped with advanced technology and will aid in our communication.

Colonel Martin's entire attention is focused on the screen, but I just wish the speaker would be quiet long enough that we can ask some questions.

At the time of your landing, a signal was relayed directly to the Financial Resource Exchange. Rest assured that even now, the FRX is preparing a shuttle filled with aid and supplies for your colony. Advanced technology means that this shuttle should reach your location very soon.

I gape at the computer screen. Soon? What does that mean? It took three centuries for *Godspeed* to reach the planet.

I glance at Colonel Martin. His hands twitch near the controls. He's torn—do we interrupt and ask for clarification or wait for the end of the speech?

The voice turns grave as it continues.

Additionally, it's essential that we inform you of what dangers exist on the planet. First we would like to remind you that both the escape shuttle and Godspeed proper are equipped with lock-down capabilities, and should the need arise, do not hesitate to seal yourselves inside until our aid reaches you.

Static interrupts the message momentarily. Colonel Martin scans the controls but isn't sure what to touch.

It is essential that you resume communication with us via the probe as soon as possible so that we may more accurately relay the information we have gathered about the current population of threatening—

There's a *pop!* and some more crackling sounds, and then suddenly the voice cuts out, drowned out by static. A high-pitched whistling sound rings in my ears as the screen goes black. The air is eerily silent, our communication with Sol-Earth severed once again.

"What happened?" I ask as Colonel Martin bends over the computer.

"I'm not sure. . . . " He types on the screen, but it goes black. "Maybe the communication systems were damaged when you almost crashed my shuttle."

Before I can comment on his claiming ownership of *my* shuttle, gunshots boom behind us, so unexpected that I jump. Bledsoe crouches on the floor of the bridge, using the wall to steady her arm as she takes careful aim. I follow her gaze and see the—the *thing*—soaring above us, its talons outstretched, already eager to rip us to shreds. Another gunshot cracks out, followed by a piercing cry. The bird-thing changes direction but isn't hit.

"What the hell is that?" Colonel Martin says. His own gun is already in his hand, his knuckles white around the grip.

"That's the same kind of creature I saw earlier," I say, trying to keep my voice calm. "Amy said that it looked like a"—I try to remember the word she used—"like a dinosaur, a, um . . . a terro . . . ?"

"I know what it looks like, damn it, but what is it?"

I hide my smirk. So we've finally encountered something that's capable of breaking Colonel Martin's cool exterior. "Before we landed, we were warned about . . . " I pause. It sounds silly to say, but there's no other word for it. "Monsters."

Colonel Martin squints up at the creature soaring overhead. It's huge—even this far away, it blots out some of the suns' light.

Bledsoe takes one last shot, but it's clear the monster has flown too far away.

"Maybe I did crash-land the shuttle," I say, "but I think maybe one of those things knocked us off course."

"Don't waste ammunition," Colonel Martin barks at Bledsoe. She doesn't lower her gun, but I see her finger slide off the trigger. "We should get inside; it isn't safe here. I want to find out more about this damn 'population of threatening' whatever," he continues, turning to me. "Bledsoe and I will go out with a group of eight more men. If we find one of the probes, we should be able to establish a secure, consistent communication link with Earth and get a better idea of what we're facing."

Colonel Martin heads to the door. Bledsoe backs up slowly, her hand still on the gun. "Elder, I need you to keep your people calm." Colonel Martin says this as a command, not a request.

"I'm going with you," I say.

Colonel Martin pauses, his hand on the door. "No civilians."

"My people need to see that we're equal. They need to know that I'm involved, and I have a right to know what you say to Earth."

"Of course," Colonel Martin agrees. "But in this moment, the important thing is for them to have someone to turn to. You need to be the strong core, the rock they can depend on."

"I—"

Colonel Martin opens the door and herds me inside, Emma Bledsoe close behind. She slams the door shut and locks it. The air inside the shuttle tastes bitter and metallic compared to the warm, fresh breeze we've just left behind.

"I need you *here*, Elder," Colonel Martin says. "I need someone I can trust to protect the shuttle."

"But—"

"I'm leaving you with precious cargo: our people. *Your* people. Are you up to the task?"

"Yes," I say, "but—"

"Good, good, glad to see you agree," he says before heading to the armory.

I can't help but think I've just become the pawn Orion feared I was all along.

9 : AMY

I slam into Emma as I round the hallway. "What happened?" I gasp. When I heard the gunshots and the cry of another one of those pterodactyl things, I broke away from my mother and raced to the bridge.

She looks surprised. "Nothing," she says. She walks past me and starts barking orders at the military men and women gathered by the cryo chambers.

I don't think my heart starts beating again until I see Elder and Dad in the armory, safe. Dad is focused entirely on selecting weapons. Elder looks resigned, almost petulant, but he shoots me a smile that makes my heart stutter all over again.

"What's going on?" I ask, still breathless. I notice that the door to the bridge is locked.

"Amy, everything's fine. Go back to your mother," Dad says.

I ignore him and turn to Elder.

"We saw one of the m—" Elder starts to say "monsters," but cuts himself off. "We saw another creature. But it didn't come close to us."

I eye the .44 in Dad's hand. "Are you going to hunt it?"

Dad looks surprised. "We're just protecting ourselves. Ten of us are going to find the probe and attempt to re-establish communication with Earth."

"Wait, re-establish?" I whip around to Elder. His eyes tell me everything

I need to know. "You talked with Earth?!" I squeal. "That's—whoa! That's amazing! What did they say? What's Earth like now? What are they going to do?"

"The com link died," Elder says. "But they're going to send help. They think . . . " He frowns. "They think they can get help to us."

My mouth drops open. *"Really?!"*

Elder nods, but he's nowhere near as excited as I am. Earth! After all this time, *Earth* is talking to us again!

"Amy, I need to work. Go back to your mother." Dad holsters the .44 and starts going through the supply of grenades and bombs on another shelf.

"I'm coming with you!" I say, stepping farther into the armory. Elder shoots me a dark look, but I ignore him. "Dad, let me come too! I *need* to go outside. The planet is right there and I haven't even seen it yet, not really!"

"No," Dad says without looking up.

I flinch as if his single word was a slap across my face. "Dad," I say urgently. "Let me come with you. I won't be in the way. I'll take a gun—I can help. Just let me come."

Dad looks up at me, and for a moment all he does is stare into my pleading eyes. "No," he says finally.

"But—!"

"No. Go back to your mother."

"Dad!"

Elder gives a tiny shake of his head, telling me to drop it. My eyes narrow. I can tell Dad's forbidden him from going too—but he just went out. He's seen the world. He didn't even want it, but he's seen it.

I spin on my heel and leave the armory. I *know* I'm being childish. I know I'm being unreasonable and immature and ridiculous. But I can't help it. Before I was just focused on saving Elder, but now I want to see Centauri-Earth for myself.

I *need* to.

I pause at the doorway to the cryo room and take a deep breath. I force myself to really see what's going on. The cryo room is crowded, but unevenly divided. The nearly fifteen hundred people from the ship gather against one wall, as far away from the cryo chambers as possible. The people from Earth are occupying themselves with menial tasks—unpacking their storage crates, setting up scientific equipment on tables made from their cryo trays, talking with each other. There is nervous energy from both sides of the room, but fear too. There is always fear for the unknown.

Emma strides past me with eight other members of the military, each with a serious expression on his or her face. The soldiers are fully uniformed now and armed to the teeth. I remember the screeching cry of the flying creatures, and an unbidden shiver races up my spine. Centauri-Earth isn't there for my amusement. I know my father was right to forbid me going with him, no matter how much I dislike it.

Still, when I unfroze him, I didn't think he'd keep me locked up in the shuttle. The cryo chambers are all empty now, like forgotten shells washed up on a beach.

All except one. Orion's.

My eyes drift to the door to the genetics laboratory on the far side of the cryo room. I slip easily through the crowd of formerly frozen people as I drift toward the gen lab. As soon as I reach the door, I type in the entry code and roll my thumb over the biometric scanner. Few people have access to this room, but Elder made sure that I could enter whenever I wanted.

Once I'm inside, the door zips shut behind me.

I am alone now with my thoughts and relative silence.

And Orion.

I stride forward, to his cryo chamber. Unlike the ones my parents woke from, this chamber is a self-contained unit. It stands upright, and a little circular window shows the man inside the ice.

My steps slow as I grow closer to him.

I don't want to admit it, but I am starting to see Orion in Elder's features. My gaze flicks to the large cylinder on the other side of the room, where dozens of tiny fetuses could be plucked from golden goo and turned into another clone of Elder.

Not another Elder . . . just another person with the same body. Elder's mind is nothing like Orion's.

I could never love Orion.

When Elder pulled me from my cryo chamber, he didn't realize that he would wake me up and I'd never be able to be frozen again. But Orion knew. And he knew when he pulled Robertson and Kennedy out of their chambers that they would die choking on the tubes and cryo liquid in their throats, their eyes bulging and their hands clawing at the glass.

He knew.

I glance down at the timer under Orion's face. 05:23:34 . . . 33 . . . 32 . . . 31 . . .

I bend over and quickly punch in the numbers to bring the timer back up to 24:00:00.

Twenty-four more hours of being frozen. Elder was able to program it to count down more time, but the timer is finicky. I check it every day now.

I force myself to stare into his frozen face, his iced-over eyes. I don't want him to be here at all, separated from the new planet by nothing but ice.

But if I can't see the new world yet, at least I can make sure he can't either.

10: ELDER

I let myself have one moment of fresh air before sealing the bridge door shut behind the ten soldiers off to face the new planet. I don't know how long I stand there, my forehead pressed against the cool metal.

It's already begun.

I can feel what little control I had over the situation slipping through my fingers.

I shut my eyes, exhale loudly. I can't let myself think this way. I can't let myself live in Orion's fears.

Noise swells from the cryo room, interrupting my dark thoughts. At first I think it's just the natural volume of fifteen hundred people cramped together in one giant room, but then a voice screams in fury over the sound of all the others. I jerk up and race to the cryo room.

"What happened?" a woman's voice shouts as I push my way through the crowd gathered around the last row of cryo chambers.

Amy stands in front of a tall Earthborn woman with long, thin arms and a giant head of bushy hair. The woman's voice is muted by thick, snotty, gasping sobs as she wails again, "What *ha-happened*?"

Amy throws up both her hands and tries to take a step back, but she's trapped by the rows of cryo chambers. The frozens are clustered around her, and my people are staring at them with nervous wariness in their eyes.

Amy says something in a voice too low for me to catch, but the woman's answer is pitched so high everyone in the cryo room can hear: "He was *murdered*?!"

Oh, *frex*.

I pick up my pace, shoving aside the people in my way as I head toward Amy and the woman. When I reach her, Amy jerks her head at the screaming lady and whispers, "That's Juliana Robertson."

Robertson—same last name as one of the frozens Orion unplugged.

"My husband!" Juliana screeches, one hand pressed against the closed door to cryo chamber 100.

Then her hand turns into a fist. She whirls around, grabbing Amy by her tunic and yanking her close. "What happened?" she says fiercely. "Tell me what son of a bitch *killed* my husband!"

Amy's eyes are wide with fear. "It was—" She pauses. I know she was going to say "it was an accident," but she can't speak the lie.

"*Who?!*" Juliana Robertson roars in Amy's face. Amy flinches, and I push Juliana aside, pulling Amy close. She loses interest in us and whips around to face the crowd of people from the ship gathering around her. "Which one of you freaks did it?" she screams, and I am momentarily caught up in the irony that she thinks we are freaks for looking similar when that's the same word people used to apply to Amy for being different. "What coward killed my poor husband while he slept? Show yourself!" She is all fury, all raging hate.

My people don't know how to respond to her. To them, the frozens are dangerous. Many of them agree with Orion and his actions. And Juliana wears the same green-and-brown clothes as the rest of the military—she is a soldier, even more dangerous for her training.

Their eyes turn to me—I am the one who is supposed to protect them.

Juliana follows their gaze to me, but she doesn't see what it means.

She thinks their look is accusatory, akin to a confession of her husband's murder.

She lunges at me, screaming, and before I have a chance to react, her fist connects with my left cheekbone, making my head snap back. I stagger away, raising both my hands in defense.

"Don't touch Elder!" one of the shipborns—a man named Heller, a former rancher on the Feeder Level—shouts as she jumps forward, grabbing Juliana's arm as she rears it back to swing at me again.

"No, wait—" I try to say.

"Don't hurt her!" another of the former frozens shouts as she jumps into the fray.

And just like that: chaos.

The people from Earth may be fiercer, but my people outnumber them fifteen to one. As the fighting escalates, the pack of frozens retreats until their backs are against the cryo chambers. Screams and shouts drown out every other sound. A woman who I take to be Amy's mother—they have the same green eyes—grabs her wrist, dragging her away from the growing mob. I swallow a lump in my throat. It's my fault the shuttle's degrading into fighting, just like *Godspeed* did. It's me who can't keep Amy safe. I jab my finger against my wi-com—uselessly; it doesn't work here.

I climb up on the nearest table, shouting, "Stop! STOP!"

But it does no good.

This is a fight born of rage and fear.

Fists slam against flesh; blood pours from new wounds. A chair is thrown into the crowd, then swung against a cryo chamber with a deafening crash. Juliana Robertson, her wild hair flying, screams as she lunges toward me but is caught by one of my people slamming her against a cryo chamber. I scramble off the table, throwing myself between fighting bodies and being beaten for my effort.

"ENOUGH!" Colonel Martin roars from the doorway. The people nearest him pause, but the fight rages. "I SAID ENOUGH!" he shouts again, walking straight through the middle of the mob. "STAND DOWN!"

And they do.

The military people who'd been left inside with us stop fighting. Even Juliana Robertson. Blood streams down both nostrils and her eyes are red, but her fists uncurl, and she steps back silently.

"*What* the hell is going on?" Colonel Martin rages. His eyes bounce between me and Juliana and back again. Behind him, the ten men and women he took with him to the probe spread out as the fighting dies.

"My husband," Juliana says through clenched teeth. "He was *killed*, sir."

Colonel Martin dips his head. "I know."

Juliana's eyes flash.

"You are dismissed. Go to the storage area and cool down."

"Sir, he was my *husband*."

"I know," Colonel Martin says. "And my friend. You are dismissed."

"They *killed* him."

"*Dismissed*." Colonel Martin's voice bodes no allowance, and Juliana spins on her heel, storming to the room where the trunks had been stored. Several other members of the military follow.

My people glance at me, and I jerk my head to the other side of the cryo room. They head back, but I notice the way their backs are still stiff, their jaws still tensed. They remain ready for a fight. It's not over, just paused.

Colonel Martin strides over to me, fury in his eyes. "This is what you call leadership?" he growls in an undertone. "This is what you call *control?*"

"No." I bite off the word, then add, "Sir."

Amy and her mother draw closer now that the fight's over. Something in Colonel Martin's face softens when he sees them.

Colonel Martin strides forward, drawing attention. "Everyone—shipborn and Earthborn alike—I have news. But first, a warning: if we don't work together, we'll never be able to survive this planet."

His words are loud and firm, but he doesn't shout. Still, I watch as the fight leaves my people, and they let go of their anger in order to listen.

"We did find the probe, less than a mile away, at the edge of the forest we landed in. We were unable to communicate with Earth, but I am hopeful that we'll be able to contact our mother planet soon."

He takes a deep breath. Every eye is on him.

"Further, we did glimpse the creatures that you've been able to hear from inside the shuttle. They are large, reptilian birds, and they do look predatory and possibly carnivorous."

At his words, a chill rushes across the entire crowd. This is every nightmare they've ever had about the planet made real.

"We must constantly be aware of the danger this planet holds. And we must fight *that*, not each other."

Colonel Martin looks around him at the chaos the fight caused—overturned tables and chairs, blood splatter, ripped clothing.

"It is clear that we will not be able to stay inside the confines of the shuttle indefinitely, despite the protection it affords us. To that end, our first missions will be aimed at survival: finding food, water, and shelter. *Everyone* will need to contribute to this task. Work will begin tomorrow."

He shoots me a disgusted look. "Don't kill each other in the meantime."

11: AMY

Dad pulls me aside soon after he breaks up the disastrous fight. "Is there somewhere we can talk?" he asks gravely.

"The gen lab," I say, jerking my head toward it. Briefly, Elder's eyes meet mine from across the crowded, tense room. If we could only have one moment to ourselves, maybe we could start to make sense of this world. But Elder has nearly fifteen hundred people who need him to answer their questions right now. And I have one.

Dad follows me to the other side of the cryo room and doesn't comment, even when the biometric scanner by the door recognizes my genetic signature. He waits for the door to seal shut behind us before saying anything.

"Who is that?" he asks, approaching the cryo chamber. Orion is caught mid-action, his hands clawing at the glass, his eyes bulging under ice.

"That's the man who killed Juliana Robertson's husband. And he tried to kill you too."

Dad turns to me. "There's a lot that happened while I was asleep. I need you to fill me in."

I don't have to ask why he's asking me and not Elder. Still, I almost hesitate to speak. Am I undermining Elder's position by telling my father what I know rather than insisting he talk to Elder directly?

No . . . no. My father needs to know the truth about Orion, and I know Elder would hesitate to explain all his faults. Dad doesn't need excuses—he needs to know exactly why Orion's dangerous. I explain, as best I can, who Orion is and why he thought murdering the frozens in the military might save his own people. I don't tell him that Elder's plan is for Dad and the rest of the frozens to judge and punish Orion. I make it sound as if Orion's punishment is being frozen—I don't want him awake, not even for judgment. I want him to live for centuries trapped in ice, just as I had to.

Dad shakes his head, trying to understand why Orion would let his friends melt to death. He reaches forward, tucking a stray lock of my red hair behind my ear. "You've been through so much," he says, his voice cracking with regret.

My right hand goes unconsciously to my left wrist, rubbing it, retracing the area that was once, three months ago, bruised from being forced down to the ground, pinned between the dirt and a man who reveled in the evil he committed.

Dad wraps his arm around me. "The shipborns," he begins gently, "they're different from what I expected."

"They're different from what I expected too."

"Anything that can help me understand them . . . "

I release my wrist and swallow the words I want to say.

Dad starts pacing—a habit that I picked up from him. "Those people," he says, "they all look the same, and they have some kid as their leader, and there are fewer of them than we expected by this time." He reminds me of a caged animal, turning sharply at each wall and stomping to the next. "And if the probe records are right, the journey here didn't take three hundred years . . . the probe indicates that more than half a millennia has passed."

So that's how long *Godspeed* orbited the planet under the tyrannical rule of the Eldest system: two hundred extra years. Six, maybe seven or eight Eldests? And one Elder who refused.

"What happened in those five centuries?" Dad continues, but he's talking more to himself than to me. "What have they done to themselves? Obviously some sort of genetic modification. But their societal rules have changed over time too . . . "

"They have been playing with genetic modifiers," I say. Dad's attention zeros in on me; he's listening to me with an intensity I've never seen from him before. "I mean, they did something to make themselves monoethnic, obviously, but I know that the babies are injected with gen mod material before they're born." Dad doesn't say anything—his rapt attention is making me a little nervous, a little babbly. "I was told that it was to prevent problems. They took out race as a source of conflict—and religion, and anything else that would make them disagree or fight."

Dad's look turns contemplative. "You sound like one of them," he says finally.

"Excuse me?"

"Listen to how you said that," he says. *"Excuse me."* He throws the words at me accusingly. "You have an accent now."

"I do not!"

He looks at me full-on. "You do."

I scowl. I don't even know why it matters. Maybe I do sound like them. Who cares?

"What else can you tell me?" Dad stares at me. "What have you learned while you were awake?"

I learned that life is so, so fragile. I learned that you can know someone for just days and never forget the impression he left on you. I learned that art can be beautiful and sad at the same time. I learned that if someone loves you, he'll wait for you to love him back. I learned that how much you want something doesn't determine whether you get it or not, that "no" might not be enough, that life isn't fair, that my parents can't save me, that maybe no one can.

"Nothing much," I mutter.

"Come on, now." Dad pauses, facing me. "Any detail, no matter how small, might help me to understand these shipborns."

I don't like the way he calls them "shipborns," as if by being born on the ship, they're somehow less human than the people born on Earth.

"What you really want to know," I say, "is how to make sure we all don't just rip each other apart, right?" The fight earlier is way too fresh in our minds. We are a powder keg; just a spark will blow us apart.

Dad nods, waiting for me to continue.

"Let us go outside," I say in a rush, my voice already pleading. "Let everyone see the planet. Let them know what's beyond the walls. These people— they've *never* had anything but a steel cage. If you open the door, if you let them see the world, they will love it, and they will do whatever it takes to make this mission work. They'll do whatever it takes to build themselves a new home."

"It's not safe—" Dad starts, but I cut him off.

"The most dangerous thing you can do right now is keep that door locked. Open it, or they'll tear through the walls themselves."

Dad sends people out in groups of a hundred or so, with one armed military person for every ten people. As he organizes the groups, I shoot Elder a triumphant smile. Elder looks away, scowling.

"What's your problem?" I ask him in a low voice as Dad starts organizing the first groups to leave.

"Nothing." Elder doesn't meet my eyes.

"No," I say, so forcefully that Elder turns to look at me in surprise. "You don't get to sulk and just not tell me what's wrong. What's bothering you?"

"Doesn't it seem a bit . . . manipulative?" he asks.

"What does?"

Elder glances at the doorway, where Dad stands, giving orders to the military personnel standing at attention in front of him.

"Dad?" I ask incredulously. "You think he's manipulating everyone?"

"It's something Eldest would do," Elder says, again avoiding my eyes. "Give the people something big to distract them from what's really important."

"And just what do you think Dad's trying to distract everyone from? The planet? Because that's exactly what he's giving them. And that was *my* idea, not his."

Elder doesn't answer at first. "I'm sorry," he finally says, although I'm not sure I believe him. He turns to face me. "I'm sorry," he says again, this time sincere. "I don't really think your dad's like Eldest."

I offer him a wan smile, but we both know where Elder's thoughts on this have really come from. Orion. Even frozen, we can't escape him.

Dad's careful to make it obvious that the first people who get to go are those from the ship, despite the protests of the scientists like my mother who are itching to start researching and exploring the planet. Elder is at least grateful for this, I think, and I know most of the people from *Godspeed* are glad for the opportunity.

Not that they all take it. Just over half the people from the ship dare to go outside, even with the armed guard. They are filled with fear and take comfort in the walls they have known all their lives. Already the shuttle is starting to stink of body odor and refuse. Dad has Emma take the three bodies of the people who didn't survive planet-landing away for burial, but there's little they can do to help with the other stenches. I don't know what Elder and Dad are going to do when it comes time to leave the shuttle permanently. Kit looks near exhausted, and her supply of yellow anti-anxiety med patches is already running out.

I notice no one wears a pale green Phydus patch.

Elder and I are in the last group to go out—along with the people from Earth, who have been waiting impatiently. The scientists crowd at the door eagerly. My mother already carries specimen jars in both hands, and the grin on her face is wide enough to make *my* cheeks ache. Dad stands at the door to the bridge, silently counting as we each pass through it.

I slip my hand through Elder's as we near the bridge. He glances nervously toward Dad, whose eyes miss nothing, but I don't let go.

"Ready?" Elder asks as we pass through the door that leads to the new world.

I'm too excited to answer. A wave of heat hits me—but it's a warm breeze of a dying summer day, not the stifling, hard-to-breathe claustrophobic air of the shuttle.

Emma Bledsoe stands guard by the control panel, a long-range rifle at the ready as she scans the forest and the sky for more of the pterodactyl monsters—or anything else that might be hiding in the twilight. I gaze out at the view before me, taking in so much more than I did the last time I left the shuttle. Then, I was too consumed by my fear for Elder and my horror at the pterodactyl monster to notice much of anything else. Even now, I have to push down my terror of what creatures could reside in the growing darkness and force myself to see what this world has to offer. The forest surrounding the shuttle is unlike any forest I've ever seen before. Instead of the trees having one thick trunk with branches that rise to the sky, each of these trees has dozens of small, thin trunks all tangled up together. The trunks are no thicker than my leg, but they twist and weave in dense groves. The branches are tangled knots with frayed ends of green leaves—but the leaves are thin and broad and look almost like washcloths draped over the sides of the branches to dry.

"Amy?" Elder says, drawing me back to reality. I take a step forward.

The marks of the shuttle landing are clear: we've decimated a huge chunk of the land. The sandy ground directly under the shuttle is burnt black and looks like it boiled and then froze again. Smoke drifts up in lazy tendrils, and I'm glad that the ramp is long enough to get us to where the ground may be black, but at least it's not bubbling.

When my feet hit the ground, I gasp. *Earth*. Real, true earth under my feet. The first thing I do is shut my eyes. I take a deep breath—I imagine filling my lungs with more than air, with dirt, with trees, with an ocean. And then I breathe out, and it's all even bigger than before. *Air*. Not recycled—a fresh, clean breeze, with scents of dirt and plants and so much more.

Even though dozens of people swarm around me, many of them glancing up at the sky or cowering close to the shuttle, waiting for one of the pterodactyl-looking things to swoop down and grab them, all I'm aware of is Elder holding my hand and the entire world spread out before us.

And I know what I told my father was true: let us taste the world, and we'll do whatever it takes to shape it into our home.

"Isn't it amazing?" I ask Elder.

He nods silently. His eyes are cast up too, but I know he's not searching the darkening clouds for a monster to come soaring down and attack. He's looking for walls that aren't there, that will never be there.

"Watch out!"

With both of us looking up at the sky, we nearly stepped on a small man crouching over the earth, a pool of white plaster at his feet.

"What are you doing?" I ask.

For answer, the man—one of the biologists from the mission—carefully lifts up the plaster, revealing a massive footprint. "Colonel Martin gave me permission to start collecting evidence of the planet's life forms," the scientist says.

I recognize this footprint—it's from the dinosaur bird that attacked Elder when we first landed. As the biologist gently lifts up the plaster cast, I can see the long gouge marks of the monster's talons. Clumps of yellow sandy soil mar the image, but as the scientist starts to brush it away, I repress a shudder. I remember when those talons curled into Elder's flesh.

Elder touches his chest, as if still feeling the pain under the bandages Kit made for him. Wordlessly, we step away as the scientist jumps up to show the cast to his colleagues. I start to head back near the ship, but Elder pulls me away from the growing crowd, closer to the forest.

"Does it still hurt?" I ask.

Elder drops his hand from his chest. "Not much," he mutters. His attention seems focused on the trees.

"What are you looking for?"

Elder shakes his head, his eyes darting along the brush at the forest floor. "When I was attacked . . . " he says slowly. "I thought I heard . . . "

He leans down, staring hard at the ground. The shadows of the tree and the fading light of twilight hinder his vision. He creeps forward. "Do you see that?" he says in almost a whisper.

I crouch next to Elder. At the base of the nearest tree, I see what might be animal tracks, although they're nothing like any animal tracks I've ever seen before. Most of the prints are indistinguishable—whatever animal walked here crossed its tracks several times. But at the base of the tree is one perfect print, embedded about a half inch into the soft soil, with crisp lines and clear shapes: three ridged toes in front of a oval marred by criss-crossing lines.

Elder's hand hovers over the print. The back half of the print is about the size of his palm; the elongated toes—or claws—extend a few inches past his fingers.

What kind of animal makes prints like this? The bird monster had curving talons, but this animal's scaly claws seem to have saw-like edges, as if they could shred my flesh just by brushing my skin.

"We should get that scientist to make another plaster cast," I say, standing.

As Elder gets up, too, a deep voice calls out, "You need to stick with the group." A young man in military fatigues steps forward from the forest—right on top of the animal tracks Elder had been examining. Elder growls in frustration, but the man doesn't seem to care.

The guy is young—he can't be that much older than me, definitely in his early twenties. He has startlingly blue eyes that belie his dark hair. I vaguely recognize him as one of the men my father brought with him on the mission to the probe, but I don't know his name or rank. When he notices me staring, he shoots me a quick smile before turning his attention back to the shuttle and giving Dad, who's watching us, an all-clear hand signal. I blush despite myself. He wears blank fatigues—no nametape or visible rank. Before I can ask who he is, Dad interrupts.

"Stay close to the group!" he barks from atop the bridge in the shuttle. The soldier turns back to continue his patrol.

Elder glances up furtively at my father as he drags me back toward the shuttle. I tug his arm, ducking around to the other side. There is military on this side of the shuttle too, but at least we're away from my father's too-vigilant gaze.

And then I notice the suns. Two of them. I don't know how I didn't notice them before—who thinks to look at the sun?—but they're low in the sky now, casting the area in a dark blue-green sort of twilight.

Two suns.

Two.

Of course, I'd known—I'd always known—that Centauri-Earth would have two suns. I'd even noticed the two giant glowing orbs from the window of the shuttle. There's a difference, though, in seeing two big stars from a spaceship and seeing two glowing suns from land.

"It's so . . . it's so beautiful," I say, unable to keep the awe from my voice. Elder's grip on my hand tightens in response.

I turn to look at him, and I see the wonder I feel in my heart mirrored in his expression. My lips creep up and up in a smile so uncontainable that I feel as if my face will never stop smiling. Elder's hand slips from my own, trails up my arm, leaving goose bumps in its wake.

My breath catches in my throat.

I lean forward, up on my tiptoes, and a warm, earthy breeze from the forest seems to push me into his arms. Our kiss holds none of the furious passion we shared at landing the shuttle. This is different—this is like an ocean's wave, washing over us, drowning us both in warmth, leaving us breathless and shiny-eyed.

One of the suns sinks under the horizon, the other still clinging to the edge of the world, spilling out its faded light. A few bright stars are visible. And one star—the brightest one that moves visibly against the sky—calls my attention.

Is that *Godspeed*? If I were to get a telescope strong enough, could I make out the broken steel of the shattered Bridge?

I move to kiss Elder again, but he steps away. I glance behind me in time to see my father silently slipping away and out of sight.

I turn my back to both of them just as the last sun falls below the horizon and the world is cast in darkness.

12: ELDER

As we walk back toward the ramp that leads into the shuttle, a woman's voice, Amy's mother's, cuts through the tranquility of our first night on Centauri-Earth. "Look!" she calls.

Amy gasps as her gaze follows her mother's pointing finger. The ground . . . is *glowing*.

It's subtle but there: under the blackened gaze of the bubbled, burnt ground, I can see, ever so faintly, a warm glow lighting up from the earth. It reminds me of when the Feeder Level burned, of how the walls of the Food Distro smoldered red-yellow under the blackened embers.

"What's making it glow like that?" Amy whispers.

I have no idea—I'm too distracted by what I see on the side of the shuttle. I step forward—the ground underfoot feels hard, like tile or glass, not like the sandy soil the rest of the world is made of. The rockets on the shuttle literally melted the dirt.

Amy follows me. "What are you looking at?" she asks.

I point.

"The symbol?"

She moves to the shuttle, touching the giant steel plate engraved with a double-winged eagle.

Underneath it, in bold, evenly spaced letters, is the name of the ship. The home I left behind.

GODSPEED

"That's just the symbol of the FRX," I say. "It was in the Feeder Level too. But that's not what—"

"It was in the Feeder Level?" Amy interrupts. "I never saw it."

"There was a little stone and metal marker in the exact center of the ship. It had a plaque; it was called Point Zero." I shrug. "It was in the middle of one of the cow fields."

Amy suppresses a shudder; she never liked the cows on *Godspeed*.

"But that's not what I was looking at," I say, pointing to the right of the steel plate, to the area that is nearly hidden behind the ramp. "Look."

Two huge dark marks scar the underbelly and side of the shuttle. They look like the after-effects of blasts—twin deep dents with black marks radiating around them.

"What is that?" Amy asks, reaching toward the dent. It's easily the size of her entire arm but too far above her to touch.

"I don't know," I mutter. "But I'm willing to bet this is what knocked us off course." I frown. I can't tell if the dents were made by our own rockets malfunctioning or if we hit something.

Or if something hit us.

"Do you think I was right?" I whisper. "That it was one of those bird-things? Or could it have been—"

"Everyone inside!" Colonel Martin barks. Lieutenant Colonel Bledsoe and her men quickly shuffle everyone up the glass walkway, all blissfully unaware of our suspicions.

Amy's mother calls to her, motioning her to the side of the shuttle. Amy shoots me an apologetic smile as she veers away from me toward her mother, who is standing near the edge of the burnt ground. When Amy approaches, she gathers her up in an excited hug. "Isn't this place *fascinating*?" her mother says in a rush. "I've been collecting specimens. I couldn't wait. Your father's furious that it's taken me so long, but he'll get over it."

"Inside!" Colonel Martin bellows again. Bledsoe waits for the three of us at the bottom of the glass ramp; we're the only civilians still outside.

The young soldier we met earlier approaches us. "Time to go in," he says. "It's not safe out here."

Amy blinks at him. "You didn't introduce yourself before," she says. There's something in her voice that makes me narrow my eyes at this intruder.

He holds his hand out to help her up the ramp, and her fingers linger on his elbow. "Private Chris Smith at your service," he says with a grin that puts me inexplicably on edge. "I report to your father."

"So does everyone else," she answers, her own smile lighting up her face.

"Except me."

My words make both Chris and Amy stop in their tracks. There is appraisal in Chris's gaze now as he looks me over, and I find myself scowling even more angrily that this person thinks he has the right to judge me.

"Let's go," I say, reaching for Amy's hand.

She deftly dodges me, new interest in her eyes as she stares at Chris. "I'm surprised anyone my age qualified for the mission," she says.

"I'm twenty." Chris's voice is deep. "Barely made the cutoff."

"You were with the group that went to find the probe, right?" Amy continues.

Before Chris can answer, Amy's mother shoves a jar of sand she collected into Amy's hands, completely oblivious to the smile Chris shoots Amy. "There must be some sort of phosphorescence," she says excitedly. "Of course," she continues on as they head up the ramp, "what I want to know is if there's a source of bioluminescence in the sand." Chris catches my gaze and rolls his eyes as Amy's mother rambles on, but I just glower back at him. "You know, maybe it was caused by a chemical reaction, perhaps the heat from the shuttle's landing. . . . " She shakes another small jar of the sand, and the glowing bits of it remind me of the stars in the sky.

Her voice trails off as she reaches the top of the ramp and sees Colonel Martin, his dark, angry eyes flicking to me, then back to his wife. Amy doesn't notice as her mother shoots a suspicious glance at me and clutches the jar closer to her as she draws her daughter into a tight, one-armed hug and leads her through the bridge to the inside of the shuttle.

Their looks were clear.

I am not to be trusted, even with samples of sand.

Lieutenant Colonel Bledsoe lingers at the door with Colonel Martin and Chris.

"I want talk more about the technology issues we've been having," Colonel Martin mutters to Chris, drawing him closer to the control panel on the bridge.

Chris nods confidently; he must be a technological expert or something. "Fine," he says, "but first you should see this." He hands Amy's father a clear cube that sparkles golden with light reflected from the inside of the shuttle. When Colonel Martin notices me staring, he slams the bridge door shut behind me.

I try not to gag when I enter the cryo room. I hadn't let myself really notice the stench before, but it's been less than twenty-four hours and already the shuttle is nearly unbearable. Nearby, one of the older men—Heller, the one who stuck up for me against Juliana Robertson—shifts uncomfortably. "Frexing stitches," he says, touching the ragged wound on his leg.

"Nothing to do but try to sleep," the man beside him says, his broad-brimmed hat already covering his face.

Heller grunts and rests his chin on his chest.

They have the right idea. Now that the shuttle doors are closed, the only things left for us are worry or sleep, and I'm sick of worrying. It's not easy to sleep on the hard metal floor, though.

There isn't enough room for everyone to lie down, especially since there seems to be an invisible wall between my people and the Earthborns, so my people try to find ways to sleep sitting up, leaning against the curve of the shuttle or each other. Opposite us, the Earthborns have lowered the tables made from their cryo trays, clearing them off and making beds using blankets and sleeping bags they extract from a storage compartment under the floor. It's not ideal, but it's luxurious compared to the living conditions just on the other side of the shuttle.

I wish I could do more for my people—something.

Without really thinking about it, I find myself heading over to Amy. When I reach her, though, I see her and her mother arguing as her mom spreads sleeping bags over the tables of cryo chambers 40, 41, and 42.

"It's not fair," Amy tells her mother.

"What isn't?" she asks, smoothing down the bag.

Amy looks up as I approach, and her mother follows her gaze. "There are only a hundred sleeping bags," Amy says.

"How is that not fair?" Although Amy and her mother sounded angry before, now her mother speaks with bland, carefully measured words.

Amy breaks in. "Mom, this is Elder. You guys haven't officially met. Elder, this is my mother, Dr. Maria Martin." I don't think Dr. Martin needed an introduction to me. She doesn't do more than nod in acknowledgment of my presence, and the polite mask over her face doesn't reveal her true thoughts. I can only guess at what Colonel Martin has told her.

Dr. Martin smoothes out the sleeping bag over Amy's cryo chamber even though it doesn't need it. Underneath her own cryo chamber, I notice the sample jars of glowing sand that she collected before returning to the shuttle. I can't help but stare at them, wondering—like Amy's mother—just what it is that makes the sand glitter like stars.

"The FRX provided the basic resources we would need when the ship landed and we woke up. There's only a hundred, enough for each of us," Dr. Martin says. "How was the FRX supposed to know how many people there would be when we landed? Besides, *they* knew they were leaving, didn't they?" She turns her attention to me, still wearing the blank expression of civility that fell over her features earlier. "Of course Elder and his people packed their own supplies and made their own preparations. They've had centuries to be ready for this moment."

I think of those last few days before the shuttle launched. It was chaotic. Everyone was still reeling from the riot in the City and Bartie's decision to stay. Some people came to the shuttle at the very last minute, running to the entrance in the pond just before I closed the door, carrying only a handful of things with them. No one brought a bed. And the few who brought blankets or quilts brought them more as heirlooms than as things to sleep with.

"There are two extra," Amy says. The two sleeping bags meant for Robertson and Kennedy, the ones Orion killed. "Elder can take one. And maybe Kit can have the other?"

I shake my head. There's no way I'm going to sleep better than my people. "We're fine, Amy," I say. "Your mother is right. We should have been prepared when we left."

Amy opens her mouth to object, but her mother cuts her off. "There, see? The shipborns are *fine*; he said so himself. Now get ready for bed."

I can tell that Amy wants to argue, but I shake my head, just a fraction. I don't want her fighting, not for my sake, not over a sleeping bag. Amy steps forward, reaching for my hand—I don't know whether she wants to follow me back to my side of the ship or keep me on the Earthborn side—but I know my place on the shuttle, and she knows hers. I reluctantly sidestep out of her grasp and walk over to my people. Dr. Martin wore a mask to hide her wariness when she talked to me; I can wear one now to hide how much I'd rather be with Amy.

13: AMY

Brrk! Brrk!

I shoot up, tangled in the sleeping bag, as an alarm blares throughout the cryo room and red warning lights flash in the ceiling.

"What's going on?" I ask my mom, rubbing the sleep out of my eyes.

Dad's already racing across the cryo room toward the bridge. A second later, Elder follows him. I throw the sleeping bag off my legs and leap up, running to the hallway.

Emma Bledsoe catches me as I reach the door. "Let Colonel Martin take care of—" she starts, but I jerk free of her and skid down the hallway. She follows at my heels.

"What is that?" I shout over the sound of the alarm. Dad looks up as Elder types a code on the bridge control panel.

"The shuttle's going into lockdown," Elder says, cursing as the alarm continues despite the codes he's punching into the computer.

"What happened?" Dad roars, and for the first time I notice Chris standing by the door.

"I was on duty all night, sir," he says, flustered. "No one was here. It just started going off."

"The shuttle sensors are messed up," Elder says. "It's detecting rapid pressure changes."

"But the pressure isn't changing," Dad says, holding his hand out as if he expects the air pressure to suddenly drop.

"I *know*," Elder says. "That's why I said the sensors are frexing broken."

"Can you cut off the damn alarms?" Dad shouts.

"Lockdown in fifteen minutes and counting," the computer's voice cuts in before the alarm continues.

Elder throws up his hands. "Even if I could fix it, there's no way I could get it working again in fifteen minutes. That door is going to seal one way or another."

"For how long?"

Elder shrugs in frustration. "I don't *know*. It depends if the problem is coming from the sensors themselves or if there's something else wrong."

"We've got to get everyone out, then," Dad says, frowning. His frustration is evident, but that's hardly fair. He can't expect Elder to know everything there is to know about the mechanical operations of a shuttle that's literally centuries old. Dad glances up at the sky, and I remember the horrible screeching cries of the alien birds, the huge dents on the side of the shuttle. Could they have somehow caused the sensors to go off-line?

Emma seems to be thinking along the same lines. "Sir," she says, "but what about the planet's native wildlife? Any alien presence could be a threat to the population."

My father looks deep in thought for a second, but then Chris interjects. "The negative ramifications of confining the ship's crew and our own to the shuttle for an indeterminate amount of time, with limited food and water and without any restrooms, will be a bigger threat than anything the planet could plausibly present. I can assure you, sir, that the biggest danger lies in trapping everyone in the shuttle, not evacuating it."

Dad whirls around. He's heard enough. "Chris, Emma, get the evacuation started *now*. Everyone—every single person—must leave the shuttle.

Immediately. All military is to aid with evacuation, then pick up as many weapons as they can carry on the way out."

The computer adds, "Fourteen minutes, thirty seconds."

"Hurry!" Dad shouts.

"I'll try to buy us more time," Elder says, turning back to the computer.

I want to help him somehow, but I know I'd just get in the way. Instead, I race after Emma. The military is already up and waiting for orders. As soon as Emma tells them what to do, they scatter, pulling people into the hallway and ordering them to the outside door. The people from the ship near the hallway are the first to go—too surprised to object, I think. The scientists try to bring their equipment with them.

I run over to Mom. "There's no time," I say, pulling the microscope out of her hand. Honestly, a microscope?

"Amy, what's going on?" she asks impatiently, as if this were all a prank that I orchestrated. The alarm pauses while the computer announces, "Thirteen minutes before lockdown."

"We have to *go*. Now!" I say.

"Why?" Mom picks the microscope back up.

"The doors are going to seal!" I shout as the alarm resumes. "You'll be trapped inside!"

Mom blanches. "For how long?"

"I don't know!"

Mom finally gets the message. She drops the microscope on the table and starts pushing the other scientists toward the hall. The door has seal locks, strong enough to keep out the vacuum of space. We're stuck on a planet with only the possessions we carry—if that door locks and the computer malfunctions, there's nothing we can do to open it again.

The shuttle will become a tomb.

"Go! Go! Go!" Emma screams at the group of shipborns clinging to the wall. I race over.

"We have to go!" I shout.

They look at me, confused. They're willing to listen to me before Emma—I'm not one of them, but they know me at least, and trust me . . . sort of. But they don't understand that the shuttle's turning against them; they see it as their only source of protection.

"Go to Elder—he's just outside, you have to get out!" Something in what I say must penetrate—they follow the scientists already evacuating toward the door.

Once some people begin to leave, others follow. Emma and the military have resorted to physically picking people up and throwing them toward the hallway. No one's moving fast enough.

The alarms dim as the computer says, "Eight minutes and counting."

We're never going to get out in time. There are too many people too scared to move. Too scared to leave.

Kit grabs me. "Tell Elder that these people are staying!" she shouts.

"What? They can't!"

"They're not leaving!" Kit says. "They're petrified! It will take weeks before they're ready to leave the shuttle!"

"They *have* to go!" I scream at her as the alarm blares incessantly. "If they don't, they might not *ever* get out! The shuttle will trap them inside!"

Chris, Emma, and a few more of the military approach the group that is backed against the wall. Their eyes are terrified, open wide and flashing white as their gazes dart left to right. A woman close to me has her back flat against the metal, her hands gripping the raised rivets along the side. Her head is slammed against the wall, and a trickle of blood leaks over her left arm—I recognize her. This is Lorin, one of the women I stitched when the ship first landed. She's thrown herself so violently against the unforgiving surface of the shuttle that some of her stitches broke.

"Lorin," I say in as calm a voice as I can muster while the alarm blares. "We need to go."

She shakes her head, eyes wide, mouth forming soundless words.

"We *have* to," I say. I glance at the others backed against the wall. They've never lived without walls—but I can't let them die behind them, either.

"Enough of this," Emma growls, knocking me aside as she grabs Lorin's wrist and starts to forcibly drag her from the room.

Lorin screams, pulling against Emma with all her body weight. She stumbles, and Emma drags her on her knees for a few steps before Lorin is able to wriggle free and run all the way to the other side of the shuttle, back against the wall as she shakes her head *no, no, no.*

"Seven minutes," the computer interrupts.

"You guys get to the armory," I say. "We need all the weapons we can carry. Kit and I can take care of the remaining people."

Emma looks as if she's about to protest, but she throws her hands up in resignation and leads the remaining military personnel to the armory.

"How—?" Kit starts, but I cut her off.

"Where are the green patches?" I scream, my voice already hoarse from trying to speak over the alarm.

"What?" Kit shouts back.

"Phydus!"

Kit scrambles for her med bag, yanking out handfuls of green patches. Willing or not, I smack a patch on each of the remaining people who refuse to leave the shuttle. Better to give them a small dose of the hateful drug than leave them here to die. They shuffle toward the door—not fast enough, and I scream at them to hurry.

I reach Lorin last—she keeps trying to dodge out of my reach, but as the alarm announces the last minute, I tackle her and slap a patch on her hand. Her eyes glaze over. I yank her up, dragging her behind me as I race to the door.

"Thirty seconds to lockdown," the computer says cheerfully. "Twenty-nine . . . twenty-eight . . . "

I run to the door, more desperate than I'd ever been in any race or sprint in high school, pulling Lorin's limp form along. I will *not* be trapped inside this godforsaken shuttle.

Elder stands in the door to the bridge. "Hurry!" he shouts.

The computer continues counting down. "Ten . . . nine . . . eight . . . "

I shove Lorin ahead of me through the door—she falls, but she's made it to the other side.

" . . . four . . . three . . . "

I dive through.

The door seals shut behind me.

The alarm stops, but my ears are still ringing with the sound of it. "You okay?" Elder asks, dragging me to my feet. Kit, panting, helps Lorin stand.

"Yeah," I say, rubbing my elbow. I must have slammed it against the metal floor.

"How long is this damn door going to be sealed?" Dad asks, glaring at it as if it's a personal affront.

"I told you," Elder says just as angrily, "I don't know."

Dad glowers. He's not happy about this at all, but there's nothing he can do. My eyes dart between the two of them. It's not fair of Dad to blame Elder . . . but at the same time, I wish Elder knew a *little* more about how to reverse the lockdown.

Dad sends Emma to gather up the military, then asks Elder to group his people together. Kit follows Elder down the ramp, leading Lorin by the hand.

Dad drops a hand on my shoulder, holding me back. "Don't do that again," he says.

"Do what?" I ask, still rubbing my elbow.

"Don't put yourself in a position where you sacrifice yourself for *those* people. If a few got stuck inside, that would have been their fault. If you'd gotten stuck inside . . . "

"We all got out in the end," I say, narrowing my eyes at him.

"Take this." Dad presses something cold and hard in my hand. A gun—a double-action .38 in a canvas holster. "Remember what I taught you," he says. "Just pull the trigger. Don't cock it. Use both hands when you aim."

"I know," I say, thinking about when I fired a gun at Doc. The bullet blew through his knee. This gun is cold and dormant, but the memory of that time tricks my nose into smelling gunpowder and blood, making my stomach churn.

"Stay near Chris," he adds in an undertone. "I trust him more than any of those shipborns."

"They're not bad," I say. "They're just people."

"They're not *our* people."

14: ELDER

Colonel Martin stands on top of the exposed bridge as we regroup. Everyone wears a glazed, shocked expression. My people spent their first day here crashing into the planet and the second day being thrust outside by an alarm.

I glare at Kit, at the green patches that are stuck to the arms and necks and hands of the last people to leave the shuttle. In my mind, I know this was the only way to get the stragglers out into the open, that if they had not been forced out, some of these people might *never* have left. Just because they had the courage to get on the shuttle doesn't mean they had the courage to leave it.

I swallow back the bitter taste in my mouth. The patches are temporary, I tell myself. They're just for now, just because they were truly needed. I turn, looking for Amy, painfully aware of how much I want her to confirm my resolution. But she's standing on top of the bridge, between her mother and Chris. She leans over and says something in a low voice to Chris, something that makes him smile.

I jerk my head away from them.

"Thank you all for helping us by leaving the shuttle quickly and smoothly," Colonel Martin shouts over the crowd, his earlier frustration with my people masked by his public military face. "For now, the best thing we can do is find a permanent home for the entire colony. We do not know how long the shuttle will remain sealed off and thus cannot rely on it for long-term shelter. As such, we need to find an area that has natural defenses and easy access to fresh water."

Nervous excitement fills the area. There are so many of us out here that we're pressed against the trees of the forest we landed in. I never thought I could feel claustrophobic off the ship, but the sheer number of people crowded together in one spot makes me uncomfortable.

"There is safety in numbers," Colonel Martin calls. "We are a large group, and it is my hope that any creature that might attack one of us individually will be scared off by our sheer size."

Around me, my people start to grumble. They've noticed Colonel Martin's choice of words—his *hope* for safety—and they are not comforted by it. Several of them turn to me, and I, like a coward, don't take my eyes off Colonel Martin. Eventually, the others follow suit.

"We're going to head in this direction"—he points ahead, slightly to the right—"as the probe indicated fresh water could be found nearby. Military: rank one in the lead with me, rank two at the tail, rank three circling remaining perimeter, rank four scout ahead."

The military immediately divides itself while the scientists stay clustered with my people in the middle of the sandy clearing near the ship. A small group of soldiers disappear into the trees, ostensibly to scout out the danger ahead. Colonel Martin starts leading the group forward, but none of my people move. On the ship, every square inch was perfectly measured. Even the hills were perfectly spaced, symmetrical rows of measured bumps in the ground. This land is nothing like that. It slopes forward randomly. Rocks and pebbles and bushes and even giant trees are scattered around with no apparent rhyme or reason.

"Excuse me," Lieutenant Colonel Bledsoe calls. "I'm sorry, could you please not wander away?"

One of the Feeders, Tiernan, stares at Bledsoe for a moment, confusion in his eyes, and then continues wandering closer to the edge of the forest. He's curious but hesitant, lingering in the shadows cast by the tree trunks that twist like knotted rope.

Bledsoe growls in frustration and starts striding toward Tiernan. Before she reaches him, I intercept. "He can't understand you," I say.

"Why not?" she snaps. "I'm speaking English, aren't I?"

"Yes. But—your accent." It's even stronger than Amy's, with a rush and lilt to the words that makes them hard to understand.

"I'm South African," Emma says, and I struggle to recall the battered globe in the Learning Center. "I spent most of my childhood in southern France, though. My ma's British. Oh," she adds, surprised. "She *was* British; my father *was* Libyan." She says the words in past tense as if they are bitter on her tongue.

"I see," I reply. I don't want her knowing that I hardly remember the names of Sol-Earth's major countries, let alone the fact that its inhabitants could speak the same language and still manage to sound different.

She nods and resumes shepherding *Godspeed*'s former passengers along, her rate of speech only marginally slower than it was before.

I sigh. At least she's trying.

I grab Tiernan, drag him back to the group, and have my people start passing on the word: stay on the path, keep up, let no one get left behind.

I make sure that everyone in the crowd is ready to go. Kit stays in the back with those on Phydus, the only people in the group who are not wide-eyed and fascinated by this new world. I wonder how much of this they will remember or if, when Kit takes their Phydus patches off, they will recall only the terror and panic they felt when the drug was first pressed into their skin.

A dark-skinned man with black hair approaches Kit. "I am Dr. Gupta, one of the medical officers on the mission," he says formally in an odd accent, extending his hand. Kit shakes it, surprise evident on her face. "I understand you're a medical professional as well?" he asks.

I watch the two of them as we all make our ways into the tangle of trees.

Kit's shy at first, but soon she's happily discussing the differences in medical technologies. Dr. Gupta is fascinated by the Phydus patches, and Kit is
eager to compare notes with another doctor—her apprenticeship with Doc
had barely begun when she left him to come to Centauri-Earth.

I can't keep the smile off my face—seeing the two of them talk makes me
hope that the people from Sol-Earth and my people might soon find some sort
of common ground.

"These trees look so familiar." I slip through the crowd, following the
sounds of Amy's voice. "But yet, somehow, different."

"They are," a deep male voice answers her.

I pause, trailing a few people behind Amy and the young military man,
Chris. When Kit was talking with the Earthborn doctor, I was happy, but seeing Amy and Chris together twists me up inside.

"I have to admit—I'm surprised," Amy continues.

The trees seem unusual to me—but I've never seen a Sol-Earth tree to
compare these to, at least not outside of pics and vids.

"They're like banyan trees," Amy says. "You know, the way that they look
like a bunch of small trees all knotted together."

I don't know what banyan trees are, but Chris nods in agreement.

"Different, though," she says again. "Everything *reminds* me of Earth, but
not quite. Like this." She pulls down a clump of straggly, string-like moss that
wafts between the leaves of the trees, dangling in our way. "It's like Spanish
moss, but purple and sticky rather than dry and gray."

Chris plucks the sticky strings from Amy's hand. "This stuff is getting
everywhere," he says, making a big show of almost getting it in Amy's face.

"Ew, get it away!" Amy says, batting at the purple strings playfully.

"Why? Don't you *like* it?" Chris teases, dangling it closer to her.

I want to snatch the purple stringy moss from Chris's hands and shove it
down his throat, but I don't. I hang back, glowering, and even though I know
I'm being loons, I can't help but to keep listening to their conversation.

"I wonder what kind of animals are on this planet," she continues, blithely ignoring the look of adoration on Chris's face.

"You mean other than large, reptilian birds that try to eat people?" Chris asks, his voice still flirting and playful. I roll my eyes.

"Yeah." Amy looks up and around at the treetops. "There should be other birds. Animals. Something to eat that purple stuff, nests within the limbs of the trees. Squirrels and snakes, deer and rabbits."

"This isn't Sol-Earth, Amy," Chris reminds her gently.

"Oh, I know," Amy says. "But it just seems like . . . something's missing."

"I'm sure there are other creatures," Chris says, and he really does sound positive of it. "But Colonel Martin was right: most animals would hide when nearly two thousand people go tromping through the forest. And besides, those reptilian birds would have needed something to eat before all of us tasty people got here!"

Amy squeals as Chris lunges at her in false menace. She jumps back, tripping on an exposed tree root. Chris grabs her and pulls her close to him, wrapping his huge, muscular arms around her in safety.

Enough. I stomp farther away, determined to get out of earshot of the two of them.

"Your eyes," she says, staring up at him. I pause, unable to make myself look away from the image of Amy focusing all her attention on another guy.

"What about them?" Chris asks, a little defensive.

"They're kind of weird."

"Wow. What a way to come on to a guy." Chris shakes his head in mock disbelief.

"No, I'm serious." Amy shoves him playfully.

"And who said I wasn't?"

"No, really. They're just so blue."

"And yours are *so* green," he says, mimicking Amy. "I don't know how you can see with those."

I don't wait for her to answer him. I can see just fine, and I do *not* need to stand around and watch as Amy admires some other guy's eyes. I circle around to the other side of the crowd, then push my way to the front of the group. I try to squelch the jealous rage that's growing in my heart.

I might have the whole world now, but it's not enough if I don't get to share it with her.

15: AMY

"Don't break formation!" one of the military guards shouts.

I pause, looking back. Kit is having trouble keeping track of the shipborns on Phydus; Lorin, in particular, is proving to be erratic. She keeps wandering straight ahead, even if the group veers in another direction. One of the doctors, Dr. Gupta, is helping her, but I shoot Chris a sympathetic smile and drop back.

"What can I do?" I ask Kit.

"Just try to keep an eye on them," she says. She pushes her hair off her brow. It's hot and humid, like a summer day in Florida.

I pull Lorin closer to me, tugging her to make her keep up the pace. If one of those pterodactyl things did actually decide to attack us, it would strike here, at the end of the group, where the weakest of us are. I glance around, looking for Elder, but he's nowhere to be seen. No—wait, there he is. At the front of the group, with Emma and Dad. With the leaders.

Where he should be, I tell myself. But I can't help but wish he was in the back with me instead.

"What's wrong with these people?" Chris asks, the joking tone he'd adopted earlier gone as he looks at Lorin intently.

I open my mouth to tell him about Phydus, then close it. How will he react? Right now, Phydus is needed, and it's too hot to start arguing philosophy.

A screeching cry cuts through the humid air.

I stop immediately, but Lorin keeps walking straight ahead. Dr. Gupta chases after her as I reach for my gun. Nearby, the soldiers closest to us pull out their own weapons.

"There!" someone calls from the middle of the group.

A huge, reptilian bird circles us slowly, like a vulture homing in on a meal. It's like it knew I was thinking about it.

I raise the .38 and am about to press my finger against the trigger when my dad begins shouting. "No one fire!" he orders from the front of the group. "Not unless it attacks!"

The *thing* screeches again, swooping down another few feet. I can see its claws—massive and curved.

Someone near the front fires a shot. Dad curses at the trigger-happy soldier.

The dinosaur-sized bird screams angrily, jerking around in another direction so quickly that I have to look away from the gun to keep up with its movements. In moments it's gone entirely. I holster my gun, and it's not until that moment that I realize Chris didn't pull out a weapon of his own, probably because he was worried about pissing my dad off.

"Move out!" Dad calls, motioning for everyone to continue following him. All the excited chatter from before grinds to a stop at this reminder of the potential dangers of this world.

Few people talk now. There's a sort of intense focus to the way we move in the trees. Everyone is jumpy, on guard.

Thunder rumbles, a low sound that rises and then fades.

Screams erupt within the group.

"What was that?" someone shouts.

"Where did it come from!?"

"What's happening?"

The entire caravan comes to a halt as the shipborns crouch, moving closer to each other, casting worried looks into the sky. I try to find Elder in the crowd, but he's too far away.

"What are they going on about?" Chris asks. Around us, the people on Phydus show no reaction to the thunder, but Kit is wide-eyed and terrified.

"It's just thunder," I tell Kit. "It's nothing to worry about; it just means it's going to rain."

She nods but still looks scared.

"These people have spent their entire lives on a spaceship," I explain to Chris, already breaking through the crowd, trying to find Dad and Elder. "They don't know what thunder is."

The trees rustle, showing the undersides of their leaves, and the wind picks up, chilling my skin, made slick with sweat from the humid air. This storm is moving fast.

"We have to keep moving!" I say as I push through the crowd.

"What if it gets us?" someone near me asks.

"What if *what* gets you?"

"The thing in the sky?" I don't know if he's talking about the reptilian bird or the thunder, but either way, standing here will do no good.

"Come on!" My dad's voice is frustrated and loud. "We need to keep going!"

Elder catches my eyes from across the mob of people. I see the same fear in them that I see in all the other shipborns. They are more scared of the thunder, which is harmless, than the alien life that might kill them.

I push through the crowd to reach Elder. He looks grateful as I approach but scowls when Chris moves behind me.

The fear I saw in him before evaporates. He calls out to his people to keep going and leads the charge himself, striding farther into the woods.

The sky continues to grow darker.

The shadows in the trees seem to have eyes, the stillness of the forest before the storm reminding me of the silence before an attack.

16: ELDER

There's desperation in the way we march through the trees now. The shuttle is far enough away that, even if we could somehow make it past the locked doors, we wouldn't be able to return to it before the storm hit, and the trees seem as if they'll never end.

"How much farther?" I ask. I don't like the way it's so humid here—the air seems to steal my breath away.

"We've gone nearly a mile," Lieutenant Colonel Bledsoe says beside me. Colonel Martin is looking at some sort of instrument, perhaps a compass, and picking out directions. Amy and Chris are behind me, but at least they've stopped flirting. "The probe sensors indicated that water would be near here," she continues. "If we can find some sort of shelter near that, it would be ideal." Bledsoe's accent is so strong, I'm grateful that she's still speaking slowly for my benefit.

She looks down at me, waiting for me to contribute my thoughts, and it hits me that if I'd met her before Amy, I would have been scared of her. Honestly, I'm a little scared of her right now. Her eyes seem too big, as if they know too much; and it puts me on edge. Despite the fact that this woman slipping through the forest is both graceful and beautiful, I cannot shake the feeling that she's also dangerous.

No. I shouldn't think that way. I saw how Amy was hurt when others flinched away from her, and I don't want to do that to anyone. I know the way Eldest, who looked just like me, was so quick to hurt others, and I know Amy, who looks nothing like anyone on *Godspeed*, never hurt any of them.

"How sure are we that the probe is accurate?" I ask.

"Pretty sure."

It's humid here in a way I never felt on *Godspeed*. The air feels thick and damp, like I could swallow it as easily as breathe it. Lieutenant Colonel Bledsoe's skin glistens with sweat. Amy called her "black," but to me, she looks dark brown, like freshly plowed earth on the Feeder Level or the darkest dyes the weavers used.

"Something wrong?" she says, scowling at me.

I blink, almost miss my step. I didn't realize I'd been staring at her. "I've never seen someone that looked like you."

"Got a problem with it?" She sounds bemused, but there's a sharp edge to the question.

I shake my head. "No," I say. "Sorry I was staring. It's just different, that's all."

Her lips spread in a smile. "'S'alright," she says. "I've been staring at you lot. Weird, the way you all look the same."

I pick up my pace again as she starts to outstrip me. "Wait, Lieutenant Colonel Bledsoe," I call.

She pauses, her lips twitching even farther up. "That's a mouthful, innit? Just call me Emma, then."

"Emma?"

"It's my first name. Lot better than 'Lieutenant Colonel Bledsoe,'" she says, trying to imitate my accent. It's so much like what Amy did to me when we first met that I am filled with an immediate sense of relief. Orion was wrong: not all frozens are bad.

The trees start to thin, the branches spreading far enough apart to make speckles of sky visible—which only makes it more obvious how dark the sky is growing. I shiver. None of the Earthborns seem upset by the changing sky, but it's . . . weird, unnatural, the way it changes so quickly.

"Look!" Colonel Martin calls from ahead. Emma picks up her pace, dodging branches as she reaches the front of the crowd.

Colonel Martin's climbed on top of a boulder at the edge of the forest, and he points down, at a wide, clear circle of blue perhaps another half mile away. A lake.

"Fresh water, enough for all of us!" Emma says.

"We have to test the water first," Colonel Martin says quickly, but he's grinning. This is a triumph for them.

The sky roars, a sound so loud and deafening that my first instinct is to cover my head and look up, trying to find the source of the sound.

"Thunder," Amy reminds me gently, touching my arm.

And then *fire* explodes across the sky, leaping from one dark cloud to another.

"The frex is that?!" I shout, leaping back.

Amy laughs this time. "Lightning," she says.

Her laughter grates on me. I'd never seen lightning before, not when it was right in front of me like this. Fortunately, only a few of my people have emerged from the trees by this point, and so only a handful saw the lightning. But their worried cries grow fast.

"We have to find some sort of shelter," I tell Colonel Martin urgently. "People are going to panic."

"From a storm?" he asks, doubt in his voice.

"They've never seen a storm, Dad," Amy tells him.

"What's that?" Chris asks, pointing to the right of the lake Colonel Martin found.

Colonel Martin frowns, but squints in that direction. We all follow his line of sight. A tall hill—or a small mountain—stands in front of a grassy meadow. Its sides are bare rock, yellowish exposed stone. And built into the stone are . . .

"Houses?" Emma asks, shock in her voice.

"Can't be," Colonel Martin says, staring harder. He snaps his fingers at one of his soldiers, and the man places a pair of binoculars in Colonel Martin's hands. Colonel Martin stares through them, then curses.

"They're ruins. Buildings built straight into the rock, but probably abandoned."

"We need to go there," I say.

"Out of the question—we don't know what kind of life-form constructed these buildings." Colonel Martin passes the binoculars to Emma—but Emma immediately hands them to me.

I stare through the lens. The side of the mountain has been carved into levels, connected by rows of stone steps. Large, even-sided buildings rise up against the hillside, perhaps made using the same stone dug out from the mountain to make the levels. I can see cutouts in the walls of the buildings: windows and doors.

Human-sized windows and doors.

Colonel Martin is right—the entire place looks dusty and old, long abandoned.

"Something could still be there. If there are sentient creatures on this planet, they had to have seen our landing," Colonel Martin says.

I think about the way the shuttle seemed to be knocked off course. Was that a malfunction of the shuttle, something to do with those giant birds, or was it an attack by whatever being built these structures?

This changes everything.

"I don't trust it," Colonel Martin continues.

Lightning cracks across the sky. Fat, heavy drops of water start to fall. My people scream. This rain is nothing like the "rain" from *Godspeed*. On *Godspeed*, rain is measured bursts of water from the sprinkler system built into the painted ceiling. But this? No rhythmic falling, no even distribution. The fat, irregular raindrops just plop down on us, clattering through the leaves, splashing against our skin, cool and slick.

"What is this?" a woman shouts. She swipes at her body, trying to get the rain off her, but of course she can't. More falls down.

I hop onto the boulder Colonel Martin still stands on. "Look," I say, "you're moments away from my people panicking. We need to get to shelter, and we need to get to shelter *now*. Those buildings are the best bet we have!"

Colonel Martin looks at me the same way Eldest did when I thought the light bulbs in the Keeper Level were real stars. "You'd really choose hiding in there with God knows what inside instead of staying out here in a little rain?"

"To us this is not just 'a little rain.' And you said yourself the buildings are probably abandoned."

"Besides," Emma says, "the lightning is dangerous. Can't stay near the trees, stupid to head into the flat areas of land or by the lake. Safest thing is shelter. Here, or *somewhere else*."

A meaningful look shoots between Emma and Colonel Martin, and from his scowl, I can tell that Amy's father doesn't like whatever it is Emma is implying.

"Rank one, rank two," Colonel Martin bellows. Emma snaps to attention and the rest of the nearby military gathers around her. "Go first, inspect the buildings. Radio back. Hurry!"

Emma races forward, followed by the rest of the military in the first two ranks. Which must not include Chris, because he stays by Amy's side.

Colonel Martin doesn't look happy, but he heads across the meadow as well, cutting a swath through the high, yellowish-green grass. Now that we're out from the trees, my people are more nervous and scared than ever. I keep looking behind me as I follow Colonel Martin, almost tripping, trying to keep tabs on everyone.

Amy sprints forward, to be beside me. I glance back but can't find the ever-present Chris tagging along. "What is this place?" Amy asks, breathless not from running, but from excitement.

"I don't know." I hate the childish way seeing Amy with Chris makes me feel, but I can't tamp it down.

The farther in the open we travel, the faster my people go until we're all jogging across the wide meadow, tall grasses whipping against our legs. The rain makes the grains stick to our skin and clothing, and a sweet smell escapes from the broken stalks as we trample the grass in our mad dash toward the buildings.

A crackle escapes the radio at Colonel Martin's shoulder. "All clear, sir," Emma's voice says through the radio.

Colonel Martin looks back. "We're heading to those buildings!" he shouts, waving his arm forward.

That's all my people need to hear. They quickly overtake him, running, racing as fast as they can to be out of the storm. The rain comes faster and harder, water pouring from the skies so intensely that I can barely see. Amy grabs my hand, her own slippery, pulling me beside her.

A bright flash of lightning illuminates the sky, casting Amy in light that seems to capture her in a single moment of time, not unlike when she was frozen.

All around us, everyone is running with terror. Blind panic, shouts of fear, our primal instincts have taken over.

But Amy runs through the rain, her mouth wide and grinning, her eyes sparkling, relishing every second.

17: AMY

I would use the same word to describe both my joy and the rain: *torrential*. This—*this*—this is all I ever wanted from the world: wide-open spaces and cooling rain and the chance to *run*.

We reach the buildings much too soon.

The Earthborns, grumbling at the rain they see as a nuisance more than anything else, stagger into the first buildings. The shipborns are panicked, but not so panicked that they're willing to share space with the people from Earth. They race past the closest buildings, the ones the Earthborns chose, then pour into the ones behind the first row, packing each building so tight that there's only room for them to stand as they watch the rain stream down over the walls.

I stop, letting the rain wash over me, and Elder watches me, bemused. I squint through the rain, trying to see the buildings clearly. They are *ancient*, far older than anything I've ever seen before. They remind me of the cave dwellings at Mesa Verde, the way they pop straight up out of the stone of the hill.

"Find shelter!" Emma shouts as she runs past me. She and the military are going to each building, checking them, trying to make sure that everyone's arrived safely.

Elder starts to pull me toward the closest building—the one packed with dozens of shipborns all standing, shivering together.

"Let's go this way," I say, pulling him in the other direction. It seems stupid to cram together with others when there's so much *space* here. So many empty buildings, with rain darkening their pale, dusty exteriors. Elder hesitates, but I slip my fingers through his, and he grips my hand in reply.

We climb the stone steps to the next level. The buildings are nearly all two stories high, with the second story smaller than the first, making a square deck. The path is paved with large, flat rocks and is as wide as a country road—a small car might be able to squeeze between the buildings if it weren't for all the stairs, but two people can easily walk side by side.

Lightning flashes.

The buildings all look hollow inside, dark, and despite the fact that there is no glass in the window or doors at the entrances, the air inside feels musty and stale. The gaping maws of the doorways remind me of monsters' mouths. And suddenly I don't want to go farther. I don't want to be here at all. Because these houses are the perfect size for people, but we're supposed to be the only people on this planet.

When I stop, Elder tugs at my arm, pulling me into the nearest building. "This happened often on Sol-Earth?" he asks as another roll of thunder bursts out overhead.

I grin at him. "Not all the time, but it happened," I say. "Isn't it great?"

Elder looks at me as if I've completely lost it.

"At least it'll be cooler after the rain," I add. "On Earth, in the summer, it'd get really hot, and then there would be a quick thunderstorm. This must be Centauri-Earth's summertime."

"So summer is a time of terrifying thunder and fire *from the sky*?"

I laugh, but when I see Elder's serious, I bite it back. "Not usually, no. Trust me, it'll be over soon. And it's not dangerous, not really."

To prove it, I step through the doorway again, twirling in the rain. I tilt my head back, looking up as the drops falls down, spinning fast on the slick stones.

Elder catches me before I fall.

The rain pours down. We're both soaked, and the rain is falling so hard that I can feel it in my scalp.

"This is loons!" Elder shouts over the downpour. "We need to get inside!" He tugs on my arm, trying to pull me into the shelter of the closest building, but I tug back, pulling him closer to me.

Another flash of this lightning. The world illuminates for just a split second—I can see each glittering drop of rain as it falls—and then another huge *crash!* of thunder.

I don't think anymore, I don't feel. I don't have time to be gentle or shy.

I just kiss him.

My lips press against his, my arms weave around him until we are so close that even the raindrops don't slip between us. My fingers tangle in his hair, then slide down the back of his neck. His arms tense, tightening his hold around me, pulling me closer, closer.

All my senses burst into life: the feel of cool rain, the thunder cracking overhead ringing in my ears, but it's all overwhelmed by the sense of Elder filling every pore of my being.

I see, through my closed eyes, another flash of lightning. It electrifies me—and Elder. He kisses me with passion that can only be described as voracious. I clutch at him the same way he clutches me: with a feeling of need, of longing, of insatiableness.

Always in the rain.

I stand on my tiptoes to reach Elder's lips better, but I lose balance, slipping on the wet stones. Elder's grip on me is so tight, though, that he easily lifts me from the ground, spinning in a slow circle, his laughter weaving in between raindrops to splash against my heart.

✳   ✳   ✳

I shiver, my rain-darkened hair hanging down in clumps as the downpour ends as abruptly as it began. Already the sky is lightening, the air cooler. I lean back, blinking in the soft light of the twin suns.

"What is it?" Elder asks, and it's only then that I realize I've sighed aloud.

"I was sort of hoping for a rainbow," I say.

He stops dead and shoots me an incredulous look. "Those are frexing *real?*"

I laugh. "Of course they are!"

Elder shakes his head, as if trying to make the idea of colors arching across the sky stick in his brain.

Up here on the second level of buildings, it almost feels as if we have a semblance of privacy. The rain has brought not just cooler air, but also a sheen of freshness to the whole world.

And insects.

I swat at a gnat—or something very like a gnat—buzzing around my face, then notice a subtle humming made by the bugs nearby. I wander along the wall of the building and find a tree, like the ones in the forest but smaller, with a swarm of gnat-like bugs hovering over beautiful, delicate purple flowers dripping from the tree branches.

I reach out to touch the petals, but then a screech cuts through the air—a high-pitched scream that fades to silence, then circles back around. I pull my hand back, instinctively wanting to protect myself even though I know I can't.

"What was that?" Elder asks in a low voice, but we both know what it was. We scan the skies but see nothing. Elder steps closer to the sprawling tree. "I think . . . I think these flowers came from that stringy stuff that was on the trees earlier."

He's right—the purple Spanish-moss-like plants that clung to the trees are the same shade as the flower petals, a delicate lilac on the edges that sinks to deep purple in the center. A few tendrils of the moss haven't blossomed, but most have unraveled, twirling into paper-thin, almost-translucent flowers. "They're lovely," I breathe.

"You like the flowers?" Elder asks, a wry smile on his lips. Before I can respond, he reaches up and plucks one from the branches of the closest tree. "Here you go. Least I could do, after I made such a mess of the last time I brought you flowers."

I look at him curiously—when did he last bring me flowers?—and then I bend my face down to breathe in the intoxicating sticky-sweet scent of the flower.

I smile. "It reminds me of—"

My body goes numb.

My eyes are still open as I fall. The ground rushes toward me, but I cannot put my hands down to protect my face, I cannot tense as my body impacts against the ground.

I feel nothing.

My eyes are still open as I lie, facedown, in a pool of muddy rainwater. I can see swirls of dirt and brown. Something sticks to my eyes, and some reflex takes over as my eyelids flutter shut.

Water seeps into my slightly open mouth and up my nose and trickles into one ear.

I try to shout, I try to move, but I can't, and it's just like when I was frozen, and I'm trapped again, and I can't move, I can't, I can't, and I have to breathe, *I have to breathe*, but there's no air, just water, and I am screaming inside my head to *not breathe* but the only things that work are my involuntary functions like my heart that's beating too fast and my lungs that have to breathe.

And then there's air.

And then there's nothing.

18: ELDER

Amy's voice drops off suddenly. Her eyes roll back in her head, and she falls to the ground, limp. For one moment I watch with horror as she lies facedown in a puddle. Little bubbles burst on the puddle's surface, then the thin layer of water is still.

"Amy?" I say, dropping to my knees beside her. "Amy!"

I roll her out of the water and swipe the water off her face. "Amy?" I shake her shoulders, but her head lolls lifelessly. "AMY!"

Nothing. Dirty water dribbles out of her mouth. I push against her chest, and more water leaks out, but she doesn't move. Her breathing is shallow but steady. Carefully, I peel back her eyelids. No response.

My heart's racing, my ears are ringing. What happened? Is she—

I press my head against her chest. No. Thank the stars, no. She has a heartbeat.

Frex! What should I do?

I scoop Amy up in my arms. I need help. *Now.*

I stumble down the stairs, shouting for Kit. She can't be that far behind. People in the other buildings peer through the windows and doors carved out of the stone walls. When they see me holding Amy's unconscious form, they gasp or scream, curse or blanch, but none of them are Kit, none of them know medicine, none of them can save her.

"KIT!" I bellow.

Someone tall and dark turns the corner—Emma, on patrol duty with Juliana Robertson. "Help!" I shout at them. Even Juliana, who wanted nothing but to fight me earlier, is worried, her face draining of color, a stark contrast to her dark, bushy hair.

From behind them, Kit comes running. She stops short when she sees Amy. "What happened?" she gasps.

"Help her!" I shout again.

"This way," Emma says as she and Juliana take off at a run toward the buildings at the edge of the ruin, where the Earthborns are. I race after them, slipping on the wet stone pavers. I twist to protect Amy's lifeless body, gouging a long scrape into my thigh that I barely feel. Kit helps me up, then runs beside me, already checking Amy's pulse as we jog toward the outer buildings.

Emma and Juliana lead us straight to the first stone building in the row, the one that's slightly bigger than the rest, and moments later, Colonel Martin emerges. "What the hell happened?" he bellows, striding toward us. I don't stop. I need doctors, medicine, something. Colonel Martin takes one look at Amy's pale, unresponsive face and curses long and loud, running beside me, shouting for assistance.

"Stand back!" he bellows once I duck into the building. Amy's mother screams. I kneel, carefully laying Amy down on the cold stone floor.

"What happened?" Dr. Martin cries as she stares at her daughter's motionless body. Kit kneels beside Amy, lifting her eyelids. Two other people—a female with narrow eyes and a short man—drop down beside Amy and take over. Earthborn doctors.

"Where's Gupta?" Colonel Martin shouts. "Where is he? He's the lead medic!"

"I don't know," the female Earthborn doctor says.

"What happened?" Dr. Martin wails again.

"I don't know," I say, my words coming out as a plea. "We were just up there, at the buildings, and there was a tree, and—"

"Could be anything," the Earthborn doctor says. His accent is strange, stranger than Amy's, but that knowledge just makes my chest ache. "There was rain—perhaps there's a toxin in the precipitation. Or a bug bite."

"Bugs! There were lots of bugs, little annoying flying things," I jump in.

The doctor nods. "Perhaps a venom that reacted strangely to her system. Anything out here, no matter how seemingly harmless, is alien to us. We don't know how we'll react to any stimuli on this planet."

"What's this?" Kit asks, lifting Amy's limp hand. The sticky remains of the purple flower petals still cling to her palm.

"A flower. She sniffed a flower and then—"

"Passed out?" Kit lifts Amy's eyelids, but much more gently than I did earlier, and shines a light in them.

I nod.

"Well, wake her up!" Colonel Martin shouts.

The Sol-Earth doctor presses a stethoscope into Amy's chest.

"You!" Colonel Martin rounds on me. His wife gives a tiny sound of fear. "You put her in this danger!" Colonel Martin's accusations slice into me, ripping my flesh to shreds.

"I don't know what's wrong with her," the Earthborn female doctor mutters.

"Where the hell is Dr. Gupta?" Colonel Martin shouts. His gaze zeros in on Juliana Robertson. "You! Go find that lazy medic and bring him here!"

I reach for Amy—I know she can't hear or see me, I just want to touch her—and Colonel Martin slams both hands into my chest, throwing me to the far wall of the building.

"Get. The hell. Out." He grinds the words out through clenched teeth.

I stare up at him, shocked at his reaction.

"You did this. If she dies, her blood is on *your* hands. You can't keep her safe. You can't keep anyone safe. GET OUT." He pushes me again, and I stumble against the wall. Kit looks up—the only other shipborn in the room— but she can't afford to divert her attention from Amy.

I drink in the image of Amy—pale, empty, lifeless on the ground. Her mother, weeping. Colonel Martin's rage.

I run from the building, Colonel Martin's accusation digging into my heart like a salted blade.

19: AMY

My mouth feels as if it's been stuffed with cotton balls. I smack my dry lips, my tongue heavy in my mouth.

Something twitches in my hand. The movement startles me, and I try to jerk my arm away, but my muscles are sluggish. I struggle to sit up, but it feels as if there's a weight on my chest even though no blankets sit on top of me.

My mother's asleep, her hand wrapped loosely around mine. That was what I felt before. I curl my fingers over hers.

Her eyelids flutter and then pop open, as if she's suddenly remembered something vitally important. She turns to me and sucks in all her breath. "Amy?" she gasps.

"Mom?" My voice is croaky.

"Amy!" she screams, and throws herself on me. In another moment, my father appears. His eyes are wet, and he seems unable to talk. I've never seen him this emotional.

My eyes skim the room. Where's Elder?

"What's going on?" I ask. My back aches. All around me, the air is cool and dim—have I slept until dusk? But no—the sky is growing lighter and lighter. It's dawn. I've slept the entire day and into the next.

"What do you last remember?" one of the doctors from Earth—I think her name is Dr. Watase—asks.

I look down at the hand my mother still holds, and it's not until I do so that I realize my body is answering for me: the last thing I remember is holding the flower Elder gave me.

No. I shudder involuntarily, swallowing down the bile rising in my throat. The last thing I remember is losing control of my body, just as I felt when I was frozen. And then the sensation of drowning, just as I felt when I first woke up.

The memories pour into me, poison my soul.

I look around me. Everyone's waiting for me to talk. "The flower," I say, because I know they don't care about how I feel; they need only a cold medical analysis. "It made me pass out."

My eyes are still looking around the room. I'm filled with disappointment. I can't believe Elder would just leave me here.

"We thought so," Dr. Watase says. She points to a line on the floor where dozens of purple string flowers are laid out. "We haven't been able to do any tests, but from observation, it seems as if the flowers are carnivorous. When they're wet, they blossom and emit a neurotoxin that causes insects to drop into their center."

"And geniuses like me to drop to the ground," I say with as much of a smile as I can muster, attempting to alleviate the tension in the room. But it doesn't work. Everyone just looks at me, gravely nodding in agreement.

"Precisely," Dr. Watase adds. She pats my hand in a grandmotherly way. I would roll my eyes at her, but that seems to take too much effort.

"I'm starving," I say.

"We all are," Dad says. "If the shuttle doesn't unlock itself, we'll have to figure out how to get food from the planet."

I close my eyes—on *Godspeed* we at least had food. If we all starve to death, it'll be partly my fault. "How long was I asleep?"

"Almost twenty-four hours," Dr. Watase says.

We've spent practically a full day and night in the ruins, and I slept through nearly all of it. I look around me, trying to gauge what's happened since I was knocked out. Everyone in the building I'm in is Earthborn. There's a rumpled sort of look to them all, even Dad. They've slept in their clothes; no one has eaten. I doubt anyone's left the buildings at all.

I stand up, my back cracking. The floor wasn't exactly a comfortable place to sleep, despite the fact that my parents appear to have padded the ground with spare coats to give me a kind of makeshift bed. At first Dr. Watase and Mom try to help me walk, but I just want to stretch my muscles, and the remaining effects of the flower are rapidly evaporating.

I wander along the walls, my fingers trailing across the dusty yellow stones of the building. The room is the same size as one would be on Earth, the doors and windows perfectly proportioned for humans. Steps lead up to a second story. "It's weird, isn't it?" I say.

Mom doesn't need to ask what I'm talking about. "It is." Her voice drops an octave. "Your father's worried."

We both stop by the window and look to him. He's talking with Emma in the doorway in hushed tones. They both look angry and tired. As if he can feel our gaze on him, Dad turns around and offers us a weak smile, a smile that doesn't reach his eyes.

I realize now that Dad has a trapped look about him. The same look Elder had, after Eldest died. Haunted.

Dad turns back to Emma and continues talking.

I trace the outline of the stone wall with my finger. Now that I'm right in front of it, I can tell that the buildings are actually made of large, handmade slabs of brick the same color as the soil. There was *intention* in the creation of these buildings, but they are empty now and so long-abandoned that there's nothing but echoes of life clinging to the stark stone.

My hand trails to the window, my fingers dipping into a depression in the stone windowsill. It's perfectly square, each line straight and carefully carved in the stone.

"We don't know what that's for," Mom says, looking at the depression in the sill, "but there's a square in every window in every building."

Dr. Watase steps forward. "Whatever built these buildings obviously had sentience," she says. "The popular theory among the scientists is that the original residents of these buildings had some sort of idol that they put here. Perhaps their gods are linked to the suns; the windows all face the light."

Emma leaves, and Dad watches her go. I step around Dr. Watase and head straight to him, wrapping my arms around him like I used to do when I believed he could solve any problem. The hardness in his face softens. "I'm glad you're okay, Amy," he says. He drops a kiss on the top of my head.

"Of course I'm okay." I shoot him as big a smile as I can muster.

He hugs me tighter. "This . . . none of this was what I expected it to be."

"Don't forget, Dad," I say gently. "This was my choice. I was the one who decided to come on the mission."

He opens his mouth, but I already know what he's going to say: that it wasn't supposed to be a choice at all, and I shouldn't have come.

I don't give him the chance.

"I'm here now," I say. "And I'm happy. I'm with you and Mom."

He squeezes me one more time, then lets me go.

"What were you talking with Emma about?" I ask.

"We have a couple problems we're working on."

"Tell me."

He looks down at me, and I know he's seeing me only as his daughter, his child. "Tell me," I say again. "Maybe I can help."

To his credit, he holds back his skeptical look. "Well, first of all, we're having trouble with the probe. We haven't been able to communicate with Earth."

My heart stops. "You mean you weren't able to communicate with Earth *again*, right? You communicated with them just after we landed, didn't you?"

"Yes," Dad says, and then, almost as if he's talking to himself: "Yes, of course." After a moment he adds, "But the shuttle's communication system is completely broken now, and we couldn't get the one on the probe to work."

"What's wrong with it?" I bite my lip, waiting for Dad's answer.

"We were able to establish a communication link—but we're not hearing anything from the other end." The look he gives me doesn't bring me any comfort.

"Is something wrong?" I ask, leaning forward, already guessing the answer.

Dad shrugs. "I think we just need to work on it more. It *is* old, Amy." He looks away from me. "But that's only one of our problems."

"What are our *other* problems?"

"One of the shipborns is missing—and Dr. Gupta. We think the shipborn wandered off and Dr. Gupta went after her, but . . . ".

"When did they go missing?"

"Sometime in the storm." Dad's eyes are distant. I know he's concerned, but his concern doesn't have the same acidic taste of the dread rising up in my belly.

They've been gone for nearly a whole day.

"What shipborn?" I ask. Dad said "her"—so it's not Elder that's missing, but maybe Kit. . . .

"Laura? Lauren?" Dad shakes his head.

"Lorin?" I ask quietly.

"That's the one."

Lorin had been wearing a Phydus patch, and I'd been guiding her before the storm, before I let her go. If she wandered off in the chaos of lightning and thunder, it's my fault.

He looks down and notices my face. "Amy, don't worry," he says, squeezing my arm. "It was rainy and dark last night, but Juliana is a good tracker; she'll find them now that the suns are up."

The radio at Dad's shoulder crackles to life. He steps away from me, pressing the button to confirm that he's ready to receive a message. Emma's voice comes out over the radio. "—Found them, sir," she says, her voice fuzzy.

"Gupta and the shipborn woman?"

"Not Gupta," Emma says. "But the shipborn and Juliana."

"Good. Send them back to the ruins."

"Sir, I can't."

"What?" Dad asks.

"Sir, they're dead. Both of them."

20: ELDER

The first thing I feel when I see Amy running up the steps to the buildings on the second level, her red hair swishing behind her, is relief.

She's alive. She's awake, and she's fine, and she's alive.

The second thing I feel is fear.

The look on her face tells me that something is very, very wrong. "What is it?" I ask.

"Dad just left with Mom and some of the scientists," she says, breathless. "He told me not to leave . . . told me not to tell you. . . . "

"Tell me what?" My insides are churning.

"They found Lorin."

"And?" I ask, already dreading the answer. Kit and I spent the better part of yesterday compiling a detailed list of every single person from the shuttle. Losing Lorin in the crowd ate away at both of us; we can't let that happen again. "Isn't that a good thing?"

"She's dead."

My eyes widen with shock, then anger. Dead? "How?" I demand.

Amy shakes her head. "She's dead, and so is Juliana Robertson, who'd been sent to find her and Dr. Gupta. I don't know how. Dr. Gupta's still missing. I just heard—"

She heard about the deaths, and even though her father forbade it, the first thing she did was tell me about them.

"Where?" I ask.

Amy shakes her head. "I don't know. Near the lake, I think."

"I have to go."

She grabs me by the elbow. "You can't. Dad would be furious—"

"So?" My mind is racing. The dangers of this planet are so much greater than I originally thought. The reptilian bird that tried to eat my face, marred footprints in the forest of something nearby, watching us, the flowers that nearly drowned Amy, and now two more are dead. . . .

There's so much we don't understand. It's our ignorance that will kill us on this planet.

Our ignorance . . .

But someone knew. There's one person here who knew what perils this world held all along. And his knowledge might save us now.

I'm reminded of Orion's last words on the floppies he left for Amy. His voice trembled and cracked with fear. *Is the ship so bad that you have to face the monsters below? Is it worth the risk of your life—of everyone's lives?*

My eyes meet Amy's.

He *knew*.

"Orion," I say. He can tell us. We won't let him speak in riddles and codes, we'll force him to tell us everything he knows. If he doesn't . . .

Amy's face drains of color. "Orion," she whispers. Her eyes focus on me. "Elder, *Orion*. We didn't—we forgot . . . his timer."

Frex. Between the shuttle locking us out and being forced into the ruins . . . no one has reset his timer.

Amy and I both take off at a run, crashing through the trees and not even bothering to look up to see if there are any more of the bird-creatures waiting to attack. For a brief moment, I worry that we won't be able to find the way back to the shuttle, but moving nearly fifteen hundred people yesterday left more than enough trail for us to follow back. Locating a place to settle seemed to take forever because there were so many of us and we didn't know where we were going—we only knew that the probe indicated water. But there are just two of us now and returning to the shuttle takes far less time than I expected.

Amy bounds up the ramp and tries the door. "Still locked," she growls.

I slam into the seat in front of the control panel. There has to be *something* I can do. I swipe my hand across the onboard controls, setting the shuttle's computer to do a full scan of all operations.

"Why weren't you there?" Amy asks as I lean back, staring at the control panel in frustration, waiting for the results.

"There?" I ask. The sensors seem to be reading fine now—but then why is the shuttle still in lockdown?

"When I woke up."

My fingers freeze over the shuttle's controls. Do I tell her that I spent the night outside the building her parents kept her in, propped under the window so I could hear if she woke up? Do I tell her that when the suns rose, the first thing I did—before checking on my people, before re-checking everything with Kit—was stand on my tiptoes so I could look at her face in the morning light? That I barely slept, racked with guilt that it was *I* who nearly killed her . . . again?

"I should have been," I say. "I'm sorry."

Amy sniffs. I glance up at her. She's looking not at me, but at the locked door. "Let's get this open," she says, the closest she'll come to accepting my apology.

I drop underneath the control panel, looking for the small box labeled FUSES AND SENSORS. The wires connecting the air pressure sensors are covered in black tape. They must have frayed or something long ago and then been hastily repaired—no wonder they malfunctioned. I'm surprised to find the tape still tacky; that repair must have been made gens ago.

But either way, they seem fine now. And if the sensors are operational—who the frex knows why they cut out in the first place—then I should be able to override the lockdown procedure.

The military authorization code request flashes across the computer screen as I crawl out from under the control panel. Shite. I don't know Colonel Martin's ten-digit secret code. I try to bypass the request. There must be some way—after all, Orion himself figured out the way to break open every door on *Godspeed*, including the ones on this shuttle.

If Orion could do it, so can I. I turn back to the computers, this time looking at the key logs stored in the computer's archives. It's a simple enough task—other than Amy and me, very few people ever came to the shuttle while it was still attached to the ship. After a moment, I find the same code entered over and over again—*K-A-Y-L-E-I-G-H*. It doesn't take that much of a guess to figure out that this is the override command Orion's programmed into the computer. He *would* pick her name, little Kayleigh, whose dead body was found floating above the spot in the pond that hid the secret hatch to the shuttle.

Amy steps aside as I jump up and run to the keypad by the door. I punch in the code, and the seal locks break.

I throw open the door and am about to step through it when Amy grabs my arm. "If he's awake," she says, "we have to refreeze him."

I shake my head. "Frex, no! If he's awake, we need to *question* him. Amy, he's the one—the *only one*—who knows what's down here. He knew there were monsters; he must know what *kind* of monsters. He might be able to help us fight them."

"Question him, then refreeze him," Amy counters. Her voice is still cold, but there is fear and pain in her eyes. "We can't afford to have him here. Imagine the chaos he'll bring . . . imagine what he'll do to the people from Earth now that they're awake."

I don't bother saying anything else. Amy will never be able to see Orion as anything but evil. She doesn't see what I see. She doesn't see herself in him.

Amy lets me go, and I push the door open farther.

"You're not going to abandon me again, right?"

I freeze. Her voice was calm and quiet, almost a whisper, and filled with more sadness than I've ever heard from her lips before.

Without waiting for my reply, Amy pushes past me and into the shuttle.

The shuttle is eerily silent. Dust motes move in the air. Even our footsteps are muted.

I half expect Orion to be casually sitting in the cryo room, waiting for us. But of course he's not.

"In here," Amy says in a whisper, approaching the gen lab door. The air inside the shuttle is musty and stifling. How could we have ever considered living here instead of outside?

Amy presses her thumb against the biometric lock. She lets out the breath she'd been holding as the door zips open.

We step inside.

"Where is he?" Amy asks. She stares at the cryo chamber. Before, Orion's face was frozen against the glass. But now—now there's nothing behind the little window. No cryo liquid. No Orion.

"That's impossible," I say.

Amy looks around the gen lab, as if she thinks Orion is going to jump out from behind the Phydus pump and say "Boo!" But I walk to the cryo chamber, dread twisting me up inside. The counter on the cryo chamber blinks 00:00:00. Out of time.

The door opens with a *whoosh* and a *hiss* of released air and pressure.

Orion is crumpled on the floor of the chamber. His skin is red and raw, and he looks like a heap of flesh, not a person. But he shivers, and that is the only way I know he's alive.

Amy gasps, and I glance at her. Her eyes are open wide with horror, her hand covers her mouth. She hates Orion, but she's not heartless. No one could look at this shell of a man and not feel pity.

"Orion?" I say softly.

One shaking hand reaches out, still damp and shimmering ever so lightly with the blue of the cryo liquid.

I take the hand. It's soft—not soft in a sweet way, but soft in the same way that a wet sponge is soft. When I try to help him stand by pulling on his arm, Orion opens his mouth, and a raw, gasping, breathless scream emits from his lips. It sounds like a death rattle.

He's dying.

The idea hits me all at once, so suddenly that I nearly gag at the thought, but I know it's true.

He's dying.

As Orion struggles to stand, all his muscles weak and atrophied, my mind flashes back to the moment when we froze him. We—I—just shoved him in the cryo chamber and turned it on. We didn't prepare his body. No electric pulse scanners on his skin to help him adjust to reanimation. No drops in his eyes or cryo liquid in his blood. His regular clothes still on.

Past our gripped hands, blood leaks out of the cuff of his shirtsleeve. His skin is fused with his clothing, and it rips away as easily as wet paper.

Amy shoves a wheeled metal table toward us, and as soon as Orion's fully upright, I help him shuffle two steps so he can sit on the low tabletop.

His back hunches. His hair, still dripping sparkling blue cryo liquid, hangs down in clumps. He's heaving, as if he's just run a great distance, sucking at the air with every ounce of energy he has. His fingers curl like claws, and he raises them to his face.

That's when I notice his eyes.

They are open and bulging, the same way they were when he was frozen. There's a pale blue film over his irises, though, like cataracts but a brighter color, the same blue of the flecks in the cryo liquid. His clawed hands run down his face, over his now-closed eyes, stopping at his mouth.

He mumbles something into his fingers.

Beside me, Amy is shaking. Her own eyes are wide open, staring at this animalistic shadow of a man.

Orion's hands drop to his side.

I lean down, trying to meet his eyes. But I can't. His eyes don't focus.

He's blind.

He's blind, he's hurt, and he's dying.

And there's nothing we can do to stop it.

It doesn't matter that I hadn't intended this. It's done.

And I was the one who did it.

21: AMY

I want him to rage.

I want him to roar, to fight, to flip the table and attack us.

That's the Orion I understand.

I don't know what to feel about an Orion who's been tortured—whose very existence *is* torture—who is dying before my eyes.

"What happened?" The words creak out of his mouth. Opening his lips causes the corners of his mouth to bleed, just slightly, barely enough to dribble down the side of his chin.

Elder keeps his voice calm, as if he's speaking to a skittish animal. "You were frozen."

Orion's body jerks, and it takes me a moment to realize that was an attempt at a laugh. "No shite. How long?"

"Three months."

I watch as this information penetrates. He seems to age those three additional months in an instant.

"Where are we?"

He doesn't mean what room is he in. He wants to know if we're still on *Godspeed* or if we're on Centauri-Earth.

"We landed," Elder says.

"Why?" Orion asks. No anger in his voice, no accusation.

"We had to," Elder says, but I'm starting to wonder if that's true.

Orion's smile is bitter, as if he doubts the need too. He lifts his head. "Why does it hurt so much?" His voice is barely a whisper. "Why can't I see?" There is fear in him now, and dread.

Something cracks inside my heart.

"You weren't frozen correctly."

"I don't . . . " He swallows, and even that action looks painful. "I don't feel well."

"I know," Elder says gently. "I know." After a moment he adds, "I'm sorry."

Orion's face tilts in Elder's direction—and mine. For a moment, his filmy eyes seem to fall on me, but no—they're blind. "I don't blame you for this," he says in a voice stronger than before.

Elder dips his head. Orion might not blame him, but he blames himself.

"Maybe I deserved it. I don't blame her either."

My heart stops. *Me.* He's talking about me.

"That girl . . . I'm glad you found her. Glad she woke up. I had tried rebelling before, you know that. Didn't have a girl like her. Just got more scars." He touches his neck. "I seem to be accumulating a lot of scars." His hand drifts up toward his eyes. He covers them with his palms and his head sinks down.

"We shouldn't be here," Orion says.

"We had to—" Elder starts to say again, but Orion cuts him off.

"No, you didn't." He coughs, a wet, hacking sound. "You saw that planet and you couldn't stay away. I know. I saw it too. But I had the sense to keep our people on *Godspeed*, safe." He coughs again, blood splattering his puffy lips. "Guess I'm not worthy of seeing it now that we're here."

There is so much longing in his voice.

And for the first time, I realize that I have something in common with Orion.

"I have my own reasons to be sorry," Orion says. Elder looks as if he wants to speak, but he can't seem to get any words out.

Blood dribbles freely down Orion's chin now, and his eyes are leaking.

He's falling apart in front of us. "I never watched them die," he croaks, echoing my earlier thoughts. "Maybe if I had, I wouldn't have let them drown."

"Orion," Elder finally says. "We need help."

Orion's hand pats the table, feeling the edges. "So . . . tired . . . "

"What can you tell us about the monsters on the planet?" Elder asks, urgency in his voice. Orion's dying—but we cannot let him die with his secrets still hidden.

"Slaves or soldiers," Orion says. He sinks against the table, lying down, his legs dangling over one side. "I told you . . . slaves or soldiers."

"Not the frozens," Elder says. "I'm not talking about the frozens. I know how they're dangerous. I need to know—what about the creatures on the planet? What did you know would be waiting for us if we landed?"

Orion's body wheezes—another laugh? Or something worse?

"Tell us!" Elder says, his voice rising. "You have to tell us! We need to know what we're up against! People have *died*."

"So?" Orion croaks. "I'm dying."

"You *have* to tell us!" Elder grabs Orion's arm.

It *squishes* under his grip, and Orion's mouth sucks in air for a scream his throat can't give life to. Elder snatches his hand away as Orion's body spasms with pain.

After he's stilled, Orion speaks. His voice is weaker than before. "Don't tell me you didn't find them?" He coughs, a dry, papery sound. "Oh, little prince, don't tell me you didn't follow all the clues."

"We don't have time for clues." Elder's voice is pleading; he sounds as if he's about to cry. "Just *tell* me."

Orion struggles to sit up again but can't. Instead, he turns his face to Elder. His blind eyes are closed, the effort to keep them open already too much. "Show me the world," he says, making an effort to make the words come out strong. "Please." There is no begging in his voice, just a simple plea simply stated.

Elder looks confused, taken aback. But I know what Orion means. He won't talk unless we take him outside.

I stand and walk as quietly as I can to the door, motioning for Elder to follow. Elder pushes the wheeled table in front of him. The only sounds in the cryo room are of us walking and the table rattling over the metal floor.

And Orion, panting, on the table, holding on to life for this one moment.

When Elder pushes the table around the hallway toward the bridge door, Orion's body slides on the metal surface. He gasps, something rattling in his chest, his blind eyes open wide as he spits blood. It's not just the sides of his mouth bleeding now; there's something inside him broken too.

We'd left the bridge door open when we'd entered, but I have to go through first, lifting the edge of the table and pulling it over the lip of the seal-lock door. If Orion's guessed that there's someone else with him beyond just Elder, he makes no mention of it.

Once we're outside, he tips his face toward the suns. They've risen higher in the sky, just above the trees. His body seems smaller, shrunken in relief against the dull metal table, but his eyes are still wide and darting around, straining to see what's happening. I pity him in this moment, but then I remember the way Theo Kennedy's eyes were bloated and bulging in death, and the pity sours in my heart.

Orion raises his arm, reaching, his fingers splayed. He breathes deeply, tasting the fresh air. His body seems to be an extension of his flared nostrils; everything is centered on his sense of smell. A warm breeze swirls around us, and he tilts his head toward it. The wind makes the leaves of the forest rustle and shake, and Orion shifts his ears to the sound.

His body is focused on every sense left to him, absorbing this world as completely as he can.

His arm slowly lowers. The corners of his mouth curl up.

He sighs—and with that sigh, the last bit of life escapes.

What little light remains in his faded eyes slowly disappears.

22: ELDER

"He's gone."

Amy says the words, but they still don't register.

He can't be gone. His blind eyes still stare, still try to absorb the world he can never see.

I don't have the heart to close them.

"He was me, you know." A me who faced the truth by himself. A me who did what he did to protect my people. Everything good in my life came from him, and I gave him nothing in return. "Technically, I mean."

"I know," Amy replies.

"I'm sorry," I whisper to Orion, because even though he was a murderer, he didn't deserve this. He didn't deserve to have the planet given to him and then stolen away.

I don't meet her eyes as I sink to the floor and roll my head against the hard metal of the shuttle. It's hopeless. We should have never come. We should have stayed on *Godspeed*.

"We'll figure it out," Amy says. "We won't let everyone die." She sits down next to me and rests her head against my shoulder. For a few minutes, we just sit there in silence—me coming to grips with the realization that I can't save my people if I don't know what it is I need to protect them from, Amy leaning against me, serving as a reminder of everything Orion didn't have.

"Elder," Amy says after a while, "what was that he called you?"

"What are you talking about?"

"He gave us a clue," she says, wonder filling her voice. "Before he died . . ." Her voice trails off as she jumps up, excited.

"What do you mean?" I ask, my heart thumping. My knees are weak with hope as I stand up.

"A clue! I don't know if he meant to or not, but he gave us a clue."

"A clue? What clue?"

"Think about it," Amy says, her eyes flashing. "Think about the trail of clues we went on."

My mind skips over that time. Harley's painting. Amy's wi-com. Shakespeare and Dante. And another book . . .

"You've forgotten—of course you have, you were distracted by the space suits at the time." Her eyes are wide and gleaming.

"Space suits?"

Amy grabs my hand and drags me back toward the shuttle door. "Remember when we discovered the room with the suits? There was a book there, just like the other books Orion left for us, but there wasn't a clue inside the book. Do you remember what book that was?" Her voice is manic, urgent.

I shake my head. My only thought had been to go outside *Godspeed* and see the universe that had been blocked out by steel walls all my life.

"I remember it," Amy says, smirking. "That book. It was *The Little Prince*." She whirls around to face me, the ends of her hair whipping her neck. "And what did he call you just now?"

"A little prince," I answer automatically. For one brief moment, the hope Amy's exuding infects me. But no— "That can't be a clue," I say. My eyes dart to Orion's body, still staring vacantly up into the blue sky. "He was just making fun of me, saying that I was, you know, the leader, but not any good at it. Besides, we already found that book and the clue in it."

Amy frowns, thinking. "What was that clue?" she asks.

I shrug. "Just some underlined text."

"No, I mean, what did that clue show us? Every single clue Orion left for us had a reason. Each one led to something else, each piece was important. How was that clue important?"

"It was where the space suits were."

Amy shakes her head. "But it's not how we found the suits—that clue came from the sonnet."

"So?"

"So we missed something," Amy says. "Orion knew something else, something about the ship or the mission that we should have discovered then . . . but we didn't. We missed a clue."

She's right. When we discovered that little book, I was distracted by the space suits, then by the planet. And Amy was distracted by the way I nearly died. Everything happened so *quickly* . . . and we missed something. Some last clue, something that will explain what we're up against on Centauri-Earth.

I head straight to the space suit room, the first door after the bridge. It's still packed to the brim with supplies we brought from *Godspeed*. I stare at the crates of food, the boxes of cloth and medical supplies and everything else we thought we'd need.

And that's when it hits me: "There's no way the book is still here." Stupid of me to come here and look, really. I knew it was gone. We cleared out this room. Crammed it full of farm equipment and livestock. At any point in time anyone could have picked up the slender volume of *The Little Prince* and tossed it away. It could be on *Godspeed*. It could be thrown away. Destroyed.

Maybe there was one more clue in *The Little Prince*. But whatever it was, it's long gone now.

Amy laughs. "Oh ye of little faith," she says. "I was in here while they packed this room. I was going to take the book back up to the Recorder Hall, but . . . " She stares hard at the crates in the way. "Give me a leg up, will you?"

"What?" I ask, incredulous.

"Give me a leg up." She puts both hands on the nearest crate, testing her weight against it. When I cup my hands under her foot, she pushes off, scrabbling to clamber on top of the crates.

"What are you doing?" I call.

She climbs over the crates, occasionally slipping and once falling through a box of cloth and cursing. "I know we agreed that we shouldn't waste space on anything we didn't need to survive, but . . . " Her voice trails off as she reaches the wall, her eyes even with the broken monitor that was supposed to show how the space suits worked. "But I just couldn't let this book go."

Amy pries her fingers under the glass monitor embedded in the wall, and it slides off its hook. She pulls out a thin volume with a hand-drawn image of a little boy standing on a cratered moon. Amy crawls back over the boxes, then leaps down, tossing me the book. *The Little Prince* is emblazoned on the cover, followed by an unpronounceable name.

I flip through the pages until I find the clue Orion had left, the underlined text Amy saw but neither of us thought to explore.

"I," replied the little prince, "do not like to condemn anyone to death."

"It's a warning," I mumble, reading it.

Amy reads over my shoulder. "There has to be something more. Orion wouldn't have left a clue that didn't go anywhere, and he wouldn't have brought it up, not as he was dying, not as you were telling him we were at the planet and it was dangerous. He might have been psycho, but he was careful with his clues. There has to be something here that links to *why* Centauri-Earth is dangerous, what it is we're really facing."

I'm not sure how much of this is logic and how much of it is just wishful thinking, but it's the only chance we have.

I flip the book closed, examining the cover. Orion called me a little prince, but I have to admit, I do not think I have anything in common with this one. This little prince stands on top of his dry, dusty rock of a kingdom, and he does not know what it is like to have a thousand people relying on him. He could step off his planet and bounce throughout the universe from place to place— and, as I start to scan the pages of the book, I see that's just what he does. He must not feel the weight of gravity on such a small planet, but there is much more than gravity that drags me down.

I start to try to read the story, but Amy's impatient, and I can't concentrate on the words. It seems silly—there's a hat and a rose and a fox, and little of it makes sense. When we get to the end, I hand the book back to Amy. "There's nothing here," I say again.

She shakes her head, opening the book again. "There has to be."

She doesn't start at the beginning of the book this time; she starts near the middle, where Orion underlined the text. Her fingers trace the circles and underlines, grooves cut deep by a heavy pen. She turns a couple of pages, running her fingers over the illustration there, a fat man in a star-strewn cape, towering above a planet even smaller than the Little Prince's.

Amy gasps.

"What is it?" I ask, leaning forward.

"Look." She holds the book out to me. I stare at the page. *"Look."*

And then I see it.

The clue isn't in the text—it's in the illustration. The man in the picture sits on a throne. "He's the king," Amy says. "He thinks he's the king of the stars." His cloak wraps around him and trails along the sides of the planet, cloth billowing out across the surface. A dozen or more yellow stars decorate the robe, giving him the appearance of being wrapped in the universe. He wears a golden crown and a scowl, and for reasons I cannot explain, his wrinkled face reminds me of Eldest.

And—right over where the king's heart should be—there's a star. It's part of the original design and is one of many decorating the robe, but *inside* the star, in very faint black ink, is a hand-drawn heart that definitely was not a part of the book's illustration.

"And look here," Amy says, pointing to the bottom of the small planet the king uses as a throne. In tiny print is one sentence, curving along the edge of the planet:

Who are the real monsters?

23: AMY

Who are the monsters. Not *what*. Who.

Elder sighs and slams the book shut.

"What's wrong?" I ask.

"It doesn't tell us anything." He looks at the book with disgust. "It's just another frexing clue. And wherever this would have led us? It's out of reach."

"We don't know that," I reply, even though deep down I suspect he's right.

Elder touches the side of his neck, where his useless wi-com is. "Amy, it's hopeless. The answer is orbiting the planet, somewhere on *Godspeed*."

"It's not hopeless," I say, even though I can't really see how it's anything but.

Elder doesn't answer me. When I look up at him, his eyes have grown serious and concerned.

"What is it?" I ask, fiddling with my hair. His intense look makes me nervous.

"You know I didn't want to leave you," he says, his gaze never wavering.

"What?"

"When you passed out. I didn't want to leave you. I wanted to stay. But your parents—"

"Elder . . ." I feel stupid for ever having brought it up. I don't need him by my side every second of the day to know that he wants to be there. I guess the only thing his absence this morning really proved was that I want—*need*—him around too.

"Speaking of your parents, we should get back," Elder says, defeat in his voice. "Your father will want to know that the shuttle is open now."

I nod—he's right. I tuck *The Little Prince* under my arm and follow him back outside the shuttle. Even though we have the thing we came for—the clue that might give us the answers we need—it feels as if we've been defeated. On the bridge, Elder pauses, looking down at Orion's body. Elder's long hair obscures his face and his shadow casts Orion in darkness, making it seem almost as if Elder is peering into his own reflection. I clutch the book against my chest, trying to dispel the image.

"Amy?" a surprised male voice calls out. Elder steps in front of me, as if to protect me from an enemy, but any enemy on this planet wouldn't know my name.

Chris walks out of the shadows of the trees.

"What are you doing here?" he asks, surprised and perhaps a little suspicious.

"I have every right to be in *my* shuttle," Elder says loudly. "What are *you* doing here?"

"Colonel Martin sent me to check to see if the shuttle's lockdown was over," Chris says. "What's that?"

He points to Orion's body.

Elder explains—partially. He tells Chris that Orion was a shipborn who'd been frozen for crimes he committed on *Godspeed*, but he doesn't tell him about the clues.

"You two should get back to the ruins," Chris says when Elder is done. "Colonel Martin is having a colony-wide meeting. He's only waiting for me to return with the voice amplifier." He runs up the ramp and to the bridge, carefully avoiding contact with the metal table and Orion's body. After withdrawing something—a voice amplifier, apparently—from a panel built into the shuttle, he tosses it down to Elder, and Elder passes it to me. I hold it next to the copy of *The Little Prince*. Chris glances at the book but doesn't bother asking questions.

"What about—" Elder says, pausing. What about Orion's body.

"I'll take care of it," Chris says gently. "I'm helping with the others."

Juliana Robertson and Lorin.

So many.

Too many.

And we don't even know what happened.

"Do we know more about how they died?" Elder asks, obviously on the same train of thought as me.

"The pteros." At our blank stares, Chris elaborates. "That's what they're calling those bird monsters. Pteros—short for pterodactyl or pterosaur or something. Because they look so much like dinosaurs."

I imagine what Lorin and Juliana's last moments must have looked like—all claws and saw-like teeth. My lip curls involuntarily in disgust, and I force myself not to think about that.

"You should go," Chris adds. "Your father hasn't noticed you're missing, Amy, but he will soon. . . . "

I nod—my dad is going to be furious if he finds out I made my way back to the shuttle, especially after yesterday's fiasco with the purple flowers. Wrapping my hand around Elder's, I gently drag him away, back in the direction of the ruins, while Chris heads up the ramp.

"What's he going to do with him?" Elder asks, looking back at the shuttle and nearly tripping on an exposed root.

"Who?"

"Orion."

"Bury him, I guess," I say. "That's what they did with the others, the ones who died during landing."

Elder frowns. He stops and starts back to the shuttle, then stops again and continues on the trail to the ruins. "I don't like that," he says in an undertone.

"What—what did your people do with the dead?" I ask, tripping over the question. I know that there was no religion on the ship, but I was never really clear on what happened to those who passed away. Harley's death left no body, and I never saw what happened to the others. When I met Steela, an old woman who was killed merely for her age, Doc hinted that the bodies were recycled, but no one, not even Elder, knew about that, I think. And that was the closest I came to discovering the truth.

"We send them to the stars," Elder says. "I've read about old religions and rituals. We didn't make a display of it—no 'prayers' or anything. We might not believe in gods, but we all could see the beauty of an eternity floating free, away from the confines of the ship, drifting across the universe."

He swallows, and I notice that his eyes are very red.

"What are we supposed to do with the dead now that they can no longer fly away?" he asks. "Burying them is the exact opposite of setting them free in the universe."

"My mother told me once that a famous physicist said we're all made of star stuff," I say slowly, trying to remember the exact words of the quote. "That the particles inside us are the same that are in stars. Maybe it doesn't matter if someone's buried or floating in space; maybe they're sent to the stars either way."

"They're still dead," Elder says bitterly.

"We all die someday." Maybe the only thing that makes that fact bearable is the idea that death is the only way we can return to the stars.

When we get to the edge of the forest, the people are already gathering into a crowd in the meadow that stretches between the trees and the ruins. They all mutter among themselves, the sounds loud but too indistinct for me to make out specific words. I don't need words, though, to know what it is they're feeling. Fear. I start to skirt the edge of the crowd, heading toward the buildings, but Elder grabs my hand and squeezes it. With a look, I know what he intends to do—stay here, where he is needed most. I nod silently and head off, dodging around clusters of worried, anxious people until I reach the buildings on the edge of the ruins.

"There you are!" Mom calls, relief in her voice. "Where have you *been*? Off with that Elder boy? You had me scared stiff! If you're going to do something like that, at least take Chris or one of the other military with you."

"I was just—um—" I start, trying to come up with a lie. Mom hasn't even noticed the tattered copy of *The Little Prince* or the voice amplifier I'm carrying. "Chris gave this to me to give to Dad," I finally say, holding out the voice amplifier while slipping the book behind my back.

Mom bustles me into the first building.

I stop short.

Two bodies are laid out on the dusty floor. One body is covered—mostly. I can still see the shock of bushy hair sticking out from under the jacket that covers half of Juliana Robertson's face, but that's about the only thing that identifies her. She's mangled and bloody in a carnivorous sort of way, and I have no doubt that it was a "ptero" that killed her.

Lorin looks as if she might be sleeping.

But she's not.

"Where's Dr. Gupta?" I ask.

Mom sighs. "We're not sure, but . . . it doesn't look hopeful. There were . . . pieces . . . of poor Juliana scattered around. We thought at first that Dr. Gupta was, er, among the pieces. But it seems as if he's missing." I look up at her, hopeful, but the look on her face makes my hope die. "Or it could just be that there was nothing of him left . . . I mean . . . Amy, maybe he was . . . "

"Eaten?" I gasp.

Mom looks grim.

"Amy! I was looking for you," Dad booms, descending the steps of the building. "Have you seen Chris? Everyone's waiting for my speech."

That's all what he wants to know? Seriously? I step around the covered bodies. "Here," I say, handing him the voice amplifier. I feel sick. "Oh, and also? Elder's got the shuttle open now."

"Does he?" Dad actually looks pleased at this. "Well, that's good. I'm glad something's finally working in our favor."

Dad goes back upstairs, and by the time I turn around, Mom is gone too. Probably outside, to listen to Dad's speech.

It's just me and the bodies—one ripped apart, the other untouched. Juliana has only one eye left, and it watches me as I run from the room.

24: ELDER

Colonel Martin stands on the roof of the closest building, the voice amplifier in his hand. Around me, my people shift nervously. In the shuttle, there was an invisible line dividing the people born on Earth from those born on the ship. Now the scientists stand closest to the buildings, and the military stands closest to the forest, trapping my people in the middle.

"Attention, all members of our colony," Colonel Martin says. My lips quirk up in a bitter smile. Smart of him, calling us one colony. As if we're united.

"It is my duty first to inform you of a sad circumstance. Last night, two members of the group—an Earthborn *and* a shipborn—were discovered dead."

Colonel Martin's words cause a flurry of chatter to rise up until he raises his hand, asking for silence. News of Lorin's disappearance had spread quickly among my people, but to hear that she's dead—that's another thing entirely.

"Their deaths remind us that this planet is full of unknown dangers. Something as simple as sniffing a flower could make you sick; wandering from the group could leave you the victim of savage beasts."

I look around me. True terror is painted on every face. I wonder if Colonel Martin knows what he's done. Fear of the unknown is the greatest sort of fear there is, and he's just ensured that *everything* on this planet is an unknown danger to my people.

"My military will be enforcing rules," Colonel Martin continues, "a cur-few, guidelines for who can go where, et cetera—for your safety."

I realize that I'm holding my breath. Perhaps it's my years with Eldest that make me wary of Colonel Martin's speech, or perhaps it's the fight with Bartie in those last days, or perhaps it's that I know what Orion would say if he were here now. But I can't shake the unease coiling around my stomach.

"We've been able to get the shuttle open again, but if the evacuation taught us anything, it's that it's unwise to have the entire colony living within such a contained area. All our eggs in one basket, so to say. There-fore, from this point forward, the shuttle will be used for storage and sci-entific research. Everyone—Earthborn and shipborn alike—is to relocate into the buildings here. Although we will all have to share our space, it will afford us much more privacy than if we were all living in the shuttle's cramped quarters."

I agree with him here; that first night was miserable.

"The first part of the morning will be spent relocating. Bring whatever supplies you need for day-to-day life with you back to the building that will be your new home. My people will distribute food rations at midday, and with them, work assignments."

I narrow my eyes.

"Every single person will have to contribute. We need basic things for our survival, and we must all work together to ensure that this happens."

I have no doubt that what he's saying is true.

But I also have no doubt that this is the first step of Orion's prophecy.

Soldiers, he warned. *Or slaves.*

As the military guides people to the shuttle, I make my way back to the ruins and Colonel Martin. I catch him as he's leaving the building. "Elder, there you are," he says. "I tried to talk to you before the meeting but couldn't find you."

I get right to the point. "How are you dividing up the labor?" I ask.

Colonel Martin holds out his hand, and Emma, who is behind him, hands him a notepad. "I've talked with your medic, Cat—"

"Kit," I correct him automatically.

"Kit." Colonel Martin nods. "She made a list that she was kind enough to share with me, indicating the labor skills of your people. I'd like to get the farmers working right away—I believe we might have landed in this planet's summer, but it might not be too late to start some crops."

"That sounds good," I say, surprised by Colonel Martin's approach.

"The other labor is menial but necessary," Colonel Martin continues. "A cleared path between the ruins and the shuttle. Toilets—toilets are a top priority. We have a pump and some water pipe as well, and I'd like to get that started so we can bring water from the lake to here."

I nod. "I can help distribute the labor among my people," I say. "But I want to know what your people will be doing."

"The FRX's primary mission with our colony was to discover new resources, so I'd like some of the geologists to be present when the latrines are dug," Colonel Martin says. "The other scientists will be performing their individual missions, and the military will be spread evenly throughout the area to protect everyone."

"From those things you're calling 'pteros'?"

"Precisely." Colonel Martin leans back, inviting me to continue, and I cannot help but feel that somehow he's using his words in the same way a spider uses a web.

"But you're not concerned about protecting us from whatever built the ruins we're now living in?" I ask.

"I'll remind you that it was your idea to settle in these ruins," Colonel Martin says genially. "And it was a good idea. But as of now we have no reason to suspect that the life-forms that built the structures we're currently residing in mean us any harm or, in fact, are even still currently on this planet."

I stare at him, waiting for him to continue. He doesn't.

"You're not even curious about them?" I ask, unable to keep the disbelief from my voice. "They're human size, they made buildings that fit our needs perfectly, and there's not a single trace of them. You don't even *care*?"

"I care," Colonel Martin says, his voice grave, "about our colony's future. Not this planet's history."

"So you want toilets and dirt samples," I growl. "And I'm guessing I can't expect any of your people to do any digging."

Colonel Martin stops. "We can provide tools, but we don't have the man-power to—"

I cut him off with a wave of my hand. I should have known. Orion's warn-ings ring in my ears. "So my people are the ones doing all the work?"

Colonel Martin shifts. "There are only one hundred of us—actually, only ninety-eight—"

"And all ninety-eight of you will be pissing in the toilets," I snap.

"We will help. I'll have some of my men help lay down the water pipe, and as I said, the geologists will be hands-on to gather the soil samples for evaluation. We have to work together, Elder." Colonel Martin doesn't sound patronizing; there's real concern in his voice, and the sincere look on his face is the same one Amy wore every time she made me a promise. He really means what he's saying.

I sigh. Would I have been so antagonistic if I didn't have Orion's words ringing in my head? If I hadn't seen him die less than an hour ago?

"I know," I say. "I understand. We're in this together."

I just wish saying that didn't make the situation feel so ominous.

Amy catches me as I'm helping to pass out our lunch rations—a single serving of dehydrated wall food that is both dry and tasteless. My people accept the packets of food gratefully, and they eat them huddled together and standing up in the bones of the buildings we'll be living in from now on.

She has *The Little Prince* in her hands.

"Let's talk to Kit," she says in an excited undertone. "She worked with the wi-coms with Doc; maybe she knows a way to amplify yours so you can reach the ship. If we can just talk to Bartie or someone still on *Godspeed*, maybe we can figure out where Orion's next clue is—"

"No," I say heavily. I hoist the bag of food rations higher up my shoulder and make my way to the next stone building. Amy follows.

"Why not?" she says. "It's worth a try."

"Maybe it is," I say. I start handing out the packets to the next group of people. "But there's work that has to be done first. I can't let my people starve."

"Elder!" Amy looks shocked. "You can't let them be food for pteros either."

I don't have the energy to argue. I just keep passing out food rations, and she leaves me in a huff, taking the book with her.

After lunch, I follow the group heading out to work on digging toilets first. It would be wrong of me to ask my people to work without working myself. I grab a pickax and spend the next several hours digging trenches, throwing every ounce of frustration at the hurt look Amy gave me into the task at hand. At first, my people freeze at each unknown noise and shadow, but as the day progresses and they realize that most of the commotion is caused by the geologists who are there to collect soil samples, they cease jumping and concentrate instead on finishing up the job ahead of them as quickly as possible, despite the intense heat.

I, for one, rip my shirt off. It's sweltering here, the air heavy like it was just before the storm. Sweat pours off me as I swing my pickax down into the yellowish sandy soil for the umpteenth time.

But this time the ax doesn't stop. It plunges through the dirt, and suddenly the ground around it breaks away, sending me and the ten or so others digging nearby crashing through the crumbling ground, falling into the darkness. For a moment I feel as if gravity has disappeared like when the shuttle was landing, but then I slam into the cold, hard earth below, dust billowing around me, clinging to my sweaty skin as the wind is knocked out of me.

"The frex?" Tiernan, one of the workers who'd been helping me, says. We both peer up—and then around. The hole we'd been digging for latrines has given way to an eerily large tunnel.

"Elder?" several of the Feeders call, peering down into the collapsed tunnel.

"Is everyone okay?" the Earthborn engineer shouts. "Someone get the medics!"

I quickly assess the damage. Three of the Feeders were injured in the fall—one's shoulder was sliced by a shovel blade, one is limping, and another has a knot on his head. We're streaked in mud, but the air down here is blessedly cooler and the drop was less than seven meters.

The others all turn to me, the whites of their eyes starkly visible in the dim light. "We're all going to be okay," I say. I glance up, and they follow my gaze. Already, the people above us are securing a rope and organizing a rescue.

My eyes turn to the tunnel. "Where the frex are we?" I mutter.

Tiernan touches the wall of the tunnel. He turns to me, eyes wide in the darkness. "I don't think this is supposed to be here," he says.

I run my hands over the hard-packed earth along the wall. It's smooth and cool to the touch. Above me, everyone is yelling and shouting—for ropes, for doctors, for the military. But the tunnel goes on and on, into the darkness and the unknown. "What made this?" I whisper.

I step forward. It's so dark—as if the inky blackness is eating the light. The tunnel's ceiling arches, but the floor is flat, with thick grooves cut along the bottom. Because the tunnel is almost three meters wide, all I can think about is that whatever creature made it must have been *huge*. My mind fills with images of worms twice as tall as me or long-nosed, sharp-clawed, overgrown moles that could eat me with a snap of their pointy jaws.

"Elder!" The voice cuts through the darkness and chaos, and I squint up at Colonel Martin, peering over the edge of the collapsed hole. "Any injuries?" he barks.

"Some!" I call.

"We're coming down!"

Before I have a chance to do more than step back out of the way, a dozen ropes are thrown into the tunnel and camouflaged military men rappel down.

They go first to the three injured men, but there's no doubt about it—they're hustling to get us out of the tunnel as quickly as possible. For the very first time, I see real fear in the military men's faces. Their eyes dart nervously as they wrap the ropes around my people and start hauling them up.

I ignore the soldier trying to get me to come closer so I can be dragged back up to the surface of the planet and instead squat down, looking at the grooves along the ground. They are cut deep and straight, almost as if wheels made the marks, but when I touch the dirt, I feel something abnormally smooth. I dig my fingers into the dirt and remove . . . something.

It's about the size of my palm, thin, and clear as glass. I hold it up to the light and see a golden sheen to the surface.

A scale? I think. At least that's what it looks like. My mental image of a massive worm burrowing into the tunnel is replaced by a monstrous snake with crystalline scales.

The scale is plucked from my open hand. I'm about to protest when one of the soldiers yanks me up—Chris. "It's not safe down here!" he shouts. He loops the rope under my arms and tugs on it to signal the people on the ground to start pulling me back up.

As I reach the surface, I blink in the bright light of the suns. I'm shuffled from Earthborn doctors to Kit, who scans me quickly for injuries. I ignore her worried fretting and keep my eyes on the collapsed tunnel. As soon as Chris is pulled back up, he goes to Colonel Martin. They talk briefly, but I notice the flash of light as the scale I found passes from Chris's hands to Colonel Martin's.

"I'm very happy to report that there are no serious injuries!" Colonel Martin booms, and the crowd around me cheers. "We're closing the dig site for the rest of the day, however, to give the military a chance to inspect this . . . unusual . . . land formation. I don't believe it's dangerous, but your safety is our top concern, and we'll make sure that there is no threat before we continue."

My people are all to happy to disperse at this—digging the latrines was hard work, and it's unbearably hot—but I keep watching Colonel Martin.

The scale-like thing is gone, hidden in one of his pockets, and he's making no attempt to hide the military involvement as he orders groups of men back down into the tunnels to inspect what's there.

"What kind of animal would make a tunnel that large?" I ask him. We haven't seen that many animals—mostly small forest creatures that scurried away before we could get a good look—and the pteros wouldn't make tunnels underground. Besides, the scale was nothing like their bumpy reptilian skin.

My mind flashes to the strange animal tracks we found near the shuttle after we first landed. There is much to this world we have yet to discover.

Colonel Martin keeps his eyes on the men descending down the hole.

"This tunnel is very close to the colony," I continue. "Perhaps the ruins aren't safe. Maybe we should go somewhere else."

Colonel Martin's mouth tightens. "It's a military matter, Elder," he says finally. "We'll determine if there's a threat."

"Really?" I ask. "That's all you're going to tell me?"

His eyes flick over to me, but he doesn't maintain eye contact. "I need you to focus on your people," he tells me. "And I'll focus on the land."

That's no answer, and we both know it.

With the latrine site closed, the only other thing I can do to help is work with the group laying water pipe. They've already set up a simple pump at the colony, and now it's just a matter of connecting pipe from it to the lake, our source of fresh water. It's much easier work, and there's something cathartic about the monotony of it. My body focuses on dragging the pipe and connecting the pieces while my mind races, trying to solve the mysteries of Centauri-Earth, Colonel Martin's strange silence among them.

Before I know it, we run out of pipe. "We'll go down and help the men laying pipe from the lake," I tell the Earthborn engineer who's managing the project.

He frowns. "Colonel Martin said no one was allowed down there."

I raise one eyebrow. "The military men are down there now."

"He meant—"

He meant none of my people are allowed down there. Just like none of us were allowed in the tunnel.

"If we all work together, we'll be done by supper," I say.

A soldier with the word COLLINS stitched on a patch on his shirt steps forward. "No one's permitted to go near the lake," he says gruffly.

"Why not?" I demand.

"Not safe," Collins says. He doesn't move from his spot blocking the path.

"But we'll be with you."

"Not safe."

I hold my hands out, asking him to stop repeating himself. "I understand that. But you have a great big gun right there, and when we reach the lakeside, we'll have at least half a dozen equally armed soldiers. We'll be as heavily protected as the shuttle."

Collins shakes his head again. I notice the firm set of this mouth, the way he grips his gun. He will fight me over this. "It is forbidden," he says.

"Forbidden?" I repeat, narrowing my eyes.

"Yes." Collins actually looks a little nervous. Good.

I lower my voice. "Do you know who I am?"

"I do, sir. And if you have a problem, I suggest you take it up with Colonel Martin."

"I'll do that," I snap. Then I turn to my people and call out, "Early supper!"

They all cheer and begin to make their way back to the ruins. But I just stand there, at the edge of the meadow that has become an unspoken border, one thought occupying my mind.

What is Colonel Martin trying to hide?

25: AMY

I'm still poring over *The Little Prince* when Mom bursts into the building I'd been hiding in. I quickly snap the book closed, but she doesn't even notice.

"It's time!" she announces with the same excitement little kids on TV back on Earth would announce that it was Christmas.

"For what?" I ask.

"Science!" she says in her best impersonation of a movie announcer. I laugh despite myself and slip *The Little Prince* under the sleeping bag Mom and I had taken from the shuttle. Maybe Elder's right—I can't spend all my time looking for clues that might not even be there, not now in the first early, crucial days of the colony.

Mom takes me straight to the shuttle to help with her research. Chris accompanies us for protection, but there are so many people now between the shuttle and the ruins that I can't help but think Chris's talents would be better used elsewhere. There are hardly any pteros in the sky, and while we've caught glimpses of other, smaller creatures—blurs of brown fur or dark feathers through the tree branches—the noise of workers and the sheer number of people here make them scarce.

Besides, I still have the .38 Dad gave me, the holster attached to the belt around my waist.

Mom chatters the whole time about the "plethora of specimens to examine on the new world." The more Mom tells me about how she wishes she had a ptero specimen to dissect, the more I wish I was with Elder, talking about what Orion's clue might hold.

The cryo chamber area in the shuttle has already been converted to a scientific laboratory. The trays that once held frozen bodies now hold scientific supplies. Several metal panels are missing on the floor and walls, exposing storage areas that hid microscopes, burners, and other scientific instruments. Some of the biologists are already preparing a trek into the forest to make casts of animal tracks. I wonder if maybe they'll find more of the strange three-clawed prints Elder found on our first day, and I'm torn between curiosity over what the creature might be and fear that whatever it was, it was very close to the shuttle we're in now.

I open the door to the gen lab for my mom and Chris. The cryo chamber that held Orion is empty, drained. It looks ominous, as if waiting for another victim, and I turn my back to it. A few other scientists are already inside— either Kit or Elder let them in, or Elder's taken down the security on the biometric lock. Two of them—Dr. Engle and Dr. Adams, who've both worked with Mom for years—are standing in front of the huge cylinders that rise up from the ground near the now-broken Phydus machine.

Each of the cylinders holds fetuses of animals the FRX felt would be most helpful to us in the new world. Livestock animals, such as cows (normal ones, not the weird hybrids they had on *Godspeed*), goats, and pigs. Predators, including wild cats, birds of prey, and trays of smaller, egg-like pouches that I suspect are snakes or insects or something like that.

Dr. Adams uses a special scoop to remove a fetus from the tube. Dr. Engle takes it from him, putting the little bean that will one day become a horse into a specially designed tube.

"What's that?" I ask, pointing to a row of twenty tubes already inserted in an incubator.

"Dogs," Dr. Adams says. "Large ones. We're aiming for a selection of animals that can be used for labor and, if worse comes to worst, food."

I don't really want to consider eating a dog or a horse, but the little tubes of bean-shaped fetuses don't look much like either. My eyes slide to the other tube, the one with yellowish goo inside. The one with dozens of tiny clones of Elder.

"Amy?" Mom says, waking me from my reverie. She's been talking with Dr. Engle. "Can you help us?"

I cross the room to the last row of cylinders. Chris follows me silently. I don't think he's ever been in the gen lab before—he's wide-eyed, taking note of everything.

"Amy, you're friends with that ship leader. Do you have any idea what this is?" Mom asks. I think for a moment she's talking about the cylinder with Elder clones, but Dr. Engle points to the Phydus pump instead.

"Yeah," I say darkly. "I know exactly what that is."

"It looks like a water pump," Dr. Engle says. "But inside are traces of a chemical we can't identify . . . "

Phydus.

"It's nothing," I say.

But of course, these are scientists. Tell them to leave something alone, and all they want to do is poke it with a stick.

"It was a water pump," I continue, sighing. "One of the previous leaders used it to distribute drugs to the people on the ship. Elder broke the pump and quit distributing the drugs. It's pretty toxic stuff; you should just leave it alone."

Dr. Engle looks even more curious than before. "What kind of drugs?" she asks. "Did they develop them themselves? What disease were they for—or were they intended for recreational purposes?"

Mom cuts Dr. Engle off. "We don't have time for that sort of thing, Maddie," she says firmly. She is, after all, the lead scientist for the group. "We have other work that requires our attention."

Dr. Engle nods reluctantly and goes to help Dr. Adams. Mom picks up a large canvas sack with special compartments for specimen jars and hands it to me. We're almost out of the lab before we notice that Chris isn't with us. I turn back to get him and see he's still standing in front of the Phydus pump, frowning, as if it's a puzzle he hasn't quite figured out.

"Come on!" I call, and he follows me outside. He grins at my excitement, and I can't help but notice that his nose crinkles when he smiles, illuminating his strangely blue eyes.

"What is it?" Chris asks, and it's not until then that I notice I've been staring at him.

"Nothing," I say, blushing.

Mom stands on the bridge, shading her eyes from the suns, a small smile playing on her lips as she watches the two of us. "I want to gather as many specimens as possible," she says. "I find it fascinating that so many plants seem similar to plants on Earth; I'd like to do some genetic sequencing and determine just how close they are. And of course, if there's any chance of catching any animal life, we *must*." Her eyes are shining; I've never seen her so excited. "We've set snares in the surrounding area, and, as you know, some of the other scientists are out searching for prints, but it would be great to see something in its natural habitat!"

Chris and I follow Mom down the ramp and into the forest. She goes the opposite direction of the path to the ruins, hoping the less disturbed areas will yield more chance of wildlife. Chris holds a rifle with a high-powered scope in front of him, and I notice that he not only has two handguns (one in his belt, one in a shoulder holster) but also carries grenades, knives, and a machete— that I can see.

"Amy!" Mom calls. I dodge around the trees to reach her. She's pulling purple string moss from one of the trees, and I hand her one of the smaller specimen jars from the bag I'm carrying. "We've got several samples of these already—Dr. Card wants to see if he can replicate the neurotoxin—but I'd like to extract cells for a closer examination."

"That," I deadpan, "is so exciting."

Mom hands me the jar. "Who knows what the DNA of this little guy can tell us!"

I squint at the plant. Although I know it unfurls to a flower nearly as big as my palm, right now it's nothing more than a bit of purple string.

Mom resumes her work, scraping off moss and lichen and bark into jars. "Just one small area, and imagine the diversity of life!" she trills.

I try to see the world through Mom's eyes, as if every *single* thing holds a new discovery, but then I stop in my tracks.

A terrible, wet, sucking sound creeps around the edges of the tree.

Immediately, Chris steps in front of me, slinging his rifle around in one fluid motion. Mom freezes, her eyes shooting first to me and then to Chris's gun.

A cracking sound. Scratching, like something hard across dry leaves.

My heart's beating so hard I can feel it banging against my rib cage. Something's out there, and it's *big*.

All I want to do is run away, but Chris creeps forward silently, his rifle raised and ready. I put the noisy specimen bag on the ground as quietly as possible. My sweaty hand pulls out the .38. I allow myself one moment to feel the gun, the heavy metal in the palm of my hand, the power behind it, and then I grip it properly, using both hands, one finger on the trigger.

Mom shakes her head at me but then stops, realizing the sense in having both me and Chris armed. She follows me as we move deeper into the forest and Chris glances back, signaling *forward* with his eyes.

A slurping, ripping sound leaks through the shadowy forest.

We're close.

Rustling. Definitely animal.

I step on a branch that cracks loudly, and an unnatural silence descends on us. The animal, whatever it is, has heard us.

Chris pushes aside a branch.

And then we see.

Dr. Gupta—what's left of Dr. Gupta—lies on the forest floor. A ptero, much smaller than the one that attacked Elder, cocks its head, looking at us as if we're a curiosity.

It bends its long neck down, using its saw-like teeth to rip away a chunk of Dr. Gupta's flesh. Blood and gore stick to the ptero's beak.

Dr. Gupta blinks.

Dr. Gupta blinks.

He's alive—he's alive, and he can feel—he can *feel*—as the ptero *eats* him. *He's alive.*

The ptero bends its head down again to its meal. A horrific crunching sound echoes throughout the forest as the ptero shatters Dr. Gupta's femur. The ptero shakes its head, worrying it like a dog with a bone, until the leg snaps off.

A small sound, a moan, almost drowned out by the sound of crunching bones, escapes Dr. Gupta's cracked lips.

Chris and I both shoot at the same time.

My first bullet hits the ptero in the wing, ripping out a chunk of the thin membrane. The ptero drops Dr. Gupta's leg and faces us. It opens its beak, foam and blood dripping from its mouth, and *screams*.

I shoot again.

The ptero's chest bursts open. It crashes to the ground. Its leathery wings flop about, and it's dead—I know it's dead—but I shoot it again anyway, right in the skull.

I'm breathing heavily as I lower my gun, the smell of gunpowder mixing with the metallic tang of blood. I look at Chris and see that he's staring at Dr. Gupta.

I realize then that it wasn't the ptero he aimed for when he pulled his trigger.

A small round hole leaks blood down the side of Dr. Gupta's skull.

26: ELDER

I can't sneak past the military to see the lake for myself, not while it's still light outside. And even if I wanted to inspect the tunnel, I wouldn't be able to. Colonel Martin's installed heavy metal panels on the collapsed ground, and his men have already erected the latrines over it. Colonel Martin acted quickly to cover up our discovery—just like he's trying to hide the lake from us.

But I think I know how I can uncover at least some of his secrets.

My first instinct is to get Amy—I haven't even told her about the crystal scale I found yet—but I'm trying to figure out what Colonel Martin is hiding, and he'll definitely have suspicions if I drag her away from her mother.

I pass Kit on my way up the paved path that runs through the center of the colony. "Don't forget to take care of yourself," I tell her as she obsessively checks over the handwritten list of passengers we made after Lorin disappeared.

"I could say the same of you. How are you feeling after the tunnel collapse? And I saw you keep working after that, on the pipes. You didn't need to do that."

"Yes, I did," I say. I cannot ask my people to do work that I won't.

Kit adjusts the white lab coat she's gotten from the Earthborn scientists, and I notice her pockets are overflowing with med patches, most of them pale green. "We need to wean them off Phydus," I say darkly, and even though Kit nods in agreement, she adds, "But not yet," in a soft voice.

I leave her to her work, feeling guilty that I'm not helping more. Finding out what Colonel Martin won't tell me is more important—I can't afford to let lies and deception rule the colony the same way they ruled *Godspeed*.

I climb past the second level of houses built into the mountainside and am glad to see that my people have spread out a little more, daring to space themselves farther apart. No one's on the third level, though, except me. I pause, looking at the few empty buildings, wondering what it was that made the original builders leave their homes. Did they die out—did the pteros kill them off—or did they move on? And how is it that they made buildings that are so perfect for *us?* That's the real mystery, the nagging thought that no one's really willing to address.

Without realizing it, I've reached the edge of the ruins. The last few buildings, the ones closest to the top of the mountain, are nothing but rubble. They look as if they've been blown apart by some force. The thought does not give me comfort.

I wonder what Amy would make of this discovery. Probably try to find a connection to it in *The Little Prince*.

I start climbing over the rubble. The suns are about to set—the sky is growing darker, the air cooler. If I'm going to find what I'm looking for, I need to do it while it's still light outside.

I find a trail that leads me farther up the small mountain. Or maybe I'm tricking my mind into thinking it's a trail—at best, this is just a path used by animals. I have to hold on to chalky, yellowish rocks and scraggly tree branches as I ascend higher and higher, grappling with the side of the small mountain.

And then I reach the top of the rocky plateau.

It feels more like a mountain now than before; I'm panting, completely out of breath, and my leg muscles *ache*. I don't know how Amy can frexing *enjoy* running.

I look up and out. This is the highest point on the planet I've been to. For one moment, terror seizes my heart. I'm so close to the sky and so exposed on the rocky bluff that a ptero could easily swoop down and carry me off. But then my eyes drift across the landscape spread out before me, and I forget about my fear. I can see now more clearly than ever.

Which is exactly the reason I wanted to come up here.

The air grows colder as something passes overhead, casting me in shadow. My stomach plummets. When I dare to look overhead, though, all I see are clouds, not pteros.

From where I'm standing, to my left is the colony, and past it, in the darkening forest that sticks out like a pointing finger, is the shuttle. I can see the scar our landing created, the burnt-out spot that seems to glitter and almost glow in the dying light. My eyes trail along the edge of the forest, moving right, looking for what I know is there.

The lake.

I don't see why Colonel Martin wants it hidden. The lake looks like any lake I've seen in pics from Sol-Earth, nothing more. It's a perfect circle, maybe a mile in diameter. One edge borders the mountain, the other edge is pale yellow, the same sort of sandy soil that makes up the surface of this planet. The shallow water all around the shoreline is pale aqua, but the lake grows deeper and darker farther in, until the center is nearly black. It looks almost like an eye, staring up at me. I wonder how deep the water is there. The suns' light glitters across the surface, making it seem as if the lake winks at me.

A scattering of pale pink dots wafts through the water. Fish of some sort, but not the quick, darting flashes of color like the koi from the pond on *Godspeed*. These fish are small from my viewpoint, but I'd guess in reality they are a half a meter or more wide, with even longer tendrils—or tentacles?—drifting behind them. They expand and collapse, expand and collapse as they float under the surface, but then the entire group of them darts sharply to the right, more suddenly than I would think possible.

I strain my eyes, moving closer to the edge of the cliff-like top of the mountain. What is so dangerous about the lake that Colonel Martin feels it needs to be kept secret?

Far, far past the lake is another forest made of darker, taller trees. And beyond that: mountains. The mountain I stand on is no more than a tiny hill compared to these jagged behemoths rising from the ground. They form a horizon that I cannot see past.

This world is so *vast*. And real. And I'm a part of it now.

Something glimmers—something between the lake and the forest. I can't make it out—it's too far out, and the trees are in the way—but something reflects from the light of the sinking suns at the perfect angle for me to see from my vantage point.

And then I realize: it wasn't the *lake* Colonel Martin didn't want me—or anyone—to find. It was the thing past the lake. The thing he found on the very first day but has been careful to hardly mention again.

The probe.

27: AMY

The gun is still warm in my hand as I stare, open-mouthed, at Chris.

"I had to," he says, his strange eyes pleading for me to understand.

And I do. Maybe if it hadn't been for the three months I lived on *Godspeed*, I wouldn't sympathize, but I know Dr. Gupta was living through the worst possible nightmare, and there was no way he could recover from such a maiming. What Chris did was merciful, and it was right . . . and it was the bravest thing I've ever seen anyone do.

I holster my gun and step forward. The muscles in Chris's arms are bunched up and tight, but his hands are shaking as I take his gun.

"Thank you," I tell him, hoping he can see the sincerity behind my words.

For the first time since the bullets left our guns, I think his eyes really focus on something other than Dr. Gupta's mangled body. Chris throws his massive arms around me and crushes me in a hug that leaves me breathless, clutching me as if I am his judge and savior all in one.

Mom steps forward, and Chris releases me reluctantly. She wears the calm, measured mask of a scientist over the panicked terror in her eyes. This is how she's always been; if she can't handle something that's happened to her as a person, she hides behind her role as a detached academic. Mom takes the lead back to the shuttle, sending more military and workers out to where we were, directing them to bring both bodies back to the gen lab before going inside herself. She breaks the news of Dr. Gupta's death to the scientists in an even, reserved tone, then starts clearing aside space in the gen lab for an autopsy of Dr. Gupta and a dissection of the ptero.

She avoids my gaze for all of this.

Inside the gen lab, she allows herself one deep, shaky breath.

From the other side of the door, we can hear the noises of the bodies being brought inside the shuttle. There are gasps of horror at the ptero—*and it was a small one*, I think—and wails of sorrow at Dr. Gupta's mangled body. Most people hadn't seen Lorin's or Juliana Robertson's remains.

Mom looks up at me, and in her eyes I see *Mom*, with all the fear that lies inside her.

I realize: she needs the mask of science, she needs the shell of Dr. Maria Martin, to separate herself from the horror of what she's seen.

We all have to find a way to separate ourselves from that.

I turn to Chris. He wears the guilt of his kill like a mantle. He doesn't hide it. Maybe he can't. My heart swells as I watch the way he straightens his shoulders as he puts one foot in front of the other.

Mom stands up and walks to the gen lab door, staring as Dr. Gupta's body is carried across the cryo room to her. "The first thing we're doing is a toxicology screen. Dr. Gupta *was* alive, but he had no reaction to the ptero . . . the ptero *eating* him." Her voice cracks over the word. "We have to find out why."

"One of the purple flowers that knocked me out?" I ask.

Mom shakes her head. "The flowers weren't open, and they don't emit the neurotoxin unless blossoming. Besides, Dr. Gupta was *awake* and even mobile, to a certain extent. When you were knocked out, Amy, it was like you were in a coma."

Finally the helpers lay Dr. Gupta's body on one of the metal table gurneys, possibly the same one Orion lay on as he was dying. The ptero is too big for a single table—we have to shove four tables together to hold it, and even then its wings and legs hang down over the side.

"We have to report this to Colonel Martin," one of the military men says. "He needs to know."

Mom nods silently as the man radios Dad.

"I'm beginning the autopsy immediately," Mom says.

The man looks up at Mom in surprise. "Bit obvious what killed him, isn't it?"

Mom gives him a thin-lipped grin. "Nevertheless, I will perform an autopsy. Please leave."

The man's eyebrows rise even more at Mom's dismissal, but he turns to go. Chris starts to follow. "You may stay," Mom says. She glances at me, and in her look is a question. I nod. I'm staying too. Seeing *that* together—it doesn't feel right that anyone but the three of us helps with the autopsy.

The gen lab door zips shut, leaving us alone with the two bodies—one the remains of a human man, the other the stinking corpse of the monster that devoured him.

Mom sighs again, but this time her breath doesn't shake. "Bring me that tray," she says, jerking her head to the tray she'd prepared on the table against the wall. I pick it up and head over to her.

It's hard to look at Dr. Gupta's remains, but not as hard as it was before, when he was alive. I try to shake the blank look in his eyes from my mind. His expression was so . . . empty. Devoid. And while he showed no pain, it makes it all the worse to think about what he felt but could not express.

Mom picks up a Vacutainer needle and carefully positions it over Dr. Gupta's heart. I try to watch as she gathers samples from his body, but soon I retreat, burying my face into Chris's shoulder while Mom works.

"I'm going to do an immunoassay," Mom explains as she leaves the body and crosses the lab with her tray of samples. "It won't tell us much; we can only test against drugs and chemicals from Earth, and I don't know of any drugs that . . . affect a person in the way Dr. Gupta was affected."

She means, she doesn't know of any drugs that let someone lie motionless yet conscious while he's eaten alive.

"Then why bother with it?" Chris asks. He stands close behind me, and I have to admit that I'm comforted to know he's there.

Mom looks surprised at the question. "Because we have to try."

She turns to the specimen bag that holds the few samples she'd taken outside before we found Dr. Gupta. I don't know who returned the bag to Mom, but everything's still there.

"Fortunately, we have an analyte generator," Mom continues as if she were speaking to a class of chemistry students. "So all I need is a sample"—she plucks one of the purple string flowers from the jar—"and then I can make an analyte to test against Dr. Gupta's blood."

Chris frowns. "I thought you said that you didn't believe the flower could have drugged Dr. Gupta?"

Mom doesn't stop as she sets up the test. "I don't believe anything I can't prove."

A few minutes later, the immunoassay machine beeps, and I shift out of the way as Mom examines the report on the screen. "No . . . " she says, frowning.

"What?" I ask as Chris hovers closer to us.

"This doesn't make sense," she says.

"*What?*"

Mom pushes a button, and a small paper readout spits out of the machine. She reads it again, disbelief written all over her face.

"Dr. Gupta had been injected with gen mod material," she mutters. "Just before he died, recently enough that it was still in his blood."

"Gen mod . . . ?" Chris says, letting his voice trail off into a question.

"Genetic modification material," Mom says. "Developed on *Earth.*"

28: ELDER

I wait until dark.

"Elder?" Amy says. I adjust the rucksack on my shoulder—filled with gear I've gathered just for tonight as I stand on my tiptoes, peering through her window.

She's made herself something of a cocoon, using strung-up tents to create walls inside the building. I wonder where the tents came from—probably more supplies from the Earthborns that they're unwilling to share.

"What did you say, Amy?" a voice—Amy's mother—calls through the tent walls.

Amy looks at me, eyes wide with surprise, then calls back, "Nothing, Mom!"

She kicks the sleeping bag off her legs and rushes to the window. "What are you doing here?" she whispers. "It's curfew."

I know—the patrol Colonel Martin's set up throughout the colony tried to cause me trouble as I snuck down here.

Amy sets down the book she was reading—*The Little Prince*.

"I'm going to the probe," I whisper back. "Your father's hiding something, and I intend to find out what."

She grabs my wrist. "Don't," she says, such worry in her voice that I'm afraid her mother will hear again.

"I have to."

"It's dangerous." There's a haunted look in her eyes now, and I'm reminded of the rumors I heard in the colony—that they found another body in the woods, one of the Earthborns.

"I have to," I repeat. "I don't think your father trusts me, and he's not telling me the whole truth."

"Dad wouldn't—"

I cut her off. "Did he show you the crystal scale I found?"

Amy frowns. "Scale?"

I describe it for her, explaining about the tunnel. From her wide eyes, I can tell Colonel Martin has kept the discovery from her—from everyone.

"We can't afford to be in the dark," I say. "We have to know what's going on."

Amy bites her lip, then nods. "I'm coming with you."

"I was hoping you'd say that." I grin up at her. Amy steps away from the window, grabbing her gun and holster from the ground and belting it around her waist before pulling another shirt over her tank top. She uses both arms to push up on the window ledge, then swings her legs over and drops silently on the ground beside me.

"What's the plan?" she whispers as I lead her away from the ruins.

"Follow the water pipe to the lake, then head back to the forest. I think the probe is somewhere around there—or, at least, *something's* there that Colonel Martin doesn't want us to find."

Amy frowns as we sneak away from the colony. "You know, there could be a perfectly valid reason Dad's made the probe off-limits. He's not Eldest. This isn't *Godspeed*."

I don't answer her as we duck around the new latrines, following the pipeline in the shadows of the mountain.

Once we're far enough away from the colony, Amy speaks again, her words cutting through the darkness. "I saw a man die today."

I pause.

"I wish you had been there." It sounds morbid to hear her say those two sentences so close together, but I know what she means. For the past three months, the walls of *Godspeed* forced us close together. Now I'm wondering if they were the only things that kept Amy near me.

"I'm sorry," I say, and I mean about more than just today.

"Maybe the only reason Dad is keeping everyone away from the probe is because it's dangerous," Amy says, her voice still distant. Her fingers touch the hilt of her gun for reassurance, and I can't help but notice that it's the weapon that comforts her, not me.

We don't speak again until we reach the lake, and even then it's in hushed tones.

"Look how exposed we are here," Amy says. "Do you really wonder why Dad's keeping people away?" She slips the gun out of her holster and carries it at the ready. She's right—there are no trees here, and any ptero circling overhead could easily strike us.

"That's not why he won't let anyone come here."

Amy's eyes dart to the sky. "Elder . . . those pteros . . . they're *horrible*."

There is panic in her eyes, something dark and scared I've never seen there before. But while her knuckles are white, the gun is steady in her grip.

"Let's get this over with," Amy says, narrowing her eyes as she starts up the hill.

I squint in the darkness. I can barely make out the black, rectangular outline against the sky, almost hidden by a small hill. If we hadn't been standing right at the water pump, I'd never have seen it.

I glance at Amy. Her face is paler than usual now, contrasting with the dark night.

We move slowly, careful to keep checking behind us to make sure we don't wander so far away that we get lost, especially as we near the forest edge and the trees obscure our path. The forest itself curves out and then back in. I try to make a mental map of where we are—the shuttle to my left, the lake to my right, the ruins we now live in behind me. And something straight ahead.

"Look at the way the land is so flat there," Amy says, pointing. Her voice is still quiet, even though we haven't seen anyone this far out.

Long stalks of some sort of grain or grass ripple in the breeze like cloth. But where Amy is pointing, there is no grain. No trees. No nothing. Something black and starless and manmade amid the sea of nature, dotted with low-roofed buildings standing up in straight edges that are in stark contrast to the swishing grass and twisting trees.

"Come on," Amy says, tugging my hand.

We race across the open meadow, and I keep thinking about how Amy said we were exposed. My muscles are tense, waiting for the outline of a ptero against the too-bright stars.

We stop short of the area where the tall grass ends.

"What is this place?" I say, my voice so quiet that even I barely hear it.

Amy steps forward, her footsteps louder as she walks across asphalt, not sandy soil. I follow after her, staring with wide eyes at a cluster of small buildings dotting the horizon on the other side. "It's some sort of compound," she whispers, "built around the probe."

I trip over a thin ridge in the pavement, and Amy and I both crouch to inspect the gleaming band of metal—a large rectangle embedded into the asphalt. There's something under the asphalt, some panel or room that can open up if we could only figure out how to trigger it.

"Look at the lines painted on the ground," Amy whispers in my ear.

Bright white lines, marking distances, with more markers embedded into the asphalt.

"It's a runway," Amy gasps. "And underneath it are airplanes. Jets. Something."

Now that she says it, it makes sense. Jets must be stored in the rectangular areas sunken into the ground so that whoever controls this compound can lift them up to ground level, position them, and use this asphalt as a runway.

"But who put it here?" Amy's voice comes out in a squeak.

I have no answer for her. This is *nothing* like the ruins we discovered earlier. The ruins were dusty buildings, long abandoned and derelict. But this runway smells faintly of oil and burnt rubber; it's been used, and recently.

I motion for Amy to follow me to one of the small buildings—not stony relics, but modern, single-storied glass and steel offices. She hesitates. Whoever made this compound has technology far more advanced than we could have guessed from seeing the ruins.

"Look." I point through the window of the closest building. "A communication system."

The room houses a control panel not that much different from the one we used on the bridge when we landed the shuttle—which is to say, it's equally confusing. But I think I can figure it out.

"Locked," Amy says as she tries the doorknob. I nod to a small square at eye level by the door. It's not unlike the biometric scanners on *Godspeed*, but there's a small thumb pad rather than a roll bar.

"Can't hurt to try," Amy says, pushing her thumb against the pad. A moment later, the thumb pad flashes a message once—HUMAN—and then the door opens.

"This door was built to only let humans enter?" I ask as we step inside the room.

Amy shoots me a worried look. If the scanner detects humanity, then that means there must be something other than humans it's designed to keep out.

29: AMY

Once inside, my first instinct is to reach for the lights, and even though my hand touches the wall where a light switch would normally be, my fingers find nothing, slipping over the smooth paint. Of course not. Stupid of me to think that. Whoever built this might not have electricity like we do. . . . Still, they have something. As soon as Elder closes the door behind us, a small panel opens up in the ceiling, exposing a softly glowing square — something like an automatic, flat lightbulb that brightens the room as efficiently as a fluorescent bulb — but with no hum of electricity or power. I blink in the unnaturally bright light.

"Do you really think Dad knew all this was here?" I ask in a hushed voice. Elder doesn't answer. He doesn't need to. Of course Dad knew about this building, the whole compound. Otherwise, what reason would he have had to stop us from coming here?

A flag hangs over the door. Two white circles, one larger than the other, are sewn into a field of sky blue. The larger circle is slightly off center, and the smaller one is just to the right, below it. I've never seen a flag with this design before.

"Look," Elder breathes.

And there, engraved on a plaque at the top of the control panel in the little building, is a symbol we both recognize.

"This was made by the FRX," I say, forgetting to whisper.

Elder leans over, inspecting it. He reads the tiny words engraved below the symbol. "On this site was discovered the first probe sent by the first interstellar mission from Earth in 2310 CE, providing the information needed to develop the first successful extra-solar colony, *Explorer*, 2327 CE," Elder reads. "This plaque is a memorial to those lost on *Godspeed*. 2036–2336 CE."

"They think we died out," I say.

I point to the end date — 2336. That's when *Godspeed* was supposed to land. But we didn't land.

"They found the probe," Elder says in a low voice. "But not *us*."

I think about the grav tube and the floppies on the ship — technology made while I slept. "Technology increases at an exponential rate," I say. "My grandparents paid thousands of dollars for a computer that was bigger than my television and had a fraction of the memory space of my freaking cell phone." I'm babbling, but I can't seem to keep my voice under control. "My grandparents used CDs to listen to music instead of downloading it, my great-grandparents used tapes, my great-great-grandparents used records."

Elder's eyes are wide and scared; he's getting what I'm trying to say. "The first airplane was made at the start of the 1900s; the first man landed on the moon in the 1950s."

I gulp. "In 2029, my grandmother took a vacation on the lunar resort, and by 2036, my parents and I were packed in ice and thrown across the universe."

Technology moves faster and faster and faster.

I look around this very modern, very well-kept communication bay.

We weren't the first colony from Earth to land here.

"We were late to our own landing," Elder says hollowly. He touches a small blinking light under the plaque. "A homing device. The same kind on the probes. This is why the shuttle landed here."

Right in the middle of a world that's already outpaced us.

The first probe was sent twenty years before *Godspeed* landed. The FRX must have liked the data it relayed and sent a faster ship to colonize before we arrived. The ruins are the perfect size for humans not because there were creatures born on Centauri-Earth that coincidentally were the same size and had the same needs as us . . . it's because *humans made the ruins*. The first colony—the real first colony, the colony that landed before us—settled there.

It happened so long ago that now the buildings are derelict and abandoned.

And in the meantime? The first colony progressed to a high-tech modern society, leaving the dusty buildings behind.

I shouldn't be surprised. It's not like they quit designing ships and rockets just because *Godspeed* left. They'd developed something better by then, and when they looked at the probe information and realized that there was something here they wanted, they sent another colony.

Why wait for us to land when this planet has resources Earth could use?

"Our whole mission . . . it was pointless," I say. "Everything we've done, everything we've sacrificed—it was all for nothing. Earth already conquered this planet. They came, they saw, they left. And now we're here. Alone. This whole damn thing was for *nothing!*" I spit the word out. "What a stupid, pointless mission. Of *course* a faster ship was invented in the centuries while we traveled. Five hundred years before the ship launched? That was freaking Shakespearean times! We're as ancient to Earth now as effing *Shakespeare!* Our ship is the equivalent of a *horse-drawn carriage!*"

Elder grabs my hands, and it's only then that I realize I've been waving them about maniacally.

"They couldn't communicate with us," I say. "Communication links were broken before the ship even got here. They probably saw us arrive, but since they couldn't talk to us and we never landed, they must have thought we were all dead." I'm crying now. I don't know why, but I'm crying. "If you're silent for five hundred years, they think you're dead." Even if we're not.

I remember then, as vividly as if I'd just woken up, the feeling of being frozen. My mind had blocked the memories as effectively as if they'd been nothing but dreams, but now, here, under a sky with stars that sparkle like eyes, all I can think about is how it felt to be frozen in ice, alive but immobile. I think about the silence of it, the way nothing could touch me. I think about how trapped it felt to be aware but unable to move so much as an eyelash.

I think about how all of *that* was worth nothing.

For the first time since leaving the ship, I feel trapped.

"The question we need to be asking ourselves is, where are they now?" Elder says. He looks through the windows as if expecting to see a modern city on the other side of the glass. "If there were people from a colony," he continues slowly, thinking aloud, "they would have tried to contact us. They had to have seen us land, this close to the compound. If they're human, if they made this plaque"—he points to the memorial embedded above the communication bay—"they would want to help us."

But no one's come.

30: ELDER

Amy is white—not pale, but *white*. "Are you okay?" I ask.

"My dad," Amy whispers.

I stop dead, waiting for her to continue.

"He knew. He's kept all of this from us. The original colony. This compound. This is what he was trying to hide from you. From all of us." She takes a deep, shaky breath. "From me."

I don't know what to say to her. She's right—she can see for herself that her father's been hiding the truth from her.

"Why?" she chokes out.

I step in front of her, capturing her wandering gaze. "I don't know. He must have had a reason."

She looks at me bitterly. "Orion had a reason. Eldest had a reason."

"Colonel Martin is a lot of things, but he's not Orion or Eldest." As I say the words, I know that I don't believe them, not entirely. He's proven already that he's willing to coerce us with lies and hidden truths.

Amy spins away from me, the red curtain of her hair hiding her face. "Do you think the colony that came before us—did the pteros kill them off?"

"There's more than just pteros out here," I say, thinking of the mysterious animal tracks I found near the shuttle and the crystal scale Colonel Martin took from me.

"There was gen mod material in Dr. Gupta's blood," Amy says. "Maybe the first colony somehow used the formula here on Centauri-Earth. Maybe that's where pteros came from. Maybe they engineered their own destruction." She makes a strangled noise, and I realize she's holding back tears. "We're alone," she says in almost a whisper. "The colony that came before—whatever happened, they died out. Just like we're going to."

"We won't—"

"We *will!*" The words rip from her throat. She whirls around to face me, and I see the raw panic in her eyes.

"Amy," I say, waiting for her to meet my eyes. "I would never—*never*—let something happen to you. You know that, right?"

She hesitates before she nods.

She looks so fragile in this moment that it breaks my heart. We both know that I won't be able to protect her from everything.

But I'll do all I can, no matter what the cost.

"Amy," I say, searching her eyes. "I lo—"

She slams her lips against mine, cutting my words off. I try to put the words she won't let me say into my kiss. Her arms snake around my neck, pulling me closer to her. There's a sort of desperation to our kiss, a hunger, one that neither of us may ever be able to satiate.

I'm not stupid.

Even as my thoughts evaporate in the flames of our kiss, I am aware that she wouldn't let me say the words I meant to say and that she has yet to say them in return.

But I don't care.

Because we can say them or not; it doesn't matter. What is in our hearts is real whether we name it or let it exist only in darkness and silence.

＊　＊　＊

A long time later, we break apart. Color has returned to Amy's cheeks, and her hands aren't trembling anymore.

"We're going to make it," I say, hoping my words reaffirm the idea within her.

She clenches her jaw and nods.

I inspect the control panel under the plaque with the double-winged symbol of the FRX. "This is definitely a communication bay," I say. "It isn't that different from the com links we used on *Godspeed*."

Of course it isn't. They were both developed by the FRX.

Amy follows my gaze. "Do you think we could contact the ship? Maybe we can get someone to help us figure out the *Little Prince* clue."

I shake my head. Even if there were a way to hail *Godspeed*, I'd have to tap directly into the wi-coms—any other type of communication system was destroyed with the Bridge. I glance at Amy. Her eyes are shiny, as if reaching the ship is her last hope. I turn back to the com bay; it isn't that different from the ship's . . . it wouldn't hurt to try.

I pull up a hard, straight-backed chair standing against the wall and sit in front of the control panel, trying to figure out what the controls are and how they're used. I recognize some—this dial searches for a signal, this one adjusts the output. But there are others—a knob labeled ANSIBLE, a gauge with a rapidly moving needle—that mean nothing to me.

Amy sits down beside me. A touch screen lights up in front of her, displaying a menu of options. Maybe the old technology is mixed with the new. Amy slides her finger over the screen, then pauses, hovering over one word.

Intercepted.

She glances at me. This doesn't bode well.

Amy presses the word, and the screen goes black with only a small red line labeled **frequency visualizer** on the top and a yellow line labeled **volume visualizer** on the bottom. As sound fills the communication room, the lines bounce up and down in a graphic sequencing of the words. In the center, typed words transcribe the audio message.

Congratulations, Godspeed! You have safely arrived at your final destination, the planet circling the binary Centauri system.

"I know what this is," I say, my stomach sinking.

"We're communicating with Earth!" Amy cries, excited, leaning forward as the message continues.

We are excited to inform you that the probes sent prior to the ship's landing have indicated not only a habitable world, but profitable environmental resources as well!

Amy turns to me, eyes gleaming with excitement.

Until she sees the look on my face.

At the time of your landing, a signal was relayed directly to the Financial Resource Exchange. Rest assured that even now, the FRX is preparing a shuttle filled with aid and supplies for your colony.

"Earth is coming!" Amy insists, still clinging to her newfound hope. "Earth will come help us out!"

"No, it's not."

"What are you talking about? They just said—"

"Amy, what was this message labeled as?" I ask.

She frowns. "Intercepted."

My finger slides across the touch screen, and the message starts over again.

Congratulations, Godspeed! You have safely arrived at your final destination, the planet circling the binary Centauri system.

"But . . . " Amy says.

"It's a recorded message." I feel sick. I heard this message when Colonel Martin typed in his authorization code on the control panel on the bridge. We both thought it was a live communication from Earth that had just gotten cut off. But it was nothing but a recording—a copy of a message being sent to us from *here*.

I scan forward in the message. In the recording Colonel Martin and I heard, the words were cut off before any details about whatever is threatening our existence were told. This message cuts off too, at exactly the same spot it crackled and died before.

I wonder if this even came from Sol-Earth originally or if it is all a part of some elaborate ruse.

"Who would do this?" Amy asks, disgusted. Her eyes widen. "Not . . . not Dad?"

I shake my head. I saw Colonel Martin's face when we heard the message on the bridge. "That message came moments after he woke up," I add. "He couldn't possibly have coordinated this."

I flick the touch screen back to the list of messages. **Intercepted** has only the message from Sol-Earth. Others are marked **Trade Negotiations, Labor Details, Manufacturing Specifications, Surveillance**—and each of these has several messages listed under each label, all marked by a series of numbers that I can't find any sort of pattern to.

I flick the touch screen back again and see a label marked **Live Feed**. I nudge Amy and point to the label. "Live feed of what?" she asks.

"Maybe the people who made this compound?"

I press down on the label. A submenu pops up showing a list of random topics: **agricultural, medical, community, maintenance, engine, control.**

Amy looks at me quizzically. These labels don't make sense. I touch the last one: **control**. The screen turns black, flashes **ERROR**, and then returns to the submenu. I shrug and touch the first label, **agricultural**.

This time the screen doesn't fade to black. Instead, it shows a rolling landscape. Perfectly even, structured grassy hills. Measured fields of grain, corn, beans. A manufactured agricultural landscape dotted with genetically engineered cows and sheep, all under a metal sky painted blue.

I touch the screen, and the image disappears, replaced by the submenu.

"Elder, that was—" Amy can't say the word.

Godspeed.

That was *Godspeed*. The labels on the submenu make sense now. I tap them quickly. **Medical** shows the Hospital from the outside, a camera angled near the statue of the Plague Eldest. **Community** is the City. **Maintenance** is the Shipper Level; **engine** shows the lead-cooled fast reactor that fueled *Godspeed*. **Control** is nothing but a blank screen because it must have been a live video feed of the Bridge, and there is no more Bridge. Doc blew it up.

"They were watching us," I say, horror creeping into my voice. "They were watching us all along."

"*Who* was watching us?" Amy asks.

I don't know. Whoever built this compound. The first colony—or whatever it is that wiped out the first colony, the thing that is *not* human, that the biometric lock on this building intended to keep out.

I click back on **community**. The City is not how I remembered it. The streets are crowded, dirty. The people—my people, the ones I left behind, the ones who stayed with Bartie—have a sort of desperation clinging to them. Some of them move too fast, rushing from one place to another as if their lives depended on it. Others don't move at all. They slump against the buildings. They have given up.

"Something's wrong," I say. I want to reach through the screen and help them, but as soon as my fingers touch the glass, the screen fades back to the submenu.

Amy puts a hand on my arm. I think she wants to pull me away from the monitor. After all, what can I do? I'm here, and they're far above me, orbiting around the planet. I can't reach them. I can't save them.

I have failed them.

I touch the **maintenance** label to see the Shipper Level. The doors to all the different offices and labs are open, but no one's there. Is it night? No, it can't be . . . the City was lit by the solar lamp. Why are there no Shippers on this level? I go back and touch **engine**. The engine room is empty as well. The camera angle is positioned so that I can see both the engine and, behind it, the massive seal-lock doors that hide the remains of the Bridge. The doors are locked. I try to look at the small screens on the control panel behind the engine—from what I can see, everything seems to be operational.

Why is no one on this level, though?

Then I see the flashing red light on the engine itself. It's massive, but the camera angle blocks most of the red glow. My mouth goes dry. I know what that glow means. The entire Shipper Level must be engulfed in a deafening alarm.

Warning us that the engine is going into meltdown.

I look closer. I can't zoom in, but I strain my eyes to see through the pixels, to understand what's happened. Amy leans forward too, her red hair sweeping across the screen before she brushes it back over her shoulder.

When Doc blew up the Bridge, the engine was exposed to space and the rapid decompression made by the vacuum sucking everything through the hole where the Bridge had been. The engine was built to last, but it was already old. It would have been easy for it to be damaged then—especially since, immediately after the Bridge's explosion, I left with the shuttle. No one did work in those days, no one bothered to check on the engine. It could have been quietly malfunctioning the entire time. Some of the Shippers inspected the engine before I left, but how thorough were they? What if they missed something?

If the engine dies, *Godspeed* dies.

It's as simple as that.

I move to close the screen. I don't want to see this; I don't want to live with this guilt.

I left my people to die.

The thought makes my hand twitch and, by accident, I bring up the video feed of the Hospital. I move to turn it off, but Amy grabs my hand. "Wait," she says, staring at the screen.

I turn away from it. I don't need the concrete face of the original Eldest mocking me.

"A robe of stars . . . " Amy whispers. She tugs on my arm. "What's the man in the statue wearing?" she asks.

I don't need to look at it to answer her. "It's the Eldest Robe."

Amy looks confused, and I remember—she's never seen it. I wore it once, when I announced the planet to the ship, but Amy wasn't there. She was afraid of the crowd, and rightly so.

"It's a heavy wool robe that the Eldest wears on special occasions," I say. I can picture it in my mind: the surface of the planet embroidered on the hem of the robe and stars stitched on the shoulders.

Stars stitched on the shoulders.

"Elder, *The Little Prince*!" Amy says, excited. "Remember? The illustration showed a king—the Eldest is like a king, isn't he?—and Orion marked the heart of the robe—a robe with stars on it."

I stare at the statue. It was made of concrete, by the Plague Eldest himself. If there was a secret about the planet, it would have been a secret the Plague Eldest kept. He was the one who started the Eldest system, he was the one who decided not to land the ship on the planet when we arrived. Of course he had to have had a reason for *why* he didn't land *Godspeed*—and what better place to hide that reason than within the concrete of the statue?

"It all fits," Amy says, wonder in her voice. "The clue, the last clue, the information about what is going on here—it's in the statue."

"In the statue," I repeat. "In the ship, which is in orbit, in *space*."

Amy sighs heavily. Knowing the clue is there doesn't help us at all.

Movement on the side of the screen distracts me from the statue. Someone's walking down the path behind the Hospital, through the garden. The path curves, and the person is momentarily out of view, but a moment later he stands in front of the statue.

Bartie.

He stops, tilting his face up to the metal sky. The camera is in the perfect angle to capture him. His face is lined with worry and sadness, with dark circles under his eyes and a new scar on his cheek. He's haggard, and his hair looks unkempt. There is no sign of his guitar. Taking the leadership from me has not worn well on Bartie.

"What's he doing?" Amy asks, staring.

Bartie looks as if he's talking to the Plague Eldest statue. I remember how I always used to stop and stare at the worn face. The Plague Eldest's open arms are benevolent, and his face is so blurred of features that I would imagine it looked on me with sympathy while I was trying to decide how to be the leader my people needed.

Bartie reaches into one of his pockets. I think for a moment that he's pulled out a floppy, but whatever he's holding is smaller than a floppy and darker. Black. A black square.

A black med patch.

Amy gasps.

And I know what Bartie's thinking, why he's come to the Plague Eldest.

The ship is dying, and he knows it. He's trying to decide how long to wait before he distributes the black med patches. The ones that kill.

31: AMY

Elder doesn't talk as he storms from the compound, heading back to the colony. I have to race to keep up with him. "Elder, wait!" I call under my breath. He slows down but doesn't stop.

His back is rigid, his shoulders stiff. When I reach out for him, he jerks away. I grab his elbow and don't let go, yanking him around to face me.

"We can save them too," I say.

Elder barks in laughter, a short, bitter sound. We both freeze, looking to the forest, waiting for a ptero's cry. But soon the soft noises of the night that I'd taken for granted return—a low, chirruping sound from a nocturnal bird, the almost inaudible shuffling of small animals on the forest floor. We haven't seen much wildlife, but that doesn't mean it's not there.

"We *can* save them," I say again, my voice lower.

"We can't even save ourselves." Elder's jaw is hard.

"We've as good as solved Orion's last clue," I counter. "We have the communication bay at the compound. We won't let them die up there."

"Yeah?" Elder asks through clenched teeth. "And how are we going to survive the frexing aliens that are down *here?*"

My heart stills in my chest.

"There's something out there, Amy," Elder says. He looks over my head, into the black forest. "Something that killed off the first colony."

"Pteros—"

"They didn't program those biometric locks to keep pteros out," Elder snaps. He's right. Those locks were for something . . . something else. "Besides," he adds, shooting me a glance and then looking away. "There are more than just pteros." I know he's thinking of that strange crystalline scale he found in the tunnel, and it frightens me, too. There's a lot about this planet we don't understand. A lot that can kill us. "Remember that footprint?" he asks.

I nod. How could I forget the sharp ridges of the three talons, as if designed to maim?

Elder continues in a hush, as if afraid of being overheard. "I thought I saw something in the forest, right before I was attacked. Maybe whatever it was *controlled* the ptero."

An image briefly flashes in my mind: a bug-eyed green-skinned alien with clawed feet, one that watches us and waits until we're most vulnerable to attack.

I don't want to think about this. I *can't* think about this. I've learned too much tonight. I turn away from Elder, and we continue back to the colony wordlessly, not stopping until we nearly reach my building on the edge of the colony. The world is silent now and dark. Elder steps closer to me, sweeping the hair I'd been hiding behind out of my face.

"Stop," a low female voice commands. I start to turn and feel the hard metal cylinder of a gun in the back of my head. I drop Elder's hand and lift my own.

"Amy?" the voice asks. The gun lowers. When I turn, I see Emma, dressed in fatigues, a semi-automatic in her right hand.

"Emma, you scared me to death!" I exclaim.

"Shh!" she says. "Or do you want the rest of the guard on duty tonight to come down here and see what you two idiots are doing?"

I glance at Elder. How much does Emma know?

"If you two can't keep your hands off each other, then go to one of the buildings," she growls. "Snogging in the middle of the night on the edge of the camp is likely to get you shot. I thought you were—" She stops short. "I thought you were an enemy."

I narrow my eyes. What enemy is she referring to exactly? Emma doesn't know what we were up to, but I have more than a sneaking suspicion she knows more than she's telling us. She was with Dad, that first day, when he went to the probe and found a high-tech modern compound.

She knows just how much he's kept hidden.

When neither Elder nor I say anything, Emma frowns. "You lot weren't just out here to snog, were you?"

"No!" I say too quickly. "Emma, we were—"

She cuts me off with a wave of her hand. "I don't care what you were doing, and I don't want to know. But you're smart, both of you, and I'm betting I can guess what's up." She glances behind her—in the direction of the compound. "Don't go out at night," she says, more sternly this time. "There're things out there you don't know about."

Elder nods solemnly, then turns to go. Emma grabs my arm, keeping me in place. "Amy, this is important," she says, her voice low and urgent. "You don't want to hear this, I know you don't, but you can't trust—"

"Who's there?" a voice—my father's—calls out.

Heavy footsteps thump their way closer to us. Dad and Chris, both dressed in fatigues, approach. "Emma? What's going on?"

Emma straightens, and whatever warning she was about to give me dies on her lips. "Sir. Found these two out here." She pauses. "Kissing."

There's a little bit of a tattletale quality to her voice at this, but I'm actually glad she's told Dad that I was out here making out. At least she didn't say what she suspected we were doing—discovering the compound and Dad's secrets.

Dad doesn't look happy, though. "I'll take Amy back up," he growls. "Chris, can you escort this boy back to his building?"

"This boy can walk himself," Elder snaps.

Dad stares him down. "There's a lot you should be afraid of out here, at night, in the dark."

Elder doesn't flinch. "I know what to be afraid of," he says. "And it's not the dark." He waits a heartbeat, then adds, "It's not you either."

Chris touches Elder's shoulder, guiding him back to the colony, but Elder shoves past him.

Dad waits until Chris and Elder are out of sight and Emma is back patrolling the camp before he turns to me. "What were you thinking?" he says. I'm shocked at how angry he sounds. "It's *dangerous* out here, Amy."

"We were still in the colony," I protest, because, as far as he knows, we were.

"And kissing one of *them!*"

This stops me in my tracks. The night is eerily silent now, the air very still.

"What?" I ask in a monotone.

"Amy, those shipborns . . . you shouldn't be with them so much." Dad starts pacing, just on the outside of our building.

"I dunno, Dad. I feel like Elder's been a little bit more forthcoming than you've been lately . . . don't you think?"

"They're not like us," Dad continues, ignoring my accusation.

"How?" I ask, my voice still cold.

"Just look at them! The way they all look the same. The way they all think a kid is their 'leader.' They're . . . strange. Different. For God's sake, Amy, the shipborns are not like us!"

"You don't know what you're talking about!" I say, louder than I'd intended. We're going to wake up the whole colony. "They're people. *Good* people."

Dad shakes his head pityingly, and it is that, more than anything else, that cranks my rage up even higher. "Oh, Amy," he says. "You weren't even supposed to be here."

Something clacks into place in my head. "Then why did you give me a choice?" I say, my voice growing louder and higher with each word. "Why even leave that decision up to me? You could have prepared me more. But no—you just waited until Mom was already frozen and then you freeze yourself, and you leave me, alone, to make up my mind on whether I should give everything up for you! And when I *do* actually do that—it's the wrong choice! If you never wanted me to come, why didn't you say so? Why did you leave it up to me at all? Why did you make it seem like I could make my own decisions when you never even packed any of my things for me? I've seen the trunks in storage—and the one with my name on it is *empty!*"

I'm breathing heavily by the time I'm done speaking, and my face is hot, and my fists are curled, and I don't care.

Dad's jaw works. "I'm sorry about that," he grinds out. "I'd promised your mother not to try to convince you to stay, and I worried if I told you what to do, you'd do the opposite. I wanted you to be able to make a choice you could live with."

"I *did.*"

"I didn't know things would get this messed up. This is not the mission I expected. And I had no idea you'd wake up early like that. I wish you hadn't. Maybe then you could see that the shipborns—"

"Don't even start," I say. "The 'shipborns' aren't a part of this argument."

"They hate you." Dad stares at me, daring me to break eye contact. "I see the way they flinch away from us, the way they look at us as if we're freaks—even you."

"Elder doesn't hate me," I say. I know this more than I know anything.

Dad barks with laughter. "Elder is a *teenage boy*. He doesn't hate anything with breasts!"

I step back as if Dad's slapped me.

"Amy, you can't trust him. And you can't—don't—I don't want you getting in over your head with this boy. I think you've let those three months you were on the ship before we landed cancel out the years you were on Earth. You're one of us. You're mine. You're my little girl."

"Not anymore," I say cruelly, sidestepping him and storming toward the building.

Dad grabs me and yanks me back. I think for one terrifying instant that he's going to hit me, but he doesn't. He wraps me in a hug so tight I can barely breathe. "I'm not letting you go away mad at me, Amy," he says softly into my hair. "We can fight, and we can disagree, but I'm never going to let you walk away from me thinking I don't love you."

He loosens his grip on me, and I step back, stunned by his words. Dad is not the mushy type. "This world is dangerous, Amy," he says. "I don't know what's going to happen. I can't let you walk away from me mad. I love you too much for that."

He holds his pinky up, waiting for me to wrap mine around his.

The ice inside me melts. "I love you too," I say, making a pinky promise just like we used to do when I was a kid. "I promise."

And I mean it: I love him.

I'm just not sure I can trust him.

32: ELDER

My eyes shoot open the next morning when I hear loud footsteps clambering up the staircase leading to my building. I stretch, my neck cracking. I used a pile of clothes as an impromptu bed, but I'm going to have to find something better—especially for the pregnant women, who must be hurting more than me.

"Elder!" Amy calls, breathless, as she runs into my room.

A loopy grin slides across my face; I don't mind being woken up this early in the morning if Amy's my alarm clock.

Then I see her face. "What's wrong?" I ask, jumping up and grabbing a tunic from the pile of clothes, pulling it over my head. The air's already humid and sticky, despite how early it is.

"Kit," Amy says, still panting from her run up to my building. "Come on."

I stagger after her, pulling on my moccasins as I go. "What happened?" I ask, my heart sinking. Other than Amy, Kit is one of the few people on this planet I actually trust—and one of my few friends. If something's wrong . . .

"I don't know," Amy says. Her eyes dart to the bottom of the hill, where Colonel Martin is giving directions to Emma and Chris, pointing out something in the distance.

"What do you mean?" I ask. "Is she all right?"

"I don't know," Amy repeats, grabbing my hand and dragging me down the stairs toward Colonel Martin. "This morning, Dad tried to find her, to go over that list she made detailing what everyone's skills are. He was going to start making permanent work assignments. But she's missing."

"Missing?" I feel stupid. It's barely morning; the suns have just risen.

"Dad thinks that she's just wandered off or something, that she'll turn up soon."

"Kit wouldn't do that," I say.

She spares a glance at me. "I know."

Colonel Martin turns as we run up to him. "Amy," he says, admonishment in his voice. "I told you not to trouble Elder with this."

"Dad, Kit wouldn't just *go*. If she's missing, that means something is wrong."

I glance at Amy. We both know if she's missing, it's probably already too late.

"I've already volunteered to go looking for her," Emma says. She scowls.

"And I've already said it's nothing," Colonel Martin says firmly. "I've sent some soldiers ahead to the shuttle to see if Kit went there."

"She wouldn't," I say.

"We don't have time to just stop all operations because one woman wandered off—against my orders, I might add."

"Dad," Amy says so forcefully that he looks a little surprised. "Kit would *not* just wander off alone. That's not like her."

Colonel Martin considers what she's said.

Chris steps up beside him. I want to knock him aside; I don't need one more person saying that Kit's just carelessly gotten lost. "Maybe she's in the latrines," he says.

"She's not; I checked," Amy says. "We need to go looking for her."

"Let's wait for the men I sent to get back," Colonel Martin says, but his voice isn't as commanding as before. "She might have gone back for more sup-plies from the shuttle . . . "

"She *wouldn't*," I insist. "Kit is one of my people, and I know her. There's no way she'd leave the colony without letting me know. I'm telling you—if she's gone, something is seriously wrong." I watch as doubt crosses Colonel Martin's face. He doesn't want Kit to have been taken; he doesn't want it to be his fault. His guard hasn't protected her. But I don't have time to assuage Colonel Martin's hurt feelings. "If you're not going to do something, I will," I say. "I'll get together search parties now."

"I'll help," Amy says immediately.

"And so will I." Emma shoots Colonel Martin and Chris a disgusted look.

We work quickly. As soon as word spreads that Kit has disappeared, people start volunteering for the search party—more than a hundred in less than an hour.

Colonel Martin casts an eye over the group assembling in the meadow. There's a grim sort of determination to the search party, and they carry tools— shovels, scythes, even, in a few cases, just a large tree branch, smoothed down on one end for a handle on a makeshift club.

"They don't need weapons. My men have guns," Colonel Martin tells me. My people, armed as they are, make him nervous. I file this information away in my mind.

"Guns didn't save Kit," I say. "Or Lorin. Or Juliana Robertson, or that Earthborn doctor."

I track down the last person who saw her—Willow, a pregnant woman who had come to her in the middle of the night with stomach cramps.

"After she gave me a med patch, she left," Willow tells me.

"Did you see anyone else?"

"There was one of *them* on patrol." Willow means one of the Earthborn military. She points at Chris, who's standing on the edge of the gathering crowd, looking worried. "That one."

I stride over to him and confront him with this information.

"I remember seeing her," Chris tells me, his hands already up as if defending himself from the accusation in my voice. "It was right before my shift ended."

"Did you make sure she got back to her building safely?" I demand.

Chris blanches. "I . . . no. I just assumed . . . "

"That's when she was taken," I say, convinced of it now. I glare at Chris. It was his job to protect the colony, and he let one of my people pay the price for his carelessness.

The question is—who took her, and why?

33: AMY

As Elder starts sending groups off in search of Kit, Dad grabs my arm. "You're not going," he says.

I stare at him, too shocked by the order to protest.

"You can help in other ways. I'm not letting you go off with them."

"I can help," I say angrily. "Kit's my friend."

Dad looks at me as if he doesn't believe his daughter could truly be friends with a shipborn. It's the same look he gives me when he sees me with Elder.

My hands curl into fists. "Dad!" I growl. "You can't just let Kit be lost because she's not one of *your* people."

"That has nothing to do with it." His voice is filled with emotion I don't understand—it sounds almost like regret, but that doesn't make any sense. He leans in closer to me. "I've already seen you wounded once, Amy. When Elder brought you to me, after you were knocked out by that purple flower. I'm not going to see you get hurt again." He hugs me tight, squeezing the air from me. "Go to the lab with your mother. Chris will stay with you two." Dad glances up at Mom as she approaches. "Got to protect my girls."

I look behind me. The search parties have already begun to disperse. With a sigh, I follow Mom back up to the building we're sharing as she gets ready for a day at the lab. I wonder briefly if Dad's going to the compound Elder and I discovered last night, if there's something there that will help find Kit. I hope so. I don't care that Dad's kept it secret, not if it helps to find Kit and bring her safely back to us.

"Okay," Mom says. "Let me just check with the geologists and see the results of the tests they ran last night. Amy?" she adds. "Want to come with me?"

I shake my head.

"I'll go with you, Dr. Martin," Chris says, standing up. I'm glad he's here to protect Mom, but it feels weird that our guard is just a few years older than me.

Almost as soon as they're gone, Emma steps into the building. "Alone?" she asks in her lilting accent. I nod.

Emma crosses the room in three long strides and presses something into my hands. A glass cube, about the size of my palm. "I want you to have this," she tells me. "Hide it."

"Why—?" I ask, peering at it. While the cube looks as if it's made of glass, it's filled with bright flecks of gold. It glitters in the sunlight, creating an entrancing swirl of sparkles.

"I've been watching you and that Elder." Emma glances at the door. "I know you lot are not going to just blindly accept what someone says is truth. And I figure maybe that's what's needed more than anything right now."

"Is this about . . . " I hesitate, not sure if I *do* want to know the truth. "Is this about Dad?"

"Your dad's a good soldier," Emma says. "He's following the mission guidelines."

My fingers curl around the glass cube. What does *this* have to do with the mission guidelines?

"I have been to many countries," Emma says, changing topics abruptly. "And now to a whole new world. But I have never felt *dépaysement*."

"What's day-pah . . . um?" I can't pronounce the word.

"*Dépaysement*. It's like . . . homesick?" Emma shakes her head, her dark curls bouncing against her cheeks. "That's not the word for it. It means . . . the way you feel when you know you're not home."

"I don't understand," I say. I don't mean that I don't understand the word—I don't understand why she's telling me this. Any of this.

"I learned long ago that *home* is a word that applies to people, not places. That's why I didn't mind signing up for this mission. Didn't matter to me *where* I was—it mattered *who* I was with."

Emma cocks her head—I hear it too. Mom and Chris are returning. "I'm giving you this," she says, looking down at the glass cube in my hands, "because you—you and that Elder boy—you two don't care about any military mission. You don't care about what the FRX may want. You care about making this world *home*."

"What do *you* care about?" I ask, searching her eyes.

"Doesn't matter," Emma says sadly. "I'm military. I have to obey the orders. *You* don't."

She glances behind her quickly. "Go," she says. "Hide it."

The urgency in her voice makes me spin around and dash to the tiny corner of privacy I have in my "room" made of tents and throw the glass cube into my sleeping bag, out of sight.

"Amy?" Mom calls.

I step back out. Emma's gone.

"Ready?" Mom asks.

I'm sweating by the time we reach Mom's lab in the shuttle—I'd love another thunderstorm to cool everything off. But then I remember the search parties and Kit, and pray that it doesn't rain.

Dr. Gupta's body is no longer in Mom's lab, and I'm somewhat grateful for that. There were too many . . . pieces. Like Juliana Robertson. I swallow drily, trying to forget the ripping, crunching sound the ptero made as it ate Dr. Gupta.

Somehow, my mind drifts to Lorin. She was found dead too, but she must not have been killed by a ptero. The horror of Dr. Gupta and Juliana's deaths has made everyone forget that it is Lorin's immaculate, seemingly untouched body that is by far the creepier corpse.

"The geologists need to run more tests before they can use my help," Mom says, already turning to the worktable in the lab. She holds out a vial of some viscous liquid. It's dark crimson, almost black.

"What is this?" I ask.

"Ptero blood."

I glance behind me. Dr. Gupta's body might be gone, but the ptero is still there, draped over the metal tables. Mom's dissected it already, weighing the organs and filling the entire lab with its foul odor, but she's not quite done with it yet.

I try not to gag at the smell of the ptero's stinking blood. When I cover my nose with the back of my hand, Chris shoots me a sympathetic glance.

"I want you to run the immunoassay on this," Mom tells me. "We've been analyzing the victims—let's look at the monsters instead."

"But we know what killed the ptero," I say. My bullets.

Mom just silently hands me the sample and we work together to test the ptero blood.

When it's all finished, Mom reads the report on the computer aloud. "Negative for everything," she says. "Except gen mod material."

I gape at her. When I talked to Elder about the pteros before, I hadn't really believed it was possible that they'd been genetically engineered by the first colony. Gen mod material was invented on Earth—*Sol*-Earth. It shouldn't be here at all, and certainly not in a native alien creature. But it shouldn't have been in Dr. Gupta's blood either.

"Is it possible that this gen mod material is from . . . " Chris trails off, looking uncomfortable. "Could it be from, er, Dr. Gupta?"

Mom shakes her head. "Too soon—the creature was killed before it had a chance to digest Dr. Gupta."

She should know. She did the dissection. She found the pieces of him in the ptero's stomach.

"But how, then?" I ask. "How could a ptero possibly have gen mod material in its bloodstream? Could it have come from the planet?"

Mom stares intently at the sample of ptero blood. "It should be impossible. I talked to Frank, the geologist. He says there are minerals in the soil he's never seen before. We're talking about whole new elements to the periodic table! Which means this planet? It shouldn't have anything that directly came from *our* planet, especially gen mod material, which was artificially created."

I don't need to wait for her to finish the tests. I already know the answer — the ptero has gen mod material in its bloodstream because humans have been here before. And they did something. Something similar to what we're doing to the horse and dog fetuses. Except they took it too far, and the creatures they made were monsters. Maybe the same monsters that killed them all, leaving behind nothing but the stone ruins.

As I watch my mother set up the rest of her equipment, I'm 100 percent certain that she has no idea what Dad knows about the compound past the lake. She still thinks we're the first people here. I open my mouth, determined to tell her the truth Dad's kept hidden, but no words come out. I have to hope that her tests can prove something, something that will save us.

There's a determined set to her jaw, an impassioned focus in the way she works now. It reminds me of Emma and what she told me this morning. It seems as if everyone knows there's *something* wrong with this world . . . we just can't quite figure out what it is.

After several hours, the lab door zips open. Chris jumps up, startled — he'd fallen asleep while Mom and I worked. Elder steps inside.

He looks a little lost as he scans the room. "Colonel Martin said I needed to come here?" he asks loudly. His eyes see mine, and his mouth curves in relief, but the smile doesn't reach his eyes. He looks tired — tired of fighting Dad, tired of peeling back the layers of this planet and finding only half-truths and danger.

"Kit?" I ask immediately.

Elder shakes his head. "Still missing. You wanted me?" There's a question in his voice.

Mom stands up. "I'm so sorry," she says. "I'd asked Bob — Colonel

Martin—to send you here before we found out that your doctor was missing. I'm surprised he still asked you to come; I didn't mean for it to interrupt the search party."

"It's okay," Elder says heavily. "We had to break for lunch."

"In that case," Mom says, standing. "This will only take a moment."

She motions for Elder to follow her back to where the tubes of fetuses are stored. Elder shoots me an inquiring look, and I realize that Mom has summoned him because I avoided telling the scientists about them earlier.

"We're beginning the incubation process," Mom says, showing Elder the tube, "and we weren't sure what animals these are. Do you know?"

"Yes," Elder says. His voice is polite but wary.

"Oh, good, I hoped so," Mom says. "So what do we have here?" She stops in front of the cylinder filled with golden goopy liquid and little beans of cloned humans. Cloned Elders. Copies of the first Eldest, all exactly the same right down to their DNA, but none of them are *my* Elder.

"They're—" Elder's voice catches in his throat. "They're human fetuses. Cloned."

Mom steps back, surprised. "Human fetuses? The FRX didn't say anything about preserving cloned human fetuses. . . . "

"They're not from the FRX," Elder says, quickly regaining his composure. "They were made by people aboard *Godspeed*."

By the Plague Eldest. He made hundreds of copies of himself, all for the purpose of ensuring that he, in some form or other, would be eternal dictator of a never-changing *Godspeed*.

"What's their . . . " Mom pauses, searching for the right words. "I'm sorry, I don't mean to be insensitive or ignorant, but what's their purpose?"

Elder stares at the golden liquid. Their purpose? To make more of him. Replacements. Eldest threatened to do just that—kill Elder and start again with a new fetus plucked from the sticky liquid. That's what he *did* do to Orion. . . .

"No purpose," Elder says in a hollow voice.

"Can I—feel free to tell me no, but can I dispose of them then? We could use the room."

Elder nods, his eyes still not leaving the cylinder. What must it feel like to see all the potential yous? I imagine Mom pulling one of the tiny beans out and putting it in an incubator next to the horse and dog fetuses. Nine months later, a little baby Elder pops out. He has Elder's eyes and Elder's face . . . but Elder's soul? No.

"Okay, then," Mom says. She turns to the cylinder, flipping up a small lid on a hidden control panel, pushes a button, and soon a soft whirring sound wraps around us. "Should only take a moment."

She steps back. A drain at the bottom of the cylinder opens up, and the chunky liquid filled with a hundred potential Elders disappears down a tube that hides their disposal under the floor.

In minutes, the cylinder is empty.

"Thank you," Mom says, heading back to her analysis of the ptero blood.

A crackle of radio noise cuts through the awkward tension my mother doesn't realize she's created. Our attention zooms in on Chris, who's standing straight, listening to the radio at his shoulder. We can't hear what's being said, but his eyes shoot to Elder.

And I know.

Kit's been found.

34: ELDER

They bring her body straight to the shuttle, so I am glad, at least, that I was already here waiting for her to arrive.

Her hair is matted with dirt and twigs and leaves. A large streak of dark brown mud is smeared on the left side of her face and down the formerly white lab coat. She'd been so happy with the coat—a gift from Dr. Gupta—that it had made me hopeful that the Earthborns and my people could really work together. It's ruined now, along with who knows what else. Over her chest is a red-and-black wound, a hole exploded in the flesh where her heart should be.

This was no accident.

This was not an attack from a beast, the vicious mauling of a monster.

A weapon killed Kit, a weapon wielded by a murderer.

"Who killed her?" I ask, rounding on Colonel Martin.

He raises both his hands. "We have no idea."

"This wound is nothing like anything one of my people could do!" I shout, pointing at the gaping hole in Kit's chest. "One of your military—in the armory—"

"Elder," Colonel Martin says solemnly, "we don't have any weapon that can make a wound like that."

I turn to Amy, who nods silently in confirmation.

The people carrying Kit's body lay her flat on a metal table, near the remains of the ptero Amy shot. My eyes are burning so much that I can barely see. Kit was kind, and good, and all she ever wanted to do was help other people. She was just like me: forced to take responsibility before she was ready, determined to do good in the footsteps of a predecessor who'd abused his power.

And she's dead now.

It's not *fair*. I am perfectly aware that this thought is childish, of no more use than a tantrum, but I can't help it. It *isn't* fair.

"Look at the way these wounds were made," Amy's mother says as she bends over the body.

"It's almost like she was shot with an exploding bullet," Amy says.

Amy meets my eyes, and I can tell we're thinking the same thing. There might not be any weapons like that in the armory, but that doesn't mean that there isn't something in the compound Amy and I discovered. Or in the hands of whatever kind of alien is out there.

Amy's mother silently starts setting up for an autopsy. Colonel Martin and his men leave, but I stay. I want to see this. I want to know what killed Kit.

Chris stays too—he's Amy's guard, after all. But I don't like the way he looks at Amy, like she belongs to him, and I can't help but smirk when he starts to turn a little green as he watches the autopsy.

Amy's mother gathers as much information from the outside of Kit's body as she can. Cotton swabs and fingernail scrapings. She labels and bags everything carefully, handing it all to Amy, who takes it without a word.

I stare over the body at Amy, who meets my eyes. Neither of us speaks, but her look is filled with sympathy—and anger. Kit shouldn't have died. Not like this.

Kit's eyes keep popping open, even though Dr. Martin's closed them twice now. Her mouth gapes as if she's screaming when Amy's mother peels her skin away, looking deep into the wound.

I try to blur my eyes, to stop myself from identifying the different shapes and colors of organs and bones and veins and flesh and fat and all those things that are not meant to be seen, that should be hidden, always, behind skin and life. I could easily fit my head in the hole in Kit's chest—there's nothing there now but scorched flesh and blackened blood.

Dr. Martin angles a light into the wound, then takes a pair of tweezers from Amy. She bags something that I can't see from where I am, then hands it to Amy. "See what you can discover about this," she says.

Amy takes the small bag over to the worktable, and I follow her. It's a cowardly move, but I don't think I can face Kit's lifelessness anymore today.

"What is it?" I ask.

"Shards of something," she says. She uses tweezers to pick up a long piece of what looks like glass from the bag. Narrow and clear, with razor-sharp edges. It's as thin as a needle, and Amy grips it as gently as possible. Too gently—the glass slips out of the tweezers, clattering to the metal table. I suck in a gasp of air, waiting for the glass to shatter.

But it doesn't.

Amy picks it back up with the tweezers, squeezing it so hard her hands shake from the pressure. The glass doesn't break.

She sets it on the table and picks up a screwdriver. Lodging the tip of the flat-head screwdriver against the center of the glass shard, she pushes down with one hand . . . two hands . . . all her weight.

The glass still doesn't break.

Amy finally puts the shard on a specimen slide and pushes it under the microscope. After looking at it a moment, she steps aside so I can see. It looks like normal glass but with thin lines of gold spreading out like sunbeams, almost invisible even with the microscope's amplification. It reminds me of . . . something . . .

"We definitely don't have any weapons that leave a wound like that, that leave behind *glass*," Amy says.

"Whatever else is on this planet has better weapons; that's what you're saying." We speak in low tones so neither Chris nor Amy's mother can hear.

Amy nods silently, worry all over her face.

I start pacing, a habit I've picked up from Amy. We're facing an enemy that's smarter and faster than us, that has better weapons and no problem using them. Not just the exploding bullets that killed Kit, but probably also some way of controlling the pteros.

If they're so smart, they must have a reason for killing who they're killing. They could have taken me and Amy last night, but they went for Kit.

Why?

They took Dr. Gupta—a medical doctor, not a scientist. They took Juliana Robertson, a military person. And Lorin. Poor, simple Lorin, who was drugged up on Phydus at the time.

I stop.

Kit's bloody, muddy clothes are heaped in a pile in the corner. I race over to them, moving so suddenly that Amy's mother squeaks in surprise. She watches me as if I'm loons as I rifle through the pockets in Kit's oversized white lab coat. Both pockets are filled with med patches of all different colors—lavender for pain, yellow for anxiety, blue for digestion.

But there's not a single green patch.

I *know* Kit had dozens of Phydus patches. I saw them yesterday. She was still giving them out; she kept them with her. I may not have approved, but I know she didn't just throw away all the Phydus after my feeble objections.

But there's not a single one here.

Lorin was on Phydus. Dr. Gupta was talking to Kit about Phydus when they were walking through the forest to go to the ruins. Maybe the aliens—the more I think about it, it *has* to be aliens that we're up against—saw Lorin in her drugged state and took her—and Dr. Gupta, who was with her and might have been able to tell them about what was happening. Juliana Robertson . . . she'd been sent to find Dr. Gupta and Lorin.

What if she found them? What if that's why she was killed?

But they couldn't have told the aliens much about the drug that controlled Lorin.

Kit could, though. She knew exactly what happened when someone put on a pale green med patch.

I might be on a whole new planet, but I still can't escape Phydus.

3 5 : AMY

I'm **exhausted by the time I leave** the lab with Mom. And we're no closer to figuring out what killed Kit—or, rather, *who* killed Kit.

The only thing we're clear on is that something—someone—is targeting us.

It was bad enough when we feared the planet. But the planet is an amorphous thing. Fearing it is like fearing nature. It did not *want* to kill us, it just did, much like a wild animal at hunt.

But to know that there's something specific, sentient, and malicious that's murdering us? Elder's theory about aliens is sounding more and more accurate.

It makes me very glad to have Chris as my personal guard now.

I don't think I'm hungry, but when we get back to the building, I find that I'm starving. I finish my ration of food much too quickly—probably for the best, given its bland taste and too-chewy texture. Even so, I'd like to ask for more, but I resist the impulse. We need to make this food last. We have yet to find anything edible on the planet, and it's too soon to tell if our crops will grow.

When I finally slink into my room, I'm ready to pass out. I pull my sleeping bag out from the corner where I shoved it when Emma came to see me this morning, prepared to collapse, when I feel a hard object inside the bag.

The glass cube Emma gave me.

It's *glowing*.

I'm so surprised I drop the bag and the cube along with it. It clatters onto the ground, and my heart stops; I'm sure the thing is about to shatter. But it doesn't. It thuds heavily against the stone floor without even a crack.

Just like the glass from the weapon that killed Kit. It wouldn't break either.

"Amy?" my father calls. "What was that?"

"Just dropped my . . . " My mind searches for an answer. "Flashlight," I finish lamely. That thud was way louder than a flashlight, but Dad buys it.

I pick up the glass cube again, staring into it. The glittery gold swirls glow brightly, casting light all around. It's as bright as a fluorescent bulb but still cool to the touch.

"Don't waste batteries," Dad calls from behind the tent walls he's erected to create a bedroom for himself and Mom.

I drop the cube back into my sleeping bag. The room is engulfed in darkness again.

"Good night, sweetheart," Mom calls sleepily.

"Night," I mutter, staring at the sleeping bag and the faint square glowing through the nylon.

My first instinct is to track Emma down. But I'm not sure which building she's in, and I don't want to call attention to the cube. She made it seem like this was a big secret, a clue to this world.

I remember the glass shards we found in the wound on Kit's chest. If this glass cube can light up my room, there has to be *some* sort of energy in it. If it exploded . . .

I stare at the floor where I dropped the cube, horrified. If it had broken, would my legs have been blown off the same way Kit's chest was blown open?

I have to tell Elder.

Before I sneak out, I make sure the .38 strapped to my waist is loaded and ready. Then I twist my sleeping bag as if it were a sack and drop it outside, grateful that the lining muffles the sound. I put both hands on the windowsill to raise myself up. My knees skim across the square depression in the stone, making me almost curse in pain.

I slink through the shadows. Elder and I have been butting heads recently, pulled in different directions by our own worries and the people closest to us. But my first instinct is to turn to him. When it comes down to it, he's the one I trust. It's barely nightfall now, but no one wants to risk going out after curfew, not after Kit's death. Chris patrols the lower level of buildings, and I'm so preoccupied that I nearly step right in front of him. I barely have time to duck behind the corner of a building, holding my breath. He doesn't have a flashlight, but he walks with assurance down the path. I count to ten before slipping back around the corner and up the stairs to Elder's building.

Elder's inside and awake, pacing his room. He looks up and grins. "I was just trying to figure out how I could get your attention," he says.

"Shh," I say, looking to the door. The near miss with Chris has me on edge. "Let's go upstairs."

Each of the dusty buildings is roughly the same design—a large room on the ground level and smaller rooms above, connected by a stone staircase. Dad has used our upstairs to store supplies, and when I helped him move our belongings in, I noticed that the back room, the room against the side of the hill, doesn't have a window. It's not much for privacy, but it's the best we can do.

"What's going on?" Elder asks as he follows me upstairs.

I go into the windowless room and set the sleeping bag on the floor. Then I reach inside and pull out the glass cube. "Emma gave me this," I say.

Elder stares at it in wonder. He turns it over in my hand, and the shadows dance chaotically along the walls. "I saw this before. Emma and . . . " He looks up at me. "Emma and your dad had this, the first night we landed."

"She gave it to me. But look—it's like the glass we found in Kit's wound," I say. The light makes dark shadows that illuminate Elder's face, giving him a creepy, unreadable look.

Elder covers the cube with one hand, and the light shines through his skin, making it appear red. "How does it work?" he asks.

I think about the way the sand under the shuttle glowed slightly the first night we landed. Glass is melted sand—the rockets on the shuttle burned their way into the earth. Then they glowed at night, much like this cube.

"Solar power?" I suggest tentatively. "The suns' light gets trapped inside the glass?"

"Maybe." Elder turns the cube over in his hand as if expecting to find an on/off switch.

"Those square depressions in the windowsills," I say, rubbing my knee where I scraped it against the windowsill as I was escaping. "The ones we thought were meant for idols or something? They're the exact size of the cube."

Elder runs his hands over the smooth surface. "Put the cube in the window in the morning so it charges with light all day and glows all night. Genius." He looks up at me. "Remember the square light in the ceiling of the communication building at the compound?"

"You think it was something like this?"

Elder nods. "I bet the top is exposed on the roof so it can charge. Maybe all the electricity—the computers, the communication bay—runs on solar energy."

Already, the light in the cube is starting to fade. It had barely been charged in the sunlight at all before I stuffed it in my sleeping bag this morning.

"The one piece of information that's been consistent since we've landed," Elder says, "is that the FRX found valuable resources here on Centauri-Earth. It's the first thing anyone ever talks about with this mission, even your dad. What if *this* is the valuable resource?"

I nod. "It makes sense," I say. "Solar energy is free. Enough of these would light up a city."

"And if it breaks . . . " Elder tips his hand over but doesn't drop the cube. "Boom."

He's thinking the same thing as me: this is what killed Kit. Whoever made the cube can also make bullets. The cube didn't break when it hit the stone floor, but if they found a way to make the bullets break on contact . . . well, that would explain why it looked as if Kit's chest exploded.

"I think there's something else," Elder says.

He explains to me his theory that the one thing linking the victims together is Phydus.

"But I don't know how we can prove that this is about the drug," he says. The glass cube is barely glowing now, making the room filled with more shadows than light.

I think about the emptiness in Dr. Gupta's eyes as the ptero ate him. The way Lorin died without a mark on her. The samples of their blood in the lab in the shuttle.

And then it hits me.

"I know how to prove it."

36: ELDER

I take the glass cube with us as Amy leads me to the shuttle, keeping it covered until we're in the forest. Amy has her gun, but I'd like to be able to see if an enemy is approaching us—ptero or alien.

As we trudge through the forest, I can't help but think about how comfortable Amy's sleeping bag looked, how nice it would be if it—and she—stayed in my building tonight rather than returned to her parents. These thoughts soon evaporate, though. The forest feels more dangerous now. When Amy and I snuck out to the compound last night, we did so with the belief that the deadliest things on this planet were the monsters in the sky. But now we know something else is out there, and the knowledge makes the shadows feel ominous, deadly.

There's a soft glow under the shuttle as we approach, and I know Amy is right: glass on this planet somehow traps solar energy. I think bitterly about the lead-cooled fast reactor in the engine room of *Godspeed*, the flashing red light that means it's in meltdown. If there was some way to make the energy in the glass on this planet fuel the ship . . .

If we could do that, then . . . what? Bartie could wait to distribute the black patches for another few years? They're trapped, and just like Amy warned when we left them there, there's nothing for the people of *Godspeed* to do but wait for death.

I have to save them.

Amy leads me to the lab aboard the shuttle. As we pass the armory, I consider pausing and selecting a gun for myself, but I keep walking. I'd rather have answers than weapons.

"Mom's been having me help her with her experiments," Amy explains as she picks up a long-stemmed cotton swab and walks over to the Phydus pump. Its wires are still exposed and broken from my hasty dismantling of the pump so long ago. Amy lifts the panel that covers the spout where Eldest used to deposit Phydus. Some of the sticky, viscous liquid is still inside, and although it's dried into stains on the edge of the valve, Amy jabs the cotton swab deep into the pump and extracts it, covered with the dark syrup.

Amy moves quickly to make sure the Phydus doesn't drip off the swab until she can scrape the liquid into a cup. Then she places the cup into a machine.

"Analyte generator," Amy says as the machine works. "It basically just makes a test so that we can see if something has Phydus in it."

The machine dings.

"Done," Amy says. "Now we need a sample to test." She opens a small refrigerator door and pulls out sample cups of blood. I read the labels one by one: RAJ GUPTA, JULIANA ROBERTSON, SHIPBORN FEMALE, SHIPBORN DOCTOR.

"They didn't even bother with Lorin and Kit's names," I say bitterly.

Amy ducks her head. "I'm sorry," she says.

She tests Lorin's blood first. "We know she was wearing a med patch, so it'd make sense for the results to test positive for Phydus," she says. We wait for the machine to finish analyzing her blood, then read the results together.

"That's a lot of Phydus," I say, staring at the report. "One med patch wouldn't make her have that much."

Amy frowns. "That much Phydus would . . . "

"It would kill her," I say.

"Lorin's body wasn't marked by attack." Amy looks at me, realization dawning. "I saw her, before they buried her. She looked like she was sleeping." Amy's eyes fill with a mix of horror and disgust. "She looked the same way Steela did, the woman Doc overdosed with Phydus."

"Test the rest of the blood," I say.

Dr. Gupta's is positive for Phydus—not as much in his blood as in Lorin's, but enough to have made him silently accept being eaten alive by a ptero. There's Phydus in Juliana Robertson's blood too. I wonder if it was the Phydus that killed her or if it was the ptero attack that did it. Maybe she had the same fate as Dr. Gupta, without a bullet in her brain to end it quickly and mercifully.

"None in Kit's blood," Amy says.

"Then it was the bullets—or the sun glass, or whatever it is these aliens use—that killed her." But that was just Kit. The others— "Amy, how did this planet get Phydus? It was developed *on the ship*. The ship that never landed here."

"*Is* there a chance the Plague Eldest landed? Maybe he landed and then went back up?"

I shake my head. "*Godspeed* was never meant to do more than reach Centauri-Earth. If it landed, there's no way it could have gone back into orbit. There's enough fuel reserved for deorbit, no more. And before you ask—the shuttle, once it's detached from the ship, can't be reattached. You heard the way the metal broke. And there's no more fuel for that in the shuttle either. *Godspeed* always had only a one-way landing process."

"Then . . . how?" Amy asks.

Neither of us has an answer.

37: AMY

The glass cube is completely dark by the time we leave the shuttle. We're both lost in our thoughts and on edge. Every noise in the forest makes us jump, every shadow makes us flinch.

Which is why I nearly scream when we get to the edge of the colony and someone says, "Amy!"

"Chris!" I say, clutching my heart as he steps out of the shadows. Elder rolls his eyes.

"What are you two doing out here?" Chris asks, looking at us both.

"None of your business." Elder steps in front of me as if he's going to protect me.

Chris ignores him. "Let me walk you back," he offers, readjusting the rifle strapped to his shoulder.

"No need," Elder growls.

I put my hand on Elder's arm. I know he's not happy about this turn of events, but I'm also not ready to battle my father if Elder's looking for a fight. "You go back to your building," I say. "Chris can walk me back to mine."

"But—" Elder starts, but I shake my head at him. He looks away, then strides up the paved path toward his own home.

"I don't think he likes me very much," Chris comments as Elder storms away.

I bite back a laugh. "No," I say. "But that's okay. He'll come around."

Chris looks doubtful.

Instead of taking me straight back to the closest building—which would take less than five minutes—Chris veers to the right, skirting the meadow at the edge of the colony. "Amy, there are things I want to tell you . . . " he says. He runs his fingers through his hair—much like Elder does when he's frustrated—and then stops abruptly, looking up at the stars.

"Yes?" I prompt.

He doesn't speak for a long moment. "I . . . I think I can trust you. You're not like your father."

This comment leaves me speechless. Is Chris saying that my father's untrustworthy? Emma said as much earlier, but it feels different coming from Chris, who has practically been my father's right-hand man since the first expedition to the probe.

The probe. Chris was there when Dad found it.

"I know what you're going to say." I ignore Chris's expression. "Elder and I . . . we've already found the compound. We know what's out there."

Chris looks genuinely startled and can't seem to form any words in answer to me.

"I don't know why Dad's keeping it a secret . . . " I continue. I look up at Chris's uncannily bright blue eyes. "But thank you."

"Thank you?" Chris echoes, still at a loss for words.

"For trusting me enough to tell me," I say. I touch his elbow, not speaking until I have his full attention again. "I mean it, thank you. It really means a lot to me." Telling me about the compound against my father's wishes would be the kind of treachery my father would never forgive. But it also seems as if Dad's hiding something even more important than Elder and I have realized. Something both Emma and Chris aren't happy about.

"Why is Dad keeping the compound so secret?" I ask. "Does it have something to do with the aliens?"

Chris's eyes round in further surprise.

"Don't look so shocked!" I say, laughing softly. "Elder and I figured it had to have been aliens that attacked Kit—that killed off the original colony."

I cast my eyes up to the buildings behind us, nothing more than a dark outline against the bright stars.

Chris touches the side of my face, his fingers sliding down my cheek and twining in my hair. My breath catches in my throat as he looks down at me with such intensity that I can barely think straight.

"You, Amy Martin," Chris says, "are one of a kind."

He pulls me closer and, like a magnet that can't resist metal, I'm drawn to him.

"You give me hope," he whispers, the warmth of his breath making the tiny hairs on the back of my neck stand up.

I think for one heart-stopping moment that he's going to kiss me—and I cannot tell my body to push him away.

But he doesn't.

His forehead rests on mine, and we just stand there, under the twinkling lights of a million stars, holding each other as if that is protection enough against the treacherous Earth.

38: ELDER

I wake before dawn and watch the morning light creep across my ceiling. There is so much that must be done, but all I can think about is Kit. I used to be envious of the way Eldest could always rely on Doc, but somehow I didn't notice how Kit had become so important to me. To all of us. I don't know how we're going to operate without her.

But we'll have to. Somehow.

I head first to the shuttle. I need to inspect what medical supplies Kit had in reserve. I'd rather use our own stuff than rely on the Earthborn doctors. My mood grows darker as I follow the path to the shuttle. Thinking about med patches reminds me of the black ones Bartie intends to use as a last resort before the engine on *Godspeed* completely fails.

I pause when I reach the bridge. The door is cracked open, and through it, I can hear shouting.

I hesitate.

Then I hear Amy's voice, practically screaming with rage.

I throw the door open and barrel inside. It's still too early for many people to be working, but the thought gives me no comfort. I race toward the gen lab, where the voices are coming from.

"Do you want to cause a panic?" Colonel Martin bellows.

"They *need* to know!" Amy yells. I pick up my pace, my footsteps clattering on the metal of the cryo room floor.

The gen lab door is open. Colonel Martin turns at the sound of my approach and rolls his eyes. "Great," he says, just loud enough for me to hear.

"What's going on?" I ask, panting.

Colonel Martin moves aside.

And I see Emma Bledsoe's body. I'm breathless from my panicked run, but I stop short at the sight of her. Emma was kind. She was the one Earthborn I trusted.

Well, besides Amy.

"What happened?" I ask hollowly. Emma looks as if she's merely sleeping.

"We're still determining cause of death," Amy's mother says, but my eyes shoot to Amy. Without saying anything, I give her a look that I hope sends her my real question: was Phydus involved? She shrugs, glancing at the machine we used last night. I can hear its motor grinding; no results yet.

"Emma was on patrol," Colonel Martin says gruffly. "She must have run afoul of something that we don't know about. That is why this world is dangerous, why no one should go anywhere alone."

"It's not like she just accidentally died!" Amy exclaims, frustrated. "Dad, there were purple flower strings on her clothing. Someone knocked her out."

"And murdered her?" Colonel Martin's voice is incredulous.

"She *knew* not to mess with the purple flowers; she saw what they did to me!"

"You're hysterical," Colonel Martin says, waving his hand at Amy as if to dismiss her.

She grabs his wrist, stopping the motion. "You need to listen to us," she says coldly.

Her eyes question me. I nod. It's all or nothing now. "Emma knew something," Amy continues. "She warned me to be careful who to trust. I thought she was talking about you. Maybe she wasn't."

Colonel Martin doesn't look any more convinced—if anything, the expression he wears now seems to indicate that he thinks either Amy is exaggerating or flat-out lying.

"She gave me a cube made of glass," Amy continues, and this, finally, makes Colonel Martin pay attention. The room is silent now, tension rising as Amy explains that she knows the cube glows, that she's linked the glass cube to the exploding bullets that killed Kit.

"There are aliens on this planet, aren't there?" I finally say, breaking in when Amy stops talking. "Sentient aliens, who have figured out how to make weapons we can't compete with."

"You don't know what you're talking about," Colonel Martin says.

"Damn it, Bob!" Amy's mother says, rage in her voice. "This is not the time for secrets! What do you know? What have you been keeping from us—from all of us?"

Colonel Martin looks cornered, trapped. When he doesn't speak, I answer for him. "I saw the compound. The biometric lock on the door to the communication room only opens for humans. That means there's something that *isn't* human out there."

"You can't expect me to stand here and listen to this," Colonel Martin interjects, but the attempt is halfhearted, and I quickly cut him off.

"I can and I will because these things—whatever they are—are picking us off, one by one." I list the names of the people who have died so far, ending with Emma, drawing her name out and watching the guilt that shadows his eyes. "And I think you know the reason why."

"Is this true?" Amy's mother asks. "Are you *protecting* these creatures?" she asks, disgusted.

Colonel Martin shakes his head in protest. "I am *not* protecting them!" he roars. "There is no *them!* I don't know any more about what kind of aliens are on this planet than you do!" And then he seems to register what I've just said about the compound. "You know about the communication room?" he asks. "You've been there?"

I don't bother denying it.

"Then you know we haven't been able to contact Earth."

Amy's mother gasps. "But you said—"

"We *thought* we had," Colonel Martin says. "But the message I heard was pre-recorded."

"And you haven't been able to reach Sol-Earth since then." It's more a statement than a question.

Colonel Martin nods.

"What did Emma know?" Amy asks. "Why was she scared?"

Colonel Martin opens his hands wide. "I don't know," he says. He sounds defeated. "I don't know why she's dead now either. Maybe she figured out something that I didn't. But she didn't tell me, and she can't tell any of us now."

3 9 : AMY

When Dad leaves, Elder follows him. I know Elder won't let go of the questions he really wants to ask, and I viciously revel in that knowledge. It's time we had some answers.

Mom, on the other hand, doesn't look happy at all about what she's learned. Or maybe she's sad to be doing another autopsy, to be prying apart another friend.

She covers Emma's body with a sheet.

"I can't do this," she says. "Not now. Every time I look at her, I think about you."

"Me?" I ask, surprised.

She nods. "When Elder brought you to us, after you passed out from those purple flowers." Her eyes are sparkling now, and I'm afraid she's about to cry. "I thought we'd lost you then. And now . . . we've had a death a day since we landed." She swallows. "We knew this world would be dangerous," she says. "But we had no idea it would actively try to kill us."

She steps away from the autopsy table and toward me, wrapping me in a hug, clutching me with something I can only describe as desperation.

"I'm starting to wish we'd never come," she says.

Her words throw me off so much that I can barely think of what to say.

"But you never wanted anything more than to go on this mission!" I exclaim. "You were working on this project before I was even born!"

Mom's grin twitches up despite herself. "I know. But that's the point: it was before you were born. Once you were born . . . how could I ask you to give up Earth? It was my dream, but never yours."

Now I really don't know what to say. I wonder if Mom knows that Dad gave me a choice to hold on to Earth, to give them up instead.

Mom leans over and wraps one arm around my shoulders. "I'm glad you're here," she says quietly, and I can feel my eyes burning and my face growing hot, so I just smile and nod and bury my face into her shoulder.

And then I know what I need to say. I pull away from her and look right in her eyes. "I'm glad I'm here too," I tell her. And I mean it. Despite the fear, despite the deaths—I'm glad I'm here. My eyes slide to the white sheet covering Emma's body. I think about what she said—the last thing she said to me. And I know it was the truth.

When Mom and I finally break apart, she seems stronger. More determined. And because she is, I can be too.

She turns back to the autopsy she doesn't want to perform. And I turn back to test the sample of Emma's blood against Phydus. I am not surprised when it comes back positive.

40: ELDER

Colonel Martin doesn't want to talk. He makes that much clear straightaway—but I don't care. I stay at his heels as we leave the shuttle.

Finally he turns to face me. "You want to know what I know? Then follow me." And whatever it is that I expected him to do, this is not it.

Colonel Martin cuts through the forest, and although there's no path and he's leading me away from the colony, I have no doubt that he knows where he's going.

To the compound.

We don't talk as we march—almost run. The tree branches whip past us; vines snag our clothing, but neither of us slows. When we reach the compound, there's only one guard on duty, Chris. He snaps to attention as we approach.

"What are you doing in the hot sun?" Colonel Martin asks, then corrects himself. "Suns."

"I was hoping . . . " Chris's eyes turn to me, confused. "I was hoping for word on Emma."

"Dead." Colonel Martin's voice is gruff. "Open up the communication room."

Chris shoots me a questioning glance, clearly surprised that Colonel

Martin has brought me here. "After you," he says, taking a step back as Colonel Martin strides forward, pressing his thumb over the scanner. The way Chris watches me makes me wonder if he only let Colonel Martin go first so he had a chance to size me up as I walk past him. I push the sweaty hair from my face and ignore him.

Chris hesitates before following us inside, but Colonel Martin's gaze softens when he sees him. "You too, son," he says, and Chris shuts the door after he enters.

"Young Elder here found the compound," Colonel Martin tells Chris. "And he found out that the first message, the one we got on the shuttle, was pre-recorded, a hack job."

Chris stands back, trying to look impassive, but I can't help but notice the way his eyes examine me, judging my reaction.

"Here's what we know," Colonel Martin says, turning to me. "We know that there was a colony before us. And we know that it made the ruins we currently live in and that it built this compound." His shoulders slump as if he's carrying the weight of the world—maybe both worlds—on him. "And we also know that they are all dead."

I grip the edge of the communication bay. I want to ask, "How?" But I cannot seem to form that simple word. Nevertheless, Colonel Martin answers.

"We found these recordings. Or, Chris here found them." He nods to Chris, and I'm surprised to see sympathy in his look.

Colonel Martin turns on the touch screen in the communication bay, but rather than scrolling through the menus like Amy and I did, he opens a cabinet to the right of the control panel and withdraws a thin, black piece of plastic about the same length as my thumb. It reminds me eerily of the black med patches Bartie has on *Godspeed*, and the thought twists my stomach. Colonel Martin presses the plastic into a slot near the touch screen, and it's only then that I realize the material is similar to the mem cards we had on *Godspeed*, used to store information.

"This is what we know," Amy's father says, punching up the screen. An image of a glass cube similar to the one Emma gave Amy appears. "Something in the soil means that any glass made here, using a specific process, will be able to easily and effectively store solar energy. The first colony discovered this, and for several years, they manufactured solar glass and shipped it back to Earth. The compound we're currently standing in was used as a transportation center. They'd ship the glass from here to an automated space station in orbit around the planet and from there to Earth."

"A space station!" I exclaim. "We didn't see anything like that when we landed."

Colonel Martin arches an eyebrow at me. "This world *is* rather big, you know." He swipes the screen, and it fades to black.

"What happened to them?" I ask. "The first colony? You said they're all dead?"

Colonel Martin looks at Chris. I get the feeling that they're both trying to decide how much to tell me. I'm very nearly at the point of demanding answers when Colonel Martin moves over to the other side of the control panel, where the audio communication is. He turns a dial labeled ANSIBLE, and static fills the air.

But—not static. Not just. Words break through, words I can almost not understand.

" . . . the danger too great . . . have received indication . . . human life once more on . . . *Godspeed* . . . survive the . . . help coming . . . "

I strain to make out the words. Through the static and the accent of the speaker it's hard to understand.

"It's on a loop," Colonel Martin says as the message starts over again.

"Sol-Earth?" I ask.

Colonel Martin nods. "It's not the same as true communication, but it's an indication that they know we've landed. And they're sending help."

I snort. "We can't wait another three hundred years for help to get here."

"We won't have to, not if we can amplify the signal enough to get a response from Earth." Colonel Martin turns back to the touch screen and swipes his fingers over it. "I don't fully understand the technology being used, but Chris here has been able to explain it to me enough that I get the basic idea. Tesseracts and wormholes and some such. Means travel is so much faster now, way beyond what we had when *Godspeed* was built."

"How much faster?" I ask, barely daring to breathe. We might just have a chance after all.

"A week, or maybe less. Once we manage to get a message back, I'd expect help to arrive at the station—it's currently unmanned—within just a few days, and they'll be able to travel to the planet from there."

"And then we begin evacuation," Chris says. I've fallen so deep into my own thoughts that I nearly forgot he was in the room with us.

Colonel Martin taps his fingers against the edge of the communication bay. I get the impression that if the room wasn't so small, he'd start pacing. After a moment, he looks at Chris darkly. "No," he says. "Then we wage war."

"What?" I say. My eyes dart to Chris—he's just as surprised as I am.

"Whatever alien being wiped out the first humans on this planet, they are, as Elder says, sentient. They are singling out my people and attacking. This isn't random assault—they're not defending their home or trying to find a peaceful answer to our presence. They are *murdering* my people. And yours, Elder."

I think about Lorin, about Kit's dead, empty eyes, the gaping hole in her chest where her heart should be.

"Whatever is killing my people, I will kill it first," Colonel Martin says fiercely. He looks right at Chris. "I will avenge humanity." His words are a threat and a promise, all wrapped in one.

41: AMY

Mom and I work in silence most of the day, too wrapped up in our sadness to focus on anything else. If I could just figure out *where* the Phydus is coming from, maybe that would tell us how it ended up in Dr. Gupta, Lorin, Juliana Robertson . . . and Emma.

Long after supper, there's a knock on the gen lab door. Before I can stand up, Elder opens it.

I take one look at his face and say, "What's wrong?"

His eyes are skittish, bouncing from me to the floor to my mom and back again. "I . . . I need to talk to you," he mutters.

"Now?" Mom's voice cuts across the lab. "Amy, we're not done with our work—"

"It can wait," I say. I drop the test tube I'd been holding onto the tray and race to the door. My mom starts to protest again, but the door zips shut, silencing her.

"What happened?" I ask Elder urgently, but he just shakes his head. There are too many people here in the shuttle. Despite the late hour, the geologists—who've set up a lab where the cryo chambers used to be—are busily and excitedly talking about something, little mounds of soil samples piled up on the trays around them.

Elder doesn't talk until we're on the path toward the colony. His steps slow as he turns to me, a wild sort of desperation in his eyes.

"Amy . . . " He rakes his fingers through his hair. "Amy, this planet isn't what it's frexing supposed to be at all."

I step closer to him, longing to take the anguish from his eyes. "I know," I say.

His eyes snap to mine. "Why?" he asks sharply. "What did you find in the bodies?"

"No—tell me what's troubling you first."

Elder shakes his head. "I shouldn't have taken you from your work."

"It's not that," I say, touching his arm until he meets my eyes again. "It's just . . . " I roll my shoulders, the muscles stiff. "Nothing Mom and I are finding in the lab really makes sense."

"What do you mean?"

"Mom's been analyzing the DNA of the pteros. She thinks they're a mix of DNA from Sol-Earth, Centauri-Earth, and gen mod material."

"From Sol-Earth?" Elder asks, so loudly that a small red bird bursts from the underbrush, chattering at us angrily as it flies away.

"It's like something from *Jurassic Park*," I say. I wait for Elder to give his normal little half grin of confusion whenever I reference something from Earth, but he's too troubled to notice. His jaw is hard, and his Adam's apple bobs up and down.

I trail my fingers up along his arm, attempting to bring him out of whatever dark thoughts are troubling him. "What did you discover today?"

"Not here," he replies. He takes another frantic look around and grabs my hand, pulling me along so quickly that we're practically running toward the colony.

But when we approach the buildings, he stops short. I follow his gaze. Dad stands in the doorway of the first building, his hand shading his eyes, waiting for Mom and me to return. My heart's pounding—I can't be with him now, not since discovering how he's kept the compound hidden. When Dad's gaze turns to us, Elder pulls me into dark shadows that envelop us.

Elder puts a finger to his lips. We wait until we hear Dad go back inside.

Thank you, I mouth silently at him. I know I'll have to face Dad eventually, but I'm not ready yet. Elder leads me behind the houses, up the stairs to his building. And I realize: he didn't do that just for me. He doesn't want to see Dad either.

"What happened after you left the shuttle?" I ask again, worry twisting my stomach.

He doesn't speak until we're inside his building. "Your father showed me the compound."

"He did?" Relief floods my senses. If he's being up-front about the compound, if he's left the secrets behind . . .

Elder's eyes flash. "Oh, yes, he told me all about it. And that the people who made all this"—Elder throws his arms up, indicating the dusty stone building—"they all died. The whole first colony. Wiped out by some alien force."

I swallow. For some reason, tears spring to my eyes. We'd guessed as much before, but to have Elder say it like that . . .

"And your dad . . . " Elder says this as if the mere thought of him fills him with disgust. "He's . . . he's bent on revenge. His first thought—the *first* frexing thing he thought of—was to kill off the aliens. Just slaughter them."

My mind's swimming with the possibility of aliens. Not just monsters like the pteros. Something sentient. Something that watches us and leaves behind weird footprints. Something covered in hard, crystalline scales like the one Elder found.

Something that wants to kill us merely because we're here.

"It's Eldest all over again!" Elder storms, his voice rising. "Eldest's first solution to anything that caused him a problem was to kill it! Orion asking too many questions? Better have Doc kill him. You show up, looking different from my people? He wanted to throw you out the hatch!"

"Dad isn't Eldest," I say immediately.

"The frex he's not! You can't just *kill* your problems away, but frex if he isn't going to *try!*" He whirls on me, and I feel the full force of his anger. "He'll use my people on the frontlines so they're the first to die. 'Slaves or soldiers,' just like Orion warned."

I flinch. "He *won't*," I say, hurtling the words in front of me like a shield.

Elder's face is contorted with rage, and I wonder how long he's been quietly stewing over these thoughts, unable to confront Dad but not able to tell anyone else. If he confided in his people, they'd panic and rebel, just like they did with Bartie. And Kit's gone now. He's been saving all this worry and fury for me, and all the while, it's been building inside him, like an overflowing cup.

"Dad *isn't* Eldest," I repeat as forcefully as possible. "We won't let him be."

This stops Elder.

"He's military. And he's always been stubborn. But he's *good*, Elder, I promise you."

I can tell he doesn't believe me. And maybe he's right — I'm not objective, not when it comes to my own father. But I also know that my dad is better than Elder thinks he is.

"Besides," I continue, "Dad's not the real problem here."

I really have Elder's attention now. He waits for me to continue.

I clench my fingers into fists so that Elder doesn't see the way my hands are shaking. "I don't know what I expected this planet to be," I say in a quiet voice. "I thought I could face the monsters Orion warned us about, and I was fine with the pteros. But . . . " My voice trails off. "I'm scared. The fact that this planet has Phydus . . . that's what terrifies me. That's worse than any monster. If there are aliens, and they have Phydus . . . " My voice cracks. Elder saw my dad talk about killing aliens, and his instinct was to rebel against the very idea. But the aliens have Phydus, and I'm afraid there's no way we can rebel against that.

"We should have stayed on *Godspeed*," I say, looking down at the ground.

It costs me everything to admit that I was wrong, that it was worth being trapped behind the walls in exchange for our safety.

"No." The word bursts from Elder in a ragged whisper of protest. "Whatever happens—it was worth it to leave the ship."

I don't answer.

Elder shifts so he's directly in front of me. When my eyes don't focus on him, he touches my face until I really see him. And that is why I know—I *know*—he is telling me the truth when he repeats, "It was worth it."

I shut my eyes, and my body melts with relief. I slowly become aware of how close we're standing to each other, the heat radiating off Elder's skin and warming me. When I open my eyes, I can see the same feral nature in my gaze reflected in his.

His hand is shaking when he trails it down the side of my face, tucking a stray strand of hair behind my ear. His fingers don't stop, outlining the side of my jaw, pulling my chin up to his.

I close my eyes.

Our lips meet. He tastes like things that have no taste: warmth and life and truth and goodness and love.

And all my other senses fade away.

There is nothing but our kiss, and in it, the knowledge that Elder wants— *needs*—me just as much as I *need* him.

But he breaks away from me just long enough to ask one thing: "Are you sure?"

And he waits for my answer.

Before, the first time, on Earth with my boyfriend Jason, I thought I was sure. But he never asked, and I never answered, and we did it all silently, in the dark, fumbling around as we tried to put our feelings into physical form. It wasn't a choice—it was just an action, a blind submission to desire.

I have made very few choices in my life. I respond to the situation, I react, but I have not set the course of my life and strode forward with the determination of a captain sailing into a storm. When my father gave me the choice to board Godspeed *or stay on Earth, I didn't decide, not really; I just accepted a fate I thought was inevitable.*

It was only Elder — it has always been only Elder — who asked me to choose who and what I am. What I do.

"I choose this," I say, my voice ragged with want. "I choose you."

I have never desired anything more than him in this moment. He leads me up to his room on the second floor, where my sleeping bag is already spread out. I thank whatever twist of fate made me leave it here last night.

We fall into each other. All the other voices in my head — the fear, the doubt, the worry — are drowned out. I die at the end of each kiss and am brought gasping back to life at the beginning of the next. I close my eyes and the entire world fades away.

There is only him and me and this thing between us that I cannot name, not out loud, but that my heart knows is love.

I shiver when I finally wiggle out of my clothes. Sweat on my skin makes the cool night air even colder. But then Elder touches me, and my skin alights with fire and warmth.

I kiss him, hard, and his hands slide down my back, to my hips. Strong hands, hands that will hold me and never let go. I feel, oddly, both safe and afraid in this moment.

He looks once in my eyes, a question still there. But we are beyond questions. We are in a place where there are only answers, and my answer to him is *yes.*

42: ELDER

I wake her with a kiss. She wiggles her nose and bats her hands at me without opening her eyes. I wake her with a different sort of kiss, and she opens her eyes with surprise before shutting them again with bliss.

And that is enough to make a smirk slide on my face that I'm sure will never fade.

"What time is it?" Amy asks sleepily.

"Just an hour later," I say, smiling.

"Mmm. More sleep." Amy nuzzles into my side.

"You need to go," I say, even though this is the last thing I want to tell her. "Your parents are going to be looking for you."

Amy glares at me.

"Hey, don't blame me," I joke, throwing my hands up in mock protest. "You know your dad's going to send out the entire military if he wakes up and realizes you're not there."

Amy rolls her eyes, but she gets dressed quickly.

"Hey." I pull her close and kiss her again. "To remember me by," I say softly.

She laughs, a musical sound. "Like I could forget."

And then she's gone.

My mind drifts immediately to every worry that's been plaguing me since Colonel Martin's announcement.

Phydus.

Aliens.

War.

Amy.

It's hard to think about all the bad when she reminds me of all that's good. I throw off the sleeping bag, shivering in the night air, and cross the hall to the other room on the second story of this building, hoping to catch a glimpse of her red hair before it disappears into the night.

My stomach clenches as I stare out at the darkness.

She's not alone.

43: AMY

The night air makes my skin prickle with goose bumps, but I relish the warm memories I've just made.

"Amy?" a voice whispers through the night.

I turn, a smile on my face, half expecting Elder to have followed me. Instead, Chris emerges from the shadows.

"What are you doing here?" I ask in a low voice.

Chris shrugs, an impish grin on his face. "I'm your bodyguard."

I roll my eyes but don't object as he starts to escort me down the steps toward the lower level of buildings and my parents' house.

He notices, though, when my steps grow slower and slower.

"You don't want to go back to your parents, do you?" he asks seriously.

I shake my head.

Chris gives me a mock bow. "Right," he says decisively. "Leave it to me. I'll convince them we have to go back to the shuttle for some reason." He darts ahead, and soon I can hear the rumble of deep male voices as he talks to Dad. I can't make out the words, but a moment later, Chris steps back out of the house—alone.

"Thanks," I mutter as Chris leads me back to the shuttle. Centauri-Earth is not the place for a nighttime stroll, but right now I'd rather face pteros and darkness than my father's lies.

"You know," I say as we approach the shuttle, "there is actually another test I could run."

Chris laughs. "You and Dr. Martin ran a hundred tests today! There can't possibly be anything else to examine from those little sample jars!"

I bump against his shoulder, which is hard as a rock. "Humor me," I say, bounding up the ramp and throwing open the door on the bridge. We tested the *ptero* for gen mod material, which led to Mom's discovery that the ptero contained a combination of DNA from Earth and Centauri-Earth. And we tested the *people* for Phydus once Elder and I came up with the idea that the people had been poisoned. But no one's tested a *ptero* for *Phydus*.

"It's probably nothing," I tell Chris, half for him, half for me. The chances of finding Phydus in a ptero? That seems impossible. But then again, if Phydus is somehow a natural part of this world, why wouldn't a ptero be infected?

I grab the ptero blood stored in the fridge and set up the test.

"What are you doing?" He actually sounds interested.

"Elder and I figured out that most of the victims have a . . . " I don't want to say "drug." "They have a *substance* in them, something that could control them. If Elder's right, and the aliens on this planet *are* sentient and they *are* attacking us, maybe the pteros have this substance in them too—and the aliens are using them to help target the attacks."

"It would be hard to control a wild animal," Chris says doubtfully.

Not with Phydus.

I'm on the edge of my seat when the immunoassay dings to let me know it's done. And even though I half expected it, I'm still surprised when I see the result.

Positive.

The pteros have gen mod material in them *and* Phydus. Elder thought he saw something when he was first attacked and later found the three-clawed footprint. The aliens are smart. They were watching us. And they *must* know some way to control the pteros, using them to attack.

"Find what you were looking for?" Chris asks, watching me closely.

I nod. "I'm ready to go back home now." Somehow, finding out the hidden truths of this world is making it easier to face the father I never thought would lie to me.

The word makes Chris pause. "Home? You've only been here a few days. Do you really already see this planet as home?"

I can tell from the way he says this that he doesn't.

But I do. I really do.

When we step outside the shuttle, it's pitch dark, a stark contrast to the electric lights inside running on the generator.

Chris stops, looking up at the starry sky. "This world really is beautiful, isn't it?"

I nod silently.

He turns to me. He has a look of intensity on his face that I cannot place. I've never seen that kind of fierceness in his eyes before.

"Follow me," he says. He grabs my hand and drags me down the ramp. I'm breathless, trying to keep up with his long legs. He veers away from the path that connects the shuttle to the colony, deeper into the forest.

"Is this safe?" I ask, touching the .38 at my hip with my free hand.

"Nothing's ever safe," Chris says.

He keeps going deeper and deeper into the trees, far away from anywhere I've dared to explore on this planet. I'm just about to jerk my hand out of his grasp and run back when he stops.

"Close your eyes," he says.

I laugh nervously.

"Seriously," Chris says. "Close your eyes."

I look at him doubtfully, then do as he says.

His fingers brush the bottom of my chin, pointing my face toward a breeze of fresh air.

"Now," he whispers in my ear, his voice tickling the side of my face. *"Listen."*

My eyes are filled with black. I breathe in and breathe out. I listen.

At first, I hear nothing. But then I notice the *drip, drip, drip* of water— somewhere. A creek or a small waterfall. The distant shuffle of leaves. A *zhrr—shh—zhrr* sound, similar to locusts. A sound that is, unmistakably, a frog's croak.

I open my eyes slowly.

"This world," Chris says, his eyes beseeching mine. "It really *is* a home worth fighting for, isn't it?"

I nod silently.

"At any cost," Chris says. He looks—tormented. As if he's trying to make a decision but cannot bring himself to it. I wonder if he knows more about Emma's death than I thought or if he's discovered the same thing that made her paranoid.

And then—before I can pull away, before I can even gasp in surprise— Chris swoops down and plants his lips on mine. The kiss takes me by such surprise that I open my mouth—and he slips his tongue against mine, hesitant at first, and then the kiss deepens, almost as if he's trying to convince me of something through the kiss. To claim me, to make me his. My cheeks grow warm, my mind spins.

I used to think that loving Elder didn't count if he was my only choice.

And here's Chris, only a few years older than me, smart and strong and brave—and I realize I had another choice all along.

I lean away from him, pulling back until he lets me go. I take several steps away from him, trying to catch my breath. Catch my thoughts. My racing heart.

"I—I'm sorry," Chris says immediately.

I'm glad it's too dark now for him to see how bright my cheeks must be, how deep my blush.

"I thought—it doesn't matter. I'm sorry," he says again. "I saw you leave

Elder's building, but I didn't think . . . I didn't know you two were more than friends. . . . " He shuffles nervously, avoiding my gaze. "I mean . . . I'd hoped . . . "

"It's okay," I say, still breathless.

I move toward the remains of the path we made, heading back to the shuttle and the colony, but nearly trip over a root. Chris dashes forward, quicker than I would have thought possible, and keeps me from face-planting.

"Thanks," I say.

Chris lets me go and steps awkwardly back. "Friends?" he asks. It's a peace treaty, an apology.

I take it. "Friends," I say, but I can't help but notice the way he's standing too close to me, as if he'd gather me up in his arms if I gave even a hint that I wanted us to be more.

44: ELDER

By the time I'm dressed and racing down the steps after them, I can barely see Chris and Amy entering the forest on the other side of the meadow. They must be going to the shuttle. Amy had an idea for another test or something. That's it. That has to be it.

I don't follow. They would see me in the meadow, and it's not safe anyway. Following them, unarmed, alone, is quite possibly the stupidest thing I could do right now.

And yet I almost have the chutz to do it anyway.

Instead, I slink back to the colony. I tell myself that all I'm doing is checking in on my people, but the truth of the matter is that I'm waiting for Amy to return. And trying not to think about what Amy and Chris are doing. Alone. In the dark. *Together.*

I skip the buildings filled with snoring Earthborns, but there's at least one of my people awake at every building I visit. I find Heller, one of the former Feeders, perched on the stoop outside his building, staring up at the sky. Behind him, I can see the sleeping forms of nearly two dozen people. It's not comfortable, but we've done the best we can, using clothes and blankets to create beds and covers.

"I can't quit thinking about her," Heller tells me in a low voice as I pass by.

I very much doubt he's thinking about the same girl I can't get out of my mind, so I ask, "Who?"

"Lorin." The first girl killed on the planet, the first casualty from an alien threat we cannot identify. "She was a good person. She didn't deserve to die."

"I don't think it works that way," I say.

Heller shakes his head. He keeps staring up at the night sky, and I wonder if he's looking for *Godspeed* and wishing he'd never come here in the first place.

After I make my rounds, I sneak back to the front of the colony and the first building, where Amy lives with her parents. I peek into the window of Amy's room, but she's not back yet. How long have they been out there? Has something gone wrong? I don't know what fills me with more dread—the thought that something's happened to them or the thought that they're just enjoying each other so much that they can't be bothered to return.

Something glows on the other side of Amy's house. I duck back down, sneaking to a window that will give me a clearer view of what's happening.

"I'm sick of lies," Amy's mother, Dr. Martin, says. I couldn't possibly agree more. I stand on my tiptoes, trying to get a better view of their conversation.

"No more lies." Colonel Martin's voice sounds sincere. "I've only been trying to follow my orders."

"You and your orders." Although exasperated, Dr. Martin sounds as if she understands her husband. "So this is what it's all about?"

The lights inside the building shift, and I see something small and flat that seems to glitter despite the darkness. . . . I gasp aloud, then clap my hands over my mouth. *The scale.* This is the thin, flat scale I found in the tunnels, just before Chris pulled me out.

"Who would have thought something like this would be so valuable?" Amy's mom says, marveling at it.

"I think—" Colonel Martin pauses abruptly. "What was that?"

I strain my ears and hear what made Colonel Martin stop. Footsteps, from the other side of the building.

"Probably just Amy coming back," Dr. Martin says. The glowing light goes dark as Colonel Martin covers up the scale.

I rush as quietly as possible around the building. I'm just in time to see Chris and Amy turn to face each other. I slink back into the shadows.

"Thanks for walking with me," Amy says. "And, you know. Earlier."

Earlier? *Earlier?* What happened earlier?

"Don't mention it. And . . . er . . . " Chris shifts uncomfortably.

And then—

—he bends his head down toward Amy—

—shuts his eyes, leaning in close—

My fingers curl into fists as I see red. I'm going to rip that frexing guy's head off—

Amy steps back, gracefully dodging Chris's attempt. "Friends, remember?" she says gently.

My hands go slack. I've been such a chutz.

Half of Chris's lips twitch up in a grin. "Yeah," he says, "friends." He watches as she disappears into the building. But I can tell by the way he stares after her that he would do anything to make Amy redefine the word *friends*.

45: AMY

I wake up well before dawn the next morning. The floor is hard and cold, but that's not why I couldn't sleep. I don't need my sleeping bag. I need Elder. My memories of last night bring an immediate, silly smile to my face.

I pull back the curtain of my tent wall when I hear low voices.

"Morning, sunshine," Mom says softly when she and Dad notice me. "Want coffee?"

I nod, yawning as I make my way over to the table. Mom dips a metal collapsible mug into a bucket of cold water, then mixes in a pouch of instant powder.

"Almost like home," Dad says, clinking his own collapsible mug against mine and taking a swig of the "coffee." He makes a face I can't help but giggle at.

Breakfast is dehydrated rations in FRX-marked packs. Powdered eggs mixed with water and biscuits that are more like crackers. I wonder how many dehydrated packs we have. The Earthborns have used them sparingly—and out of sight of the shipborns, who've shared their rations of wall food.

Dad dunks his "biscuit" in his "coffee," something he always did at breakfasts back on Earth.

"Well," Mom says, wiping crumbs from her shirt, "I'm heading to the lab."

At the mention of this, I think about what I discovered last night, with

Chris. The words are on the tip of my tongue, but at the last moment, I bite them back. I'm not ready to tell them this. Not yet. I want to tell Elder first.

Dad peers outside, then calls back to Mom, "Chris isn't here. I'll escort you to the lab. Amy, are you going?"

I'm not—but I follow them outside to say goodbye just as the suns start to rise. Around us, we can hear signs of others waking, soft chatter and shuffling as people greet the new day. It's amazing to me how quickly we've fallen into this role of colonists. How quickly we've made this our home.

I smile.

And then the forest explodes.

Dad acts first—he throws Mom and me to the ground, covering our heads with his massive, strong hands. The air burns white hot over the forest, and the ground beneath our feet—solid stone, sturdy—rumbles and shakes. I can hear screams and shouts of panic, sounds echoed by my own heart as I whip my head around, wondering where Elder is. A high-pitched ringing pierces my eardrums, and I don't know if it's coming from the explosion or if this is a sign that my eardrums have ruptured.

A cloud billows over the forest, blotting out the suns and casting a dark shadow over the whole colony. Chunks of stone and whole trees fall from the sky like hail. The big pieces rain down in the forest, but even here, in the colony, dirt and charred remains of trees clatter down on the stone path.

"What the hell just happened?" Dad roars. The military starts to assemble around him just as another, smaller explosion erupts like an aftershock, shaking the remaining treetops.

I cannot rip my eyes away from it. The big, black, scarred earth.

Right where the shuttle used to be.

46: ELDER

The military tries to stop me, but—short of shooting me or tying me up and leaving me behind—they can't. As soon as the explosion goes off and I realize what's happened, I race out of the colony and toward the shuttle. Amy's been at the lab with her mother every morning. Every frexing morning. If she was there *this* morning—my heart bangs against my ribcage, and my eyes burn. She can't have been.

I catch up with Colonel Martin and his task force before they reach the forest.

"Where's Amy?" I ask, panicked and breathless.

Colonel Martin stares at me as if he doesn't understand my words. "Amy?"

"Yeah, is she okay?"

"Amy's fine. She's not here."

My knees go weak at his words. *Thank the stars!* Colonel Martin shoves past me, not bothering to waste the time it would take to send me back to the colony, and I get a hold of myself enough to follow him toward the site of the explosion. We move forward, the acrid smell of smoke burning our noses and blurring our eyes.

We continue as a tight group, me in the center. Everyone except me has a gun out, and they use the guns like eyes, always pointed forward.

When we reach the blast zone, the smoke billows around us, making it almost impossible to see. My eyes water as we creep forward, and I've never been more grateful for wind than when a breeze dilutes the smoke, making the world visible again. The trees are nothing but charred, blackened sticks in the ground. The ground itself is lumpy, like freshly plowed soil, but scorched and marred.

We stop when we see the shuttle.

The elegant, smooth lines of the shuttle have been ripped into three sections. The bridge is the farthest away but least damaged, as if a child snapped it off and tossed it into the trees. The rest of the shuttle is split in half longwise, the roof blown apart like a blossoming flower made of burnt, smoking metal.

"Spread out. Look for casualties. Look for perpetrators. Look for evidence," Colonel Martin orders.

The ground directly under the shuttle—the blackened, burnt sand that was turned into glass by the rockets of the shuttle landing—is cracked open and shattered, little beads of charred glass no longer with a trace of the suns' light in them. I wonder if the explosion made the glass break or if the aliens used the glass already here to set off the explosion.

I avoid the empty shell of the shuttle. It is ragged metal edges and burning aftermath. The cryo chambers are all blown apart, the glass boxes shattered and strewn everywhere. The gen lab is split nearly evenly in half. The embryos of animals from Sol-Earth are gone. I can see the heavy cylinders cracked open, leaking yellow goop and little beans of fetuses on the burning ground. The incubators—the scientists had started making horses and dogs— are burnt to a crisp.

Most of our food supplies were there. Irreplaceable equipment. And—the realization hits me like a punch in the gut—Harley's last painting, the one he made for Amy. Amy had brought it with her but kept it in the shuttle. For safety. Nothing but ash now.

I stumble and nearly fall over a heavy metal plaque. A double-winged eagle and the word *Godspeed* engraved on one side. The nameplate of the shuttle. Scorch marks along one side, making it illegible.

It wasn't much, but the shuttle was my last tie to *Godspeed*. It was the last piece of the ship I had. The last remnant of the place I called home.

And now it's gone.

I flip the nameplate over with my foot. Under it is a perfectly curved piece of glass.

I pick up the glass carefully. Once it's out of the debris, I can see that it's a globe. I don't remember anything on the shuttle in this spherical shape.

The light catches it just right, and I see the swirling liquid gold inside. The solar energy.

Shite.

"Colonel Martin?" I call nervously.

One of the other military men looks up at me. When he sees what's in my hand, he shouts for Colonel Martin and races to fetch him.

The ball of glass in my hand is about the same size as my head, but I can tell that it's made of thinner glass than the cube Amy has. I have no doubt in my mind that it will break—it's a miracle it hasn't broken already.

"Son of a—" Colonel Martin curses when he sees me. "Why did you pick that up?"

"I didn't know what it was . . ." I say. My hands are slick with sweat, making the glass ball even harder to hold.

"Put it down . . . gently . . . gently . . . " Colonel Martin says. "Back up, everyone."

Out of the corner of my eye, I see everyone else nervously moving back, looking for cover. I bend at my knees, bringing the glass ball down as carefully as possible. An inch above the ground, I hesitate. My face is less than a foot away from a glass bomb, the same kind that must have been used to blow up the entire shuttle.

"Careful," Colonel Martin calls.

"I *know*," I snap.

The glass ball makes a soft *clink!* when it touches the ground.

I step back. It rolls a few inches. Everyone gasps, but the ball stops as soon as it reaches level ground.

Once I'm behind a tree, Colonel Martin takes his handgun out of its holster and points it at the ball. He pulls the trigger.

The glass ball blows apart like a punctured balloon, the energy inside it bursting forth in an explosion that momentarily blinds me. Blinking, I look at the damage.

A two-foot crater is all that remains.

Colonel Martin strides forward, scowling at the debris. He swears, long and loud.

"Right, men," he commands. "Now you see what we're up against. Keep looking, and be careful."

They disperse.

Colonel Martin moves over to me.

"That proves it," I say. "This is the work of the aliens."

He doesn't answer.

"Do we have any weapons that would match something like that?"

He turns to the remains of shuttle. "If we did, they're gone now."

Frex. He's right. The shuttle housed the armory. The only weapons we have left are the ones the men are carrying.

"Good thing this happened so early in the day," Colonel Martin says. "There could have been massive casualties otherwise."

Amy. Amy had spent nearly every day in the gen lab, with her mother. I shut my eyes, and I see her in the explosion, just as I did the second the bombs went off—her caught in the middle of the ship as it's torn apart, her burnt beyond recognition.

"We have to do something," I say, emotion making my voice as ragged as the edges of the shuttle.

Colonel Martin looks me right in the eyes. "I know."

I used to think that Orion's warning about us becoming slaves was the greater possibility, but I'm starting to believe Colonel Martin's determined to turn us into soldiers instead.

47: AMY

I push through the crowd waiting on Dad and his men to return. But it's not Dad who emerges from the smoking forest.

It's Elder.

When my eyes meet his, we rush to each other. Elder crushes me in a hug so fierce that I'm left breathless.

"What happened?" I ask when he finally releases me.

"Your father wants me to bring everyone out."

"Out? Where?"

He looks grim. "The compound."

I nearly stop then, I'm so surprised. "But Dad—"

Elder shrugs. "He told me to get everyone there."

"*Why?*"

He shoots me an inscrutable look. "I don't know."

Everyone grows more anxious as Elder gathers us all together and leads us away from the forest and past the lake. Once the compound is in sight, the nervous energy has made us all as combustible as the bombs that ripped apart the shuttle.

Chris stands outside the communication building. "What's going on?" he asks Elder as we approach. He looks tired and dirty.

"I don't know," Elder says. "Didn't Colonel Martin tell you?"

"He just said to meet you here."

Dad strides out of the forest then, followed by the men he took with him to the explosion. He doesn't speak until he reaches Elder, Mom, and me. He looks a bit surprised to see Chris, but he doesn't comment on it as he presses his thumb over the biometric lock. When it flashes **HUMAN**, the door unlocks. He motions for Elder to join him, but I walk right in behind him, looking at Dad defiantly and daring him to exclude me. When I go through the door, Mom follows, then Chris. Dad opens his mouth—to kick us out, I think, but with a look of defeat, he just closes the door.

"What is this, Bob?" Mom demands the minute the door locks behind us. Through the big glass windows, I can see Dad's military directing people to the far side of the compound, just off the asphalt.

"Maria—" Dad starts.

Mom looks as if she would very much like to hit Dad. "*This* is the compound you told me about? Why didn't you tell me it was so—so advanced?!"

"I had orders."

"Orders! Screw the orders! I'm your *wife!*"

Dad crosses the room and grabs hold of Mom's hands. "Maria, let me explain."

She rips her hands out of his grasp and throws them in the air. "Fine! Explain!"

Dad heaves a sigh. "This compound was built by the first colony from Earth." Mom opens her mouth to shout something else, but Dad silences her with a look.

"The first colony encountered . . . problems. Aliens. Highly intelligent, aggressive aliens. They killed everyone in the original colony. And it's clear that, since we've landed, they're intent on doing the same to us."

Mom opens her mouth again, but Dad raises his hand to silence her. "We had trouble establishing contact with Earth, but last night my tech crew figured out how to amplify the signal. We were able to send one message through, and we got one message back."

"You did?" It's Chris who's spoken this time, his voice shocked. Dad smiles at him, and I can't help but wonder if the two of them, both military, know something that they're not telling us.

"We were able to tell Earth that we had landed and were being attacked by the native population. And Earth sent back an answer."

Dad turns to the touch screen panel on the communication bay and swipes it to life. After scrolling through the menus, he brings a block of text up on the screen, then steps back. We all crowd around it to see.

Message received.
Aid deployed; estimated TOA five days.
Station contains life support for five hundred humans
and a weapon to eliminate threat.

We each notice a different thing. Chris asks Dad about the weapon that's big enough to "eliminate threat." Mom asks about the station. Elder asks about what kind of aid is being sent.

But me? I'm stuck on the first line. *Message received.* Dad spoke to Earth . . . and Earth responded. I breathe a sigh of relief I didn't know I'd been holding.

"Here's all I know," Dad says, stepping away from Chris, Elder, and Mom as they barrage him with questions. "There's an auto-shuttle under the compound, and it's designed to ship cargo—and people—to and from the space station over the planet. It isn't large enough to hold all of us, but we'll send the most at-risk, the weakest members of the colony, the ones who can't fight. And a few of the military, arms specialists who can inspect whatever weapon the FRX has made at our disposal."

"What is this weapon?" Elder demands immediately. Chris watches us all silently, an unreadable look on his face.

"The message came with instructions on how to remotely detonate the weapon from the communication bay, but I don't like how little information the FRX has given us. I'll have my men tell us more after they inspect it."

The others all have more questions, mostly about the weapon, but I have just one.

"When?"

The word slices through the chaos, and everyone stills to listen to Dad's answer.

"Now."

48: ELDER

Amy grips my hand so tight that I lose the feeling in my fingers as Colonel Martin uses the voice amplifier to explain the situation to the crowd outside—that we weren't the first humans to land on Centauri-Earth, that the others were killed by aliens who want to kill us too.

The sky is a cloudless blue, the air mild and calm, the trees vibrant—but no one sees this. They still see the dark gray smoke, they still hear the explosion. I watch my people's faces carefully as Colonel Martin tells them that they'll be relocated to the station. I can tell immediately that some of them—many of them—are happy to hear this. They want safety, and to them, living in space is safe. They cannot wait to go to the station. It won't be *Godspeed*, but it'll be better than this planet. At least to them.

But more of them balk at the idea. And that gives me courage.

"Once aid from Earth arrives," Colonel Martin calls over the loudspeaker, "we will have some options. Those in the station will be able to board the next interstellar ship immediately."

There's confusion over this, and Colonel Martin quickly clarifies. "Back to Earth. You will have the option to return to Earth."

This is something else entirely. Many more of my people aren't happy about this. If going to the station means they have to go on to Earth, they are far more reluctant to do that. At least this planet is theirs; Earth definitely is not.

I step outside the communication room to help control the crowd. As soon as I do, my people descend on me like birds of prey.

"They can't make us go!" one of the former Shippers shouts in my face. "This planet is our home, and they can't make us go!"

"It's for our safety!" another man counters.

"And for our children," says a nearby woman.

"Ain't safe nowhere!" a Feeder shouts. "Might as well be here as there."

"We can't trust the FRX!"

"Sol-Earth don't care about us!"

"But we can't stay here!"

"Enough!" I shout as loudly as I can. I grab the voice amplifier from Colonel Martin. "No one is *making* you go!" I shout into it, and my voice is enough to drown out the crowd. "But if you *want* to go—the option is there."

Someone yells from the center of the crowd, "What will you do?"

"Me?" I say into the voice amplifier. My words sound brittle coming from the gadget, and I wish—again—that the wi-coms still worked. Colonel Martin frowns at me. "I'm staying here."

Cheers—and shouts of protest—break out over the crowd. They're already dividing themselves between those that want to stay and those willing to go. I cannot help but feel triumphant at the number of those who don't care about the danger, who are willing to fight to claim what's theirs.

"Silence!" Colonel Martin shouts into the voice amplifier. The crowd settles—but they're still muttering and worried. Colonel Martin switches to the radio at his shoulder, giving instructions to the military, then he goes inside the communication room to the control panel. I watch as he punches a series of buttons and dials. Outside, the ground rumbles, and the crowd screams, thinking this is another aftershock of the earlier explosion. Amy and her mother rush to the window of the building, the first time Amy's left my side.

Outside, the asphalt runway shifts, opening like a hinged door on a pair of hydraulic lifts. A grinding sound leaks out from under it. I watch, open-mouthed and wide-eyed, as a humongous shuttle rises from the ground. It looks like an oversized fighter jet with a fat, pregnant belly under sleek wings. The bulbous underside of the shuttle opens up as it rolls forward onto the asphalt, exposing hundreds of human-sized vertical boxes. The panel closes, leaving only the shuttle and the runway.

Colonel Martin said it was an auto-shuttle, designed to use homing signals to fly straight up to the station and back to the compound here, but all I can think about is whether or not it can take a detour, to *Godspeed*, so I can save my people still trapped on the ship. From the size and shape of it, I think it must soar like an airplane until it reaches atmo, then shift its rockets down to reach orbit.

While Colonel Martin's explanation of the situation and my words did little to make the crowd outside calm, the presence of the shuttle silences everyone.

Before, it was just words. But this is reality.

The auto-shuttle represents a parting of ways. Some will leave, and we'll never see them again. They'll go to Sol-Earth, a whole separate planet, and they will no longer be a part of our colony.

Colonel Martin strides forward. Using the military to take count, he organizes which of the "civilians" should enter the shuttle first. Pregnant women are instructed to leave and able-bodied men to stay, but families and friends don't want to be divided. They hang back or refuse to separate, while others, more eager to go, take their place.

Sorting who will go and who will stay seems to take forever. Finally, people are sent to the shuttle. The small vertical boxes I noticed earlier are lined up in the belly of the auto-shuttle, each one designed to hold one person.

"They look like the automatic racks that dry cleaners use," Amy says, a high-pitched, nervous giggle escaping her lips.

The first people get in. A small ledge sticks out in the center of each box, similar to a bicycle seat. Straps pull down over each person's chest and waist, securing them to the box before a thin, transparent, plastic door seals them inside.

"See?" Colonel Martin calls to the group of nervous shipborns as he loads up the first round of Earthborn scientists into the auto-shuttle. "Nothing to be afraid of."

After the first row of individual compartments is filled, the next one drops down automatically. My people move forward nervously, hesitant to trust another ship, one they don't know.

Just as some of my people draw closer to the auto-shuttle, I notice how others slowly separate from the group, stepping back. Their eyes keep going to the left, past the trees and the lake, where the ruins are. Where their home is.

Hours go by as the shuttle's loaded. Amy stands beside me, watching, an unreadable expression on her face. I touch her hand, but she jerks it away. A worrisome feeling I can't name starts to gnaw at the inside of my stomach. She . . . she couldn't be thinking about leaving me, could she?

When there are two spots left in the rockets, Colonel Martin stops taking volunteers.

There's a roaring in my ears. Something's wrong, but I can't quite pinpoint it.

Colonel Martin walks over to the communication building, where Amy and her mother and I are standing.

Oh, no.

He holds his hand out to Amy's mother. "It's time," he says.

She nods.

They both turn to Amy.

"It's time to go," they tell her.

And then I realize: they want to send Amy back.

49: AMY

I knew this was coming.

As soon as Dad started talking about who would stay and who would go, I knew what he expected of me.

They want me to go.

I glance at Elder. A look of dawning horror grows on his face as he realizes what Dad means to do.

"Amy." Dad's voice is stern. "Come on."

I hesitate.

"It's not optional this time. I'm not giving you a choice. You're going on the auto-shuttle." He pauses, searching my eyes. "It's for your own safety."

I step forward.

Elder makes a sound as if he's being choked, and he lunges toward me, but I'm already out of his reach.

All the sounds around me fade to background as I approach the massive auto-shuttle. I know what I must do, I just don't know *how* to do it. I can see the people inside their individual transport boxes, staring at us through the clear, thick plastic that seals them inside. The little boxes don't look comfortable, but the journey won't be long. Just a short trip up to orbit, then to a space station. In a few days, another ship will arrive, and it will basically zap everyone waiting at the station back to Earth.

This—all of us, packing ourselves up into boxes and returning to space—feels like running away.

I don't like that—it's as if the aliens have won. They didn't want us here, and they chased us off their planet.

I feel dull and senseless as we stop in front of the transport boxes. Out of the corner of my eye, I can see Elder. He looks pained and wounded.

My heart aches for him. I didn't even tell him what I planned to do. But it's too late now.

"I'll go first," my mother says, stepping forward. Dad nods in agreement. Mom looks up at him, an expression I can't read on her face. "Let me tell Amy something." When he doesn't move, she adds, "Girl talk."

Dad steps back.

I look into Mom's glistening eyes. I think about the words I have to say to her, the way I have to break her heart. I reach to my neck, pulling out the little gold cross that, three months ago, I took from her cargo box. "This is yours," I say. "I'm sorry I took it." I start to undo the latch.

She touches the cross, pressing it into the skin on my chest. "Keep it," she says. "I've known you had it since you passed out from the flowers. It's yours now. My mother gave it to me, and now I'm giving it to you."

"Mom, I can't—"

She nods, and I think she understands what I cannot say.

What I cannot do.

She steps away from me, smiling, her eyes watery. Then Dad straps her into the transport box and seals it shut.

He turns to me.

"I'm not going," I say.

I take a step back—toward the crowd, toward Elder.

"What did you say?" Dad already sounds angry.

"I'm not going." I don't leave any room in my voice for doubt.

Dad strides forward, twin infernos in his eyes. "For *him?*" he asks furiously, pointing over my shoulder to Elder. "Are you throwing away your family for *him?*"

"No," I say, and the answer is enough to shock my father from his rage. "I'm not staying for him. But I'm not going to go for you."

"I will make you go," Dad says, grabbing my arm. He yanks me a few paces closer to the auto-shuttle before I have a chance to jerk my arm free.

"You can try," I say, retreating several steps. "But I will fight you every step, and I will find a way to come back here."

"You're going back to Earth!" Dad shouts. "You're going where it's safe!"

I laugh, a bitter bark sound that sounds ugly. "It isn't safe anywhere. You want to know what I learned in the three months I was awake and you weren't? That's pretty much it."

Dad looks as if I've slapped him across the face. "You're going," he says. "We all are. I'll go up as soon as the mission is done here. We're going to be a family. Together."

"You were willing to give me up once before," I say.

"And what? Now you're willing to give us up?"

The words cut into me, make my heart bleed. But I step back again, farther away from the auto-shuttle. I glance over Dad's shoulder, at Mom in her transport box. She smiles at me again and mouths three words. Even though I can't hear them, I know what she's saying—*I love you.* I touch the gold cross around my neck and mouth the words back to her.

Then I turn from my father and walk away.

I stand beside Elder. I don't look at him, I don't look at the crowd of people behind us. I watch my father. I wait.

He's madder now than I've ever seen him before.

But he turns to the controls in the asphalt and starts the process of launching the auto-shuttle. Without me.

I watch Mom, who stares at me with sad, forgiving eyes. A *whoosh* comes from the pipes plugged into all the boxes—oxygen for their journey to the space station in orbit over Centauri-Earth.

Something in Mom's face changes.

A small red light starts flashing on the control box at Dad's hand.

A knocking sound diverts my attention. *Bang! Bang! Bang!* People in the transport boxes beat against the plastic sealing them inside.

Horror washes over me.

The transport boxes jump on their tracks as the people inside shake and pound at the plastic, trying to get out.

My face whips around to Mom. Her mouth is hanging open oddly, as if she no longer has control of her facial muscles. Her eyes are staring straight ahead. Empty.

"Something's wrong!" I scream, running forward. "There's something wrong with the air!"

Dad's cursing, trying to make the controls work, but that little red light just keeps flashing, and the gas—the gas that I fear is not oxygen at all—is whooshing inside the sealed transport boxes.

I hurtle myself against Mom's transport box with all my might. The plastic bends but doesn't break, doesn't unseal. "Open the boxes!" I scream. "Open them all! It's poison!"

"I can't! I can't!" Dad shouts, pounding against the control and cursing.

I use all my strength to pull against the box door. My fingernails break off, but I don't care. I can't get it open, my mom's inside, and she might already be—

A loud hiss erupts from the boxes, and all five hundred open at the same time.

"Mom!" I scream as a wave of the gas that had been inside the transport box washes over me. I collapse, dimly aware of my senses deadening. Dad rushes to me, picks my head up from the ground. Elder's on my other side.

"Amy? Amy?" Dad asks, shouting in my face, but the gas has made me frozen.

I can't move.

Everything seems so

slow.

I've felt this before.

Like living underwater.

The sky is so blue.

Daddy. Daddy yells at me.

I wonder why.

There's Mommy.

She's quiet.

Still.

50: ELDER

Screams and shouts erupt around us as people rush to the transport boxes, trying to save the people strapped down.

But it's too late.

They're all already dead.

I don't need a sample of the gas to know that it was a high concentration of Phydus that killed them—and since the lab in the original shuttle is gone, we couldn't test a sample anyway. But Amy's reaction tells me all I need to know. I kneel beside her. In my head, I know there's nothing to do but wait for the effects to wear off. But my whole body is shaking with fear. She could have been inside one of the transport boxes. She could have been . . . I taste bile and swallow it down. I can't break down because of what might have been.

Colonel Martin checks Amy's mother's vital signs before collapsing at her feet, but it's as I feared. She's gone. Her mouth and eyes are open, as if she were screaming, but it's too late. She's dead, the same way Eldest died and Lorin—an overdose of Phydus.

Any doubt that the aliens on this planet have access to Phydus and know what it does evaporates.

They killed four hundred and ninety-nine people in one fell swoop.

The medical doctors who weren't packed into the transport boxes—only three left now—are racing from person to person, trying to see if anyone is alive. Some of my people, panicked by the massive death toll, race to the ruins, screaming. Some of the military dispatches, trying to keep everyone together and at a safe distance from the transport shuttle. The gas is gone now and only oxygen blows through the vents, leaving just the trace of a sticky sweet scent in the air before evaporating.

Chris moves beside me; I hadn't seen him approach. He looks stunned, and he struggles for words as he stares down at Amy's body, hardly even noticing those who actually died.

I watch her too, even as I take in the chaos that surrounds us. She stares vacantly ahead. Right at her mother.

I know exactly the moment when the drug wears off. I can see the look in her eyes change from empty idleness to dawning horror at the sight of her mother's dead body. She curls up, a gasping, choking sob escaping her lips as she clutches her father and cries. A part of me rejoices—the drug didn't kill her, didn't deaden her mind—but part of me wishes she could be spared the pain of her mother's death.

"We're too much in the open," Chris says, looking up. The blue sky feels ominous, as if the pteros could just swoop down out of the sky or the aliens could attack us at any moment. We have to get out of here.

"The ruins?" I ask Chris. My eyes flick to Colonel Martin—he should be giving the orders now—but he's crouched in front of Amy's mother, sobbing. I am surprised by the cold, emotionless part of me that's detached itself from sympathy.

Chris frowns, thinking.

I answer my own question. "It won't be safe there," I say. "The—aliens, whatever is attacking us—they blew up the shuttle. They're trying to kill us all, and they *must* know where the ruins are. They could be waiting for us."

"It's that or nothing," Chris says grimly. And he's right. Where else can we go? To the forest—where the flowers make us sleep and the pteros fly overhead? Here, in a wide, open space where already five hundred have died?

The ruins aren't much, but they're the only place of security we have, and the stone walls might provide us with some cover.

It'd mean returning to walls, but what other option do we have?

I rush to the communication room and grab the voice amplifier. People have scattered already, some panicking in the woods, some just *running*, and I hope my words can reach them all.

"Everyone! Go back to the ruins! Do not stay in the open! Get to the buildings!"

Through the big glass window, I can see a shift in the group as they swerve back the way we came, toward the ruins. The military acts as one, rounding people up and herding them to the relative safety of the stone structures.

Chris is trying to talk to Colonel Martin, but none of his words are breaking through his grief.

"Amy," I say, "we have to go." I grab her by the elbow, but her arm slides out of my grip like water streaming through a sieve.

I seize hold of her again, sure of my grasp, and yank her up. She stumbles, but I don't let her go. "There's nothing we can do!" I shout, hoping she can hear my words through her sorrow. "We have to go."

Colonel Martin stands too. We've made it halfway across the compound when Amy gasps and turns back. "We can't leave Mom!" she says wildly, turning her head to her father. "We can't just leave her there!"

Chris wraps his arms around her to keep her from running back to the auto-shuttle. "We have to," he says, gasping as he struggles to hold her back.

"We can't leave her!" She reaches blindly for her mother.

"Amy." Colonel Martin's voice is heavy and broken. "We have to go."

She sags, the fight leaving her so suddenly that Chris staggers under her weight.

"Follow me!" I call. My heart breaks at the way Amy's entire body is limp with grief. We start out across the meadow after the group heading back to the ruins. Soon we're running, Amy's steps only occasionally tripping when her eyes, blurry with tears, don't see a root or stone.

When we reach the first building, the one that had become Amy's home with her parents, Amy collapses in one of the little camp chairs the Earthborns had packed with them, crying softly. Colonel Martin turns to Chris and me. His cheeks are sunken, dark circles under his red-rimmed eyes. He's shaped his grief into battle-ready armor; he looks more deadly and dangerous in this moment than I've ever seen him before.

"I'm sending out a group of military to scout the nearby area, to look for anyone who got lost in the panic, with orders to capture any sentient alien life-forms they can find." He glares at Chris, a wild fierceness in his eyes. "Is there *anything* you can tell me about what attacked us, anything that can help us track them down and kill them all?"

Chris shakes his head mutely.

I narrow my eyes, unsure why Colonel Martin thinks Chris is the expert on this.

"Is there anything you're keeping hidden?" I ask. We don't have time for secrets and subterfuge. If there's any other information that can be helpful . . .

"You know what I know," Colonel Martin replies. "Earth is sending aid. We only have to survive a few more days, a week, max."

I snort. "Oh? Well, they killed off a third of us in one morning. A week shouldn't be too hard."

5 1 : AMY

I try to look interested.

I try to care.

I *should* care.

I was prepared to say goodbye to my parents. I *did* say goodbye to Mom. And when I did, I never expected to see her again. She'd go to the space station and from there back to Earth. It was a forever sort of goodbye.

But there's a difference, isn't there? Between saying goodbye and death.

Dad and Chris and Elder argue about something. The weapon on the space station, the Hail Mary that's supposed to be able to wipe out the aliens and save us all. Elder and Chris don't want to use it. They say we don't know what it is, how much damage it will cause. If it kills the aliens, couldn't it kill us too?

But I don't think Dad cares about that sort of thing anymore. About casualties. Not now that Mom's become one.

At one point, Elder brings up our idea that there's something still on *Godspeed*, some sort of clue that will tell us what the aliens are and how to defeat them.

"I don't need any damn clues," Dad growls at him. "I don't care what the aliens are. All I need is a big enough gun to kill them all. And that's what I've got on the space station."

"You would commit genocide?" Chris asks softly.

"They would do the same to us."

Elder tries to bring me into the conversation. Maybe I could soften Dad, make him listen.

But I just stare at the floor.

"I'm so sorry," Chris tells me as Dad dismisses him and Elder.

I look right through him.

Sorry? It's just a word.

Elder doesn't use words. He just wraps his hand around mine and pulls me until I stand. He keeps pulling, and I stagger behind him. At the doorway, he stops.

"I thought I was going to lose you," he says softly, not letting go of my hand.

Like I lost my mother.

"Amy," he says, and then he waits until I meet his eyes. "I can't lose you. I can't ever . . . "

But death doesn't work like that. It doesn't care if someone loves you, doesn't want you to go. It just takes. It takes and it takes until eventually you have nothing left.

Elder seems to realize that nothing he says can penetrate the darkness that has wrapped around me. He just tugs me closer to him, and he wraps his arms around me, and he holds me up while I sag against him, biting my lip as hard as I can to keep from crying because I'm afraid if I do, I'll never ever stop.

After a long time, Elder says, "Do you want me to stay?" He glances past me, at Dad. "I will, no matter what he says."

I shake my head and step back from him. Elder squeezes my hand one last time, then disappears into the night.

Then it's just me and Dad in this cold, stone building, made by people long dead.

Dad hugs me, and we stand together like this for a long time. And even though we hold each other tightly, it still feels as if there's something between us, something that makes us unable to really reach each other. And I realize there *is* something between us, something that will always be between us: the ghost of Mom's memory, reminding us of what we've lost.

Dad goes to talk with the military. About guns, and how many remain. And how to arm the big one on the space station.

And then it's just me.

I sit on the floor and pull my knees up under my chin. The .38 digs into the soft skin of my belly, and I pull it out, staring. Inside it are five hollow-point bullets . . . the only bullets I have left.

I set the gun down beside me. I wore it before because it made me feel safe and it appeased my parents' worry. But now I think about those five bullets and what they can do. It is no longer simply a precaution. I intend to use them, and I will.

I understand the part of my dad that wants to kill the aliens, even at the price of blowing up the whole planet with them.

I hug my knees, burying my face in my arms.

This room feels very large, and I feel very small.

52: ELDER

I know what I have to do.

The question is: can I?

I wait until night falls. The entire colony has spent the day fluctuating between tension and grief, fear and panic. The military is on edge, more people than usual during each shift of patrols.

But I know I have at least one ally.

Chris.

He might not be my favorite person, but he was with me when I argued with Colonel Martin and I know that, like me, he'd do anything in his power to protect Amy.

He waits for me about an hour after the suns set. "What have you got planned?" he asks me softly as we head down the path through the colony.

"Neither of us wants Colonel Martin to play around with whatever bomb the FRX has up at the space station, right?" I ask him.

Chris nods. "I don't trust the FRX."

"Good," I say. "Neither do I."

We sneak through the alleys of the colony, then I duck behind the first row of buildings so I can get to Amy's window. Chris frowns at me—Amy was too caught up in grief earlier today; how can we expect her to help now? But I can't imagine doing this without her.

"Amy," I hiss. I think Colonel Martin is assisting with patrols, but I don't want to risk it.

Amy sits in the center of her room, her knees drawn up to her chin, her eyes sunken and hollow. But she looks up at me and, after taking a deep, shaky breath, stands and crosses the room to the window.

Her eyes spark with curiosity when she notices Chris standing nervously behind me.

"What's going on?"

"I have a plan," I say. "Come with me?" I try to hide the hope and trepidation in my voice. Amy has every reason to say no—her mother just died, and we're all scared of whatever the aliens are planning for us next.

But a moment later she's lifting herself up on the windowsill and jumping outside.

"You okay?" I whisper.

"No," she says simply.

It is the honesty of this statement that makes me know that although all of this has cracked her, she's not broken.

"But I want to do *something*," she says for my ears alone. "I can't stand the thought of being alone right now."

"That something you want to do," I say. "It's not the same plan Colonel Martin has, to detonate whatever weapon that is up in the space station, right?"

Amy gives me a look that is wholly her. "Of *course* not," she says. "I'm not Dad."

"Let's go," Chris says, looking around. Helping me now isn't exactly against Colonel Martin's orders, but getting caught would lead to questions he probably doesn't want to have to answer.

I lead them both in the direction of the probe, not bothering to sneak through the tall grass of the meadow. Two guards are on patrol on this side of the colony, but they don't dare stop us. We are the leader of the shipborns, the daughter of the colonel, and a soldier—they have no reason to doubt us. We walk straight toward the compound as if we've been ordered there, and the guards don't even stop to ask questions.

I let out a sigh of relief when I see the outline of the giant auto-shuttle on the compound—and no guards. I glance at Amy. Her eyes are glass, her face slack as she stares at the rows of boxes, each carrying a person, one holding her mother. I touch the back of her hand, and her watery eyes focus on me. "I'm okay," she lies.

We may have made it through the colony without arousing suspicion, but if Colonel Martin or any of his people were to see us *here* under the shadow of nearly five hundred dead people, they wouldn't let us pass just because we pretended to have confidence.

"What's the plan?" Chris whispers. I pull out the glass cube Amy gave me earlier and use it to light our way to the communication room, covering it so only a dim glow escapes. I hold it so tightly my fingers ache, trying not to imagine just how much damage it could cause if I dropped it against the cement floor.

Chris stands back, looking around us nervously as if expecting Colonel Martin—or worse, the aliens—to show up. Amy presses her thumb over the biometric scanner. It flashes **HUMAN** and unlocks. It's not until the door is shut again that I feel safe to speak in a normal volume.

"Here's what we know," I say. Our faces are lit eerily by the glass cube on the floor between us. "We know that the aliens are smart, and they have better weapons and technology than us."

Amy stares over my shoulder toward the auto-shuttle. Chris just watches me.

"But we don't know what they are. We've never seen one. We don't know what their weaknesses are. And while the FRX has promised us a weapon that can kill them, we don't know what the weapon is."

"Which is why it's so dangerous," Chris adds.

"I agree," I say. "A weapon that can wipe out an entire alien species? Why wouldn't it wipe us out too? Or destroy the whole planet? It's not safe to use something that powerful that we don't understand."

"So—what? What are we going to do?" Amy asks.

"Not 'we.' Me. I'm going back to *Godspeed*."

Amy's eyes widen and her mouth drops open. Chris just stares blankly at me. "How can going back to the ship do anything?" he asks.

"I have very good reason to think that the ship holds the answers we need. First, the drug that was used to kill . . . " My voice trails off as I glance at Amy.

"The drug used to kill my mother," she states flatly.

"And the others, yes. I want to know how we have that same drug on the ship. And Orion's last clue that makes me think the answer to everything is still on *Godspeed*." I pause. Outside the window, the auto-shuttle looks huge and dark. I try not to look at the hundreds of dead bodies still strapped inside the transport boxes.

I turn to Chris. I don't want to confess this to him, but I have to. "Also, I left some of my people on the ship." I think about the video feed we saw before. I hope I'm not too late. I hope Bartie's kept the black patches to himself. "I can bring them back here, along with more supplies. We need their help. We barely have any food left."

All of that was stored on the shuttle.

"You're going to take the auto-shuttle?" Amy asks. "What about . . . " She swallows, and when she speaks, there's an odd tremor to her voice. "What about the people in it now?"

"I thought . . . " I force myself to look her in the eyes, to recognize the pain I find within them. I know of no way to make her feel better about what's happened, but at least I can give her some peace. "I thought I'd release them to the stars."

Amy bites her lip and looks down, then nods.

"But . . . how can you take the auto-shuttle?" Chris asks.

"It's automatic, right? I don't have to actually fly it."

"Yeah," Chris says, "but it's designed to go between here and the space station. Nowhere else."

I nod. "I'm hoping I'll be able to reprogram it," I say. "There is—we found live video feed of *Godspeed* being sent here. If we can manipulate the signals to reprogram the auto-shuttle to go to *Godspeed* rather than to the space station—"

"Then you can fly there, get the information you need, and return with your people," Chris says, excitement rising in his voice. "Yeah, I think that could work!"

"And Dad won't set off the weapon, not when there's a chance your information could stop the aliens without resorting to it," Amy adds. She pauses, determination flashing in her eyes. "We won't *let* him set off the weapon, not till you're back."

"Let me work on the programming," Chris says, striding toward the control panel. In a few minutes, he has the screens lit up and is typing rapidly.

"Wow, you're good at this," Amy comments.

Chris pauses without lifting his fingers from the screens. "Oh, it's not that complicated," he says. Soon he steps back. "Okay, I've got it! You should have no trouble getting the auto-shuttle to *Godspeed*."

I take a deep breath. "Good. Let's do this."

Amy looks anxious. "That's it? You're going right now?"

Chris looks at the two of us. Even though he's just triumphantly programmed the auto-shuttle and is helping us to find a way to stop the aliens without relying on some mysterious FRX bombs, he looks defeated. "I'll go prep the shuttle," he says, leaving us behind in the control room.

Amy grabs both of my hands tightly. "You come back to me," she says, the words fierce. "You do whatever it takes; you come back to me."

"I will," I say.

"I mean it." Amy says forcefully. "I've lost nearly everything else I love; I can't lose you too."

"I'll always come back to you," I say, pulling her close.

She kisses me, and just as I'm about to lose myself in it, I taste salt. I step away from her and see that she's crying again. I wipe away one tear with the pad of my thumb, and she swipes her arm over her face, embarrassed.

We walk to the shuttle, Amy a few paces behind me. I can hear her sniffling, trying to cover up the tears she can't keep from falling.

Chris pushes a button on the controls embedded into the asphalt by the auto-shuttle, and the transport boxes disappear, metal panels automatically enclosing them with a reverberating slam. Next, he motions for me to follow him to the front of the shuttle, where a small metal ladder extends up into the bridge. "It looks like you're right; everything *should* be automatic," he explains. He says this as if there's no doubt in his mind that I'll be able to fly myself into orbit around Centauri-Earth, but there are worry lines at his eyes and every muscle is tense. "There are simple flight controls in the bridge and a manual override if things go wrong."

I nod, trying to look confident. Landing the shuttle from *Godspeed* was automatic too, and three people died.

"When I was looking at the bridge, I discovered this," Chris says, drawing me around the corner of the ship. "An emergency distress rocket. It's designed as an escape for one person, in the event something malfunctions with the ship. It only has two settings—to go to the space station for aid or to go back here. If something goes wrong, just get in the distress rocket and come back."

I look up at the escape rocket. It's claustrophobically small, a paper airplane in comparison with the auto-shuttle. It looks like nothing more than a ridged bump under the bridge of the auto-shuttle, and I somehow doubt it could ever survive detaching from the auto-shuttle, much less a journey through space.

Chris steps back, giving Amy and me privacy again.

"Promise," Amy says, wrapping her pinky finger around mine. "Promise to come back."

I look her right in the eyes. "I promise."

53: AMY

As I watch the transport shuttle roar to life and shoot away, an ominous feeling sickens my stomach. I am hollow inside. I try to shake off my worries, but all I can think is, *That was the last time I'll ever see Elder.*

"Colonel Martin will be here soon," Chris says. "He can't have missed that."

"Let him come," I say. It's too late. Elder's already gone. I move to the communication bay, waiting for Elder to start talking to us over the radio. Chris stands by the window, waiting for Dad.

Sooner than I'd expected, Chris says, "There's Colonel Martin."

I squint through the glass but can't make anything out.

"There." Chris points, but it's just darkness and shadows to me.

I turn back to the control panel. A warning flashes over the communication link with the auto-shuttle: Launch in Process. I don't want to distract Elder when he needs his attention on the controls.

I glance back to the window, and I finally see what Chris is pointing at. Dad, and about ten other men, all with guns, running toward us.

"Great," I mutter.

A moment later, I hear Dad's voice booming, so loud that it's like the glass and walls aren't between us. "Come out now!" he orders. "The building's surrounded."

"He doesn't know it's us," Chris says. There's real fear in his voice. The glass cube is still illuminating the room, but the shadows it's casting must have made it impossible for Dad to see inside. I go over to the door and throw it open. For a split second, I can only hear the metallic rattle of nearly a dozen guns aimed at me.

"Dad, will you put the guns away and be quiet?" I say impatiently.

"*Amy?*"

"Yes. Now put the guns down and come inside before the aliens see us out here!"

Dad curses roundly, and he and his men crowd into the communication room. "Do you really need everyone here?" I ask. "Wouldn't these people be better off guarding the colony?"

Dad turns back to the military with a command, and one woman and one man break off from the rest of the unit while the others return to the colony. "Amy," Dad says, turning to me. "What the *hell* are you doing here? And where did the auto-shuttle go?" He eyes Chris, and there is such furious rage in his look that I'm afraid Dad's going to punch him—or worse. "What did you tell her? What did you do?"

"It was Elder's idea, Dad, not Chris's." I can feel the fight rising within me. Dad might object, but Elder's a leader, too, and in this case, he was right. We shouldn't rely on weapons from the FRX. And although Dad will never admit that Elder might be able to save us, I believe he can.

Dad looks around him. "Where *is* Elder?"

I point out the window, toward the far-distant stars. And even though I'm proud of Elder in this moment, it's not until now that I realize just how out of reach he is. It takes a moment for Dad to realize what I mean.

"Did he go to set off the weapon?" he asks. "That's a damn stupid thing to do! We can operate it remotely, right here from the compound. I was only going to send a few arms specialists there to inspect it."

"No," I say, squaring my shoulders. "He went back to *Godspeed*."

"What? Why?!"

I try my best to explain the clue, and the fact that the people on the ship need to be saved before the engine goes into full meltdown, and that they can bring back supplies for all of us. I can see that Dad thinks we're being foolish and wasteful and that the only answer that could have brought him any happiness would have been if I'd told him that the weapon was launched and targeted at the aliens right now. He doesn't care so much about our survival, not compared to revenge.

"That isn't going to save us, Amy," he says, glaring at me. "We need to get rid of the alien threat once and for all. That weapon—"

"Is something you don't even understand," I say, cutting him off. "All you see is the possibility of destroying the aliens. You're not even thinking that it might hurt us too! What kind of weapon picks and chooses who it kills?"

Dad opens his mouth to protest.

"At least let Elder try to find more information," I say. "There's a chance he can figure out what the weapon is and how it works—*then* we can detonate it."

"The aliens have killed a third of the colony already," Dad says. He stares at me with hard eyes. "They've killed a third of our *family*."

"You think I don't know that?" I'm barely able to get the words out.

"How are we going to protect ourselves while that boy is up there playing the hero to the ship that should have landed with the shuttle?"

That? That I don't know.

54: ELDER

The auto-shuttle ascends much faster than I would have thought possible. It climbs higher and higher until I'm competing with the falling suns—as they sink below the horizon, I shoot above it, leaving the whole shuttle in perpetual twilight until I break atmo. My stomach jerks and my hair lifts as I rise slightly from my seat before the grav replicator kicks on.

My heart thuds around inside my chest. *I'm going back to Amy,* I tell myself over and over. It's not just a promise to her; it's the vow I make for myself too.

The auto-shuttle slows as I hit orbit. A flat screen on the control panel lights up. A red bar of light illuminates the curve of the planet on the lower half of the screen and two blinking dots above that. This must be some sort of locator system. **Interplanetary Preparation Station—Centauri—FRX** flashes under one dot. **Unidentified Orbiting Satellite** is under the other.

That must be *Godspeed*. Downgraded from ship to satellite, nameless.

I peer out the window of the bridge. When the shuttle from *Godspeed* landed, I remember seeing a bright flash against the horizon. As I squint into the star-speckled darkness now, I see neither the space station nor *Godspeed*. From the looks of the locator, I'm between the two.

The control panel lights up again, flashing a message:

Manual Input Required

Beneath that, I'm given the option to direct the auto-shuttle to *Godspeed* or
the space station. Briefly, I consider going to the station. What *is* the weapon
there? Could it really eliminate the alien threat? It can't be that far away,
despite what Colonel Martin's said.

But then I remember Bartie and the black patches, and I know even if I
could wipe out the aliens and keep the planet for myself, I have to get to *Godspeed* first. But before that, I have one more task to do.

The ship is silent, and that seems appropriate. I click open the panel of
controls. It still looks intimidating and complicated, but I'm looking for one
thing specifically.

Finally, I find it. A tiny label. **Cargo Evacuation.**

I close my eyes after reading the words. Amy was once labeled as nones-
sential cargo, and I promised her that she was so much more than that. But
the four hundred and ninety-nine dead bodies in my cargo hold cannot hear
my promise now.

First, I flip the switch to undo the safety harnesses around each body, then
I open the doors of the transport boxes in the hull. The grav replicator affects
only the operational level of the auto-shuttle, and the bodies below deck float
effortlessly into space. The release of air causes the bodies to drift, like lotus
flowers floating in water, toward the cockpit. Weightless, the bodies rise from
the bowels of the ship past the window before me. I recognize individual faces
as they waft up before floating into the abyss of space. I try to say a silent
goodbye to each of them, the Feeders who had only a few months without
Phydus before being overdosed by it, the women who came here to give the
babies growing inside of them a home without walls, the Shippers, the workers in the City, the engineers, all of them *my* people, gone. But I won't forget
them. I force myself to say their names aloud, memorize each one—Rhine and
Lucien and Cessy and all the rest. I will never forget them.

Four hundred and ninety-nine people.

I lean up, pressing my face against the window as I seek out individuals,
begging each person to forgive me for my part in their disastrous end.

A flash of red glints out of the corner of my eye, and my head whips around.

Amy's mother.

Her pale skin and red hair are just like Amy's, and though her eyes are open, she is too far away for me to see the green that lies within, though I know it's there.

Amy almost entered the five-hundredth chamber. If she had . . .

Amy's mother's body moves like a dancer in the weightlessness of space. Her arms stretch out, pale skin against the blackness of the universe, and I imagine that starlight makes the golden highlights of her hair gleam.

I stand there, watching the bodies float past, until the very last one is gone, and all that's left in the sky are stars.

My eyes are burning and watery as I sit back down in front of the control panel. I touch the **Unidentified Orbiting Satellite** dot on the locator screen. From the edge of the cockpit window, I see rockets burst along the right side of the auto-shuttle as it slowly turns around. More rockets kick on, and I soar closer and closer to *Godspeed*.

Soon I can see it.

Godspeed looks ravaged. The shuttle's gone, of course, and the Bridge is nothing but mangled ruins. Still, my heart sings as I peer down at the ship I thought would be my home forever.

The auto-shuttle gets closer and closer—so close that I start to worry it won't stop and I'll just crash right into the ship. Instead, the rockets reverse thrust, and the auto-shuttle stops. I'm still several meters away from *Godspeed*, but I'm close enough that my window is filled with the image of it.

The red-and-white location system flashes a message: **Destination Arrived.** Another panel lights up. **Disembarking Process Initiation.**

Frex. I hadn't thought of this. The only door to the outside of *Godspeed*, the hatch from which Harley threw himself, was a part of the shuttle that landed on Centauri-Earth, the same shuttle the aliens just blew up. The auto-shuttle is designed to automatically dock in the space station.

The problem?

I'm not at the space station.

Beep, beep-beep! My wi-com jumps to life just as I'm pondering whether I'll be able to connect to the hatch inside the koi pond. I touch my neck. I'm close enough now to pick up the signal directly from the ship, just as I'd hoped.

"Com link req: Bartie," I say.

I wait, a silly grin plastered on my face.

"Elder?!" a voice—Bartie's voice—says into my ear.

"Hey, Bartie," I say.

"The *frex!* Elder! What? How?!"

I'm so happy I laugh out loud. Bartie's not just the rebel who took control of the ship after me. He's my friend, the one who used to chase rocking chairs with me across the porch of the Recorder Hall.

"Doesn't matter how," I say. "I just wanted to see if the new leader of *Godspeed* would be willing to let the old one back on the ship."

After a moment's pause, Bartie barks with laughter. "Good one! Tell you what, you figure out how to get up here, and we'll throw you a party."

"Start baking a cake," I say, grinning widely. "Because I'm already here."

55: AMY

Dad keeps us close to the trees as he escorts us back to the colony. Part of me wants to fight him on this point, stay in the communication room. What if Elder needs us? He's farther away from me now than he's ever been before—the least I could do is keep the communication link open. But Dad leaves one of his military guards there and the rest of us return to the ruins.

I wish we could take the quick way, straight through the meadow and up to the buildings. But it feels so *exposed* going that way, and while the trees are dark and dangerous, they give us the illusion of safety. I keep my eyes cast down. Every shadow reminds me of Elder, each warm breeze that brushes against my skin makes me wish I could fly up to him.

A light spritzing of rain starts to fall.

"Be careful of the flowers," Dad whispers to me. I'd almost forgotten about the purple string flowers. I watch them out of the corner of my eye. As soon as water touches the delicate petals, the flowers unwind in an elegant twirl, blossoming into a beautiful, nearly transparent bloom. So beautiful . . . but I remember the way they made my mind go numb, the way I couldn't move my body. One of the flowers hangs low, nearly at the level of my face. I grab it and crush it in my hand, the purple petals sticking to my skin.

We creep back to the ruins. Everything is silent. The air is pregnant with expectation, as if the silence is just an indicator of something worse to come.

Dad doesn't speak to me again until we're in the building, safe from the pteros and the aliens who must control them somehow through the gen mod material. Chris follows us inside. Dad starts to object but then gives up, collapsing into the same chair he sat in just this morning, dunking a cracker-biscuit in his "coffee" as if everything was normal.

And I guess that in a way, everything was. We still had Mom.

And I still had Elder.

My eyes burn. I look away. I cannot let myself crack.

"We'll have to go into hiding," Dad says heavily.

I look up at him.

"If we're waiting to detonate the weapon, we'll have to go into hiding. Only for a few days, a week maybe. Until the aid from Earth comes."

"What's wrong with the buildings?" I ask.

Dad shakes his head. "The aliens know we're here. They can attack us anytime. The only weapons we have are the ones my men carried with them — and once the ammo runs out, there will be nothing left." Once he lets his words sink in, Dad adds, "Got any ideas?" I look up — but Dad's asking Chris, not me.

Chris shakes his head. I look down at my hand, stained purple from the flower I crushed earlier. "The flowers," I say.

They both turn to me.

"The purple string flowers," I repeat, excitement growing in my voice. "Dad, what if we made a weapon using those? They knocked me out immediately! We could use them to make the aliens pass out if they get near the colony."

"*How?*" Dad asks, clearly frustrated with me. "Even if we got the flowers, they only bloom when wet. And even if we made them bloom, how could we force the aliens to sniff them?"

I pick the petals stuck to my hand off my skin, setting them in a little pile on my knee. "We could grind them up," I say, thinking aloud. "Throw the dust in their faces."

"While they shoot at us with exploding bullets," Dad says.

"We could hang them nearby, keep them wet with the water pipe from the lake. . . . "

"And they'll see them and hold their breath," Dad shoots back. "Or just attack us from a distance. We don't have time for this, Amy. We have to come up with a real plan."

"You could smoke them," Chris says.

For a moment, I have an image of rolling the string flowers into cigarette paper and lighting them up.

"I mean, we can use the smoke as our weapon," Chris says. "Not that *we* would literally smoke the flowers, but that we could blow the smoke on the aliens. They'd be forced to breathe at least some of the air, and hopefully the properties of the flower would still exist—perhaps even be stronger—in a smoke form."

"But you can't control smoke," Dad protests. "It can just as easily knock *us* out as the aliens. And we still don't know if the creatures—whatever they are—are affected by the neurotoxins in the flower."

But he's thinking about this plan, I can tell. He jumps from the chair and starts pacing. He pauses when he notices me watching, then looks straight into my eyes—the same jade green as Mom's—and says, "Your mother would like this plan."

"It could work," I say, hopeful.

Dad's voice is filled with doubt. "Your mother would know how to test the flowers and smoke, figure out the effects of it on the aliens. If she were here . . . "

"It's a better plan than trying to run," Chris says quietly. "Think about the way the aliens have been attacking us. They know what makes us weak— which means they probably share the same kinds of weaknesses."

It's not hard to be weak compared to an attacking ptero, but the aliens' interest in Phydus does make me think that Chris is right.

"I don't know. . . . " Dad starts to pace again.

"You don't think the aliens are watching us?" Chris says angrily. "They are. They're just toying with us at this point. Waiting. If we try to run, they'll mow us down. Our best bet is to be aggressive—they won't expect that. Do something, anything, to buy us time."

Dad glowers at Chris. I don't think he's used to having someone younger boss him around, especially not someone under his command. But whatever Chris has said is starting to crack through Dad's doubts.

"I think we should stay too," I add. "We've got a mountain to one side— probably not going to be attacked from that angle. They'll come from the front, and at least here we have stone walls to protect us."

"Against weapons that can explode a steel shuttle," Dad points out, but he's softening to the idea.

"Better than nothing," I counter. "Look, they hate us. They want to kill us. There're more of them, they have more supplies, and we have nothing. I've got five bullets in my gun. How many do you have?"

Dad frowns, and I know I've hit on his biggest worry. If we run, we can't defend ourselves. We just have to hope we can outrun them.

"We *can't* fight. We can't run, not really. We have to hole up here, where we at least have access to fresh water and the possibility of surviving an attack."

Dad snorts, a bitter facsimile of a laugh. "Survive?" He looks around at the old, dusty, yellow stones of the building. "That worked out well for the first colony."

Chris looks grim, and for a moment my father almost seems to regret what he's said.

I brush the little pile of torn purple petals into the palm of my hand. "This is the best chance we have," I say. "It's our only chance."

56: ELDER

"What?" Bartie says so loudly that it hurts my ear.

"I'm in a shuttle—not the same one we launched from *Godspeed,* a shuttle from Centauri-Earth—"

"How the frex did a shuttle get on Centauri-Earth?"

"Look, it's a long story, but—"

"What the frex are you talking about?!"

"Bartie! Calm down!"

"The frex ever! You're in a frexing *shuttle?* And you're *here?!*"

I grin. "Technically, yes."

"Technically? The frex is going on?!"

"Bartie, *listen.* I took a shuttle from Centauri-Earth—never mind how I got one, just listen—and I came up here. I'm right outside. I can see *Godspeed.* I'm almost close enough to nudge it."

"Frex!" Bartie exclaims. I would give anything to see his face right now.

"Now here's the tricky part," I continue. "I have a sort of tube thing that I need to connect to the ship. It's not exactly designed to go to *Godspeed,* but I think I can make it work."

"How . . . ? Elder, are you serious?" Bartie's voice is filled with incredulity.

"Very," I say. "You make sure the area around the hatch at the pond is clear. I'm going to see about the tube."

I disconnect the wi-com link and make my way from the bridge to the boarding chamber, which, according to the maps and diagrams on the wall, should have an automated connector I can use to get to *Godspeed*. My feet echo down the hall, and I feel very alone here.

For a moment, I wish I could have Amy with me now. The auto-shuttle is so massive and, after sending the dead to the stars, so empty. But I also know that this is something I have to do by myself—*Godspeed* is my responsibility, not hers—and she is the only one who could pacify the rage in her father's heart enough to quiet his desire for immediate revenge. That weapon from the FRX makes me nervous. We don't know what it is; all Colonel Martin's said is that it can be detonated remotely and it will wipe out the alien population. I half believe the FRX would be willing to wipe us out too, just to cut down on complaints.

The boarding chamber is just behind the bridge, just as the little map on the wall by the door indicated. The door has a seal lock, but it opens with a press of a button. On the wall to the right is a small cabinet filled with emergency oxygen tanks. To the left is a control panel. And directly across the door is my ticket off this shuttle.

I step inside. The boarding chamber is small, with a round porthole sealed with metal flaps taking up nearly the whole wall. A chart beside the large porthole illustrates how a tube made of some sort of metallic fabric will shoot out from the porthole into space and lock onto the side of the space station with magnetic-seal locks.

But I'm not trying to get to the space station. And *Godspeed* wasn't designed to work with the auto-shuttle.

I touch my wi-com and reconnect with Bartie. "Are you at the hatch?" I ask.

"Yeah," Bartie says. "Elder, are you really—"

"*Yes*, I'm here. If all goes well, you should be able to open the hatch in a few minutes, and I'll be on the other side."

"If?" Bartie asks.

"Don't break the com link, okay?" I run my fingers through my hair. "I'll need you to open the door for me if I'm on the other side."

"*If?*" Bartie repeats.

"Be ready, okay?" I mute him without waiting for a reply. I need to focus.

I turn on the control pad by the tube. The screen lights up immediately. Once I figure out the controls, I turn on the mechanical arms.

There's a grinding sound, and the tube starts to extend from the auto-shuttle. The screen shows an image of the area outside of the ship; there must be a little camera embedded into the tube door. The tube stretches out, closer and closer to *Godspeed*.

Matching seal lock not discovered, the display reads. **Automatic connection not detected.**

Of course it's not detected; we're not at the space station, we're at *Godspeed*, which doesn't have a matching seal lock. I pray that my guess is right and the magnets on this side are going to be enough to lock into place in *Godspeed*'s hatch.

Manual connection required.

I try to push buttons to operate the arms, but the same message displays across the screen: **Manual connection required.**

I check the display from the outside. It looks as if the mechanical arms have extended the tube, but the end of the tube is still several yards off from the hatch on *Godspeed*.

I go back to the control panel. Nothing works. Every button I push that would move the tube around just makes the screen flash the same message.

"How the frex do I make a manual connection with this frexing thing?" I mutter, staring at the screen.

The end of the tube isn't that far off. If I could just give the tube a good push to the right . . .

I go over to the porthole. The metal flaps closing the door are firmly shut.

If I open the door, the boarding chamber will be depressurized, and I'll be sucked out into space. Can't move the tube from here.

I briefly consider trying to move the ship. But the tube is off the hatch by no more than a few yards at best, and I don't think I can control the ship to move in such a small space.

I just need to wiggle the bridge, just a little, to make the end meet up with *Godspeed*'s hatch. The hatch on the ship side is much smaller than the opening on the bridge tube. All I have to do is get the larger end of the bridge tube to cover the smaller hole of the *Godspeed* hatch and the magnetic lock will create a seal against the ship's metal surface.

I bite back a little laugh.

All I have to do is somehow move a tube a few yards to the right. In the vacuum of space. Without a space suit.

Just to be sure, I check the rest of the transport shuttle, looking for an emergency space suit. The closest thing I can find are cans of oxygen strapped to the wall of the boarding chamber, but that does me no good. If I try to go into the vacuum of space breathing oxygen, my lungs will blow up like balloons and burst inside my body.

Staring at the tanks of oxygen gives me an idea, though.

A dangerous idea.

A *stupid* idea.

But an idea.

I know what I need to do.

I push my wi-com. "Bartie, you there?"

"I'm here, Elder," Bartie says. "Are you at the hatch?"

"Not yet," I say. "Look, it's a bit more difficult than I thought. I'm going to have to . . . anyway, listen. I need you to stay very focused and don't break this com. I'm going to try something. When I say go, start counting. If all goes well, before you reach thirty, I'll ask you to open the hatch."

"What happens if I get to thirty and you don't tell me to open the hatch?" Bartie asks.

"Nothing," I say. "Keep the hatch closed."

"And we'll try something else?"

"There is nothing else. I've only got one shot at this," I say. Bartie starts to protest and if Amy were here, she'd kill me, but still I add, "Please. I need to focus. I say go, count to thirty. Open when . . . if I say anything."

I head over to the emergency oxygen. Pressurized tanks are connected to tubes and face masks. I grab an oxygen tank and yank out the tube but leave the valve closed. I won't be able to breathe this in space, but I don't need the oxygen for breathing. I strap four tanks around my body, two at each hip. Each tank points down to the floor.

I head back to the control panel.

There's one button I didn't push. *Open Portal.*

Pushing this button will make the round metal flaps move away. It will open the door—and I will be sucked out into space. I'll have maybe half a minute, but probably less than that, to grab one of the loops on the inside of the tube and move the bridge over the hatch. There will be no oxygen—no air at all—and I would have no protection. And I know just how quickly someone can die from being in space without a suit.

I've seen it happen.

I suck in a deep breath. Shut my eyes. Blow out all the air in my lungs. Count how long I can go without breathing.

Twenty seconds.

My heart's racing.

I breathe in. Breathe out. Hold. Count.

Twenty-eight seconds.

I silently apologize to Amy.

That will have to do.

57: AMY

Dad consults with a handful of scientists who worked with Mom to see if Chris's theory of using smoke made from the purple flowers will work against the aliens. While the smoke seems even more effective at making *people* pass out, their study doesn't really tell us anything. The aliens *aren't* people. They have strange crystal-like scales and leave weird footprints. That's about all we know. We've never even seen them, let alone analyzed their weaknesses and susceptibilities. Maybe they don't even breathe. Maybe the purple flowers make them stronger rather than make them pass out. We don't know.

And that's the worst part of all this.

We don't even know who—*what*—we're fighting.

They know all about us, though, and exactly how to kill us.

"I don't like it," Dad growls at me as he sends five of his military to the forest to collect strands of the purple flower. "I don't like building the colony's entire defense around some *flowers*."

"Running away and hiding is no defense at all," I say. "We have to try."

"It will only work once—if it works at all," Dad says. "Once they see what we're doing, they will know how to avoid the smoke the next time."

"It only has to work once," I reply. "We only have to survive a few more days before Earth arrives, right?"

"And we might be able to take some hostages." Dad's voice is softer as he thinks aloud.

I hadn't thought of hostages.

I glance at Dad. I hadn't thought of Dad as the kind of person to take hostages.

Once we have enough of the purple string flowers gathered, Dad has his men start digging a shallow trench. The idea is that we'll load the flowers into the trench along with a fuse and if we see the aliens approaching, we'll light the fuse and smoke them out.

We rip up anything that would be flammable—paper, cloth, dried leaves— and roll it around in the sticky purple string flowers. One of the Feeders has a small jar of petroleum jelly, and we use it sparingly, spreading a thin coat on the flammable mixture so that the fire will burn hotter and spread quicker. It takes hours to set everything up and place it in the trench.

We're hoping that if the aliens are already watching us—which, let's face it, they probably are—they'll assume we're just making a runoff ditch or something similar. We're also hoping that the fuse will light up quickly, the wind won't blow the smoke back on us, and the plan actually *works*.

Basically, we're hoping for a miracle.

58: ELDER

"Bartie?" I say into my wi-com.

"Yeah, Elder?"

"Start counting."

I unscrew the tops of the oxygen tanks so they blow oxygen straight down. I hope to use them as jets to help propel me where I need to go, but the force isn't that strong, and the decompression of the boarding chamber will likely be more than I can handle. I bite back a grin, imagining how many ways Amy would call me an idiot if she saw me now.

No going back now. Breathe in. Breathe out.

Oh, stars, Amy, I'm sorry.

I slam my fist into the OPEN PORTAL button.

The metal panels on the opening to the bridge zip open and I hurtle into space. My vision is filled with chaotic flashes of the shiny metallic cloth of the tube. I tumble through it, banging against the side of the tube, praying I don't make everything worse. Things smack into my head—the loops of ropes along the top of the tube, used for handrails. My brain plays tricks on me: I'm flailing about, tumbling in every direction, but I feel as if I'm constantly falling down, a sick feeling in my stomach. Despite the fact that I can see the rippling cloth of the tube and feel the looped ropes, there's no sound. My brain is screaming at me: This is *wrong!* Everything is *wrong!*

The gaping maw of the end of the tube rushes toward me. Frex! *Frex!* The decompression of the boarding chamber was so much more violent and quick than I thought it would be. The tube is acting like a wind tunnel as the air from the boarding chamber pours out all at once. I twist my body, and the air rushing from the oxygen tanks strapped to my hips slows me just enough that I'm able to wrap my fingers around one of the looped ropes. . . .

My body feels puffy, my joints slow. The rope slips out of my grasp.

I scramble, trying to grab another loop.

My lungs scream at me. *Oxygen!*

I feel cold, and my mouth feels fuzzy. My vision is blurring.

My hands grab for another loop of rope.

No.

My shoulders ache. I feel as if I am being pulled apart.

I lunge, twisting my body. I can feel the oxygen tanks, still pouring air out against my legs, and they help propel me up—to the very last loop. I stick my whole arm through it and push my palms against the huge metal edge of the magnetic seal. I can barely see; my vision is red and watery.

But I'm almost at the hatch.

I shift, pointing my hips—and the oxygen tanks—down. The end of the tube moves to right. The hatch. I can . . . almost . . . My body feels as if it will break in half, but I reach for the hatch anyway.

I cannot hear the click of metal on metal because there is no sound in space, but I know—the magnetic seal locks into place.

But there's no air in the tube.

No air in *me.*

59: AMY

All that's left is to wait.

And so we do.

Dad distributes water—a bucket to each building, with a warning that going to the latrines might be dangerous. We finish the last of the rations we had stored in the colony by noon—all the rest of the food was in the shuttle. We thought sealing the things we needed the most, like food and medicine, behind the steel doors of the shuttle would make it safer. The irony of it makes me want to vomit.

There's only Dad and me in the first building. Without Mom, the building has no chance of ever becoming a real home, so for now it's our base of operations. All the military checks in with us here, for new assignments or permission to rest after patrol.

The nervous tension in the air is stifling.

We're all waiting—for an attack we aren't even sure is coming, against an enemy we've never seen, using a weapon made of flowers.

And, despite the waiting, none of us are prepared when the radio at Dad's shoulder crackles to life.

"We see them," the solider on patrol says over the radio.

Dad shoots up immediately and rushes out of the building, binoculars already in his hand. He scans the forest, but I don't need the binoculars to see the flashes of *something* emerging through the forest.

They're coming.

I squint, trying my best to see them. They're forest green from head to toe, so dark that they blend in with the trees. I don't know if they're made of dark green skin or if they're wearing something to camouflage themselves. Flashes of gold gleam around their waists—scales, like the one Elder described. The aliens are tall, but no taller than Elder, with smooth, bulbous heads and a big round eye that flashes when it catches the sunlight.

"Get inside," Dad orders. Over the radio he barks, "Prepare to light the fuse! Get the snipers on top of the buildings. This is it!"

I go inside, just like Dad said, but as soon as I reach my window, I lift up on the sill and jump out the other side of the building, just as I did when I snuck out to be with Elder. The thought of those nights makes me pause. If he were with me now like he was with me then, I don't think my heart would be racing with so much fear.

I force myself to focus on what's happening as I sneak around the wall. I'm not going to miss this.

I stick to the shadows in the corner, between the buildings and the mountain. The aliens creep closer. A part of me feared they'd be bug-like, crawling on the ground with spindly spider legs or slithering like a snake. But they walk with two legs and carry their weapons with two arms, just like us.

If we hadn't been watching for them, we might have missed them—maybe that explains why we've never seen them before. Their skin seems to shift, turning a lighter shade of green as they wade through the tall grass of the meadow between the forest and our homes.

They stalk closer and closer. A couple dozen, maybe thirty. That's all the troops they felt they needed against nearly a thousand of us. But they know—they must surely know—that of the thousand, only a handful are armed, and of those weapons, only a few bullets remain.

And then—I only see it because I am looking for it—a flash of light. The fuse is lit.

I hold my breath.

It works. The fuse flares brightly, and the fire catches quickly. Smoke wafts up and up, trailing through the sky, almost invisible.

This is it.

They're close enough to be seen clearly now.

They reach the smoke.

And they walk right through it.

It does *nothing*.

My eyes widen with shock, but the military scattered throughout the colony don't even hesitate. Pops of gunfire go off immediately—Dad's snipers, from the roofs of the buildings. Not a single alien falls, despite the fact that enough bullets are raining down on them to stop an army. I stare at the aliens incredulously—how is this possible? Neither the smoke nor the bullets stop them?

There's no way we can win this.

One of them lobs a glass bomb at the colony, and it shatters against the paving stones in the street, bringing down half the building I am standing beside with it. I can feel the rumbles through the stone as the mortar cracks and fails, the rocks tumbling down. If I'd still been inside, I would have been crushed.

"Fire! Fire! Fire!" Dad shouts from the street. More gunshots ring out as a bright, yellow, glowing object arcs across the sky toward the colony. Another solar bomb. It hits higher now, and there are screams as the people inside the buildings try to run away.

"Up the mountain! Farther up!" Dad shouts.

But I'm not listening to him.

I'm behind the building, and the path Chris and Elder and I used to sneak to the compound before is clear. No one's looking this way; the fight is focused on the streets and the center of the colony. I can go behind the latrines, cut down near the lake.

If I can reach the compound, maybe Elder can tell me what he's learned.

And if I can't reach Elder, maybe I can detonate the weapon that will kill the aliens.

I take a deep breath.

I have to make a run for it.

Another solar bomb goes off, this one behind me. The aliens are nearly at the colony's edge, lobbing their solar bombs as far into the buildings as they can.

I tell myself I can do this. I'm a runner. I can outrun an alien army.

And then I go.

60: ELDER

I wake up with four tanks of oxygen pointed at my face, blowing cool air right at me.

"Thirty-seven," Bartie says, leaning over me.

I blink.

"Shite, Elder, your eyes are red."

"His ocular blood vessels burst," a familiar voice that I can't seem to place says. "Subconjunctival hemorrhages."

My body shifts, but my shoulders roar in protest. I whimper, sinking back into the ground.

Doc leans over my body, concern on his face. He presses a med patch against my skin. I look through blurry eyes at my arm and see that three other med patches are already adhered there.

"What the frex happened?" I wheeze, my voice raspy.

"I counted to thirty, like you said," Bartie says. "But you never commed me."

"Then how?" I croak, unable to finish the sentence.

"I kept counting. I had my ear pressed against the hatch door. At thirty-seven, I heard a dull thud."

"You opened it?"

"I was scared as shite, let me tell you! But I figured I could close the hatch again if I needed to, and . . . "

I shut my eyes; the light hurts them too much.

The tanks aimed at my face sputter, then hiss into silence. I take a deep breath, imagining the last of their oxygen filling my lungs, filling my whole body.

"The effects of your little adventure should wear off in time," Doc says. "Your heart didn't stop, and although you exhibit signs of decompression sickness, you're surprisingly well kept for someone stupid enough to jump out into space."

I crack my eyes open, but I'm not looking at Doc. I'm looking at Bartie. "It worked?" I say.

He grins at me, and I see my old friend, the one I had when I was thirteen and neither of us thought a world existed beyond the ship. "It worked," he says.

I struggle to sit up, my shoulders throbbing, my skin too sensitive, my joints aching. I risk opening my eyes more fully and find that I am lying at the bottom of a hole that was once the pond. The hatch in the center is flung wide open. Bartie pulls me up so I can stand, and I peer down into the darkness. The tube from the auto-shuttle is securely locked in place. "I can't believe that frexing worked," I say, turning to Bartie.

He cringes. "Your eyes look like shite," he says, but he's grinning too, just as excited as I am. "I can't believe you had enough chutz to do that!"

I look around the ship. It's so much bigger than I remembered it, but at the same time, so much smaller. Everything looks exactly the same, but strange somehow. It's as if I stepped into my bedroom, and even though everything is exactly where I left it, I can tell a stranger invaded my privacy.

"Let's get you to the Hospital," Doc says. "I have some eyedrops that might help."

"I'm really thirsty," I say. I take a step and nearly fall over. Bartie grabs me by the elbow, holding me up, and even though I want to shake him off and tell him I can walk on my own, I'm not sure I can.

When we get to the Hospital, Doc hooks me up to a saline drip, despite my protests that I don't need it, and he shoots more medicine directly into the line. Then he hands me a small mirror so I can get a look at my face. There are bruises on my skin, and I can see little red strings of veins standing out. The whites of my eyes are completely red, as if they are filled with blood. No wonder Bartie kept mentioning them. Doc puts two thick, yellow drops of something in my eyes. It makes them burn, but he assures me it'll help.

"Dismissed," Bartie tells Doc.

Doc looks as if he's about to protest, but Bartie's face is unforgiving. I'd almost forgotten—Bartie is in charge of determining what punishment Doc should pay for the crimes he committed on the ship just before we left.

Doc carefully takes off his stethoscope and places it neatly on the table. He adjusts the medical instruments on the small table, checks my IV, nods once to me, and goes. Before he rounds the corner, two Feeders—they used to be butchers, before Bartie's revolution—start walking on either side of Doc, escorting him . . . somewhere.

I wonder if that's Doc's life now—a prisoner, until he has the rare chance to work his medicine. Does he have an apprentice who will take over after him, making his one skill redundant?

That thought reminds me of Kit, and when I think of Kit now, all I can envision is the way she died.

I swallow back my questions about Doc and his punishments. That's not important compared to the matter at hand.

Bartie pulls up a chair closer to me. "How did you know?" he asks.

"Know?"

"That the engine's failing. That we can't survive on *Godspeed*." Bartie states this with such sincerity that I know he's already come to terms with it, and with the black med patches.

I smirk at him. "Knew you couldn't handle the ship without me."

Bartie tries to laugh, but this is not something he can discuss lightly.

"It's because of Doc," Bartie says. "When he blew up the Bridge"—*killing Shelby and the others*, I think—"the engine was damaged."

"Damaged?" I ask.

Bartie nods grimly. "So you came to save us." There's a tone of defeat in his voice, one that I understand all too well.

"The auto-shuttle's big," I say. "We can put five hundred in the transport boxes and the rest in the cargo hold. There won't be much room for cargo, and in what room there is, we need to pack away every single bit of food we can. All our supplies on the planet were destroyed. Whatever we can take from the ship in terms of survival will make a huge difference for us all." I hesitate. "But you should know, the 'monsters' Orion talked about—they're very real, and they are very good at killing us. Before I came here, I released nearly five hundred bodies to the stars."

Bartie doesn't look at me when he says, "If it's a matter of dying here or dying there, I think I'd like to at least see the world first."

"You didn't always think that way," I comment dryly.

Bartie's gaze doesn't flinch. "That was before I knew the ship would fail so frexing soon."

I explain everything to Bartie, from Orion's dying words to the latest alien attack on the colony, my strength returning to me as the meds and fluids enter my system. I start with the destruction of the shuttle and the deaths of so many of our people. We continue talking as Bartie and I walk outside, to the garden. There are oddly few people here, but Bartie tells me that most tend to stay on the City side of the ship. There are too many dark memories leaking from the hatch in the hole that used to be the pond. People don't like to be reminded of the choice they made, the friends they let go.

We stop at the Plague Eldest statue, and both of us stare at it silently for a moment.

"It all begins and ends here, huh?" I can't tell what Bartie's thinking of, but I'm remembering the way I used to view the Plague Eldest, as if he was the model of everything I should be, an ideal I could only aspire to. But then I found out I was made of the same stuff he was and that it wasn't either of our DNA that made us the leaders we had to be for our ship.

It doesn't matter now. The Plague Eldest statue is only made of concrete, not replicated DNA and broken promises. The statue's face is worn away, rivulets embedded into his cheeks as if from tears. "He knew," I tell Bartie. "The Plague Eldest. He knew whatever it is that's down there. He *must* be the king Orion refers to with that clue, and the only thing missing from Orion's puzzle is information about who the aliens are and what they want. How to stop them."

Bartie looks doubtful. "You got all that from a scribbled-in illustrated children's book?"

I shake my head. "You don't know how Orion played with us. It was all a game to him, always a game."

"And this . . . whatever . . . that Orion has hidden is supposed to be some sort of way to . . . fight these 'aliens'?" Bartie sounds skeptical—of both the clue and the threat on the planet.

I sigh, looking up at the concrete face of the Plague Eldest. The truth is, I don't know. At all. Maybe it is. Maybe it's not. I wish Orion was here to tell me himself . . . but now it's too late. "I don't like your odds of survival." Bartie leans forward. "But I think they're better than ours." He jerks his head toward the statue of the Plague Eldest. "So what do you think is inside?"

"No idea," I say. "Maybe a vid recording or a book. Maybe another frexing clue that will lead us down another 'rabbit hole,' as Amy likes to say." I grin at him, but the smile's really for Amy, even though she can't see it. "Either way," I say, "let's find out."

61: AMY

I sprint to the meadow, dirt raining down on me as one of the glass bombs explodes in the hill above. I cover my head with my arms and run as fast as I can, holding my breath when the smoke blows in my direction. I hope the latrines can provide me with a little cover before I dash to the lake, then up and around the forest to the compound. If I can make it to the communication room, I can lock the aliens out. That was what the biometric lock was for, to make sure that only humans got through.

I think about the big windows in the communication building. I hope they're made of something stronger than glass, or else the aliens will just smash their way inside. I shake my head, refusing to think about this. I will go to the communication building, and I'll talk to Elder, and we'll figure out a way to stop the aliens, and everything will be fine.

I jog in place a few steps, ready to kick off and sprint to the lake, when someone grabs my arm. I nearly scream, but I'm yanked back, a hand covering my mouth.

"It's me!"

I struggle free and turn to see Chris, his blue eyes shining.

"What are you doing?" I gasp, slinking closer to the shadows at the latrines. The tall meadow grass does little to hide us.

"*Shh!*" He looks around him.

There's so much noise from the battle that I doubt anyone can hear us, but I lower my voice. "I was going to the compound," I say.

He nods. "Good idea. I'm going with you."

I start to protest. I was able to make it to the latrines because they're close and there was so much chaos. But there's nothing to cover me as I run to the lake, and two people will stand out more than one.

Chris raises his gun, a high-powered rifle. I pull out my own .38. If it came to bullets, I'd rather have another gun with me.

We both run straight for the lake. I keep turning my head, trying to see if anyone's following us, but there's so much happening at the colony that we're ignored. Smoke billows up from the first couple of buildings. My heart breaks for a moment. The aliens have completely breached the colony. A group of people are running up the mountain, a line of soldiers at the bottom, trying to protect them. It won't be much longer before they're all taken.

Or killed.

"Ready?" Chris asks when we reach the lake, his voice still low.

I nod. We don't have time to stop.

I've never run faster than now. There is no pacing to the way I run, no method. I just race, as fast and hard as I can, until I reach the asphalt of the compound.

Sweat drips off my body, making dark circles on the black asphalt. I lean over, my hands on my knees, gasping for air.

Chris stands at the communication room door. "What are you going to do?" he asks.

"See what Elder's discovered, first," I say automatically. If he's solved Orion's last clue, he might have the information we need to stop the aliens. And even if he hasn't . . . I want to hear his voice again.

"And then?"

"Activate the weapon, if I have to." I swallow hard. I don't want to be responsible for a genocide, even of alien creatures who are trying to annihilate us. But I'm not going to let them kill my father and my friends, not when I could stop it, not when they've already killed my mother.

I open the biometric lock, and Chris follows me inside, his rifle still at the ready. I holster the .38 and go straight to the communication bay.

My hair sticks to my brow, and my shirt is drenched. The air inside the communication room feels stuffy and humid. I lift my shirt away from my chest, flapping the cloth as I try to cool down. "I don't know how to operate any of this," I say, staring at the control panel.

Chris steps forward. "It's not that complicated," he replies. "I already programmed Elder's auto-shuttle into the network, here." He flips a switch, and static fills the air. Another press of a button, and a steady *beep-beep-beep* interrupts the static. "I'm hailing him. He should answer as soon as he sees my signal."

I move over beside him, looking down at the control. "I wonder which one of these operates the weapon," I say.

Chris looks at me with his startling blue eyes, an unreadable expression on his face. "I don't think it will be safe to detonate," he says. "We don't know enough about it."

My hands curl into fists. I remember Dad giving attack orders, but after the first bomb, I didn't hear him again. Is he, even now, gasping for breath, his blood leaking on the dusty yellow stones as an alien crows in triumph over him?

"What *were* those things?" I ask softly.

"They looked humanoid to me," Chris says. "Maybe they're not that different from us."

"Good," I say. "If they're not that different from us, they'll be easier to kill."

62: ELDER

Bartie glances up at the weathered concrete face of the Plague Eldest. "So . . . should we get some chisels and hammers?" he asks sarcastically.

"Oh, no. I was thinking we'd go a little bit bigger." I look past the statue, barely able to hide my excitement at my plan.

Bartie follows my gaze across the ship to the grav tube clinging to the side of the wall. His eyes round. "You're going to *smash* it?"

"Got a better idea?"

Bartie laughs. "I think it's frexing brilly."

It takes both of us the better part of a half hour to move the statue from its pedestal onto an electric cart. We use crowbars and wedges, but in the end, we both jump on the pedestal, pushing, before the whole statue crashes down. It lands on the electric cart with a thud and a crack. Bartie jumps down from the bench to inspect our handiwork.

"One arm broke off!" he says, picking it up and using it to wave at me. "Look, it's hollow inside."

The arm has exposed a narrow hole in the side of the statue, and it is, indeed, hollow inside. I try to wiggle my fingers in, but the concrete is thick, and without tools, there's no way to break it open.

"I guess we *will* have to smash it," Bartie says in mock reluctance.

"Such a shame," I comment.

"It's a great work of art."

I nod sagely. "It's a sacrifice we'll have to make."

Bartie's smile cracks through his false sincerity. "Come on!" he says, excited.

We practically run up the path between the Hospital and the Recorder Hall with the cart trailing behind us, but some of the fun of breaking apart the statue dissipates as I think about how, when I leave *Godspeed* this time, I'll never come back to it. I have been on this path countless times. I walked along it with Harley and Kayleigh, before they were both gone. I used to race it with Bartie and Victria. I kissed Amy, right there, by the pond, in the "rain."

I'm going to miss it. I thought I said goodbye to *Godspeed* when I left, but I realize now that I always believed *Godspeed* would still be here, that I would be able to look up at the stars and see it floating, a beacon in the sky, a reminder of the home I once knew. But now I know that this goodbye will be the final one I say to the ship.

Bartie and I have to shove the cart to get the statue fully under the grav tube. Bartie locks the cart down so it won't get sucked up, then orders the grav tube on at low levels. The tube sucks the statue up a few meters, enough for us to slide the cart out of the way.

"Would you like to do the honors?" Bartie says, grinning.

"Gladly." I push my wi-com. The familiar *beep, beep-beep* fills my ear, and although I once longed to hear it again, it sounds strange to me now. "Grav tube on, stationary transport to Shipper Level," I say.

The tube switches fully on, and the statue is sucked up.

"We better get back," Bartie says, pulling me behind the cart. "That thing's going to shatter everywhere!"

The statue soars up and up, scraping along the clear sides of the grav tube as the tube curves along the contours of the ship.

I push my wi-com button again. "Grav tube *off*," I say.

"Caution: transport material is currently inside the grav tube. Eldest override?" the computer voice in my ear says pleasantly.

"Override confirmed," I say, grinning. "Grav tube operations off."

The familiar sound of the tube cuts off suddenly. Bartie and I both look up. The statue stands, stationary, for just a moment, then plunges down, twisting in the tube. Some of the acrylic material of the tube breaks as the statue's edges crash against it. The statue picks up speed as the tube straightens out, nothing but a gray-black blur inside.

BOOM! The statue crashes into the grav tube base and *explodes*. Gray dust and chunks of chalky concrete fly everywhere, and Bartie and I both duck behind the cart as gravel rains down. Before the air is clear, I jump up, racing to the debris.

Amid the cracked concrete and broken grav tube, I can just make out a shiny silver box. I reach for it, gray dust sticking to the sweat on the back of my hand.

"What is it?" Bartie asks. His voice is low and breathless.

I lift the latch on the box, and the lid creaks open.

Inside is an old vid recorder and AV display, the kind they used before floppies. It's about the size of both my hands put together and is nearly an inch thick and heavy. Underneath it is a small book bound in brown leather. The pages are yellowed with age, but the writing inside is clear. A formula of some kind and detailed scientific notes.

"I haven't seen one of these in ages," Bartie says, picking up the AV display. "I think there are a few old ones in the Recorder Hall."

Bartie's right. No one's used this tech in a long time. Maybe not since the Plague Eldest.

The recording is labeled, a white note with handwritten information in black ink:

These are the original recordings collected by Captain Albert Davis, the first Eldest of Godspeed, *as he established Eldest rule. Additional copies will be passed down to each successive Eldest, and this will be preserved, hidden in the event of mutiny.*

Orion must have known two things when he left the clue for me in *The Little Prince*. First, that copy intended for the Eldests was gone. Second, that the original was kept here—probably another Eldest secret that never made it to my ears. I guess the Plague Eldest figured that if people ever revolted against the Eldest system, they would destroy his statue and discover the truth he hid behind his concrete heart.

I load up the AV display and hold it in my lap so Bartie can see.

A man's face fills the screen. It's a face that looks mostly like mine, but lined with age and worry. He's somewhere between Orion's age and Eldest's, maybe fifty or so, but he has a scar on one cheek that makes the left side of his lip hang down in a perpetual frown. His fading hair is peppered with strands of black, and he wears it cut short, but I can trace the angles of his face and know they match my own.

He is the Plague Eldest. The first of us. The original, from which I, Orion, Eldest, and all the others are just cloned copies. He might have "improved" on us over time, adding gen modifiers to our DNA to make us better, stronger, more monoethnic in appearance, more charismatic in personality. But I can still see myself in him.

"I'm afraid," the Plague Eldest says in a deeper voice than mine, "that this is the end."

63: AMY

"—lo?" Elder's voice crackles over the radio from the auto-shuttle. Chris and I both lunge toward it.

"Hello? Hello?" I say anxiously, my heart sinking as I envision every worst-case-scenario possible.

"Amy, is that you?"

"Yes!" I nearly cry with joy. "Elder, you're alive! I was so worried."

His laugh comes to me from miles away, but it's still *his* laugh. "Of course, I'm alive. What did you think happened?"

I can't even put those fears into words.

"Amy, I have to tell you—" Elder's voice pauses, and for a heart-stopping moment, I think our communication link has been severed. "I've found the last clue," he says.

I blink, surprised. He doesn't sound very happy about this. "You did?"

"Yes, and you're . . . you're not going to like it."

"What is it?" I ask. My mouth is so close to the intercom that I can taste the metal cover of the microphone. Chris moves behind me, and I nearly jump in surprise. Once I heard Elder's voice, I forgot he was even in the room.

"I think . . . I think I can show it to you. Give me a second."

Chris touches the screen on the control panel. "He must have a video he can show us," he says. "I might be able to help him load it from here." He swipes the screen, bringing up a menu.

"Are you okay?" I ask Elder.

"Yeah." He sounds distracted. After a moment he adds, "Why? Are you guys okay?"

I glance at Chris, who shakes his head slightly. We shouldn't tell Elder about the attack now, not when he can't do anything about it. Past Chris, I can see the trees of the forest and beyond that, a trail of smoke. Not from our smoke screen—something much larger is burning at the colony.

"Got it," Chris says, tapping on the touch screen as a video feed loads.

"Did it load?" Elder asks.

"Yeah," I say.

"You guys watch that; I'm going to go back and help with the packing. Everyone from *Godspeed* is coming down with me, and we're bringing supplies for everyone."

I look at the smoke again. There might not be anyone to give supplies to.

The intercom cuts out, and Chris moves aside, letting me have the chair in front of the touch screen. He stands behind me. He picks his rifle back up, casting a nervous look outside the window.

A man's face fills the screen. "That must be the Plague Eldest," I say aloud. I glance behind me at Chris. "He's the last captain of *Godspeed*, the one who decided not to land the ship when they arrived at the planet."

"I'm afraid," the man says, "that this is the end."

I lean forward, listening as hard as I can.

"My name is Albert Davis, and I am the captain of *Godspeed*. This is what happened."

The camera immediately shifts images. This footage was filmed in the Bridge. The image wobbles a bit as the camera is stabilized on the control panel. It sweeps the Bridge, showing everyone standing inside. This is before monoethnicity. The crew gathered on the Bridge are of several different races—and religions too, judging by the Hebrew star one of them wears as a pendant around her neck. My fingers go up to my own cross pendant, a small smile on my lips. It makes me happy to know that once, *Godspeed* wasn't as messed up as it became.

Everyone is chatting, but it's too soft to understand individual words. They seem excited or, perhaps, nervous. The camera swivels back into place, facing the planet.

Godspeed is in orbit now, hanging over the blue-green-white of Centauri-Earth.

"There it is!" a woman's voice says from behind the camera. A moment later, I see it too—a sleek silver shuttle, zooming over the horizon toward *Godspeed*.

The camera cuts to black, and I gasp in recognition as a new image fills the screen: the hatch where Harley died.

The camera is pressed against the porthole window, and the hatch is open, showing blackness.

"A little history," Captain Albert Davis says from behind the camera. His voice sounds bitter. "Twenty years before we were due to land, we sent a probe to Centauri-Earth. The plan was that we'd get an idea of the environment, adjust our studies so we'd be ready for the planet when we landed. Instead, Sol-Earth discovered that there were some valuable resources on the planet. And they figured out a way to make transportation there even faster. They landed first. They built a colony."

Something metallic lowers over the hatch. Not the door, but something cylindrical that locks onto the side of *Godspeed*. It's the bridge between the ship and shuttle that was shown earlier.

Captain Davis laughs bitterly. "And now they have to figure out what to do with us."

A tall, slender woman with jet-black hair and cheekbones sharp enough to cut glass steps out of the shuttle bridge and into the hatch, adjusting her tight pinstripe skirt. Captain Davis opens the hatch door after checking the pressure, and the woman steps out, smiling. Behind her, several men carrying thermal crates emerge from the shuttle. Captain Davis frowns at the crates.

"I would prefer our conversations be off the record," the woman says. Her voice is kind, but even I can tell this is an order, not a request.

After a moment of blackness, the camera switches back on. It's higher up now and stable—mounted somewhere, and, from the way the others ignore it, I suspect that the woman from the shuttle doesn't know it's there. Captain Davis has set up a meeting with her in the navigation room on the Keeper Level of the ship. Above them, light bulbs map the stars. A table is in the middle of the room, and Captain Davis sits opposite the woman.

"The original colony proved . . . difficult," the woman says.

"In what way?" Captain Davis leans forward. He is clearly someone used to having authority, but I can tell that the woman intimidates him. I notice a flash of silver on her lapel—a small double-winged eagle pin. She's the representative from the FRX.

"The solar glass this planet can produce has provided us with nearly unlimited pollution-less energy. It's revolutionized the way Earth produces and consumes energy; it's the answer to the prayer we've been saying since fossil fuels ran out."

Captain Davis nods solemnly. The woman has yet to answer his question.

"The problem," she says, sighing dramatically, "is that the original colony limits the type of production it's sending to us. We need *more*."

"More solar glass for energy," Captain Davis says, "or more for weapons?"

The woman's eyes narrow, but she laughs genially and waves her hand, dismissing the question. "I know you're opposed to the weapons manufacturing we've implemented, but rest assured that your people will not be asked to produce weapons. Just energy cubes, as we discussed before."

Captain Davis looks skeptical, but he doesn't comment again.

"As I've said, the problem is the production rate. Our people—the original colony and, when you land, all of your people—are having problems with solar radiation. Too much sun; it makes people sick."

My jaw clenches. This isn't true. We've been on Centauri-Earth nearly a week, and none of us have gotten sick from sun exposure.

The woman waves her hand, and the men who came with her from the shuttle appear, carrying the thermal crates. They open one of them and hand the woman a syringe filled with golden liquid.

"This is a genetic modification vaccination. I assume you're aware of gen mod material?" the woman asks.

Captain Davis nods. "The livestock were modified to better adapt to life in the bio-dome of the ship. We've used it sparingly on some crops throughout the years."

The woman smiles. "Gen mod material has been *enormously* helpful in this situation," she says. "We grafted a vaccination to solar radiation onto gen mod material. We simply inject a person with this vaccination . . . " She reaches for Captain Davis's arm, but he snatches it away. The woman laughs as if this were all a joke, but it is clear neither of them trusts the other. "Once someone is injected with the vaccine, it grafts to the person's genetic code, ensuring that not only will that person be vaccinated against solar radiation for the rest of his or her life, but all of their descendants will be born immune as well. One shot, and every generation that lives on the new planet will never have to worry about solar radiation again!"

Captain Davis doesn't speak.

"I've got enough vaccine for everyone on board *Godspeed*. I'll leave it here with you." The woman waves her hand again, and the men cover the crates and take them away. "Once your ship is vaccinated, we'll talk again and help you land the ship on the planet's surface." She looks around her, her eyes lingering on the curving metal ceiling. "I imagine you'll be glad to get off this outdated hunk of metal. Bit claustrophobic."

The image cuts to black.

"What is this?" I ask softly. "None of this lines up with what we thought happened. . . . "

Chris doesn't respond. I glance back at him. His jaw is fixed in a hard line, his startlingly blue eyes flashing. He looks *furious*.

The screen's image shifts, and I turn to it again. Now Captain Davis is in a laboratory—the gen lab, on the cryo level. Two men and a woman in lab coats stand around a young girl, maybe fifteen or so, with long dark hair and narrow eyes that remind me of the captain's. She sits on a chair in the center of the lab. Behind her, I can make out the Phydus pump—but it's not pumping Phydus. Instead, a large vat labeled VITAMINS AND SUPPLEMENTS stands next to it. Over the girl's shoulder are the cylinders of fetuses from Earth, but none of them contain clones of Elder. Not yet.

"Is it reversible?" Captain Davis asks one of the men in the lab co

He shakes his head. "From what we can tell, the 'vaccine' does nothing but turn a person into an obedient dog." He hands Captain Davis one of the syringes the woman with black hair gave him.

The man in the lab coat shakes his head sadly at the girl. "We'd tested it . . . we had no idea our volunteer would be affected in this way."

"Maybe you should have tested it before you accepted my daughter as your volunteer," Captain Davis growls. "You should have known better than to test it on a human subject so quickly."

The scientists look nervously at each other, all scared of the captain's wrath. The only person in the room who doesn't show any emotion is the girl. His daughter.

"We've isolated the compounds within the 'vaccines,'" the woman continues, her voice high and scared. "There is gen mod material there and another drug, one we've never seen. When injected, a person becomes . . . well, a person becomes this."

They all look at the girl on the chair. She stares vacantly back.

"What is this drug?" Captain Davis grinds out, furious.

"We're calling it Phydus. When taken orally or injected into the bloodstream, it makes a person temporarily obedient. When it's combined with gen modifiers, though, the condition becomes permanent."

"This is what the FRX wants from us. Mindless workers. Perfect slaves."
Captain Davis looks bitter and enraged. I think for a moment he's going to
punch his own daughter, but he spins away from her instead.

"You know from our communication with the first colony on the planet
that the FRX was pressuring them to increase production of solar glass and
make more weapons," the woman in the lab coat says. "After trade negotiations crumbled, we never heard back from the colony again."

Captain Davis gapes at the woman. "Do you think . . . the entire first
colony? They're already drugged into slavery? Transformed into something
not entirely human?"

"It must be," the woman says. She sounds as if she's about to cry. "Maybe
the FRX tricked them like they tried to do with us, calling it a vaccine. Maybe
the FRX found a way to force the drug on them. Either way . . . "

"Either way, it's too late for them." Captain Davis's face crumples. "And
her."

"We're working on a drug to inhibit the properties of Phydus." One of the
male scientists steps forward. "We might be able to find a cure."

Captain Davis whips around to his daughter, a sudden look of hope crossing his face—one that fades just as quickly. "And if we land and give the cure
to the first colony?" he demands. "The FRX will just do it again. They want
their glass, their weapons. There aren't enough of us, even if we joined forces
with the colony, even *if* we could cure them."

"If the FRX is that determined to control us," the woman says, "what can
we do to save ourselves?"

The camera shifts again. A group of people are at the table in the naviga-
tional room, deep in conversation.

"They voted," a young woman says. "The majority of the crew want to
land the ship." She is fierce, this woman, tall and dark with wild hair. She
wears vivid red, but everyone else in the room wears muted colors. And they
all already look defeated.

Captain Davis slams his fists against the table. "Don't they see the danger in that? Don't they see the terrible fate that's befallen my little girl? The FRX doesn't want a colony, it wants slaves!"

"We can fight—" the young woman starts.

"How? We don't have many weapons, not ones like the FRX has. If they can't control us with Phydus, they'll drop solar bombs on our heads." Everyone but the young woman seems to agree with Captain Davis.

"So—what? We're going to just stay on the ship? *Forever?*" she demands.

Captain Davis spreads his empty hands out in front of her. "What other option do we have?"

"We will fight," the woman in red says. "We'll fight *you* if we have to!"

"No," Captain Davis says simply. "You will not."

The image fades out, but it doesn't matter, I know what happened next. I can see it in my mind as clearly as the images on the video. Captain Davis uses Phydus—not the drug mixed with the gen modifiers that the FRX gave him, but a variation of it—to control the rebels and contain the ship. Fear of Phydus kept them from landing, then use of it kept them subdued.

This is where Orion's twisted mind latched onto the idea of us all being turned into slaves or soldiers. Because it already happened once before.

Suddenly, another image appears on the camera. No sound. Just the girl, Captain Davis's daughter. She looks leaner and fiercer, but at the same time, she's subdued, controlled. A tame lioness. She sits on the stool, staring vacantly ahead. I wonder what happened to her. I wonder if the Inhibitors ever worked on her.

The camera zooms in closer to her face. Her startling blue eyes. Such a strange color, almost clear, with irises . . . unusual irises . . . .

I've only ever seen eyes like that once before.

I'm suddenly aware that Chris has not spoken in a long time. I turn slowly.

His gun is leveled at my head.

64: ELDER

Bartie stands by the door to the bridge of the auto-shuttle. His eyes are still wide and disbelieving as the vid feed continues playing for Amy to see on Centauri-Earth. *Godspeed* is our—*his*—home. It's a spaceship, yes, but also part farm, part bio-dome, and all used and old and lived in. The auto-shuttle is made of gleaming chrome and white. It looks pristine, especially compared to us, covered in gray dust from the destruction of the Plague Eldest's statue.

His eyes linger on the window over the control panel. He's seen the stars and the planet once before, from the bridge of the shuttle before we departed. But since then, he must have given up any hope of seeing them again. There were no hatches, no workable doors on the rest of *Godspeed*.

"I'd almost forgotten . . . " he says, staring.

I grin at him. "Wait till you see it from the planet's surface."

I can tell by his face that he's not quite registered what's in store for him.

"We should leave as quickly as possible," I add, bringing us back to the serious task at hand.

Bartie makes an all-call to the ship's inhabitants, letting them know first of my arrival with a new shuttle and second that he's planning on moving everyone out to it. He gives orders to slaughter any remaining livestock and package it for transport and that only items linked to our survival can be taken.

I watch him as he commands his people — because they are *his* people now, not mine. Bartie recognizes something in my look because he smiles at me. "I know, when we land, it can't be like it was before," he says. "I don't plan on overthrowing whatever rule you have on Centauri-Earth. I just want to make sure we survive."

I shake my head. "It's not like that. The frozens woke up, and they have their own ruler. Amy's dad actually. And it's not like we're sitting around trying to make a government. All we've been doing is surviving, and we haven't been very good at that."

"Maybe we'll be able to help when we land."

"Will they fight against leaving?" I ask, remembering the last time we tried to land.

Bartie shakes his head. "I've already told them about the black patches. They've all known the end was coming. This . . . this is the only hope we'll have to survive, and they know it." He shifts. "I should help prepare everyone," he says, heading to the door.

"I'll make sure everything's ready here," I say. The auto-shuttle was designed specifically for people and cargo transport, but I want to make sure everything's packed as efficiently as possible. I don't want more guilt on my hands, not after letting three people die in the original shuttle landing.

As I turn to go, I notice the vid feed I'd played for Amy on the planet finishes. I move to disconnect the AV player — why didn't she say something when the vid stopped?

I touch the controls for the com link. Amy's voice fills the bridge. "What are you doing with that gun?" she says, her voice crackling over the intercom.

I freeze. Something is very wrong.

"You've realized, haven't you? Looking at that video. You realized my eyes are like hers." Chris's voice sounds harsh — desperate. "You didn't want to see before," he continues. "You and your father — you didn't want to see what was always right in front of your faces."

"Oval irises," Amy says, then pauses. "I'd noticed your eyes were different, but not that they were . . . "

"That they weren't *normal?*" Chris spits out bitterly.

I try to remember Chris's eyes. I never really looked at him that closely
before, and when I did, I was distracted by the way he seemed to show Amy
special attention. He has oval irises? Just like . . . just like the girl who was
injected with the gen mod compound.

"How?" Amy asks, her voice taut with fear. I imagine Chris with a gun,
pointing it at her. "You're—you're in our military," she stutters. "You were one
of our people—frozen. . . . " Her voice trails off.

I try to remember the list of military personnel that Orion gave me. There
were so many names on it—but was there a Chris? No . . . I don't think so. . . .

Why had I never thought of that before? Orion taught me to question
everything.

Chris echoes my train of thought. "It was easy," he says. "Your father
left the shuttle the first time, looking for the probe—do you remember? He
left with nine people but came back with ten. With *me.*" His voice is mocking, gleefully crushing Amy's trust. "I'm a descendant of the original colony
that you *humans*"—he says the word with disgust—"decided to genetically
modify."

My hands are clenched into fists so hard that I can feel the nails of my
fingers cutting the skin on my palms. I'd do anything not to be miles above
Centauri-Earth, trapped in space, unable to save her.

"But . . . the Phydus . . ."

"That's really all you can say, Amy? I expected better of you. But no, as
you can see, I'm one of the few that isn't affected by what you call Phydus."

"How's that possible?"

"Genetic defect. The compound they gave to my people genetically modified the adrenal and pituitary glands. Instead of a 'fight or flight' option, my
people are programmed to 'accept and obey.' Lucky for me, my adrenal gland

is broken. Makes more adrenaline than Phydus. After a few generations of being mindless Phydus-controlled freaks, my ancestors started to mutate."

"Are there others like you?" Amy asks. "I mean, others who aren't affected by Phydus?" She keeps her voice very calm—unnaturally so. It's not hard for me to imagine how much that placid voice is costing her. It reminds me of the lightning in the storm—the thunder was loud and terrifying, but it was the silent lightning that broke through the dark sky.

I am waiting for her lightning to strike.

"Dozens," Chris says, and even though he's speaking miles below me, I can hear the sneer in his voice. "The ones the FRX hasn't found and killed. You met a bunch of us earlier tonight. They call us rogue hybrids, the ones that have the genetic modification but aren't under their control. And they've been trying their best to kill us off for years."

"Why?" Amy's only speaking in short quick words. I wonder if she's trapped or worse, if Chris is hurting her.

"Don't you see? Those monsters you've been so worried about. Not aliens. *People.* The monsters have always been people."

She is silent for a long time, absorbing this information. I unclench my fists, my knuckles cracking, but that doesn't stop my hands from shaking.

"That's not an explanation," Amy replies.

"Why does any master hate a slave that won't work? We've been sabotaging the shipments, destroying whatever equipment we can."

The screen on my console lights up. Amy's kept the communication link between the auto-shuttle and the compound open, probably hoping that I can see what's going on. I know better than to try to talk—there's nothing I can do here. I can only listen as Amy does her best to show me what's happening on her end.

"I thought you were different." Chris's voice is so soft I almost don't catch his words.

Amy's voice, however, is loud. And angry. "Get away from me," she shouts.

I taste blood—I've been biting my lip so hard I didn't notice I'd broken the skin. If Chris touches her . . . if he hurts her. . . .

The menus on the console scroll quickly. This must be Chris's work. The screen stops at **SECURITY FEED: COMPOUND**, then a recorded video showing the outside of the communication building at the compound starts playing. It quickly reverses—I see Amy and Chris running—*from what?*—then a night goes by. The auto-shuttle launch. Me, Amy, and Chris with the glass cube, sneaking inside. Military. Amy and I discovering the compound. Military. Military. And then—Chris.

The video stops rewinding as Chris hits play, showing Amy what happened. In the vid, Chris is not wearing any of the military clothes I've seen him in; he's dressed in a dark, camouflage uniform, one that looks vaguely like green skin. He tries to get into the communication building. He presses his thumb across the biometric scanner. Instead of flashing **HUMAN**, it shows a warning light and the words **ACCESS DENIED**.

The Chris on the screen hits the door with his fist—and a sound that bursts over the intercom tells me that Chris has hit something in the compound, something metallic and hard. If he dares to hit Amy . . .

"But . . . you're human," Amy says, but it doesn't sound as if she believes the lie she's speaking.

"Not according to *them*." Chris spits out the word. "*They* genetically altered us. We're hybrids, no longer fully human."

"Why?" Amy asks. I think she's trying to distract Chris, calm him down, temper the vitriol in his voice. "Why would the FRX mess with your genetic code . . . ? There's no real risk of solar radiation, right? And they could just control you with Phydus." She pauses. "Not that I approve of Phydus. But they didn't need to make you something . . . other than human."

I notice Amy's choice of words, but I don't think Chris has. Amy didn't say the FRX made the hybrids *less* human, just *other than*.

"They wanted to make efficient workers, so they enhanced our bodies.

But that's not all," Chris says bitterly. He sounds louder now; he must be closer to the intercom than before. "They did it so that we don't *technically* count as human anymore. At least, not according to them. It helps them sleep at night, I think, to believe that their slaves aren't people."

I don't want to think it, but I do: would the FRX classify me as less than human too, just because I'm a clone?

There's a note of pride in his voice now. "We have all the strengths the FRX genetically engineered to make a better, stronger slave, but none of the mind-control."

"You can see in the dark," Amy says slowly, thinking. "That night, at the shuttle . . ."

I have no idea what night at the shuttle she's talking about. It's taking everything I have not to steer the auto-shuttle down, *now*, straight back to Amy and the compound.

"Better night vision—better senses in general. Strength. Speed. Agility. The FRX thought they were making something less human, but really they *improved* upon the original model."

"You still look human to me," Amy says, her voice soft.

"Shut up!" Something loud pops over the intercom. I think he hit her. I see red. I will kill the frexing traitor.

The recorded video continues. After being unable to get into the communication room, Chris looks as if he's going to strike the door with some sort of weapon—is that a scale, like the one I found in the tunnel? Suddenly, he looks up. He quickly hides the solar glass—because that's what it must be—and Colonel Martin and his military approach, guns out. There's no sound on this video, but it's obvious that Colonel Martin is shouting, pointing a rifle directly at Chris's heart. Chris slowly raises his hands, but I notice that there's a small, flesh-colored device in his right hand. He quickly sticks it in his ear.

This must be how he can talk like us, I think. If our accents evolved on the ship so that the Earthborns have trouble understanding the shipborns, it must be even more different for people who are born on Centauri-Earth. That device enables him to understand us and reply in our language. The FRX is made up of many nations; no doubt they needed something like this.

Chris starts talking on the screen, but with no sound I can't tell what he's saying. Soon, though, Colonel Martin lowers his gun.

"My father knew?" Amy asks, shocked.

"Of course he did—at least, he knew what we wanted him to know. I told him I was a survivor of the colony, that we'd been wiped out by *aliens*. It wasn't hard. My people hacked the system—we interrupted the automatic message Earth had set up for you on landing. We manipulated the information, made it seem like aliens were the threat. I gave him some solar glass. But then a real message got through. Colonel Martin was persistent—far more so than I thought he would be. The FRX knows you've landed, and they're on their way."

There's a pause. Amy and I are both trying to sort this information out, I know it.

"The message about the weapon," Amy says slowly. "That's the real one. That's the message the FRX sent to us."

"We tried to block it, but enough of the message transmitted before we could stop it. There aren't many of us. 'Rogue hybrids,' or whatever you want to call us. But there are more now than ever before. And the FRX—they've figured out a way to kill us all."

"The weapon."

"Exactly. Problem is, we have a slightly different genetic code than humans now. And the FRX knows it. The weapon? It's a biological bomb. There's a disease in there that will attack anyone with mutated DNA—all of us hybrids, rogue or not. It will kill us all."

That means—everyone the FRX has enslaved, all the people with the Phydus implanted into their systems as well as all the ones like Chris, who aren't affected by the Phydus—they will all die. This is why the FRX didn't worry about the weapon killing us. We don't have the mutation that makes Chris and his people susceptible. They will die, and we will live.

My stomach drops as I realize what that really means: As soon as the FRX wipes out the hybrids, they'll turn to us. We'll be their next slaves.

Orion was right all along.

"But then why—why did you kill *us*?" Amy asks, and the sorrow that leaks out of the intercom brings me back from my dark thoughts and into hers. "Why did you kill my mom?"

"You heard Colonel Martin," Chris says, his voice crackling over the intercom. "He intends to fire the weapon."

"You killed my mother because she was on a ship to the space station." Amy's voice is hollow now. "She just happened to be there. She had nothing to do with the bomb. But you killed her. You killed nearly five hundred people!"

"It wasn't just me!" There's panic in his voice now, fear. "I've reported everything back to my people. They—they think you're with the FRX, that you'll do whatever they say. And they're right, aren't they? Colonel Martin *was* going to set the bomb off. And he still plans on doing it."

"If he's even alive anymore!" Amy shouts. "You told your little friends about the plan with the flowers. That's how they knew to wear gas masks." A pause—much longer than I'd like. "That's what they were wearing, right? Gas masks? Pretty convenient that they made them look like 'real' aliens."

Amy taunts him, the way that she says the word *real*, and I'm so worried about what Chris will do next that I can barely breathe. I don't know what she's talking about now, but I know that if nothing else, I've got to do *something*.

My knuckles are white, gripping the edge of the console. I have never, *never* felt so helpless. I think about the escape rocket Chris showed me, the thing I'm supposed to use if something goes wrong. Maybe I can use it to go to the space station.

I can set the weapon off.

I don't want to kill them all. I don't believe in the FRX, and I don't want to be responsible for the deaths of countless people, especially innocent, mindless drones already destroyed by Phydus.

I look at the little brown book that was in the box with the AV display from the Plague Eldest. In that book is the formula for Inhibitor meds. There's a chance. . . .

"It's us or you," Chris says, his voice high.

"Only because that's what you've decided."

"Colonel Martin has made it clear, time and time again, that if he can, he will use the weapon. It will *always* be a threat he can control. And when the FRX gets here—because they *are* coming, Colonel Martin made sure of that— they will kill anyone else they can find. This is about *survival*. This is our *home*, and you are the trespassers." He says the words as if they are weapons, each syllable another stab, each pause a blow.

"Don't—" Amy says, squeaking in terror for the first time. "Please, don't."

And I know: she's begging for her life.

I flip on the intercom. *"WAIT!"* I bellow.

65: AMY

Chris looks from me to the intercom and back to me. He'd forgotten about the communication link; he didn't realize I'd kept it going.

He grips the gun in his hand.

"If you kill Amy," Elder says through the intercom, his voice filled with passion and rage, "I *will* kill you. I will take the shuttle straight to the space station, and I'll set off the biological bomb, and you and all your people will die."

Chris does not lower the gun.

"But if you let her live," Elder says, "I will land this shuttle. We've found more than just the video from the Plague Eldest. We also found the formula for the Inhibitor medicine we developed to counteract the effects of Phydus."

"A . . . a cure?" Chris says. The end of the rifle dips as he starts to lower the gun. "You'll be able to fix my people, the other hybrids?"

The door to the communication room bangs open, and my father races inside. "You bastard!" he shouts, slamming into Chris and knocking him to the floor. The rifle skitters away. Chris shakes Dad off and lunges for it.

"Amy? Amy! What's happening?" Elder says anxiously over the intercom.

I rip my .38 out and aim it at the floor, near the rifle, my finger already pulling the trigger. The bullet embeds itself in the ground, and Chris stops. He turns around to see me, my finger on the trigger, my gun aimed at his chest. Dad gets up and grabs the rifle.

"We've got Chris," I tell Elder.

"You're okay?"

"I'm fine."

Dad sits down at the communication bay. "Just so you know," Dad tells Chris over his shoulder, "I never really trusted you."

I don't know how true that is—I think Dad *did* trust Chris, rather a lot. Not at first—Chris didn't have a gun that first day. But later, Dad *wanted* to trust him. It's the only reason I can see why Chris has been able to deceive him for so long. That, or Dad's planning something. I watch them both carefully, waiting for the moment when Dad will strike.

"You were working with the FRX," Chris says. "I knew better than to ever put my faith in you."

"Yeah, well, now we're going to have the FRX kill you all, so there's some comfort in that. For me, anyway." There's a smirk of triumph on Dad's face as his fingers punch the numbers and letters on the screen to enable the remote detonation of the bomb on the space station.

"Wait!" Chris says. He makes a move to reach for Dad, but I adjust my position, making sure he remembers me and my .38. "Just—I want to show you who you'll be killing first. We have video feed from security cams—you can access them from here."

Dad's gaze flicks to me. There are black gunpowder marks on his hands and face, and I notice a bloodstain on his left shoulder. He must have barely escaped the fighting at the colony. And for him to leave the colony to come here, the fighting had to have been bad. Setting off the bomb must be his last chance.

"How's the colony?" I ask softly.

"Mostly prisoners," he says.

"Prisoners," Chris says. "*Prisoners*. We tried not to kill—"

"You didn't try that hard," Dad says. "Not in this battle and not before, not with Emma or Dr. Gupta or the shipborns or the five hundred people in the auto-shuttle *including my wife, you sick bastard.*"

Dad looks so—I can't even describe it, the rage on his face, the fury in his eyes. I think he would kill Chris right now, with his bare hands, if I weren't here.

Chris's body sags in defeat. "Just—just look at the security feed of the city, where the other hybrids live," he says. *"Please."*

I nod to Dad. I want to see.

Dad scrolls through the menus on the control panel, finding the security feed. After a moment, the screen comes to life.

The city the hybrids live in must be in the valley of the mountain range I spotted well beyond the colony and the lake—that's why we never noticed it before. I can see tall, jagged mountains rising in the background.

There's no sound on the video. But I think even if there was, there would be little to hear. The people on the streets move robotically, emotionless. They stare straight ahead as they walk. The screen shifts from camera to camera, showing a street, a packaging factory, people pushing wheelbarrows full of yellow sand, a glassmaking factory. The people in the factory are hand-blowing glass sculptures. They move methodically, with perfect rhythm, as they make dozens of identical glass figurines—flowers of some kind. If I had just seen the glass flowers by themselves, without knowing how they were made, I would call them works of art. They are perfectly balanced, delicate and lovely, with a string of liquid gold inside that I know won't fade—it will make the flowers glow from within, lit petals that almost look alive. But having seen them made with such emotionless exactitude, the flowers now look creepy and false.

"They're all like that," Chris says after we stare at the screen. "Thousands of people, born to be slaves, so used to rote repetition that if something goes wrong, they don't know what to do and so they end up injuring themselves or . . ." Chris stands up, glancing at the screen with the glassblowers, "dying. Sometimes, they stick their hands in the fire or touch the molten glass without gloves. They only know how to work, and if their tongs go missing, they work with their bare hands. They don't know any better because the FRX has ensured they'll never rebel, they'll never think for themselves."

I have seen this before. On *Godspeed*. I'd hated it there, but I hate it more here.

"Every few years, representatives from the FRX come and check up on us, make sure that everyone's still working, still controlled. If they see any children like me—born without the control of Phydus—they just kill them. I watched them kill my little sister. They shot her in the head, and they left her on the street, and everyone on Phydus just stepped over her body until it rotted away."

I swallow dryly.

"This is what I wanted you to see," Chris says to back of Dad's head. "I wanted you to know what organization you're supporting."

Dad swipes his hand across the screen, making it go dark.

"At least they're alive," he says bitterly. "Unlike my Maria. You've killed too many of my people for me to have any sympathy for yours."

Dad's hands move quickly, tapping codes onto the screen and swiping across new menus.

"What are you doing?" Chris says urgently. He steps forward. I wiggle my gun at him, making him freeze. *"What are you doing?"* he asks again, fear in his voice.

"I'm arming the bomb," Dad says matter-of-factly.

"You're committing *genocide!*"

"I'm protecting my people," Dad says. "What's left of them after *you* tried to kill them all."

Something on the screen beeps, and Dad starts pressing more buttons.

There's a bang on the door, and I turn, startled. Chris takes that moment to knock aside my arm, making me drop the .38. We both dive for it. Dad lunges for Chris—and that's what saves his life. A second later, the glass window over the communication bay shatters and three men in camouflage suits—I can't believe I'd thought they were green scaly aliens—jump through it. They step over the control panel, and I hear Elder call out my name in a desperate cry as the red flashing light that shows his communication link with us cuts out.

I wonder if that was the last time I'll hear Elder's voice, if this is the point when I die.

One of the men rips Dad off Chris, and Chris stands—with my .38 in his hand, pointed at me. The men are all tall—taller even than Elder—but much stockier, with muscles that look like carved stone under their skintight shirts. But Dad doesn't cower before them, and neither do I.

"This ends now," one of the men in camo says. He points his own gun at Dad, a weapon that is slim and light, with disks inside it instead of bullets. He wears more ammo around his waist—rows of thin, flat glass circles that glow golden. I gasp. This is a weapon that uses more of that exploding glass, and the disks . . . they're the exact size and shape of the scale Elder found in the tunnel. But it wasn't a scale. It was part of a weapon. And it won't just kill Dad—it'll blow him apart.

The man who spoke dips his head at Dad in a mock show of civility. "I am in charge of the rogue hybrids." I notice his crystal-blue eyes, his oval irises identical to Chris's. Now that I see them on a stranger, I'm even more shaken that I never let myself recognize just how unusual they were.

The two other men with him stand on either side of the communication bay, their own guns out.

"I am the leader of the people you've tried to kill," Dad says.

The man barks in laughter. "You have courage, I'll give you that. It is your misfortune that you landed your shuttle now. A few decades earlier, and there wouldn't have been as many of us. A few decades later, and the revolution would be over. We could have been friends then. But now? Now you're aligned with the FRX, and we can't have that." He sneers at Dad. "You're going to do two things for us," he says.

"I would rather die than do anything for you," Dad growls.

The rogue leader looks at Chris. Chris steps forward until the round end of the barrel of my .38 is pressed against my temple. I can feel the cool metal circle digging into my skull; I can smell the remains of gun oil and powder.

"What do you want me to do?" Dad says.

"We'll start with your surrender. You're going to call the FRX from this compound, and you're going to issue your surrender to me and my people on your behalf *and* on the behalf of the FRX."

"They'll come anyway," Dad says.

"The only weapon that could do us any harm is the biological bomb. We've been stockpiling solar bombs for decades. Not to mention all the human hostages we'll have to negotiate with. Without the biological weapon, they don't stand a chance against us."

My stomach drops. Outside the window, the world is calm and peaceful. I imagine it exploding, torn apart by bombs and warfare.

Dad sits back down at the communication bay, wiping away the shards of glass scattered over it. We all watch as he types in his military codes.

"The disarmament function isn't there . . . " the rogue leader says. "What are you *doing*?" A new voice fills the communication room. "Colonel Martin, we have received your distress call," a voice says. "The FRX stands ready to aid you."

"The hybrids have taken over!" Dad shouts as the rogue leader lunges for him.

"Do you want us to remotely activate the biological bomb?" the man on the other end of the line says. His voice is utterly emotionless. "Please give your military authorization code."

"No!" the rogue leader shouts. He shoves Dad away from the communication center.

"Zero-alpha-four-two-gamma," Dad shouts. Half of the ten-digit code.

The rogue leader slams his fist into Dad's face before he can finish speaking. The two of them grapple a moment, Dad's hands around the man's right arm, trying to wrest the weapon free—then the solar gun goes off, exploding a hole into the side of the building. Dad finally knocks it away from the rogue

leader's hands. One of the other men that came into the communication building with the rogue leader jumps into the battle. Chris watches, my .38 pressed
hard against my head.

"Please note," the voice on the intercom says, "without the full code we
will not authorize the remote launch of the bombs. We do not wish to destroy
our slave labor force except as a last resort."

And I know: the people who sent us here in the first place, the ones that
promised to protect us, have absolutely no problem sacrificing us. Not if it
would mess up their "production." They would much rather have us and the
rogue hybrids kill each other off than to lose all the resources they could har-
vest from the planet. Using Phydus—if anything, that would solve their problems for them.

The third man who came into the communication building with the others
steps toward Chris and me. His neck muscles are tense, and he seems to be
silently asking Chris some sort of question.

Chris nods, then turns to me. "You know what? I thought . . . I thought
we could be something."

"We can *never* be what you want us to be."

Chris sneers. "Because I'm a hybrid?" he asks. "Or because of that *boy*?" I
wonder if he even notices that he's used the same word to describe Elder that
my dad uses.

I glare at him, hoping he can see the hate in my eyes. "Your DNA has
nothing to do with the reason why Elder's a better man than you."

The other hybrid has moved out of my line of vision. I gasp in pain as
something sharp pierces my arm. The man grabs hold of my shoulder firmly,
digging his fingers into my arm so that, between his grip and the gun at my
head, I cannot move.

But I can tell what's happening. The other man has a syringe, and I can
feel icy-hot liquid being injected into my bloodstream.

The rogue leader and his lackey have Dad back under control, and they
slam him into the chair and turn his body to look at me.

The liquid feels like ice, and I have a sudden and sickening flashback to being pumped full of cryo liquid.

"What is that? What are you doing to my daughter?" Dad roars, trying to jump up and save me, but the rogue leader throws him back, grinning maliciously.

"In just a few moments, she won't be human anymore. Not genetically at least. You set that bomb off, you kill her as well. She's a hybrid now too."

"No!" Dad jumps up, throwing the rogue leader out of his way. "Amy!"

My eyes are burning, streaming with water. I squeeze them shut, unable to bear how bright the light is.

"The pain will pass," Chris says to me softly. Sympathetically. His gun lowers as the other man steps back.

I dry heave. It's the idea of my body being *changed* irrevocably. I can't bear it. And I can't bear the way Chris looks at me now, as if I'm already *one of them*.

"Amy!" Dad shouts. It's taking two of the men to hold him back.

"She'll be fine," the rogue leader says. Their voices sound metallic, too loud. I clutch my hair, pulling my head down, rocking. I can't bear this, I can't bear this. "This compound only has the gen modifiers in it, not the Phydus. She'll have all the genetic modifications but none of the mind-altering control."

"You bastards," Dad snarls. "How dare you! My daughter!"

"Sit *down*, Colonel Martin," the rogue leader orders. "Or I will make you."

I slide to the floor. Chris says something, I can't understand what. My bleary eyes can barely blink, but I can't help but notice that the rogue hybrids all wear the same kind of boot, ones with metal grippers, three long, sharp pieces curving over the toes of their shoes. Ones that would make the same footprints we found outside the shuttle. Elder was right all along. They've been watching us since the very first day.

It *hurts*. My body's DNA is rearranging itself to become some mutated hybrid, and I'm not even sure what's happening, I just know it's not *human*. It's painful, as if there is a fire inside, burning up my blood. I try to open my eyes. Dad's fighting against the hybrids while I'm becoming one.

Dad knocks aside the rogue leader, sending him crashing against the communication bay.

I think for one wild moment that he's coming for me. He will pick me up and carry me away and make the hurting stop.

But he's not coming for me. He lunges at Chris, grabbing for the .38 in his hand.

The gun goes off.

Dad lands with a thump on the ground, his eyes open and staring, inches away from my face but already out of reach.

66: ELDER

I try to re-establish the communication link, but it's gone. All I heard was glass shattering and loud thumps and bangs, and then I was disconnected.

It's not too late, I tell myself. *Amy's not dead.*

I tell myself this, and I force myself to believe it.

I rush out of the bridge and back up to *Godspeed*. Bartie's standing near the hatch, looking happy. "I don't think it will take that long to load up the autoshuttle," he says, grinning at me.

"Now," I gasp.

"What?"

"*Now,*" I say. "We have to go now. They have Amy, they've taken over the whole frexing colony."

"What are you talking about, Elder?" Bartie asks, grabbing my shoulders. "Calm down."

I shake him off. "You don't understand! I heard it over the com system — Bartie, they have Amy. They've taken the colony."

"*Who?*"

"The hybrids!" I throw up my hands. "The aliens! Whatever you want to call them! The *monsters* we've been fighting, the ones that have been attacking us! They have our people!"

A line of worry mars Bartie's brow. "What can we do?"

"We have to go *now*. Get the people out. Whatever they can carry. But we have to go now."

To his credit, Bartie does the all-call. Some people are already crossing the fields, heading toward the hatch, and I see them pick up their pace, running closer.

"But what can we do?" Bartie asks me. "Even if we left in the auto-shuttle right this second, what could we possibly do?"

"Come with me," I say.

Bartie has to run to keep up with me as I tear back down through the hatch, running to the control panel on the bridge. "Here are the controls," I tell him. "This is how you can fly the auto-shuttle back."

"Me?" Bartie steps away. "*You're* going to be flying the auto-shuttle!"

"No," I tell him. "No, I'm not. You are. Now pay attention."

I show him everything as people from *Godspeed* start to load up the shuttle. I show him how to operate the controls and the communication system. It's really simple—the auto-shuttle was *designed* to function without human operations. Once I'm sure he knows what to do, I race out of the bridge, past the crowd that's already gathering at the transport boxes, and down a flight of stairs.

The escape rocket Chris told me about is smaller than it seemed from the ground. I have to shimmy through a hatch opening that drops me straight into the seat. The controls are the same here as on the auto-shuttle but more compressed and with an additional "manual maneuvering" control that looks like a joystick. I'm not comforted by the simplistic controls, but they'll have to be enough.

I flip on the communication system and hail Bartie, just above me in the bridge.

"Yes?" his voice says immediately. He sounds anxious.

"Just checking," I say. "I wanted to be sure that the controls worked."

"Elder, this is insane," he says. His voice sounds a little tinny over the intercom, but I can understand him loud and clear.

"Yeah," I say. "It probably is. But it's my only chance of saving Amy." I can go to the space station, and I can detonate the weapons there myself. I will protect Amy, no matter what the cost.

I turn off the communication link with Bartie and flip it to the compound's system. A red light blinks several times as the communication link with the compound on the planet is established.

"Don't break this communication link," I say quickly once the controls tell me I've connected.

"And why not?" a voice I don't recognize drawls.

"I am currently in the escape rocket. I will head straight to the space station. I will dock. And I will set off the biological bomb myself."

"Elder, don't!" a voice screams. Amy.

"Amy, what's going on?"

"They've injected me too," she says, then her voice is muffled. It sounds as if she's being dragged away.

"What do you mean?" No answer. "What the frex is going on?"

"Amy has been injected with the hybrid compound. She will be susceptible to the biological weapon. We tried to negotiate with the other leader, Colonel Martin. We are done negotiating."

"Let me talk to Colonel Martin," I say.

"He's dead!" Amy's voice cries out over the intercom. Her voice sounds rougher than I remember, perhaps a bit deeper. "They've killed him!"

More muffled sounds. I have no doubt now that they're trying to silence Amy, drag her away from the intercom. But I also have no doubt that Colonel Martin's dead. Amy would never say that—not with that much anguish in her voice—unless it was true.

My hands are shaking. I have never been more scared.

There's only one thing I can do.

"Here's the deal," I say. I hope I sound convincing. We don't have much to hold over the hybrids, but we do have one bargaining chip. "We have the plans for the Inhibitor medicine. Chris can tell you that *Godspeed* had Phydus too, and you'll just have to trust me when I tell you we have an antidote that fights the drug's effects."

No one answers me when I pause, so I just plow through. "My friend Bartie is going to land the auto-shuttle. He carries the plans for the Inhibitor drug with him. Shoot the auto-shuttle down—kill my people as they land— and you'll lose the formula."

This time, a voice answers. "We will not destroy the auto-shuttle."

"I'm in the escape rocket right now," I say. "I'm going to disable the bio- logical bomb. If I do that, you let Amy and the rest go."

The sound of the man's laughter over the intercom chills me to the bone. "It's not just the bomb we fear," he says. "The FRX is coming, and now the one man who might have been able to call them off is dead. If the FRX arrives, it will be war for all. They'll *decimate* this entire planet."

"We'll com them!" I say desperately. "We'll tell them not to come!" I don't know if the FRX will listen to my pleas, but I'll try. I'll do anything; just let Amy be okay.

"It's not enough," the man says. "The only thing that could stop them is if the entire space station is destroyed. The tesseract-based high-speed travel requires the signal from the space station for it to work. If the station is gone, the FRX can't reach us, not for decades. But I don't think you have any weap- ons on that ship of yours, do you?"

There's a lump in my throat, and I can't speak for a moment.

Then I say: "What if I can?"

"What if you can what?" the man barks into the intercom.

"What if I can destroy the space station? If I do that—I'll take out the threat of the FRX being able to reach us, and I'll eliminate the biological bomb. If I do that, will you agree to leave my people alone?"

"If you do *that*," the man says, "I'll write the peace treaty myself."

I don't reply immediately. I sit in the cockpit of the escape rocket, and I think about what I'll be sacrificing to make peace between us. I stare at the stars, and I silently say goodbye.

Amy will never forgive me for what I'm about to do, but *Godspeed* is dead. Just floating here. All it needs is a little nudge. I can use the escape rocket to get behind the ship, then push it to the space station. Inertia will take care of most of it — *Godspeed* will crash into the space station, then the station — and its weapons — will be destroyed, Sol-Earth's military won't be able to come here and frex things up.

"Just give me a little time," I say into the intercom. "And let me speak to Amy."

67: AMY

Chris grabs me by the arm and drags me to the communication bay. I can feel the pressure of each of his individual fingers gripping my skin. Colors swim before my eyes; scents I don't recognize fill my nose. I stumble and Chris jerks me up as I realize with horror that I'm sniffing the air like an animal on the scent—because that's what I am now. Not human. Animal.

It feels as if ice is shooting through my muscles, ripping apart my flesh. When I yank away from Chris's grasp, I'm surprised to realize that I'm strong enough to do it—he has to use all his strength to keep pulling me forward.

We have to step over my father's body to reach the communication bay, and I nearly break then. My new eyes don't let me miss any detail: the sweat still clinging to the bridge of his nose, the flatness of his face against the floor, the pinky finger curled on his left hand, as if waiting for me to wrap my own pinky around it and whisper promises that I'll never be able to keep. Not now that he's dead.

"Elder?" I say, my voice cracking, unfamiliar even to my ears . . . my ears that are suddenly picking up more sound than they ever have before.

"*Amy.*" There's relief in his voice, something else I can't recognize.

"What are you going to do?" I ask. An ominous dread flows through my veins, poisoning me.

"I'm going to crash *Godspeed* into the space station."

Chris slides his hand on the touch screen near me. The rogue leader looks over my shoulder as a map of the satellites in orbit around the planet lights up the communication bay. The screen fades in and out, updating every few seconds. The auto-shuttle is right next to *Godspeed*, their dots so close together that their labels overlap. I imagine the evacuation as people scramble from the ship into the auto-shuttle.

Nearby, only the space of four inches or so on the map, is another dot, labeled **Interplanetary Preparation Station**.

"You still there?" Elder asks, his voice small and scared.

"I'm here," I say.

"I have to tell you—" he says, then stops. I inspect the screen under the intercom. There's nothing wrong with the communication system; Elder's struggling to find the words he wants to say. Finally, he speaks.

"I'm sorry," he says.

The line goes dead.

"What happened?" I ask. I want to slam my fists into the controls, make Elder's voice come back to me, but I don't know how.

Chris looks at the controls. "Nothing," he says. "Elder must have disconnected the communication link. He's not answering my calls now."

I look up at the rogue hybrid leader, who's watching me intently. And my stomach twists as I see the pity in his eyes.

68: ELDER

It takes time to load up the auto-shuttle, and the delay makes me anxious. Now that I've decided what I have to do, I just want to *do* it. The waiting is miserable.

Before Bartie gets everyone and everything strapped down, I get inside the escape rocket and detach from the auto-shuttle. Using the manual controls, I maneuver the escape rocket directly behind *Godspeed*. The map on my screen shows a line of dots: me, then *Godspeed*, then the space station. I just have to move the dot in the middle until it crashes against the other dot.

Simple.

Bartie coms me from the auto-shuttle. "We're loaded and ready," he says. His voice sounds worried. "Are you sure about this?"

"Very sure," I say.

"I'm departing now," he says.

"Bartie?"

"Yeah?"

"Thanks for everything."

"I'll see you on the ground, right, buddy?"

I don't answer him. I disconnect the com link and watch as the auto-shuttle breaks from *Godspeed* and shoots away, a stream of rocket fire blasting out as it heads for the planet.

* * *

Godspeed floats before me, hanging impossibly in the black sky. It looks broken, the jagged bottom lacking the shuttle, the Bridge blown out so that it looks like twisted scrap metal. And even though I cannot see through the metal to the emptiness I know lies inside the ship, it *seems* hollow in the same way a dead body looks soulless.

Godspeed is dead.

But it has one last task, one last service for the people it lived to protect. And so do I.

It was not an official part of the studies Eldest taught me while I lived on the Keeper Level with him, but Orion once slipped me a book about the *Titanic*, an old ship on Sol-Earth that sank and killed many of its passengers. Looking back, I wonder if Orion had some deeper meaning in giving me the book, perhaps something about the different classes or that those stuck in the bowels of *Titanic* were frozen. Or maybe just that we were all destined to die, like the people on board.

But the thing that really stayed with me was the way the captain went down with the ship.

This escape rocket seems tiny compared to the hulking mass of *Godspeed*, but I know, from that same book that Orion gave me, that a tiny tugboat can move a massive ship. *Godspeed* needs only a push from me.

I go slowly, very slowly, until I'm only a few meters away from *Godspeed*. I don't want to crash into the side; I need to push the giant ship toward the space station. I take a deep breath and check my seat belt. Fortunately, the bottom of the escape rocket extends farther out than the cockpit, but it'll still be a near thing, especially if I have too much speed.

Adjusting the output of the orbital maneuvering rockets, I nudge the escape rocket forward.

Even though I expect the impact, it still knocks me breathless and rattles me to my bones. My eyes search the seams of the cockpit window frantically, looking for any crack in the heavy glass.

Impact detected, a computerized voice says. Red lights flash all along the dashboard.

The computerized voice continues: *Warning: external damage. Warning: external damage.* It repeats this message over and over, and I have no idea how to silence it.

"You're going to get a lot more damage before this is done," I say, and I increase the outputs on the orbital maneuvering rockets. The blinking dots on the screen that represent me and *Godspeed* jolt to life, moving closer and closer to the station.

It's not long before I can see it, my view obscured by the husk of *Godspeed.* The station is large, but no bigger than the ship. It reminds me very much of the Sol-Earth insects called dragonflies. The center is long and cylindrical, with mechanical arms and circular hatches dotting the top, clearly intended to connect to the tube from the auto-shuttle. The central area is large enough for people to live there comfortably, but no one is there now. Maybe the FRX once thought it would be a place for peaceful communication between humans and hybrids, but I don't think that's a possibility anymore.

The space station itself doesn't just store the goods of Centauri-Earth, it also operates the communication link between the planets, and the flat "wings" extending out on either side of the station are lined with satellites and relay receivers. Somewhere inside its metal body is the tesseract-relay device, the thing that enables high-speed travel between planets. Destroying it will isolate Centauri-Earth from communication and eliminate any chance of visitation from Sol-Earth for decades, if not longer.

Underneath the space station, aimed directly for Centauri-Earth, is a massive missile. The biological bomb, the one that will kill every single hybrid.

Including Amy.

I have one shot at this.

Godspeed careens toward the station.

* * *

I imagine it all in slow motion, each cause-and-effect scenario playing through my mind. *Godspeed* will crash into the station. The station will rip apart, fall in on itself.

Possibly the missile will go off without launching at the planet, setting off an explosion bigger than I can imagine.

Or maybe the ship's engine, a lead-cooled fast reactor fueled by recycled uranium, will explode first.

And there will be me, in my tiny rocket, swallowed whole.

"I'm sorry, Amy," I whisper, despite the fact that I've cut off all communication. I know she won't hear me, but I also know one day she might forgive me for breaking my promise to her.

I'm not going to come back from this one.

69: AMY

I don't think I really understood why Elder cut the communication link until I see the dots on the electronic map start to fly toward each other. The escape rocket and *Godspeed*, on a crash course toward the space station.

And then I realize: he didn't want me to hear him die.

I shut my eyes and cover my ears, trying to hold in the scream that is rising from within me.

I can't breathe. I can't breathe. I'm going to be sick.

"Look," Chris says, pointing as the map flickers and dies, showing nothing but a black screen.

I rush to the door of the communication room and throw it open. The hybrids don't bother trying to stop me. I suppose it's because I'm one of them now, or maybe they just know there's nowhere for me to run. A blast of cool air hits me, making my hair swirl in front of my face. I swipe it away and run to the center of the compound, where the auto-shuttle stood not too long ago, before Elder boarded it.

I throw my head back and stare into the sky.

And I see.

The dark sky.

A hundred million stars.

More stars than I've ever seen before. My eyes let me see farther, but they don't show me the one thing I want to see. I would trade all the stars in the universe if I could just have him back again.

Wind whistles through the trees nearby. Birdsong weaves in and out of the sound.

The hybrids emerge from the communication building, heads tilted to the sky.

And then we see the end.

Godspeed's engine was nuclear; who knows what fueled the biological weapons. But they explode together. In space, they don't make the familiar mushroom cloud. They don't make the *boom!* of an exploding bomb.

There is, against the dark sky, a brief flash of light. It is filled with colors, like a nebula or the aurora borealis, bursting like a popped bubble.

Nothing else—no sound of an explosion, no tremors in the earth, no smell of smoke. Not here, on the surface of the planet.

Nothing else to signify Elder's death.

Just light.

And then it's gone.

And then he's gone.

71: AMY

I am numb, inside and out.

I stare up at the cold night sky until it is as empty as I am.

Behind me, the hybrids talk. I suppress a shudder. I am a hybrid now too. My eyes see far better in the dark than they've ever been able to before. I notice each leaf of the trees in shadow, I hear the tiniest sounds distinctly.

I hear the hybrids talking.

"The threat is eliminated; our communication specialists confirm it," one of the hybrids says.

"Elder saved us all," Chris says.

The rogue leader grumbles something.

I turn. I have lost everything I have ever loved. But in the absence of love, a resolve made of steel fills me up. I stride toward the rogue leader. Chris halfheartedly raises his gun—my gun—the gun used to kill my father—toward me, but I knock his hand aside as if he held nothing more dangerous than a flower. I stand directly in front of the rogue leader and look him straight in the eyes. I'm uncomfortably close to him; I've invaded his personal space, and he doesn't like it, but he's unwilling to step back.

"I believe," I say flatly, "that we have a peace treaty to negotiate. And I think we can start with the release of my colony, the people you are currently holding in captivity."

"That can wait until—" the leader starts to say.

I cut him off. "It will not wait. You have imprisoned my people, abused us, and killed us. You're going to *start* by letting them go. *Now*. And then we can talk about the rest of the retribution you owe my colony."

The rogue leader cocks his head, looking down at me. Finally, he extends his hand. When I take it and we shake, he adds, "My name is Zane. And now that the FRX is out of the equation, I think both of our people can learn to live together very well."

Zane has some sort of communication device that is far beyond the radios and even wi-coms that we had. He calls for trucks to come to us while at the same time sending information to release the colony and bring the people back to the ruins to live.

"How many of the buildings still stand?" I ask. When I escaped, at least three of the buildings—including the one I had lived in with my family—were destroyed.

"We tried to keep damage minimal," Zane says. "And whether you believe it or not, we tried to keep deaths at a minimum, too."

I don't believe that, not at all. They could have destroyed the auto-shuttle rather than kill everyone inside it when my mom was leaving. But they didn't. They wanted to intimidate us, take us by force so we could surrender. Or maybe killing us was just simpler.

I narrow my eyes. Killing us *would* have been simpler. "You tried to wreck the shuttle before we even landed," I say, remembering the way we were knocked off course.

Zane nods slowly, watching me as if he's afraid I'm about to attack him. But I'm too busy lining up all the pieces. The hacked communication Dad and Elder heard when we first arrived. The shuttle lockdown. Every stumbling block and miscommunication. All because of the rogue hybrids.

"You know," I say bitterly, "if you'd just been honest with us from the start, we could have worked together."

Zane raises his eyebrow. "Colonel Martin did not seem the kind of man to abandon his mission."

I force myself to look at my father's body, and I can't seem to quiet the part of myself that realizes Zane might be right. Maybe my dad *wouldn't* have negotiated with the rogue hybrids. I don't think he agreed with the FRX and their program of forced slavery, but it *is* possible that my father, who was in the military all his life and whose first instinct upon landing on Centauri-Earth was to get his orders from the FRX, would not have been able to think about peace without first seeing bloodshed.

I tell that annoying—but truthful—part of myself to shut up.

Trucks arrive, and even though they're larger than the biggest gas-guzzlers on Sol-Earth, they move across the rough terrain silently. Cubes of solar glass line the roof of each truck. I suspect the hybrids have figured out a way to use the suns' energy to fuel the vehicles, but I don't bother asking about it as Chris and Zane usher me into the first one. Zane leaves the other at the communication building with orders that, when the auto-shuttle lands, they are to take Bartie and the formula for the Inhibitor medicine to a secure location.

"I want to take you to the city first," Zane says eventually. When I don't respond, he shifts uncomfortably, looking out the window at the passing landscape. He and Chris are both nervous around me—they're waiting for me to break down.

But I won't.

Not in front of them.

The truck takes us past the lake and toward one of the tall, jagged mountains behind the colony. Even as I contemplate how a whole city within reach of the colony has been hidden, I realize how unnatural it is that the hybrids haven't spread out more. Phydus didn't just make them obey the FRX—it killed their sense of wonder and exploration.

We don't speak again as the truck drives through a long, dark tunnel cut into the mountain and emerges into a populated area. We are the only vehicle on the street but are surrounded by people and vast buildings made of glass and steel—factories, mostly, judging from the grime and sweat on the people who emerge from them.

They shuffle straight ahead, their eyes and faces directed forward. Even though they all seem to have a purposeful direction, their shoulders slump and their arms hang limply at their sides. They look more like zombies than any monster I've seen in a horror film. The driver stops the truck in the middle of the largest intersection of the city. There are so many people around that I expect the city to be loud, but when Zane opens the door, the only thing I hear is the rhythmic pounding of feet on pavement.

Something bumps into the door Zane still holds open. A woman with short curly hair and blank eyes—they're crystal-blue eyes, with oval irises, but blank all the same. Her feet keep going up and down, up and down, but she doesn't seem to notice she's not moving forward. She doesn't even really notice the door that's blocking her path. Zane slams it—no one even flinches at the reverberating sound—and the woman plods forward as if nothing was ever in her way.

"Why are you showing me this?" I say, my voice barely a whisper.

"I wanted you to see what we were fighting for," Zane says. His voice carries, but no one even seems to register his presence.

I've seen Phydus. I saw the City on *Godspeed*, I saw the blank stares, the empty expressions.

This is worse somehow. I think because of the open sky above us. Eldest had made the use of Phydus almost excusable behind the steel walls of the ship. But nothing like this can ever be excusable in a world without walls.

Zane turns his attention to me. He's trying to make his face as emotionless as those of the people walking around us, but it's not working. "Did you know the drug you call Phydus—it was developed in part from research the first colony did on some of the plants they discovered here? Phydus wouldn't exist without this planet, and yet it's caused . . . all this." He moves his hands weakly, indicating the whole city.

I look up and out, trying to determine how many people are in this sprawling city. Thousands, at least. All drugged by Phydus.

Zane takes in my reaction before continuing. "They mixed the Phydus—which I suppose they eventually wanted to test out for use on Sol-Earth—with gen mod material."

I flinch. I don't know what's worse—his assumption that much of the population on today's Earth might be just as doped up as the zombie-like people before me or his mention of the same gen mod material my mother helped develop before she ever set foot on *Godspeed*.

"The combined drug was designed to attack the adrenal and pituitary glands, as well as the senses, and as a result, Phydus becomes a natural part of the body's response to stimulation, creating passivity instead of individual thought."

"The first people were infected generations ago," Chris says. "The FRX didn't count on people like us—the ones who have defective glands."

"It's a mutation." Zane shrugs. "It would have happened eventually."

The empty shells of people move robotically down the street. They hardly seem human.

I look down at myself. My muscles still ache, my bones still throb from the effects of the hybrid solution I've been injected with. Who am I to judge who seems human or not?

Zane stares at something high up, and it takes me a moment to realize he's looking at a pole embedded into the sidewalk with a giant speaker perched atop it. "They used to have people from the FRX here at all times," he tells me. "They would live here until a shipment was done, then new masters would come to give orders until the next shipment was complete. Now they don't even bother with that. They know all they have to do is say what they want, and my people will do it."

The way he says that—*my people*—reminds me of how Elder felt about the shipborns. I swallow down the lump rising in my throat.

"For at least a decade, they've just used the satellites to issue orders. Now they can't even do that, but my people keep working anyway."

And I know they will all continue working, because even without the FRX telling them to do so, the Phydus in their systems won't let them stop. "The Inhibitor formula Bartie's bringing will work," I assure Zane.

Zane shrugs. He's not willing to get his hopes up. "I am glad, at least, that the humans from the FRX aren't here anymore." He looks down at me, forcing me to meet his gaze. "It was bad when they were here. I wonder, sometimes . . . "

"What?" I ask. It takes me a moment to recognize the feeling that's welling up inside me. Sympathy.

"I wonder if the only reason the rogue hybrids like me mutated is because the humans from the FRX . . . " He turns away, unable to finish speaking.

I don't need him to explain his thoughts, though. If there were FRX leaders here, seeing to the day-to-day operations of the colony they'd turned into mindless slaves . . . I rub my wrists. The women who lived here, born with Phydus already in their systems, were nothing more than dolls to the slave masters on Centauri-Earth. The kind of men who had no problem turning people into mindless automatons would have no problem doing exactly what they wanted with the women, the women who could not even think to protest.

I swallow dryly. I can do nothing about the past. But I won't let this sort of thing ever happen again on my planet, my home.

73: AMY

The peace negotiations go surprisingly well. Zane has a team of his own scientists read over the Inhibitor formula that Bartie gives him, and they seem confident that the meds will work.

Even so, negotiations take hours. Mostly because I insist that everything be written down, witnessed, and signed by all present. I leave nothing to chance or spoken promises.

"And one thing I want to make clear," I say as we near the end. "My people are independent from yours. We are not merging colonies. We are our own. We will elect our own leaders, have our own laws."

Zane starts to speak, but Bartie cuts him off—one of the few times Bartie has spoken at all. He and the other people from *Godspeed* are still recovering from their journey. "Elder would want that," he says.

I raise my eyebrow at Zane, waiting for him to object to my demand. But he doesn't. He just nods, adds it to the contract, and signs his name.

The worst part was the first night. When I really came to realize that I'm here, and he's not. That I'm alive and he's . . .

I let myself cry that night. Alone, in one of the stone buildings not destroyed by the hybrids, I weep until I have no more tears left, ever.

I have the whole world now, but I don't have him.

Zane is true to his word. On the first day after our peace treaty, he sends half his group of rogue hybrids to help clear away the damage of the battle at the building. None of my people—Earthborn or shipborn—want to work with them.

"They killed our people," one of the shipborns, a man named Tiernan, says. He has a gun, a weapon he plucked from one of the dead military, in his hand, pointed at the trucks arriving from the rogue hybrids. "They killed Elder!"

"They did kill our people. And my parents," I say, looking evenly into his eyes until he flinches, unable to keep staring at my oval irises. "But they didn't kill Elder. Elder chose to die. And he did it so we could have a life here. With them."

A crowd of shipborns gathers around. The sky is cloudy, the air humid. It'll storm later. But they know what a storm is now and how to survive it. One of the women drops her hand protectively over her stomach, and I'm reminded that most of the female population is pregnant. In a few months, there will be babies born in our little village who will never know *Godspeed*. Their parents will tell them stories about metal walls and a painted sky, and they won't understand, not really. They'll never know a cage for a home.

They'll never truly be able to comprehend how much was lost for their limitless sky.

"We can't trust them . . . " Tiernan says, lowering his gun but not releasing it.

"We have to," I say, putting a hand on his arm. "We will *not* survive in this world without help. Look around you. We have almost nothing. The supplies brought from *Godspeed* helped, but we need more. We need knowledge and help and training."

"I don't like it," Tiernan growls.

"Neither do I." I cast another look behind me—and then look past Tiernan, to the other shipborns that are crowding around him, their wide-open eyes, the fear they wear on their faces. "But it's time for us to work together," I say, more loudly so the others can hear. "It's what Elder would have wanted."

And this is the true legacy of Elder: his people are willing to accept peace.

A few days after the peace treaty is drafted, Zane comes to the colony in one of his big trucks. "I wanted you to see the first treatment," he says. "We couldn't have done this without you."

Bartie and I both go on behalf of the colony. Zane and Chris sit across from us. The tension is palpable—not just between us and them, but also in the way Bartie is afraid to sit too close to me. He keeps peeking up at me when he thinks I'm not looking, comparing who I am now to the girl he used to know.

He thinks me even more of a freak than before, I can tell that much.

Zane's set up his base in the old tunnels used by the first colonists for their mining operations—an extension of the same tunnels Elder discovered when he helped dig for the latrines. The entrance is blocked off by a high-tech door that reminds me of the one at the compound. Zane scans his thumb at the keypad, and **HYBRID** flashes across the screen. I look down at my hands. They don't *feel* different, not now that whatever transformation I underwent is over, but I know if I pressed my finger against the lock, it would flash **HYBRID** too. Not human. Never human again.

I wonder what Elder would think of me if he were still alive. My eyes are blue now, not green, with oval irises. I can see so much clearer now, so much farther. I can sense from which direction the wind blows before it touches my face; I can shut my eyes and still tell where everyone is based on their scent alone.

Elder is a clone; he must know what it feels like to wonder if your DNA even belongs to you anymore.

And then I remember: Elder's gone.

Something inside my soul snaps like a string pulled too tight, but I put one foot in front of the other and stare straight ahead.

Zane strides off to the laboratories—despite the fact that his headquarters are in abandoned mine tunnels, he's been stealing from the FRX for long enough to make this base camp just as high tech as anything we had on the shuttle. Rogue hybrids pop out of rooms built into the walls of the tunnel, greeting him as he walks by them.

He is truly their leader. In his late twenties or early thirties, it can't have been easy for him to assume control of the entire rogue hybrid population. I wonder what it was like for him, realizing that he had control of his own mind but his parents did not. Hiding when the FRX came to inspect the glass factories. Wanting to save his people, a people that, for the most part, aren't even aware they are enslaved.

He reminds me very much of Elder.

I chew on the inside of my cheeks until I taste blood. I will *not* cry. I will *not* show emotion. Not now. Not here.

Chris sidles close. His presence makes me uncomfortable, but I'm not willing to let him know that. I turn my back to him, but that doesn't stop him from talking to me.

"Look at the way Bartie flinches from you," Chris says in a whisper so low that no one else can hear. *I* wouldn't be able to hear it if it weren't for the fact that my ears have betrayed me, becoming bat-like in their hybrid clarity.

I ignore him.

"I saw the way they treated you before. You lived with them for how long? Months? And they were still scared of your perfectly normal skin color. What will they think of you now?"

I stare straight ahead.

"They'll never accept you."

I whirl around and grab Chris's collar, all in one swift motion that startles Bartie so much he curses in surprise, jumping back to the far wall so there's plenty of space between us and him.

"If you have something to say," I growl, "say it to my face, you coward."

Chris jerks free, and for a moment he looks angry. But as he smooths down his shirt, he says, almost as if it is an excuse for me, "A violent temper. Side effect of hybridization. Your adrenal glands are more likely to make you fight than run away, in other words."

What I don't tell him is that I was always more likely to fight.

"There's a difference between you and me," I say. "I know that one day, my people *will* accept me again. They've done it before. They'll forget about how I look because they'll remember who I am and how I act. But they won't forget about what you've done. You're the one who'll never be accepted. Not me."

Chris's eyes slide away from mine.

I can *feel* my muscles flexing, still shifting, growing stronger as my body comes to terms with the fact that I'm no longer just human. And I can smell the fear radiating from Chris.

Chris doesn't whisper any more cruel words to me. But the fact remains: a part of me got angry because I know what he's said is true.

75: AMY

Zane finally takes us to the laboratories and, just as I suspected, they're far more advanced than the simple tunnels would imply.

A man stands in the center of the lab. He stares blankly ahead.

"Sit," Zane says, and the man sits immediately, almost missing the chair Chris rushes to put behind him.

I wave my hand in front of the young man's face. Nothing. He's as empty as a blank sheet of paper.

"We're experimenting with methods of mass distribution," Zane says, "so I've been giving this subject a diluted version of the Inhibitor drug through the water supply."

I grin at Bartie, who—despite hesitating initially—grins back in response. This was our idea, inspired by the water pumps that distributed Phydus on *Godspeed*.

Zane hands the young man a tall glass of water. "Drink," he adds when the man does nothing but stare at it.

The man guzzles the water.

Zane and Chris monitor the man's vital signs on their computers, but Bartie and I know where to look when the Phydus wears off, and so we're the first to notice as life returns to his eyes.

"What's happening?" the man asks, his voice cracking from disuse.

"You've been drugged—all your life," Chris explains in a kinder tone than I've ever heard him use before. "And now you're regaining your autonomy."

The young man's eyes are wide and fearful, darting around the lab.

"Have some water," I say, handing him another glass. "It'll make you feel better."

While Zane and Bartie discuss ways to distribute the Inhibitor meds more broadly, Chris motions for me to follow him out of the lab.

"There's something I want to show you," he says.

I hesitate.

"Come on, Amy," Chris says, a touch exasperated. "We're friends."

"We are *not* friends," I say. "We will *never* be friends."

"But—" Chris's face looks devastated. His oval irises stand out in his watery eyes, but all this does is remind me that he's not entirely human and neither am I, not anymore. "I did what I thought I had to do," he says.

"Like killing both of my parents."

"I want you to know . . . " he says, "I *need* you to know—I'm sorry."

Sorry means nothing coming from his lips.

Chris heads down the tunnel, and I follow—not to hear any more apologies, but so that I can understand just why he did what he did. We walk in uncomfortable silence.

I sniff the air. Something's different.

"You noticed," Chris says.

I smell . . . copper, and something . . . something animal. It's nothing I recognize, but it's still familiar, like the memory of a scent I've never noticed before. The little hairs on my arms rise and my skin prickles with gooseflesh.

It can't be. Not here. We're underground. This is the one place on all of Centauri-Earth that can*not* be . . .

"Pteros!" I scream as Chris leads me around the corner and I see them, all clustered at the end of the tunnel. I'm about to run when I notice the glass between the monsters and me.

"It's okay, that's solar glass," Chris says. "There's no way they can break through."

A ptero—one of the smaller ones in the group—hops on its massive hind legs, coming closer to the window. I creep forward too. The ptero extends its wings slowly—just to stretch them; there's nowhere for it to fly. The hooked claws at the end of its wing joints scrape against the glass, and I cringe at the sound.

"The pteros—they were made by the first colony, before the gen mods and Phydus," Chris says. "The scientists in the first colony were trying to see if extinct animals from Earth could be resurrected here on this planet."

Mom knew, I think. The closeness between the pteros and actual pterosaur DNA. "The pteros also had Phydus, though," I say. Chris was *with* me when I ran that test.

"I wanted to tell you before, but . . . " Chris doesn't meet my eyes. "That was us. The rogue hybrids, I mean. That's one of the reasons I brought you here—I wanted you to know that you were right: we figured out a way to control them. To use them to fight for us." He pulls out a tiny silver tube like a dog whistle. He blows a few notes on it, and the pteros all look up at him, swaying at the high-pitched sound until Chris pockets the whistle again.

The littlest ptero rubs its head against the glass, turns around three times, and sinks to the ground, curled up.

I shut my eyes, and I remember the other ptero, the one I shot in the head, the one whose mouth dripped with the blood and gore of the remains of Dr. Gupta.

"You used them against us," I say flatly. "Is that what you brought me down here to show me?"

Chris throws up both his hands. "No! I mean—yes, but not that—I just . . . I wanted to explain."

"So explain," I growl.

"I didn't know it would be so bad. I . . . Zane and the others . . . they were just supposed to *take* that shipborn woman on Phydus. But the doctor was with her, so they took her too. And then the military woman showed up, and—"

"And they killed all of them." Maybe the pteros ripped Juliana Robertson apart after she died, or maybe the rogue hybrids made it look like Juliana's death was because of them, but either way, she's dead.

"The shipborn woman was an accident. We didn't mean to make her overdose on Phydus."

"And Dr. Gupta?"

Chris frowns. "I didn't know they would kill him. They—they thought he knew more about Phydus because he was with the shipborn woman who had the green patch. When he didn't tell them . . . "

"They thought they could control him. Make him talk, under Phydus's influence." My words are bitter. I think about what Elder said once, how different everything would be if people just told the truth.

"Dr. Gupta," I say. "Was eaten. *Alive.*"

Chris's mouth turns down. "It wasn't supposed to be like that," he says.

"But it was."

"I'm trying to apologize," Chris says in a small voice.

"You're not doing a very good job of it." I can barely stand to look at Chris. I wonder if the bullet he put in Dr. Gupta's head was supposed to grant him a merciful death or to ensure that he couldn't tell us the truth.

"I told them that the Earthborn doctors didn't know about Phydus, that only the shipborn doctor did. . . . " Chris's voice trails off.

"I guess Kit couldn't answer all your questions well enough. She was barely a doctor herself, you know—she'd been an apprentice until just before the shuttle launched. So they just killed her?"

"It wasn't like that!" Chris starts to protest, but I can see from his face that it was *exactly* like that.

"And Emma?" I ask.

Chris is looking at the sleeping ptero on the other side of the glass now. "She knew too much."

I frown at this. Chris starts walking again, away from me. He pauses, and I can tell that he hopes I'll follow, that he hopes I'll forget about all this.

And then I realize what he doesn't want me to know. "She didn't know anything about Phydus. She knew too much *about you,*" I say. "She didn't trust *you.* You were the one she tried to warn me about. She guessed that you were a traitor."

"I wasn't a traitor!" Chris says immediately, and I know he wants to believe that. He did what he had to do for *his* people, the rogue hybrids.

"You were a traitor to her," I say. "And to me."

"No," Chris says, his voice pleading. "Amy, just listen —"

"*You* listen." I glare at him. "If you had been honest from the start, none of this would have happened. *None* of it!" Emma would be here still. And Lorin and Dr. Gupta and Juliana Robertson. And Mom and Dad.

And Elder.

"We didn't know!" Chris is nearly yelling now. "Your father worked with the FRX military; he trusted them blindly!"

"But I didn't. And Elder didn't."

"How was I supposed to know that?" Chris asks in a desperate tone.

I shrug. "You could have asked."

"But —"

I stop. I'm tired of hearing excuses. I'm tired of words. "You could have tried," I say in an even tone. "You could have valued our lives more than your secrets."

I walk off silently.

77: AMY

Sol-Earth—and the FRX—tries to contact us one last time. Zane comes to fetch me in one of his trucks.

"I don't know how they did it. There must be a smaller communication satellite still in orbit around the planet, or they found a way to boost the signal from their end. All the communication systems in the city turned on at the same time. It's a sign—they're trying to reach us."

He takes me to the communication center in the compound. The auto-shuttle, now empty, still stands on the asphalt, overshadowing the communication building. I'd nearly forgotten the shattered glass, the hole in the wall. We step through it to enter the building. The biometric lock would have kept both of us out.

Red lights flash on the communication bay. Not much still works—the space station housed the biggest satellites—but when we turn the dial for the ansible, we hear a voice.

"—trying to reach any remaining survivors of the *Godspeed* mission. Message repeats: this is the FRX, trying to reach any remaining survivors of the *Godspeed* mission. Message repeats—"

I press the intercom button. "Hello?" I say. "This is Amy Martin, daughter of Colonel Martin."

The message on repeat dies. "Hello?" the voice barks into the intercom.

"What do you want?" I ask, unable to keep the anger from my voice.

"This is Chairman Li of the Financial Resource Exchange, representative of all the nations under the FRX."

My eyes drift up to the silver double-winged eagle engraved on the memorial plaque above the communication bay.

"What do you want?" I ask again.

"We would like to know your status. All communication was severed. We no longer have remote control of any previously active functions of the space station—"

"The space station blew up," I say flatly.

"Did the hybrids revolt?" Chairman Li says. "What happened? Are the rogues greater in number than previously thought?"

"We have joined forces with the hybrids," I say. "We have a cure for the 'vaccine' you gave everyone." I raise my voice as Chairman Li tries to talk over me. "We are making sure all the hybrids are able to think for themselves, and so far none of them have elected to remain your slaves."

"Confirm that you are acting commander of the *Godspeed* mission," Chairman Li shouts into the intercom.

He thinks the rogue hybrids are talking to him—that they hacked the system.

"I am the acting commander," I say. "I don't have a code for you, but I do have this: we have united forces with the hybrids—rogue or not—and none of us are any longer under your control."

"We have already sent ships toward the planet," Chairman Li says angrily. "If this is the way you and your people feel, we will treat you all as rebels and act accordingly!"

"That's fine," I say. "You should know that without the space station, I'm told it will take you the greater part of a decade to reach us. And while you will only have the weapons you can carry, we're going to spend that decade making as many solar bombs and missiles as we want. And we'll point them all straight up to the sky. As soon as your ships get here, we're going to blow them up."

"This is *our* planet! *Our* solar glass! You can't just cut us off like this!"

"*His* planet?" Zane says beside me. He glares at the intercom. It's a very good thing—for Chairman Li, at least—that he's so many light-years away from us.

"Just try to take it," I say into the intercom. "But I somehow think our missiles are bigger than yours. Here's the thing you never expected: if you enslave an entire group of people for as long as you've enslaved the hybrids, they're a bit angry. And personally? I'm angry too. So if it's a war you want, please, *please*, come over here. We'd be happy to fight it."

Static crackles over the intercom. I turn the dial until it clicks, severing the last connection we had with Sol-Earth.

Zane crows in triumph. "That? That was brilliant!" he says.

I grin at him weakly. I might have just caused an inter-planetary war. In a decade, when—if —the warship from Earth arrives, he might not be so happy with my rebellious streak that has been amplified by my new hybrid status.

But I also meant it. If it comes to war, we will fight. I will fight.

I will never give up my home again.

79: AMY

"What's that?" Zane asks, pointing to one of the few lights still blinking on the communication bay.

I clear away the dirt and debris accumulated on top of the control panel.

"Homing signal," I say, reading the label under the light.

"A homing signal?" Zane asks. "What's it detecting? The auto-shuttle landed, the shuttle from *Godspeed* is gone . . . "

A ringing fills my ears, making me dizzy.

The escape rocket only has two directions: to go to the space station or to come back here, to the compound.

The homing signal continues to blink.

"Could it be . . . ?" Zane asks, looking at me.

He presses a button, and a small, compass-like gadget like the one Dad used to find the probe ejects from a slot under the flashing light. It blinks on and off, showing a spot maybe a mile away, in the forest.

It can't be, I think. *It's impossible.*

But I snatch up the compass and race out of the room.

The homing signal's beeps grow louder as I crash through the forest. I run without thought or fear. I carry one of the solar guns now, but I don't even think about the possibility of danger as I dodge tree limbs and jump over exposed roots. I run past the burnt-out area that holds the remains of the *Godspeed* shuttle, past the little grove where Chris kissed me. I don't care how lost I get, if I ever find my way back.

I have to know what's on the other end of this homing signal.

As I run, the tree branches whip around me, scratching my arms and face, snagging my clothes. My heart thuds in my ears, in perfect time to the beeping homing signal from the compass in my hands. For the first time, I'm grateful to be a hybrid because it is my hybrid muscles that make me run faster than I ever could before.

I'm closer.

Closer.

I slow down, turning on the spot, trying to figure out where the signal is pointing me. I sniff the air, my eyes focusing on every detail. I push through more branches. I can hear rustling and movement as small animals and birds skitter out of my way.

And then I see it.

The escape rocket.

It clearly crashed, taking out half a tree with it. A jagged scar in the earth shows where the escape rocket skidded to a halt against the ground. It long ago quit smoldering, but I can smell smoke clinging to the burnt-out trees that must have been engulfed by the flames shooting out of the thruster at the back of the escape rocket.

The front of the escape rocket is crumpled like paper, the pointed nose flat, sharp edges of metal exposed. The cockpit is encased with glass, but dirt and debris cover it so completely that I cannot see inside.

I drop the compass onto the ground.

I shut my eyes.

I try not to think that I'm about to find Elder's dead body.

I climb over the broken wing of the escape rocket, grappling to find something to hold onto as I make my way to the cockpit. I slip, slicing my arm on exposed metal, blood making my hand slick.

When I reach the cockpit, I wipe it with my hands, smearing my blood with the grime on the glass. I strain my hybrid eyes, begging them to see what lies inside.

Nothing.

No Elder—no one at all.

The cockpit is empty.

"Amy?" a voice says from the forest. I whirl around so fast that I lose my tentative hold on the edge of the escape rocket, crashing down and landing with a metallic thud on the wing. I scramble up, looking frantically in the direction where I heard the voice.

A person emerges from the trees.

Tall, with dark brown skin and dark hair and dark, slightly almond eyes. High cheekbones and full lips.

And even though my body is screaming at me that this isn't *possible*, my heart is singing one name:

Elder.

I stand slowly. And then he's running toward me, and I'm running toward him, and we don't stop, we crash into each other, and I'm laughing and crying, and he's dirty and limping; there's dried blood on his head and one arm hangs funny, and he cries out as I touch it.

My hands shake as I raise them to frame his face.

It *is* him. It is. It is.

"As soon as *Godspeed* hit the space station, the escape rocket lost its connection," Elder says as soon as I relinquish his mouth so he can talk rather than kiss me. "It locked onto the homing signal in the compound instead and headed straight to it. I got caught in the blast, though, and knocked off course."

"Why didn't you come back sooner?" I ask.

Elder's voice is cracking and raspy. "I tried. I didn't know where I was." He looks around the forest. "I found a creek nearby, so I had water. And my leg." He looks down, and I see the crude splint he's made for his leg. He couldn't walk, and he didn't know where to go.

"I just had to hope you'd find me," he says.

Then he can't talk any more, because I'm kissing him, and I don't think I'll ever stop. But I do. I lean back and stare into his eyes, and it's not until I see the light within them that I realize the truth of it. *He's back.*

He's skinny, far skinnier than I've ever seen him. I think his arm is broken by the way he holds it against his body, and his leg definitely is. He's bedraggled and wounded and dirty, but he's *here.*

He blinks. Touches the side of my face, near my eyes. My eyes that are blue now, not green. With oval irises.

"I'm still me," I say, because my greatest fear now is that he doesn't want a hybrid Amy.

He cocks an eyebrow. "You think I care if your eyes are blue or green? I just care about *you.*" His hand slips down my arm, and he wraps his pinky finger around mine.

"You came back to me," I say, my voice breaking over unshed tears of joy.

"I'll always come back to you," he tells me, pulling me close.

Always.

ACKNOWLEDGMENTS

When I was writing *Shades of Earth*, it felt like something of a miracle to me that I could build a whole new world with ink and paper and have my characters discover it. But the truth of the matter is that ink and paper aren't enough, and Centauri-Earth—and indeed this entire book—would not exist without the help of some amazing people.

Thanks always to my wonderful agent Merrilee Heifetz, who knew the story would take me to the planet's surface even before I did, and Cecilia de la Campa at Writers House for taking the books all across the surface of *this* planet to get it into the hands of international readers.

The problem with discovering a whole new world is that it could be *anything*, and without the guidance of Ben Schrank and Gillian Levinson, Centauri-Earth would be nothing but a pale imitation of what it is now. They made me dig into the sandy soil and uncover what lay beneath the surface of the planet; they tilted my head to the skies so I could see the pteros flying there, and they led me to the poisoned heart of the world and helped me to discover a way to cure it. And extra thanks to Gillian, who never let me rest with "good enough," but pushed me to make it even better. Even when I complain, that is the quality I love the best about you.

I thank the stars that I landed with such an amazing publishing team as Razorbill. I don't even know where to start—you're all so wonderful! Thanks to Natalie Sousa and Emily Osborne for the covers that captured the spirit of each book; Erin Gallagher, Courtney Wood, Emilie Bandy, and Anna Jarzab for all the help with the online marketing; Jessica Shoffel for organizing the Breathless Reads Tour and working on publicity, Erin Dempsey for always being in my corner, and everyone else at Razorbill—you're all frexing brilly.

I have the best friends on Sol-Earth, and I can't thank them enough. Laura Parker, thank you for lending me your French. Jennifer Randolph, thanks for being there for me when I need you. Lauren DeStefano, you're my kind of crazy. Carrie Ryan, I want to be you when I grow up. Stephanie Perkins, you're too awesome for words. Elana Johnson, you inspire me. Heather Zundel, you have the biggest heart of anyone I know. Erin Anderson, may the zombies never eat your brains. Christy Farley, I'm so glad I stole you!

The Breathless Girls were with me during some of the hardest and best times of writing *Shades*, and their friendship made this book even better. Thank you so much Andrea Cremer, Marie Lu, and Jessica Spotswood: may our adventures continue!

Special thanks to the students of Burns High School, who are still asking me to kill them off in my books. I hope you enjoyed your gruesome deaths!

Bookstores and libraries are magical places, and some of the most magical ones include Malaprops, Books of Wonder, Fireside Books and Gifts, Little Shop of Stories, Anderson's Bookshop, Politics and Prose, Towne Center, Doylestown Bookshop, Blue Willow, Barnes & Noble (especially the Dallas branch), Once Upon a Time, Blue Bicycle Books, BookPeople, Morganton Public Library, Irving Public Library, and so many more.

The deepest place of love and gratitude in my heart belongs to my parents, Ted and JoAnne Graham, who are worth crossing the universe for, and my husband Corwin Revis, whose love is brighter than a million suns. You are the ones who help me create every shade of Earth.

Thank you all.